MacLyon

MacLyon

A NOVEL

Lolah Burford

Macmillan Publishing Co., Inc.
NEW YORK

Macmillan Publishing Co., Inc.
866 Third Avenue, New York, N.Y. 10022
Collier-Macmillan Canada Ltd.

Library of Congress Cataloging in Publication Data

Burford, Lolah.
  MacLyon; a novel.

  I. Title.
PZ4.B947Mac   [PS3552.U714]   813'.5'4   73-21292
ISBN 0-02-518190-4

FIRST PRINTING 1974

Printed in the United States of America

Dedicated to the Scotch-Irish

"Sergeant Mhor," 1753

I singly suffered the wrongs of many upon my person,
And for this, I was made a hero,
And sung songs about,
Stories told of me, even that I still held the glens in spirit,
Tho' I had died, as bravely as man might,
At rope's end, dangling my long length like a little weight,
A savage pleasing a savage law.
All our heroes and our gods come from such acts
And from such deaths, the one standing for the many.

Contents

I   Prologue: April 14, 1746   1
II   The Wedding   7
III The Wedding Feast   14
IV   What Followed   24
V   The Aftermath of That   29
VI   Monstrous Fruit   40
VII From the Military to the Civil, Diar's
     Wife, Perth   46
VIII A Civil Jail   50
IX   Diar's Wife, Ft. Augustus to Inverness   58
X   Carlisle, The Castle Gaol: The High Road
     and The Low Road   68
XI   Diar's Wife, Inverness to Carlisle   78
XII Diar's Wife: The Judge   89
XIII Carlisle Castle Gaol   100
XIV Diar's Wife: Carlisle, London, Carlisle   104
XV   Prisoner Lyon   110
XVI On Board the Transport   118

XVII   *Wecomica—Annapolis: An Indenture Bought*   126

XVIII   *Diarmid Indentured*   135

XIX   *Georgia, 1747*   143

XX   *"I will not bend my back."*   155

XXI   *The Field*   164

XXII   *Diar's Wife Travels Again to Carlisle and Again to London*   172

XXIII   *Diar's Wife: London*   184

XXIV   *Diar's Wife: Across Atlanticum*   193

XXV   *Diar's Wife: Boston, New York, Philadelphia, Fort Christina*   205

XXVI   *Diar's Wife: Annapolis*   216

XXVII   *Diar's Wife: Virginia, North Carolina, South Carolina*   228

XXVIII   *Diar's Wife: Chicali*   235

XXIX   *Diar's Wife: Charles Town*   241

XXX   *Smythe's Plantation*   252

XXXI   *"I do not work tobacco."*   258

XXXII   *Diar's Wife: Journey's End*   267

XXXIII   *The Remeeting*   273

XXXIV   *A Gift*   282

XXXV   *The Shed*   286

XXXVI   *Epilogue: Eighteen Months After*   294

XXXVII   *Lovers' Meeting*   303

   Author's Note   309

MacLyon

I: *Prologue: April 14, 1746*

OWN THE HILL, OVER THE SHORT SPRINGING GRASS OF
EARLIEST SPRING, CAME THE ELDEST SON OF MacLYON,
RIDING SOFTLY, HIS SKIRT BLOWING IN THE MILD EVE-
NING WIND, HIS BONNET COCKED ON HIS BLACK HAIR AS RAKISHLY
as the look sparking his black eyes in the dark night air. He
was more than half drunk, but for Diarmid MacLyon the
world looked best that way, and he saw it in that condition
three quarters of his waking life. It did not affect his riding or
his carriage, and he sat easily, swaying slightly, not from that
but for the pleasure of the feeling of the bare flanks of the
mare beneath him moving against his bare thighs and bare sex.

She was stolen, reived, he would have said, to use the
gentler word, and strange to him, but he rode her with only
the tight bit and an easy hand, and he thought she would
do. He had taken her for his share of the raid, liking her
looks, and left his uncle and his cousin and his two brothers
to take the other cattle home. Half were theirs, the long-
haired long horned blond cattle of the Highlands, and half
were pure gain and black Angus, which they would kill for

meat and skins, a friendly retaliatory raid for old Times on Jock Armstrong's stronghold, who had visited them in the early Fall for old times' sake.

He threw back his head and laughed, for the pure joy of it, the memory of the soft rushing sounds of the animal herd, for the escapade swiftly and silently carried off, almost too easily, it seemed now, and for life itself, which he loved living. The falls of French lace at his throat shook with his silent laughter, and the jewelled pin that held it caught the light in broken sparkles of amethyst and ruby ringed with pearls and diamonds. It was not his, he had taken it too, on a raid the Spring before on the MacDonalds, but he had not told his father that. Cattle yes, and horses sometimes, though very seldom, but nothing else. Only Armstrongs would loot, if even them. But the pin had caught his eye, and he had made it his. God in heaven, he hoped his father would not drown him for it if he found it out, the way MacDonald of the Isles had drowned the silly women who broke his laws. He'd like to see his father try. He laughed again, his white strong even teeth parting.

The grass beneath the mare's hooves gave way to cobblestone striking spark like flint beneath the mare's shoed hooves. When he got her home, he'd take the shoes off her feet, he thought, and show her what life could be like. But not now. The raid had bored him, being in the end like all the rest, and too easily accomplished, and after he had ridden a few miles North, and seeing no pursuit seemed to be developing, he had waved his hand and trotted off towards the East, thinking he would pay a call on Edinburgh, and see what he could stir up there.

He edged the mare away from the sewer running down the middle of the street, pausing in the shadow cast by the castle on the hill, and heard music sliding down the planes of the dark air. "Georgian," he thought, his eyes narrowing, "Georgian grace, by God," his ears pricking to determine the direction of the sound. It was coming, not after all, from the Hill, he decided, but from a house with a garden he could see a little way below him. The lit windows were large and glassed, in the style of French doors, standing a little ajar, and with no hesitation he left his mare, the bridle tossed about a branch of rowan, and walked towards the nearest window as though it were his own, and entered it, standing unnoticed in the curtained alcove, observing the company.

He saw none of the King's soldiers, the Hannoverian soldiers, that is, and he did not expect to, for they had moved up into the North towards Inverness and Nairn after Charles' descent in October into Edinburgh with his army of Highlanders, pushing down as far as Newcastle and farther. He was not himself much interested—less interested even than the Lowlands and than Edinburgh. MacLyon, that old lion, his father, had kept his clan in, and sat home, when the Highland Armies went out. His wife, the MacDonald, whom Diarmid favoured, rather than his tawny father, was dead now, and he wanted peace and a surcease from altercations and disturbances. He had not gone with any of the Mac-Donalds, and had refused to let Moidart or Keppoch round up any of his crofters or his men. Diarmid, lazy in communal warfare, and disinterested in the Prince, had applauded the decision of neutrality, and assumed, as his father did, that it was possible.

He moved out now, full in view of the room, and stood negligently by the heavy curtains, eying the figures moving in the dance with insolent young interest, so confident in his air and in his bearing it did not immediately occur to any of the eyes drawn towards him that he did not belong there by right. He was worth looking at, and he knew it, did Diarmid MacLyon, but he had known it for so long that he paid it now no more mind than he did the glances directed at him. Tonight, however, there was a different quality to the looks directed towards him, and to the quick murmured whispering, half-suppressed behind words and hands of those not dancing. It was, tonight, half-frightened, had he been less drunk enough to catch it, with wondering if he was alone, or if the town was full of Highlanders, and bent on what or whom. But for what their thoughts might be towards an uninvited Highlander or guest of any sort, Diarmid had no mind. He put his hands on his kilt, his arms and legs akimbo, and cocked his head, wondering whether he would try the refreshments first or a partner in the dance. The question was settled quickly for him by the passing of a very pretty girl right by him, and without a word, or bow, he hooked his arm through hers, and led her off from her surprised escort into the middle of the floor, turning his head to throw a sweet mocking smile that showed his teeth back towards the man whose face was turning thunderous.

He turned then, back to the girl whose arm he held, to bow and speak, his eyes warm and laughing and alight with pure mischief: turned straight without warning into the palm of her hand drawn back and meeting his face in a stinging slap. He heard the sound of laughter, low, and not so low, infuriating him, and his good humour evaporated like his smile. His instincts quicker than his thoughts, his eyes kindling, he lifted his own hand and struck her back, full force across her cheek, leaving the marks of his fingers like a red rake cutting the skin tender as a child's.

Well, he thought vaguely to himself, he'd done something now, aware for a brief moment of soft drowned eyes staring up astonished at him, behind the red welts, but he had no time to speak or to collect his wits, for several of the Gentlemen who had observed the episode, besides the pretty girl's former escort, had drawn their short dress swords and advanced upon him, ringing him. For all the fierceness of their points, they did not apparently expect him to fight them in their show of concerted force, and when he drew his dirk from his stocking, and with the same upward movement knocked a hole in the wall of the swords, uttering his first sound, a wild savage yell his father's gillies used on occasion, it needed only a few menaces from the tall and brawny savage, laced and jewelled, in their midst and the ring fell back a little. With a bound, his kilt flying up, he was through them, and through the curtains and out the windows again, into the gardens, falling into the yew bush spreading below them.

He sat perfectly still, inside it, the feathery green branches brushing his face, while boots trampled the garden about him, content to stay where he was and catch his breath, with no misplaced notions, drunk or sober, that honour demanded he show himself for a fight he would win only by a second flight. Let them trample the earth if it pleased them, slash with their swords at shadows, in whispers and muffled shouts, muddy their shiny boots. It touched him not a whit. As for himself, he would do what he chose to do, himself, as he chose, on his own terms, and no one else's, on the ground of his choosing. So he sat under the yew bush and waited, until after a time the commenting voices grew faint and the boots went away and the garden was quiet again. After another little time, he pushed the branches aside and put his head out, and then all of him, and walked back over to the window, gingerly, and stood looking in.

He was as puzzled as he was angry, for the idea of being unwanted had not occurred to him. His own house, like all Highland houses, was open, to the stranger as to the invited guest. He should not, of course, have slapped the girl, but then he was not used to being slapped himself, or slighted, or refused.

"Well," he thought, in so far as he was thinking at all, "I might show them a thing or two." His eyes were busier, looking through the glass, searching the room among the dancers, until they found the girl he'd slapped who had slapped him and would not dance with him. In fact, as he looked, she turned towards him and began to walk with her escort towards the window and towards him. He moved a little away, back into the shadow below the window ledge, and watched them walk out into the air.

He could not hear what either was saying, but he could see her fanning herself, her scarf slipping from the low-cut laced neck of her white dress. They were unaware of him, and irrationally he felt fury rise in him that they should be able to be. Action and resolve born in an instant and meeting, he leaped out of concealment with the advantage of surprise, and with an outflung arm and leg vaulted onto the little platform of the veranda, crooking the arm about the neck of the man. In a rude wink he had thrown the man backwards into the same yew bush, not looking to see if he had broke his neck for him, and knocked the lady into an unkind heap with a rough direct swing of his fisted hand. He picked her up, his esteem and his good spirits instantly restored by his actions, slung her over his shoulder, and strode off back across the garden towards his mare.

II: *The Wedding*

H E HAD RIDDEN SOME FEW MILES WITH HIS PRIZE SLUNG
ACROSS THE MARE IN FRONT OF HIM, WHEN SHE
STIRRED, AND CAME TO HER SENSES, AND TRIED TO SIT
UP. HE PUSHED HER DOWN WITH A ROUGH HAND.

"You will lie still now, and not be moving," he said, "for I
am not trusting you to not be slapping me again, and I'll not
have you upsetting my mare," and began to whistle. Whatever words she might have said were lost in the noise and in
the jolting as she bounced face and head downwards across
the mare's bare sides. But after a time of that, drunk as he
still was, with the wine and self-conceit at his prowess, he
relented, and slowed the mare, and turned the limp girl and
raised her so that he held her just against him.

"I think," she said, "that I am going to be sick."

"The Devil you are," he retorted. "I'll be putting your head
down again then, it's good for both kinds." He made to suit
his actions to his words, but she held his hands frantically
off.

"I will be quiet," she said, without having been asked to

7

be, desperately, "if you just won't hit me again or carry me like a sack. I cannot bear it truly."

"Is it still sick you're going to be?" he replied dubiously. "I'll not be having that on me, now I tell you."

"Not if you say not," she whispered, and he laughed aloud.

"O the pretty one!" he exclaimed joyously. "Then put your arms around my neck, my dear, and your legs too, and hold to me, my dear, for I'm going to let my mare loose now."

He had slackened his pace, before, but now he shook the mare on, and had she felt any loathing to obey, she had no choice except to cling hard to him or be thrown off, for his hands were on the mare. His sex was hard against her, but when she tried to move, he took a hand from the mare and held her closer yet against him.

"O my heart," he said into her hair, "I'm going to marry you, and now. We'll go wake parson for it first."

"You are drunk!" she cried, trying to twist away, unable to.

"Ay," he agreed, "but all the same I'm going to marry you, missy, and it's marry me you will, too. And that's to-night. And there's no say you'll have about it, and if you're wise, m'dear, you will not try to, for I will hit you if you do."

She did not say a word, but she began to shiver, against him and his plaid. He loosened it a bit and wrapped it about her, wrapping her against him more closely, one arm supporting her in its crook, and then he threw back his head and began to sing, in the Gaelic, a song she could not understand. The first dews were beginning to fall, and she shivered again, from them as well as fright, beneath the warm plaid and the warm arm.

Yet all the same, with the length of the ride and the rocking motion, she was half asleep, in a strange man's lap, against altogether too much of him, when the horse slowed at a command and she felt her cramped legs lifted down to the ground. They were slipping from under her, but he had sprung lightly after her to the ground and held her up.

She did not resist him. If she seemed spiritless, she had no strength to waste in spirit then. Her jaw ached where he had hit her as if it would split, as if it were split, and her temples were splitting with headache from the jouncing ride following hard on the blow. Her legs ached from the ride and the posture forced upon them, and the joints of her thighs, and her back. There was nothing she could find about her that did not ache, and she looked at the tall laughing Scot beside her and found nothing to admire. But she would have given him almost anything then just for a drink of water, or of wine, to quench the parching in a throat mingling with the held down fright in a rigid constriction threatening to turn to panic and choke her. Almost, not quite. She stood waiting, not asking where they were, or why, as he rapped peremptorily on the door, wondering in a faint sick way who he thought would answer in the middle of the night, so, to him.

After five minutes or so of knocking and hallooing, the chain was pulled back from inside with a little rasping sound, and the door opened a little way, and an elderly man in a nightcap put his head out, cautiously and dubiously, holding to the door.

"Bestir yourself, parson," cried MacLyon jovially, "I've a fine girl here that I'm wanting you to wed me to!" He felt the fine girl stiffen, and he took the arm he was supporting and gave it a hard twist behind her, smiling all the while.

"You are drunk, young man, I think," the parson said, his face settling into even more disapproving lines, "and I cannot imagine such a young woman wishing any such thing."

"Oh, but she does," MacLyon said, trodding hard with the heel of his shoe on the young woman's toe, "Indeed it is her earnest wish, and we have come express to you just for this purpose, and a long ride it has been, and a weary one for this poor girl. And will you be making us go back all the way again?"

"I will that," said the parson, "and you can come again to me in the morning, when you are sober, if you both be of a mind to it still then. And I'll tell you goodnight now, and beyond time for it."

MacLyon looked crushed, but his eyes were dancing under his lowered lashes as he looked compassionately at his bride.

"It is entirely crushing me, you are," he said, "and this poor disappointed lass who's as hot for it as I. For it's bedding her tonight I'm bound to be, with your blessing on the bedding or not, parson. And will you be making a dishonest woman of this poor girl for lack of a few words when we've come this long way?" The poor girl's eyes lifted in a stricken glance that seemed to confirm his words, and the parson seemed to waver. MacLyon pressed his advantage.

"Only give this poor thing a glass to drink, parson, and let her rest a moment, before you send us on, then. And maybe it's doing it after all you'll be."

The parson shook his head, but they were a pretty couple, and the girl clearly weary, and after a moment he did open the door to them, somewhat more awake, thinking perhaps to dissuade them.

"These dances," he observed, "are the devil's instrument."

"Then be God's," said MacLyon, "and amend us." With a sudden swoop he lifted his bride-to-be in his arms, pressing her face in against his chest in a tender picture, and carried her in. As the parson departed to fetch what refreshment he had, with an amused grin MacLyon set her down in a chair and stood looking down at her. She looked back up at him steadily, rubbing her bruised wrist.

"Abductor!" she whispered.

"Yes!" he agreed.

"You will never do it," she whispered again, more strongly.

"Oh, but I will," he whispered, his finger on his merry lips.

"I will scream," she said.

"Scream away," he agreed. "But look you," he said as an afterthought, "I may have to shoot the old gentleman if you do. I have my pistol and my dirk, and I will use them on you both." He saw her blanch.

"I will not answer," she said, "I won't speak the words. You cannot make me do it, and I won't."

"Oh, but you will," he said. She shook her head. "I think you will," he said again, "when you know that if you don't, I'll just take you to another parson, but before we get there, I'll have beaten you again, and so, and so, and so, until you do agree to say them." He paused, and said thoughtfully, his eyes fierce but dancing, "I wonder how many parsons I will have to wake tonight."

She looked at his face, and she believed him. "I'll scream. He'll tell. He'll send men after you."

"He'll not be able to," he assured her with a smile. "Hush now, I hear him coming back. Make up your mind, and quickly now."

"Why should you do this to me?" she whispered. "Why should you want to? I don't know you, I've never hurt you." She flushed as he looked at her piercingly.

"You struck me, Missy, in front of all that company. If you've forgotten, let me tell you, I have not."

Her hand went to her mouth in a frightened little gesture, but it did not touch him. "And you've taken my fancy, but it's not my way to take a woman of your quality rough and ready. I'll have it parsoned first, and papers to show it, and take you to my hall, and bed you proper there." He looked at her sharply. "I'll teach you to slap men you don't know, my dear."

She thought it a troublesome way to himself to teach her, but she knew well he was drunk and she despaired of reaching through to any sanity to him. She was frightened of him, and she believed his threats, and so again she said nothing. She drank the wine the parson brought her, looked at his aged querulous face, seeing no help to be had there, and overtaken by a curious fatalism decided if it had to be, it might as well be sooner rather than later, this wedding. She did not think she could bear to be struck again or carried about like a sack from place to place.

When MacLyon's tongue and the offering of his jewelled

brooch had persuaded the parson to administer the short form of the sacrament, still silent, she made no demur, and when he came to her, she let him take her cold hand in his, letting it lie there unprotesting in his strong warm one, while the parson put on his surplice.

He laughed suddenly, and looking down at her, said, in a whisper, "I never asked. What's your name, my dear?"

"No," she said, and felt a light slap to her cheek.

Her eyes flew into his, startled, grey meeting grey, hesitating, as his hand tightened on her fingers, before she whispered, "Mary Elisabeth."

He nodded approvingly, his grip still painfully tight.

"Grant," she finished.

"Mary Elisabeth Grant. And I am Diarmid MacLyon. You may call me Diar," he added, "as my friends do. Are you protestant, Miss Mary Elisabeth?" he added with a glint.

She nodded her head slightly.

"I thought you might be. Myself, I'm not. We'll do it sometime again my way, but not tonight. This parson's a Dissenter, but I thought he'd do."

His rational concerned voice conflicted sharply with his lunatic action, and she looked at him wonderingly, in puzzled dismay. But she made the answers required and expected of her, only once pausing as if she would say "No," but the fingers holding hers held her, and he took a gold ring with a ruby in it from his little finger and set it on hers.

With a flurry then they were out and off again, in the dark night, and she was riding again, seated this time in front of the man, her legs falling on either side against his, leaning back against him in weariness, unable to believe she had married him, unable to think. She was falling asleep again when she heard his voice in the dark.

"Tired, Mrs. MacLyon?"

She sat up with a jerk. "I am not Mrs. MacLyon," she said with a sudden show of spirit.

"Oh?" he said lazily. "I thought you were. I thought that's what it was we did."

"You tricked me," she said stormily. "And coerced me, and my father will have it set aside."

He began to laugh again, loudly and uproariously, his body shaking behind hers.

"If he reaches you in time," he said, "which I doubt he will do." He put his arm around her and drew her back against him, holding her. She tried to push away from him, but she could not.

"You may have wedded me, you drunken Highland Scot," she said bitterly, "but you will not bed me. I will die first."

"We will see about that," he said comfortably, "Miss Mary Elisabeth." He tightened his arm around her stiff shoulders, and drew her closer yet against him. "But I will feed you first, in style." He put a quick kiss upon her hair. "And now, Mrs. MacLyon, I will take you home."

III: *The Wedding Feast*

WHEN DIARMID ARRIVED BEFORE THE DOOR OF HIS HOUSE, HIS WIFE WAS ASLEEP IN HIS ARMS, AS DOCILE AS MAN COULD WISH FOR. HE GRINNED, TIGHTENED HIS ARM ABOUT HER, AND RODE THE MARE DIRECT INTO THE hall, through the door the sleepy gilly flung open at his call, the mare side-stepping delicately over the threshold in the unaccustomed place.

"My God, Diarmid!" cried his cousin who had returned already from the raid, "what are you doing, and what have you got!"

"Diarmid is up to his tricks," said his second cousin, lifting his head, from the table where he sat, "and his father will not put up with them this time, I am thinking."

"It is no trick," Diarmid said, "or it is the best of tricks this time. I've got a wife," Diarmid announced to his cousins and to the hall at large, "and what I'm doing is calling on my hall to welcome her, as the wife of Diarmid MacLyon should be welcomed. Hist, love," he said in a fierce whisper to the girl he held, who had wakened up at the commotion, her face wan and her eyes heavy with weariness and the hard sleep on the long ride, looking about her bewildered and then in fright, tightening his arm about her as she tried to sit up. "Be still and behave as you ought. We are at my house, at our house, where you will one day be lady. And my house is here to welcome you. If you disgrace me," he added, "I will strip and beat you before them all. And they will none of them lift a finger to help you, for they know who I am, and they do not care how I came by you."

"Who are you?" she whispered, looking up then into his face, wonderingly then.

"I am Diarmid MacLyon," he whispered back, "MacLyon's son, and it is no mean thing that I am, or that you will be."

She looked about her at the large darkened hall, that seemed to her exceedingly unwelcoming, her eyes wide now, but the arm about her waist threatened to cut her breath off and she said nothing at all, trying to loosen it with her small hands, but she found she might as well have tried to loosen the ring of iron around a cask with her bare fingers. He laughed softly and kissed her hair, pleased at her quietness which he took to be a proper awe, and shouted out for lights and food and the tables to be set up, and the pipers and the harper brought, and all to be set in order. "Logs," he shouted, "fresh logs for the fire, to warm my bride who is cold!" feeling her shiver under his hands.

"Diarmid!" said his cousin, in the midst of the bustle, "Are you mad! What are you thinking of with your father away at my father's tonight? And what will he think?"

"Is it my father or yours? And is it my house or yours?"

"Yours, Diar, of course, but—"

"Then do not behave to me as though either were yours. I will do here as I wish, and you will dance at my wedding feast, Cousin Cameron, for I wish it! There is no father can object to his son's wedding feast."

"Diarmid is more than head over," said his cousin Nial

softly to his cousin Cameron, coming up and taking his arm. "I have seen him like this, and there is no dealing with him in this humour. Leave off," he said, in something of Diarmid's state himself already, "and let's enjoy ourselves. It bids to be a bonny night." He added his voice to Diarmid's shouts for his pipers, and in the confusion of voices, his bride's attempts to make herself heard went unheard by all except her husband who took her wrist in his hand and twisted it behind her back, while he continued to shout out his commands.

To her amazed eyes the sleepy hall sprang to life before them, trestles were set up, covered with cloths, silver goblets brought and pitchers of wine, meats, breads, candles. The fire blazed, the hall filled. And in the midst Diarmid sat his horse with his bride and watched and approved.

"I shall take you to my mother's room," Diarmid whispered, "where my sisters stay when they come, and you shall brush your hair, and wear my mother's wedding necklace."

"No," she whispered in terror, "no."

"Yes," he whispered. "Come with me now, or shall I make you?"

"I will not come," she said, "I will not leave this room and go off in a room with you, I will not, I will not, you will never make me."

He threw back his head and laughed, his chest shaking behind her, with amusement.

"Very well," he said, "fierce little thing, you shall attend your wedding feast without the necklace and your hair uncombed." He did not trouble to explain what he found so funny, but he stroked her hair, where it curled about her temples, with his fingertips, combing it lightly with his fingers, letting them travel then lightly down her face and across her lips. It was like an invitation to bite, and bite she did, to find her own fingers imprisoned.

"Shall I do that too?" he said, a gleam in his eyes, raising them to his lips, and he opened his mouth invitingly. But he did not bite her. He only laughed again, and said, "When I bite, I shall bite you somewhere else, but not yet, not now, not here." As she caught her breath, he said, his laughing eyes crinkling on her, "And it is Maeve herself I have, the great-bladdered Queen. But remember what I have said, Queen Maeve."

He set her down on the floor, and leaped down beside her, and led her to the center table that had already been set up when he arrived, where his cousin had been sitting, drinking. There he welcomed his younger brothers who had returned, blond and unlike him and with little to say but their eyes admiring and uncritical, and sat his bride down in her crumpled white satin laced dress, and sat himself down beside her, and called for the Harper to come to him.

"I'll have some songs," he cried, "to honour me and my bride, sing me," he said, his voice quietening, thoughtful, "sing me the glories of my name that my bride may know what she has. Sing for her the story of King Diarmid mac Murchada of Leinster who stole his bride from her husband and lost the whole of Ireland to the English for it, and thought it little cost."

"You are mad," she whispered, "you are drunk and mad."

"Hist," he whispered back, pinching her knee beneath the table so hard she caught her breath, "be still now, like a proper wife, and listen to the story of a wife-stealer." He began to laugh so hard, at his own humour, that he was near to drowning out the voice of the Harper, took a drink of wine to steady himself, and offered the same to her.

"Drink," he said, "where my lips have been, and I will drink again where yours have touched."

"No," she whispered, "I will not," and felt the cold rim at her lips. "No," she cried, desperately, and knocked the cup down. It rolled across the white cloth, spilling the claret as it went, staining the cloth like thin clear blood, falling to the floor and denting its side. She felt the man beside her stiffen and grow quiet, and she was suddenly afraid to raise her eyes. Without a word, he took her hand that had his ring on her finger in his left, while the hall watched, and with his right, picked up her cup of wine and poured it over their two hands, hers clasped in his, and over the ring, and threw the cup then after the first. He put her stained hand to his mouth then, and when he had taken the wine from it, he put his hand to her mouth in turn, but she would not do the same. He wiped it then against her lips, despite her, his eyes on her all the time.

"Bring my wife another cup," he said quietly when he had finished, "she has spilled the first in her joy at my touch." He took the silver stemmed cup brought to him, raised it a second time to his lips, this time formally, and as formally offered it to her to drink. She was frightened by the look on his face and in his eyes, and by the broken cup, and she took the second cup in her hands as he offered it, and felt his two hands encircle hers as she lifted the cup, lifting it with hers gently, until the rim touched her lips, where his had been, and she drank, a swallow only but it satisfied him, for he took the cup from her, his eyes on her, not it, and turned it until the side she had drunk from faced him, and then drank himself, his eyes still on hers, until hers fell, and her breath began to quicken. His hand slid down to hers, and clasped it, where his ring was, holding hers in his large one, and brought it again from beneath the table and laid it still crossed in his upon the cloth.

"Sing us the story of Diarmid and Grainne," he said softly to the Harper, "of black-haired Diarmid with the love-spot on his forehead, whom all women loved, who was reared by the Ever-Living in their house, and Grainne the High King's daughter, let my wife hear that too, for she is a Lowland Scot, and I doubt she knows it," he said. "Sing it first in the Gaelic and then in the English. So let her hear it now, that story of the Diarmid who was Finn's nephew who took Finn's betrothed at her request, breaking his ties for her, and breaking the Fianna, and bringing war upon the land."

("Diarmid is as drunk as a loch loon," said his Cousin

Cameron aside, dispassionately observing the pair, "when he will begin to quote ancestral verse. I think his wife is stolen, she looks none too happy."

"I think so too," his cousin Nial agreed, nodding his head sagely, "but Diarmid has a way with him, I hear, and in the end she will not mind. Besides, she has gotten in Diarmid a good thing. It is someone else, I think, who will be minding this impromptu festival. But it is a good claret, and I shall myself drink it.")

"Your stories are all of wife-stealers," Diarmid's wife said, her voice more of a hiss than a whisper, "but I do not wonder. You are well named." If she wished to provoke him, she could not. He looked down at her, and smiled softly, and said only, "Fierce wee thing, we shall see what your fierceness is made of by and by. Listen now, and hear the story, how he was killed by treachery by the tusk of the boar of Beinn Gulbain."

"I would that tusk were in your heart now," she said, her voice rising a little, pulling her hand from his.

He put a finger to her lips. "Hist, love, and listen. It was in the groin the tusk took him, and Finn would bring him no water. Would you bring me water, love?" he asked, his eyes laughing into hers.

"No," she said, "you might die thirsty for all of me. I wish you were dead now."

"That is an unlucky wish," he said, his eyes not laughing now, "an unlucky wish at my wedding feast, and I require a forfeit for it now, to unsay it. We will make another little death in its place, but it is a different tusk shall wound you in another place, and not to death, but life."

"No," she said, her breath uneven, "you must not talk this way. I will not listen." She tried to rise, but his hand caught her wrist and held her down.

"I am not asking you to *listen*," he said, pressing his lips a little together, his eyes on her. "But you have eaten nothing," he said, his mood suddenly shifting. He clapped his hands and had meat set before her, and taking his short dirk from his stocking and a fork he carved a slice of the cock for her, and offered it to her on the prong of the two-tined fork.

"I cannot," she cried, her hands gripping the table.

"Eat, Mary Elisabeth," he said softly, "eat, it is your feast night and you must partake too."

"I will be sick," she whispered, "I cannot. Oh, will no one help me?" she cried, looking about her wildly.

"Eat, Mary Elisabeth," he said. "I do command you do. The hall is watching you to see you eat.'

He held it to her lips, and she choked, and suddenly she pushed back her seat from the table and stood up, her eyes desperate, overturning the stool, and ran from him into the middle of the room looking desperately and hopelessly about her for any sober face among the laughing singing eating crowd gathered at the trestles, for any one to turn to among them for help. To her horror, she saw the man who called himself her husband leap to the seat of the stool he was sitting on, onto the table itself, where kicking off his shoes and signalling to the pipers, his eyes upon her, he began to dance, his hands raised in the air, his feet lithe and nimble among the dishes, overturning nothing, in front of the laughing faces of his two cousins and his brothers who began to clap their hands and shout. The exhibition, which it was at that height, leaving little undisplayed, brought a fiery blush to her face as she stood frozen before him. Abruptly he stopped, though the pipers continued to play, retrieved his shoes, and vaulted over the table itself to her, where he held out his hand to her to take.

"No," she cried, white-faced now, her face as white as her dress.

"Have you then finished eating and drinking?" he said, his eyes glinting. "Are you hot for it too, like myself? Then come, little wife, we will be at it now. My wife," he cried to the company, "will have no more of eating or of drinking in her impatience, and I am of her mind. Bring torches then, and light us out."

He continued to hold out his hand.

"No," she cried, her face whiter yet, and she pulled out from the fold of her skirt the knife he had cut the meat with, holding it against her, its point towards her. It was a gesture only, for almost before it was seen, he had pulled it from her, his wrist snapping about hers, and while he held her, with his other hand, hurled it across to the door of a room where it stood quivering in the wood.

"That door," he said, his eyes dark, "leads to my room, and it is there we are going."

She fought him then, in front of all the assembled men, with nails and teeth and fists, striking his face and his hands, unable to hurt him.

"They think you're shy, Mary Elisabeth, as brides are meant to be," he whispered, "and they don't care how I got you. Don't you know that? Are you shy?" he asked, his face alight, his mouth laughing at her. She struck him, full on his laughing mouth then, but he only laughed and caught her hands and gathered her in, and pinned her arms behind her.

He called for torches again, and his tacksmen came then, taller than he, each with a pine-torch in their uplifted arms held high in hand, encircling the two. She grew quiet then, for the moment, at the strange sight, its savage beauty awing her. The man beside her put his hands on her shoulders, holding her against him, her back against him, his intention hard and evident against her.

"Be still now," he said, "it is the hymeneal they will sing. It is always done. If you fight me now, within this ring, within this blessing being made for us, I shall fight you back." He picked her up in his arms and carried her, very quiet now against him, believing him and knowing his blows and fearing them, down the hall surrounded by the torches to the door where his knife hung.

He turned then to the crowd following them, grinning like a boy, and waved to them.

"Go on with your eating and drinking," he said. "You will excuse us now, my wife and I have other things to do. And pipers," he cried, "my wife is shy, play loudly and do not let her little cries of fright disturb the company."

He closed the door behind him, pulling out his knife, and let her down and stood before her then, only the two of them, and the bed with its pelts of wolf and deer and cat. He put his hands on her shoulders, where he had set her down, and there he stood still, his eyes looking into hers until hers fell, before their look, and then he put his hand beneath her chin and raised her face again to his until she had to look.

"You are my wife, Mary Elisabeth," he said gently, "there is no shame in it. Do not be afraid of me. I shall love you always and live always in this house with you."

"But I do not want you to love me," she said piteously, "I only want you to let me go."

He shook his head and picked her up again, as unresisting now as a terrified bird, and crossed to the bed of skins.

"I caught them myself," he whispered, laying her down on them, and sitting himself beside her, "as I caught you, and I let none of them go, though they cried and looked at me too with their big eyes." He took her wrist in his hand, holding it, and then before she knew what he meant to do, with a sudden movement of his knife he had cut it, a slight gash. She sat up in surprise, and began to cry with the pain of the wound and the free-flowing blood and its unexpectedness on her tight nerves.

"Hush," he said. "Now do the same to me."

"I cannot," she said shrinking.

"Quickly," he said, making no humour over her past threats, taking her hand and putting it over the knife and helping her to make the cut. He placed then his bleeding wrist against hers and bound the two together with the light scarf he took from the neck of her dress and wrapped it around them with his free hand. But before he had done that he had put the tip of his tongue delicately to his wrist and then to hers and back to his, and had required her silently to do the same, his eyes fixed on hers and not letting them go, and then he had made her, his eyes silently still requiring, to touch the tip of her tongue with his, the silent ceremony shaking both him and her, but with different emotions.

"It is thus," he whispered, "that we shall be, you and I, Mary Elisabeth, always, bound, and of one blood."

He turned then, his wrist still bound to hers, and took her to him, holding her against him, making no move, while their pulses bound together at the cut throbbed in a rhythm of their own.

"If I break this bond," he said, "or play false to you, Mary Elisabeth, with any woman, take this knife and put it in me, for I shall let you, and so shall I do the same by you." He took it then and threw it back into the door. "It is sheathed now," he said, "and at rest, so sheathe me, so let you and me have peace and rest."

At the words, she pulled her wrist free from his.

"Oh God," she cried, "Diarmid, do not do this to me," her hands pushing against him, as he bent to take her lips with his. He did not answer. If his conversation in the hall had seemed rational, though wild, he had no conversation left. At first she cried bitterly, clinging to him, fighting his lips, pleading, and weeping. When he laughed at her, she struck him, and he struck her back, place for place, hit for hit, until she broke from him and ran from him. He followed her with light running steps as he would have chased a deer on the hills, and caught her. She struck him again, sobbing wildly, and he struck her back, and she began to scream then, her screams drowned in the skirling din of the pipes outside the door.

IV: *What Followed*

WHEN MACLYON HIMSELF CAME HOME, HE FOUND HIS HALL AND HOUSEHOLD IN DISARRAY. HE STOOD AT THE OPEN DOORWAY AND SURVEYED THE SCENE.

THE BANQUETING TABLES WERE SET UP, AND COVERED WITH clothes and his silver and crystal, and the remains of shank and legs of ham and beef, knives and forks stuck in them, beaks and feathers of fowl, wine and brandy bottles tippling, spilled on the clothes, the French wax candles guttering, and his kin and retainers lying back in their chairs and on the floor in various attitudes of languor and repose. A duel or a practice with dirk and claymore was taking place between two of his sons in one darker corner, watched by a ring of admirers, in another corner a group of three bagpipes screeching as though to cheer them on or drown their noise. A strange mare was standing patiently, tied to a sconce, surrounded by her droppings on the carpet.

Rage held him speechless, unobserved, standing in the doorway. Then he strode into the midst of his tacksmen, humblies and kin, his grey eyes colder than the pale grey dawn. As he passed the mare, with his dirk he cut the ribbon of rein holding her, and with a slap of his hand to her rump, sent her out of the door, and then he passed to his fighting sons and with a rough hand on their shoulders, sent them sprawling.

"Where is my first son?" he demanded, his voice cold with rage, "and what is this noise in my house? Where is Diar?" he demanded again peremptorily. "Is he here? And does he then permit this?" his anger mounting as the noise continued about him unabated, and as neither one answered.

They looked up at him, in bemused stupefaction, their mouths open. The amusement of the night had begun to wane, to gutter out like the white candles: Diar's command for the sudden wedding feast, for pipers and harpers, the entrance of the silent white-faced white-dressed bride, her fight before them all with her new groom with nails and teeth and fists, and his removal with her, himself laughing, to the inner room, while the bagpipes played louder at his command to drown her screams, which had risen above them and mingled with them, with the sound of running scuffling feet, and slaps. It stood in its proportion now before the owner of the house, their chief and father, and they looked up at him in sobered and speechless fear.

"Where is Diar?" Diar's father shouted above the tumult, "and what is this racketing of music in my house?"

In the silence that fell, then, in which the silence of the room beyond, silently indicated, made itself felt, he strode to the door, and pulled it open. Taking in the situation at a glance, he walked to the bed, and pulled his son up and off the now silent girl, except for the soundless sobs shaking her in shudders.

Without a glance at his eldest son or a word, he went to the girl and with knowledgeable fingers parted her thighs, examined them quickly, his face without expression and then covered her nakedness with a sheet, still without a word. Then he turned to his son, standing both defiantly and sheep-

ish in the middle of the floor. With his short sword and his
fists he advanced upon the unarmed young man who did not
try to fight him, and with his sword cut through his plaid,
letting it fall to the floor.

Diarmid's eyes flashed, and he gasped involuntarily, anger
rising like a molten tide in him at the shame done him, but it
was his father and so he stood entirely still, before the anger
rushing out unchecked against him. His father took his open
hand then and slapped his son with it with all his strength,
the blows falling on one cheek first and then the other, and
across his mouth, but the young man did not lift his hands, or
move, except to turn his face a little aside with the blows.

"Fight me," MacLyon said between his teeth, "won't you?
I want you to fight me."

"No," Diarmid said, between his teeth, setting his bruised
mouth, his eyes fixed on his father, grey meeting grey.

"No?" his father exclaimed. "Not men? Only women?" He
did not glance towards the bed, nor did his son, at the girl
watching them with enormous eyes, unable to understand
their speech.

"I do not fight *you*, sir, I cannot, as you know," Diarmid
replied.

"No? But you can turn my house into a brothel, can you
not, into a drunken stable. I think you can do that. It seems
you can."

Diarmid did not answer immediately, but after a minute,
as his father continued to lower upon him, breathing hard,
sword still out in hand, he said in a low voice,

"You want me to do something, I think. What is it you
want me to do?"

"I want you to apologize to me, Diarmid Lyon."

The young man looked back steadily at the older, and then
he slowly shook his head.

"No," he said, "No, I won't do that, and you know I won't.
You struck me before you spoke to me. It is for you now to
apologize to me."

The faces of both were white now with a new anger, of a dangerous kind, and the girl lying in the bed sat up, drawing the sheet and the rugs about her, wanting to intervene between them and not daring, feeling almost sorry now for the young Scot who seemed for the first time entirely sobered. She was to feel sorrier yet.

"You won't fight me, and you won't apologize," Mac-Lyon said slowly, contemptuously, "and I can't make you?"

Diarmid shook his head. His father stretched out a hand then and picked up Diarmid's plaid from the floor where it had fallen, and with his sword he cut it in four pieces and dropped them again on the floor. Then with his sword he cut through his kilt and his laced shirt, ripping them from him with his hands and letting them fall to the floor.

"Get you gone now, Diarmid," he said bitterly, "no son of mine now. Naked I took you from your mother and naked I send you out. You are proud of that instrument, so display it now. Let the world see it, and let the world know what you value. Go down to the Lowlands or the Sassenachs, and do not show your face about me any more. For if you do, I will sell you across the ocean, and put you to the ship with my own hand. It were better you had died in place of Glengarry's son, in place of the young Angus Og, so had I then been spared this shame. You have broken my ways, and I have broken you now. I do not want to see you in my sight ever any more."

"Did I think I loved you?" Diarmid answered no less bitterly. "I never knew you. The man I thought my father would not have so treated me. I am indeed going now, and I shall not come back until I see you dead, until I see you hanging from that tree by your door as naked as you have made me. I shall never for any words return here or speak words with you again."

"So be it," his father said. "Go with my curse. May all your undertakings come to naught and smother and die beneath you and you with them, until you repent these words to me and what you have done to this poor child and brought her to."

"I shall never do it," Diarmid said, his voice flaming with anger then, "though my heart leaned towards it as it does not and it never will, yet should I never do it, for the outrage you have done upon me. I shall never speak words with you again."

He turned on his heel then, and left through the door his father, turning from him, silently indicated, his face proud and unseeing, his cheeks flaming, and the tears falling down them, as they were falling down his father's, walking through the silent rows of listening men inside the house who did not dare laugh or smile, wrapped only in his dignity, and out into the misting rain of the early morning air.

His father stood, his face turned away, not watching him go, as if turned to stone except for the tears that continued to run down the grooves of his face. But when some time had passed, and there was no sound from anywhere, he remembered himself and turned to the girl in the bed.

"I am sorry, my dear," he said, in her own tongue. "I am Glenlyon. I will make what amends to you that I can. Will you tell me your name, and where you live?"

"I live here now," she said bitterly, her feelings beyond her unravelling. "My name is Mrs. MacLyon. Unless you want to send me after my husband."

If her words shocked him, he did not show it.

"You shall tell me the entire story another time," he answered, "but not now. I find I do not want to hear it now. The graceless boy I once called my son has mistreated you, and we will make what amends to you we can. Are you certain there is nowhere else you'd rather go?"

She shook her head. "There is nowhere I can go now that will receive me where I am not ashamed to go."

"Then I will take you to my oldest daughter, who is married, and she will care for you, my dear. But you will not use his name again while you stay in my house."

V: *The Aftermath of That*

DIARMID, LYING NAKED IN THE HEATHER ABOVE WHAT
HAD UNTIL NOW BEEN HIS HOME, IN A TEARING BITTER-
NESS OF SPIRIT THAT DID NOT ADMIT OF ANY SENTI-
MENT THAT HE MIGHT HAVE DONE WRONG, WATCHED UNTIL HE
saw there was nothing to see, and then he continued to watch.
He was startled by a cold nose nudging his shoulder. He looked
up to see the mare he had stolen who had come up beside him.
"Women," he thought to himself, in disgust, "all of them, all
alike," remembering the look of pity he had seen without
seeming to see it in the dark-fringed grey eyes watching his
disgrace. But he mounted the mare, and rode off on her, careless of who might see him go, towards the little wood to the
south.

Once inside, he put his mind upon his plight, and what he
was to do to amend his situation. The first thing, he clearly
saw, was to find himself some clothes, someway, from someone, and until that was taken care of there was very little he
could do of anything else. He had just formulated this
thought to his now sober but very tired brain when he saw
coming down a small hill directly towards the spinney he

was in a cousin with whom, with others, he had joined in the raid the night before. He whistled softly to himself, at his luck, and quickly scaled a little ash tree overhanging the path down which, if this luck held, as it did, his cousin should come riding. With no compunction, he let himself fall directly on him, as he rode directly beneath the little ash, knocking the breath from him and then with his fist, quickly, the senses. He had no desire to be seen, either in his state or in his action.

He knew his cousin's strength well, from other scuffles, over the years, and he knew his own. Without haste, he stripped the other young man completely, who was much his size, close enough for one ready to take a humbly's strip, of shoes, stockings, trews, kilt, shirt, and plaid, dirk, dag-pistol, gold and silver coins, bonnet, and all.

"There," he said grimly, "see how *you* like it." He was no more fond of his cousin than blood required, and he rather hoped his father and his men would think the poor figure staggering in was himself, and would plan a reception. But he was delighted to have his plaid again, as near as made no difference, and a good shirt and something to conceal his offending member. He began to feel more himself again, and he thought of the old tag of his schoolmaster, "Clothes makyth man." There was something in that, after all.

He went back to his mare then, who looked at him enquiringly. It was an unexpected piece of fortune, in the midst of a bad time, to have found not only a plaid, but his own. His father had not succeeded in "breaking" him there after all.

So he rode on South, and bought himself breakfast with a penny, and then, feeling suddenly tired, a bed, at a cottage, in which he stretched out his long length comfortably and forgot himself for the rest of the day, and all those he had left behind him.

He awoke in the late afternoon, and putting his head out, charmed the housewife into heating him a bath, and making him some thick oatcakes and tea to which she added slices of thick ham and cheese and a bowl of cream on her own thought. He ate heartily and cheerfully, his troubles if he considered them so forgotten in the comfort of the moment, and joked with the housewife, with no premonition that it was to be the last such meal he would eat for a time past remembering. He could tell by the glint in the woman's eye that he could have had more than the oatcakes, had he tried, but he had for once had enough of women, and he merely bussed her cheerfully, took his bonnet, and set off.

He had no idea where he was going, altho' he had a hazy notion in his head that he might join up with one or the other of the armies, if it suited him, the Royal Scots of Charles or the Royal Scots of George. His loyalties with either being unengaged, and with only the present necessity of finding money when his cousin's ran out, no desire to spend his life in outlawry, or no skills or resources other than a strong arm that he was willing to hire out in a work not below a gentleman's pride (albeit a gentleman thrust on hard times), he went South, away from the two armies rather than North towards them. The coins in his pocket gave him a short time of grace without the pressings of an empty stomach, to think things out in, and his present plan was to take service with the army which in that week appeared to be winning. He took himself therefore again towards Edinburgh on his mare with the thought of most quickly becoming in possession of accurate facts. The only emotion he could find in his breast was a slight disappointment towards his father's neutrality. Had his father chosen a side, with any luck he could have arranged himself on the other and possibly looked forward to the pleasure of officially looting or sacking his father's house, once his and once to be his, and possibly, just possibly, showing mercy to the cowering old man. He erased the adjective, both of them. In honesty he could not imagine his father cowering, and he was yet in his prime, although Diarmid had been a late son.

On arriving in Edinburgh, two days later, his plans and his

attitudes underwent an abrupt change. He heard reports there of the Prince's defeat at Culloden Field, on Drunmossie Moor, between Inverness and Nairn, a defeat already rumoured to be decisive, and that the victorious army, as drunk with triumph as he had been two nights before, wading in blood, was giving scant respect to claims of uninvolvement or neutrality. The eyes he met looked on him with a hostility and a suspicion he had not encountered. He was unable to find anyone who would serve or sell to him openly. His lips set, and his heart strangely turning, he turned the mare back again towards the North, curbing his desire to push her into a gallop.

He felt an unreasonable, unreasoning desire to hurry, but when the next day he came to a halt on a precipice overlooking his father's house in the vale below, there seemed no reason to have come. He could see small figures below him, going about ordinary activities. The Glen was quiet, there were no sounds except the lowing of the cattle, borne to him on the wind, the creak of a windlass and rope at the well. He did not see his father, but neither did he see anyone strange. Life was going on, and going on without him. His lips stiffened, and he turned away, and walked back to his mare.

But having come so far, he thought he would ride yet a little farther North, and see what truth there was in the reports. He discovered quickly that his neutrality which in Edinburgh had closed the King's doors on him in his Highland dress here in the Highlands closed the crofters' cottages and huts on him.

"Have you come from the big battle?" he was asked twice, and in all honesty he said he had not.

"Why not?" they had asked, and then shut the doors in his face. It was not a time, he discovered, for explanations, and he began to doubt they would do much good, either way. He shot a woodpigeon, and a rabbit, using his shot, and made a fire near a burn, and roasted them on a green stick, and while he waited, he sat by the burn tossing pebbles in it, his mind blank of thoughts or images, and yet in a turmoil of hurt. He had almost gone down, almost, but then, in the doorway he had seen the chestnut hair of the girl he'd brought there, who seemed to be still there. So he had not gone. It was as well. He'd made an oath, and it was a weakness that he had for a moment thought to go back from it. He threw the little pebbles harder, and then he rose and went off with his long strides to walk on the hills before he ate, to bring back the appetite that had suddenly left him.

It was a beautiful afternoon, and despite the situations in and around him, he felt his heart lightening in the sheer joy of mid-April in the hills, the twigs touched with colour, sallow and rose, the tender buds in sight, swelling, ready to burst their cases, the deer's horns glimpsed through the thickets in fur, the brown heather softening, and he began unconsciously to whistle softly.

He was startled to hear a voice suddenly calling him, calling his name, urgently, the voice low and frightened. He stopped, and turned, locating the direction of the voice as he thought.

"Diar," the voice cried again, a sob of relief underneath it, "oh Diar, I am over here."

He walked over to a little hollow, almost a gully, and saw his young cousin Rawn MacCullough lying in it among the stones, his foot twisted under him, and wedged in the stone.

"Rawn!" he exclaimed, "What's happened to you, Rawn, how did you come here?" He had leaped nimbly down the scree into the little gully, and was pulling the rock off the boy's foot, even as he spoke, not waiting for any answer.

"Oh, Diar," the boy said, "I heard you whistling, and I knew your whistle, so I thought I dared to call."

"Thought you dared to call?" Diar said slowly, his face blank.

"Oh, Diar, I have been so frightened. I've heard people, and feet, and horses, but I didn't dare to shout. I've been here two days now, since my horse threw me, and I fell. I think I've broken my foot, but I can't tell, for I couldn't draw it out."

Diar's hands had been busy all the time at the sharp rocks, pulling them off the boy and off his foot.

"I didn't know I was whistling," he said noncommittally, his voice lighter than he felt. "You were in a rock fall, weren't you, Rawn?"

"I suppose," the boy said wearily. "I don't know. My horse slipped and we fell, and he stepped on my foot trying to get up, and the rocks fell." He began to cry a little. "Oh Diar, I thought I was going to die here, and then I heard your voice." He winced, as Diarmid felt his foot. "Don't, Diar, it hurts so."

"I don't think it's broken," Diar said. "I think you've turned it, and it's just a sprain and badly bruised, Rawn. Try to stand, now, holding on to me. I've got a dinner roasting now, if I can get you back to it before it burns, and if you've been here even one day, you must be hungry."

"Oh, Diar, I can't," the boy said, his eyes filling and his lips quivering. "It hurts too much."

"You, Rawn?" Diar said, hiding his concern under a surface roughness. "You, acting the infant on me now? Brave boy that I know you are. I'll pack you, if we can just somehow get you up this scree. I can't get the balance to go up, if I carry you now."

But in the end that was just what he had to do, the boy clinging to his neck, and his weak fingers loosening their hold and letting him fall back twice, until his big cousin took his plaid and tied him to his back in it, pulling himself up by little twigs that broke, unable at first to get a purchase, the rocks slipping underneath him too.

"Well, young man," he said, depositing him on the ground, when they finally did reach the top, "you made a deal of trouble. What were you doing down here by yourself, and why didn't you call out when you heard horses yesterday?" But he knew the answer before the boy told him.

"I thought it might be soldiers," Rawn said, "and I didn't know which ones they were—if they were," he added. His face was crumpling childishly again, and without a word, Diarmid picked him up over one shoulder and started to walk back towards his fire and his glen.

"We'll feed you first," he said simply, "and then you'll tell me. I suppose you'd mind," he added, "if I left you here and went to get my horse? You could ride her then."

"I don't want you to leave me, Diar," the boy said, his voice trembling and very small.

"Well," Diar said, lengthening his stride. "It will be about the same, this way or the other."

He could smell the rabbit beginning to char, as they came in sight of the burn, where the stick had broken and let it drop, and putting the little boy down, he fished it out of the embers.

"Here," he said, his eyes kind, trying to smile at the pitiful figure with its helpless foot, "try some burned rabbit leg, just the thing to cure a foot."

The boy fell upon it as though he were starving, much the way Diarmid himself felt, and they both wished the rabbit had been two, and the woodpigeon four. When they had finished, and taken water to drink in their hands from the burn, the air was growing darker, and colder. Diarmid looked at the boy and said,

"Now, Rawn, tell me all about you, where you've been." As the boy hesitated, his eyes enormous, Diar said gently, "You were at the battle, weren't you, Rawn?"

"Yes," the boy gasped. "Yes, I was. I saw it all, almost."

"How would you be doing that?" said Diar. "Were they so short on men that they took children?"

"No," the boy said, "we were supposed to be at school, but we didn't go, a friend and I, we thought we'd rather see the fighting, and see our fathers go in, and so we hid in the heather and the bracken on a hill to one side, and we did see." He stopped, and he couldn't seem to go on.

"Yes?" Diar said. When the boy didn't speak, he said, "I know. You saw them lose."

"You don't know," the boy said, "and I don't know how to tell you. Then, when we went home, when we could, my mother was afraid I'd been seen or afraid I was too old to be safe, and so she sent me away on the only horse she could find, that she had left, but I couldn't ride it very well, and it threw me, when I got to where you found me."

"Is your father safe, Rawn, do you know?"

The boy shook his head, his lips white.

"I don't know, Diar, I don't know. My mother went to see, and I went with her just behind her but she didn't know, but they had put a ring of soldiers around the field, guarding it so that no one could get in or could get out. I could see the heaps of men, lying there, in the dark, Diar, they were groaning and crying out for water and for help, and no one could go to them, they were not allowed to. And when anyone tried to leave, when they went crawling or stumbling to the edge, the soldiers standing there just shot them or ran their swords right through them. It was dark, but I saw them, the shapes, and I heard them, and I had seen it earlier, it was nothing any more but blood and mud, on all their clothes, and on the soldiers' boots up to their knees." He rubbed his sleeve across his eyes. "My mother stayed, and I went, as she told me to. There was nothing I could do. She told me that. She said she didn't want to see me killed. They're all blood-mad. And so I went. I don't know about my father, Diar, I just don't know. But I saw people killed all along the road, just ordinary people, Diar, old men, and women, and little boys younger than me, and not even any clothes left them, and some of their heads split in two, and their things cut off and put in their hands. So I left the road, and I went through the rough. I saw some soldiers going into a cottage, and when they came out, Diar, one of them had a little baby on the sword end of his gun." The boy began to cry again helplessly, and Diarmid, cursing softly under his breath, said,

"Hush, now, Rawn, hush now. Battles look worse than

they are. I doubt not you'll find your father will be all right, but your mother was wise to send you off. She'll have enough to do with my girl cousins. I'll take you to my father—" he broke off—"Oh, my God, I can't."

"Can't what, Diar?"

"I can't take you to my father, and you can't walk." He drew an unamused laugh. "Well, I'll think of something."

"Why can't you take me to your father? Have the soldiers gone there, too?"

"No, Rawn, they haven't. And I don't think they will. He has a letter, if they do. He didn't call his men out, as your father did. You remember how they argued about it, when your father came to persuade mine, but he could not do it." He sighed. "It seems so long ago now. But when was it? In October? And it is now just April. So you should be safe there, if I can just get you there.— I wish your mother had come with you."

"Oh, Diar, I want to go. Can't we go now, tonight? Can't we? Is it so far? Can't you take me? Can't you pack me, as you did before?"

"No," Diar said shortly, "I can't." He paused, and then, seeing no help for it, he said, without expression, "My father has thrown me over."

"I don't believe it," the boy Rawn said, looking up, not certain how to take the older man's remark. "Thrown you over?" he repeated uncertainly. "Whatever for? I don't believe you."

"I assure you it is quite true," Diar said, even more bitterly. "Though it will seem a little thing to you, after what you've seen."

"But why? Whatever for, then?" the boy asked in amazement.

"You are too young, you would not understand," Diar said roughly, and then as the boy looked at him, he added, "I married without his consent, without asking him. There. That's all, or almost all."

Young Rawn shook his head, looking at the cousin he had

idolised all his life, as had they all. "I can't believe it, that he really has. Why, Diar, you were, you are, the one he loved best of all, you were his white-haired boy, the apple of his eye, and you know it."

"I knew it," Diar said, "and I suppose I presumed upon it, always perhaps a little far. Two nights ago, too far. You would believe it, had you been there. He threw me out. I soiled his house. You know the way he feels about his house. I could do anything but that, I knew it, but I was drunk and I forgot. He thought I hadn't married the silly girl. I don't blame him for it now. But we have both said and done things now, we can't go back on. I know I can't, I know that he cannot, Rawn." He smiled bleakly at the younger boy. "You see now how foolish men grow when they grow up. Do you think you can help it? I hope so, but I doubt if you can either, if you will be able to. I don't care about the girl. I never did. I don't even know her, I'd never seen her before that night, I was dead drunk and mad, all ways mad. I hurt his pride, and he hurt mine, and yet he's all I care about. That's funny, don't you think, Rawn?"

"No," the boy said, "I don't think so. I wish I could do something."

"You can," Diar said. "You can 'not talk' about it any more to me. I have to forget about it now. Tomorrow I was going away. I just came to be certain the old gentleman was all right, in this stir, and he seems to be. I will think of some way to get you to him. I'm going to sleep now."

"I can't go to sleep," the boy said. "I'm hungry, and I'm cold." The words trembled like his lips. "And I'm afraid my father's dead."

"I'm hungry, too, Rawn, but I have to thole it myself. You can go down, if you like, and wake up one of the tawnies, if you can't wait until morning. I will take you part of the way. But I can't go with you all the way, you see. If I did, they wouldn't give you anything."

The boy shook his head. "I don't want to do that." He sighed. "I think I'm not so hungry after all."

"Are you afraid, Rawn?" Diarmid asked gently. "They won't hurt you, you know."

"I seem to have gotten to be afraid of the dark," the boy said shakily. "I keep seeing things in it, all those arms and legs keep flying up at me out of the dark, and I hear the cannon and the cries and the sounds of the grape splattering against them, and they just standing there, surprised-like, and taking it, because they were told to." He began to shiver, and the older man put his arm around the boy, and drew him against him, wrapping his plaid about them both, letting the calm rise and fall of his broad chest calm the child's thin shaking one, until he fell asleep, and Diar then fell asleep too.

VI: *Monstrous Fruit*

IN THE MORNING, WHEN HE WOKE, THE LIGHT WAS NOT OVER
THE HILLS BUT THE SKY WAS LIGHTENING. DIAR DID NOT
WAKE THE STILL-SLEEPING CHILD, BUT SLIPPED OUT FROM
HIS PLAID. HE MEANT TO TAKE A LAST LOOK AT HIS FATHER'S
house, before he turned his back on it, a look without the
child's eyes on him. But when he reached the rock at which he
had stood the night before, he saw the soldiers had come before
him, sometime in the night. He saw them, a group of them, all
about the house.

He did not go back to the child. He stood there, helpless,
and knowing he was helpless, and watched what took place
below him. He saw two of his brothers come out, unarmed,
and he saw the soldiers shoot them, and his brothers fall, and
the soldiers go inside the house. He saw the woman he had
taken to wife brought out, and stripped of her clothes, as he
had stripped her, and from the tugging at her fingers, he
supposed of the ring he'd given her, and thrown down in the
dirt before the door, and taken in turn, one after another, by
the company. He did not see his sisters, he did not know

where they were, or where his other brothers and his cousins were, whether they were at home or not, whether they had left, after the cattle raid and his disgracing, or whether they were dead too, where he could not see them. He saw his father come out, helpless to stop the outrage on his steps, a paper in his hand, the letter of immunity, Diarmid thought, without mirth. He saw the letter taken and torn in strips, and his father stripped like his wife, and taken to the ash tree by the front of the house, and a rope slung across it and put about his neck, and his father hung from a branch of it, by a group of soldiers who had finished with his wife. He watched the anguish and the ribaldry of the separate little figures, knowing he could do nothing to prevent it, one man, without even bullets in his pistol any more, or reach them in time, were he fifty men.

"I said I would return when I saw my father dead, when I saw him hanged," he thought to himself in shock, his lips moving silently with the words, his anger and grief beyond caution or self-preservation or thought for the child with him, "and I will keep that word."

He stood up and walked down the hill towards his house, where the soldiers were milling in and out, careless of himself, until he reached the cleared space before the house. He paused only a moment, looking at the house, at the orchards beyond it ready to bud, knowing he would not see it again or much longer, and then he walked towards the tree where his father hung. He did not expect to find life there, or if life, awareness of him or his presence, and he did not. He did not know whether his father yet lived or not, he could not bring himself to look upon his tortured and distorted face beyond his control now. He knelt for a moment beneath the feet above his head, and then standing up, he gave a great shout of rage and anguish and crying "MacLyon avenge MacLyon!" he took the dirk that he had concealed in his sleeve, seeming unarmed as he walked up, and struck the soldier approaching him through the red cross on his breast, and pulling it out, flung it like an arrow through another, as he felt arms take him from behind and hold him. He stood there, panting, his head thrown back, braced in their grip, beside his dying or dead father, not caring what they did to him, expecting to feel the sword.

So his wife saw him, pulling herself to her feet, and saw them strip him, as they had his father, binding his hands, and bringing a second rope.

"You carry ropes aplenty with you, ready," she cried in a ringing bitter voice, and pushed her way through them, as if her stained dusty body were covered in court robes. "You have taken my ring from me, and my honour, and you take now my husband. Is not his father's life enough for you?"

Diarmid turned blank eyes upon her briefly as on a stranger, and then looked away.

"She is not my wife," he said, "Pay no attention to this woman or what she says."

Nevertheless, unaccountably, the soldiers let her meet him, and stand before him, and drew themselves a little back. Perhaps they thought his speech was meant to deceive them to protect her, but if they did, they misjudged it.

She stood before him, looking at him full in his white nakedness where his kilt and his shirt had covered his skin.

"Have you come to taunt me, madam?" he said bitterly, his face as rough and bleak as the North Sea. "Make haste with it then. This should give you pleasure, and amend my sins. These men are in a hurry, and I am too."

She shook her head slowly, her eyes upon him. "No," she said softly, "I have indeed not come to taunt you. You have a bonny body, Diarmid MacLyon, and I wish they would not spoil it, but I am not sorry that I met you, for our meeting, or that we came together. I am only sorry for this ending."

"A pretty speech, ma'am. I wish I could make you a pretty speech in return, but I cannot. I only wish I had never met you. So should I have been here then to stand as I should by my father's side. I wish you joy of the bastard I saw recently gotten upon you."

He turned and went with the soldiers as they directed him, to the limb of the tree by his father. She saw him gasp, as the rope tightened, and his eyes widen in pain, and other signs of visible distress she could not bear to watch. She turned away from the sight, and saw to her astonished eyes a man she knew, her cousin, Colonel Grant, approaching.

She ran to him, oblivious of her nakedness, and caught desperately at his cloak, as he reined in his horse.

"Why, Mary Elisabeth," he cried in startled surprise to see her, beyond speech, reaching down to clasp her hands, "my dear, my dear, what is it?"

"Oh, Colonel Grant," she cried, "make them stop, oh make them stop, they are hanging my husband now, oh please make them stop!"

He could not help believing her, however incredible her presence and the fact, the tears streaming now down her face. Without a word, he spurred his horse into the ring of soldiers by the tree, and drawing his sword, cut both ropes in two, that of the young man first. She had come running, and was there almost as he fell to the ground, her fingers frantically pulling at the rope about his neck, unable to release it. The Colonel had dismounted, and his fingers and his knife did what she could not. He was experienced both in taking and in restoring life, and with sharp tapotements, and a quick extempore bloodletting with his knife, and then his brandy flask, he had the young man breathing again. The older man, however, as she knew, was dead.

"He will do now, Mary Elisabeth," the Colonel said, standing up, "this young fellow." He stood uncertainly beside her, his face a little flushed, his eyes averted.

Diarmid opened his eyes in pain, and looked at her, his eyes full of angry pain. "Why could you not let me be?" he said in an angry whisper. "Now it will just be to do again, a second time." He shut his eyes, and turned his head away.

"The fellow's right, you know, Mary Elisabeth," the Colonel said, not ungently. He took his blue cloak off and put it about her shoulders and put his hands under her arm to lift her to her feet. "But it's done now. We've got him back now, for the time being."

He gave orders to two soldiers to carry the living prisoner to a horse and into camp and to secure him there under guard, and to bring the dead for burial.

"Who is this other man they hanged?" he asked her curiously. "Did you know him?"

"Yes," she said with a sob, "he was my father-in-law. He was my husband's father. He had a paper of immunity. And he was very kind to me."

"Well, my dear," he said, patting her shoulder gently, "these are not sights for you, and I am sorry you have seen them. Have you things in the house?"

She shook her head, and he looked at her more curiously still. "Only my clothes," she said vaguely, "they are about somewhere. And Diar's are there too."

"I will have them taken to him," he said. "I am under orders to fire this house," he said, "and all that's in it that I do not take. There is nothing of yours, you say?"

She shook her head, not explaining. "Except my ring," she said suddenly. "Oh, Colonel Grant, I want my ring, my wedding ring. Can you not make the soldier give it back to me who took it from me? I know the man, I know which one it was."

"Show him to me and I will see to that," he promised. "Now put your clothes on, my dear, if these are all you have, and when we get to camp, as soon as I may, I'll send you down to Edinburgh to your home."

She did not attempt to argue then. She dressed herself inside the house, in the white finery of the assembly ball and her wedding, and let him lift her in front of him on his white horse.

"Your soldiers have hurt me, Colonel Grant," she said, wincing.

"I was afraid they had," he said, embarrassed. "They did not of course know who you were." The scene he had come across was a commonplace one to him now, except for her presence there.

She leaned back against him wearily. Nothing was safe any more, and she saw no comfort and no help anywhere, but she had done what she could for the present. Behind her, she saw flames rising, from Diar's house and orchards, and she felt the tears sting her eyes, for the little thing of their destruction, after the destruction of their owners.

VII: *From the Military to the Civil, Diar's Wife, Perth*

COLONEL GRANT TOOK HIS RELATIVE TO HIS QUARTERS OUTSIDE THE CAMP IN PERTH, AND MADE HER COMFORTABLE THERE, HIRING A DOCTOR TO ATTEND HER AND A WOMAN TO WAIT ON HER, AND SENDING A DRESSMAKER TO FIT her out, and when he came to see her again three days later, she was more like herself in looks, in a blue and white sprigged muslin morning dress, and her curls combed and brushed and held back with a blue ribbon.

"Where is Diar?" she asked him at once. "Can I see him?" She spoke hopefully, but in her heart she was full of terror, waiting for the answer, knowing the rough peremptory justice of the camps.

"He is in the camp, my dear, under my protection, for what that avails him," he looked at her searchingly, "but Mary Elisabeth, my dear, your stories do not gibe. You say he is your husband, and he says he is not." He sighed and put aside his wig and his laced hat and sat down in a chair, sandy-haired, his red face clean-shaven above his blue coat red-faced and gold-laced.

"Never mind what he says," she said. "Just believe what I tell you." She sat very close to him, her face pleading. "What will happen to him, Colonel Grant?"

He looked embarrassed. "I wish you wouldn't ask me that, Mary Elisabeth. I don't know how to answer you."

"Can you save his life?" she asked directly.

He looked relieved by her directness. "No, my dear, I really don't see how I can. He has killed two of my men, and altho' admittedly he had provocation, the law won't excuse him, the military or the civil."

"Which has him now?" she whispered.

"The military."

"And which is quickest?"

"The military, my dear, always."

"What will you do with him?"

"If he were not your husband? We would already have questioned him, and hung him then." He looked at her searchingly. "And he says he is not. Every one about him hears him say it. It puts you, and me too, my dear, in a position of some ridicule and more awkwardness."

"Can you not have him transferred to the Civil?"

"I could, perhaps, my dear, but the end there would be the same, only slower, and the jails are worse. He would not thank you for it."

"I know that, Colonel Grant." She sighed. "You have been very good to me, Colonel Grant, and we are hardly relatives. Can you not do just this one thing more?"

He sighed in his turn. "I think not, my dear," he said baldly and frankly. "I could lie to you, of course, until after the thing is done, but that is not my way. He is being questioned now, and tomorrow morning he should hang." He winced at her face. "I told you," he said gently, "at the time, it was not a service to him. But with the questioning, it may be of some to us."

She grew even whiter, and without other warning, she fainted.

"I did not know it would be so soon," she said, when he had brought her to her senses with a hartshorn and a cloth on her forehead.

"I do not understand this," he said, sitting beside her. "You act as though you were his wife and he your husband, and yet he does not act as if he is or as if you are. He does not want to see you, Mary Elisabeth. He has made as his request that you not be allowed in to him again."

She brushed the remark aside, as unimportant. "I know," she said. "I know how he feels. Colonel Grant, what are you going to do with *me*?"

"Why, send you home to your mother and to your father," he said, "what else?"

"I watched your face," she said slowly, "when you found me. I thought"—she looked at him quickly, and then away— "I thought you might like it if I stayed with you."

He blushed a fiery red, and stuttered, and ran his fingers under his tight stock, but he did not deny what she said. He looked as if he were going to rise, but she reached out and caught his hand and held it in hers, and kissed it.

"Oh, Miss Mary Elisabeth," he gasped, but not withdrawing his hand, "you must not. We are related."

"But not so very closely," she murmured, drawing him by his hand nearer to her, and putting her other hand against his cheek, guiding it to her. He knew what his soldiers had done to her, and she knew that he did. On that score no explanations or reassurances were needed.

"I do not want at all," she said softly, "to go back to my mother's and my father's. I am not at all a little girl any longer. I would much rather stay with you"—she paused— "as long as you want me."

"I know what you want," he said, his voice low, his eyes upon her too, now.

"Do you," she said, bringing his hand upon her breast.

"You want me to turn this fellow over to the Civil."

"Yes," she said. "That's all. I know that's all you can. I don't expect you to do any more."

"And when I've done it, will you leave me?"

"No," she said, "I will stay with you as long as you want me to, or until his trial begins."

"Oh, Lord," he said, his hand against her breast, "what will your ma say?"

"She will not know. I am not going home, no matter what you do, or what you do not do." She held out her arms then and clasped them about his neck and brought his lips down against hers, but after a moment, seeing their intention, she whispered, "Only first, stop the questioning, Colonel Grant. And oh, do not let them whip him."

"I think you love the fellow, whoever he is," the Colonel said, looking at her.

"I don't know," she answered, "but I wear his ring, and I don't want him to die."

The Colonel was not an unkind man, as he had shown, nor dishonest. He said to her very gently, with a question in his voice: "Do not deceive yourself. He will only suffer more, in the end he will die."

"But not yet," she said, a fierce determination in her voice.

When the Colonel returned, she fulfilled her part of the bargain, as well as she could, and after Diarmid had been sent off under military guard, one the Colonel trusted to exact no executions on their own, she continued to keep it, to his satisfaction if not to hers.

VIII: *A Civil Jail*

Lodged in Carlisle Jail, Diarmid was unaware of his wife's efforts in his behalf, and had he known them he would, as the Colonel said, have been unappreciative. Had he known the means, he would have killed her, had he the means himself; and the ends he did not like either. Death had no more terrors for him than for most Highlanders, a commonplace accepted thing to be got through as well as one's nerves allowed. But the elusiveness of the unpleasant death he knew he had to go through was wearing his nerves.

He had endured the questioning and the stripes given him, without giving any satisfaction, since he had none to give. He had attempted once to explain MacLyon's attitude of neutrality, but when he reminded the soldiers of the paper some of them had torn up, he was gagged summarily with a drum stick for impudence, and after that he confined his answers properly to *yes* and *no*. He had endured the binding on his hands, and the thought of the neck binding to follow that would bind off his breath finally. His grief of spirit at the loss of his father and the burning of his house was too great to allow lesser griefs to prick him. But then, instead of what he had expected and braced himself to meet, his hands had been bound in front of him, and he had been set like a figure of fun, he thought bitterly, on a Galloway pony, his legs tied underneath the animal's belly, and he had been led off then, on an endless and uncomfortable journey through Ft. Augustus, where he had lodged for a night in a cellar and been carried in triumph through the streets and pelted with refuse, on up to Inverness, and put in that vile hole. He feared imprisonment and rot more than death and its pains, which in foreseeable time ended, as this did not.

The ropes on his hands were exchanged for iron fetters, needlessly heavy, in his eyes, since he could see no way out of the jail, and his feet were fettered. They were not all ironed, there were too many of them, but he had killed two men, not in the battle itself, and being sure of death, it seemed, and strong in his youth, he had been heavily ironed as the dangerous and the condemned were.

He had seen, in those few days since his taking, sights he had never seen in his twenty-two years, or thought to see. He had been bedded in Inverness in a room he would have considered small for one, with ten, which he would not have left his horse in because of the damp, ankle deep in the uncleaned mire of ten men's necessities, there for days before him. He had stood against the wall, his ankles in it, his face a mask, and of necessity added his own to it. The weight of the irons on him pulling him down, still he stood, refusing to sit in it like those too weak to stand, with fever or mistreatment and their wounds. One of the prisoners, a Frenchman, an officer, was dying, he thought, and he lay unattended, his legs covered with the muck, and with blood. He would have thought it impossible to breathe the air of the place, but he breathed it. He had yet his clothes, but half of them had not. They took the measure of dry meal thrown to them, catching it as they could, eating it with their fingers, even the bits that dropped, those there before him having been left the first days with nothing. He had been beaten himself, before the questioning had been abruptly stopped, cruelly enough in his opinion, and having no interest in either side, had he had anything of interest to them, he would have gladly let them have it, but he hadn't. But he saw then the sides of men, old and young, torn open in ways two days before he would have retched to see. Now he merely turned his eyes a little from their blackened opened sides, or stared up at the ceiling, at the little unconcerned spiders running on their strings now.

In the beginning he had been hungry enough to have swallowed one of the beasties, had it chanced to fall on its thread into his mouth, but after a time, with the sights and smells about him, and his stomach growing more used to the little it was to have, he felt no appetite. From time to time the door opened and other prisoners, men, women, and children alike and together, were added, but those who died were not removed. So April outside the walls turned to May, and as the days grew milder the smell of illness and rot and unburied death from the overcrowded prison grew so strong that the crowds that had in April come to watch them like caged animals or savages, hardened as they were to bad smells and odours, in May no longer filled the streets about the prison.

The week after May Day, which was celebrated in the South with an unusual merriment that year, he was taken without any reason for it that he knew, or questioned, out of the stinking hole, his clothes a grey shadow of themselves, a figure of such unpleasantness he saw faces turned away from him as he passed, his strength still with him, dragging his chains through the street. They had been tight when they were first put on him, and caused him much discomfort, but there was only bone now, and a veil of flesh, inside the iron. It seemed to him that all of Inverness had been after all loyal to King George. It was full of citizens who were going about their business, as well as crammed with redcoated soldiers wherever he looked, and yet he had thought all Scotland was in the jail. He was not even of much interest now, it seemed, except to the children. One spat on him, and he spat back. Then he held his head up, and did not look at anyone, as he was taken with the other twenty, down to the Quay.

He did not know where he was going, and he did not care. He knew when he was put in the boat with the twenty that the boat was overloaded, but for all he knew, the purpose was to drown them, and he was hardly surprised when once out of the shelter of the quay, the wind and the ruffling waves did overturn the boat.

The stinging coldness of the icy water brought him to his senses. They were in deep water, and he felt the weight of the irons pulling him down like a kitten weighted in a sack to drown, and he knew, like the kitten, he was only one of many, unwanted and uncared for, drowning suddenly in the dark airless waters, without warning, without preparation.

"I could be free now," he thought dimly in the rushing tumult striking against him, "I could be free and no one would know, if these irons were not dragging me down." Those on his feet had been taken off, for the walk, and had been piled in a corner of the overweighted boat. His hands now with the help of the water pulled free of the heavy shackles on his thin wrists, scraping in the stinging salt which roused him again, and he struck out towards the surface, the only thought in his bursting brain under the weight now to pull up where he could find air.

The waves were tossing and choking him, when he found it, throwing spray against him and into his mouth, but he had swum in icy lakes and tarns all his life, he had been baptised in cold spray, and the chill briefly revived him, washing the blood and filth off him, fresh and cold in his nostrils. He struck out strongly now for the shore, hoping he would not fall into waiting hands, not knowing where he was going, until the waves flung him against a rock and knocked his senses from him. He thought even as they fell away, that he heard his name called, by a voice he had known somewhere, and he tried to reach the voice, but the pain in his head was too great and it took him away.

When he came to his senses he thought he had been dreaming, or he would have thought so except for the cold clamminess of his wet clothes on him, and the ringing pain in his head. He was lying in a cradle like a helpless child, rocking to and fro, shaking him, and then his senses returning told him he was in a boat again, another cockleshell, and his hands and feet were bound. He could have cried then, for weariness and vexation and disappointment, had he not been past crying age. He might as well have drowned, and he wondered why he hadn't, forgetting the struggle his still strong unconscious senses had made for him in their brief hope. Except that the twenty had drowned and he had not, his situation was just the same. He shut his eyes against the sharp pain in his head and bones and the sharp cold of the wet and the wind, and wished he were one of the twenty, instead of in the second boat with twelve going out to sea to what he did not know. He opened his eyes and saw the other chained men whose eyes were not looking at him, and he shut them again. God alone knew why he lived. He did not.

They were taken then on board the transport, hauled aboard like baggage, the fetters returned to their feet, and a pair found for Diarmid to replace those he had lost, and sent down to the hold.

It was already filled, as the jail had been filled when they were dropped into it, with naked ill bodies that had once been proper men, and with all the filth and smell of nature and of illness they could not rid themselves of in the natural ways of privacy, all there together, nothing but the cold earth and colder stones of the ballast to sit on or lie on or die on. The dark air all around was full of little whispering sounds, pulling at his ears, until he thought he would go mad, with that, and the rocking motion of the anchored ship, and the cold, and the dull slap-slapping of the waves echoing down against the sides. He sat on a stone in the dark, beside the other bodies, pale stones and pale bodies, and put his head on his chained hands, and wept.

But he did not die. He ate a biscuit when it was tossed to him, and his legs swelled, and his stomach cramped, and the days passed, four of them, in a delirium of nothingness, as painful as death and as ugly as hell. There was nothing he could do about it. He could not even die, his body being yet too strong. Then miraculously or by chance the ship, unlike the other transports, received its orders and set sail for Carlisle where a week later it dislodged its passengers into the Castle Gaol.

He did not know where he was, or that for the first time in his life he had entered England, until he was told, and then he did not care much. He did not talk, and he did not listen. In the day, now, he was allowed to move free, but at night he was stapled to the floor. He sat there, among his fellows, and wished for death, like a wild free creature trapped.

The place itself, though bad, though dirty and cold and with no fresh air and little light, was not the impossible hell of the jails he had been in. He was in England, and neither the streets nor the jails there were sewers. In it, he did not wade in filth or blood, and when men and children died about it, after a reasonable time they were removed; and the women with their different necessities were in another part. But those places had had one virtue that the jail in Carlisle where he was lodged now did not: they had been temporary, makeshift prisons, and in them he could believe he would be released out of them, if he could endure, in a day, in an hour, into something different, what he did not much care. But in this jail meant to house robbers and murderers and those dominant society put away out of its sight, permanently forgotten, he felt for the first time in his life despair.

Against it, he whistled, when his mouth was not too dry, or when things weren't thrown at him. He stood against the wall, whistling, except at night when he was forced to sit down, chained to the staple. It did not occur to him then that his ducking had lost him his identity, and that he was no longer the Diarmid MacLyon who had killed two of Colonel

Grant's soldiers, that that man had been drowned, and he was only an unnamed Rebel, suspected.

On the third day that he was there, the door to their ward was opened and three soldiers from the Manchester Brigade were added, and the boy Rawn MacCullough, whom he had left on the hillside, limping on an improvised stick. His eyes, frightened and unseeing, did not light on Diarmid, or if they saw him, did not recognise him.

Diarmid watched the boy, just a child, not yet twelve, thin and reedy and undangerous, and he felt rage welling up within him, the first emotion he had felt since his father's death, turning his blood and increasing the flow, for a moment, as full of life as a dinner of meat, and then it ebbed, leaving him weak, as he realised his helplessness to translate that rage into any effective action.

"Rawn," he called softly, from his corner of shadows, "Mac-Cullough there, hillo!"

The child lifted his eyes, as if he had been struck, and covered them with his arm thrown suddenly over them, shrinking away, his stick clattering on the floor.

Diarmid walked forward a step, and picked it up and held it out to the child.

"I'm not a ghost, Rawn," he said, his mouth twisting into a wry smile, "not yet. Did you think I was?"

"Yes," the child answered, his eyes enormous and dark, looking anxiously at his big cousin, "yes, I did, Diar." He put out a hand timidly, and Diarmid took his cold shaking ones in his own, warm with that rage. His face relaxed at the reassuring touch, and he ran limping into his cousin's arms, against the chains, and began to cry, painfully, trying to hold the sobs back.

"There now," Diar said, his own throat dry and empty, beyond tears, "there now, Rawn, you should be angry with me, I think. I left you there asleep, with never a thought to you, or what you would do."

"The soldiers found me," the boy said, his face buried.

"Oh, Diar, I thought you were dead. I saw—I saw what they did to you. I woke up, and you were gone, and after a little, I made a stick and walked to the edge, and I saw what they did to you."

"Then you didn't see it all," Diarmid said, "you see, for here I am."

"I couldn't watch it any more, I went away," the boy said. "I didn't know what to do. And then the soldiers found me, and they made me come with them here." He began to shiver, under his cousin's hands.

"And here you are. Good friends together again," Diarmid said lightly. "Well, Rawn, now that you are here, perhaps I'll give a mind to our escaping."

But they did not escape. There was no way. They stayed, and were ill, eating unfit, unclean food, skins, and offal thrown to them, and the maggoty spoiled meal, and soiled themselves like all the rest, and grew too weak to stand easily. Diarmid had seen one man, unironed, escape through the privy closet in Ft. Augustus in the officer's house he had been kept in one night, but there was no such means here, and the walls were solid.

"Here, Rawn," Diarmid said, with grim determination and humour, "eat maggots. They've more to them than the meal." He protected the boy's share for him and coaxed him, and somewhere, out of the caring, came without his knowing an intention and a determination just to live, until someone killed him, that stood them both in needed stead.

IX: *Diar's Wife,*
Ft. Augustus to Inverness

I N PERTH AND THEN IN FT. AUGUSTUS, DIAR'S WIFE STAYED
IN HER QUARTERS AS COLONEL GRANT'S MISTRESS. SHE WAS
SEVENTEEN, AND HE WAS FIFTY. AFTER DIARMID HAD BEEN
REMOVED, WHERE SHE COULD NOT PERSUADE HIM TO TELL HER,
she had ceased to woo him, although she kept without complaining to her bargain. When the call came in May for the
army to move North, to Harry the Glens, they parted company, without ill feelings on either side.

"I'd like all the same to send you back to your Ma," the
Colonel said. "I wish you'd let me. You needn't tell her about
this."

"No," she said, a little smile at her lips, "I'm past my family
now."

"Well," he said, "I can at the least give you money."

"Oh yes," she said, "I'll take that, whatever you will give
me."

"Where will you go, then?" he asked curiously. "What will
you do, Mary Elisabeth?" He felt a little pricking of shame,
but there was not much use for that, now, and he had only
continued what others had begun.

"I am going to find Diar," she said, her mouth obstinate. They had been through the subject before. "I think you might tell me where you sent him."

"Mary Elisabeth," he said impatiently, "that young man doesn't want to see you. And you know that. God knows why you want to see him. He doesn't love you, he doesn't even own he married you. I would bet money on it he is not thinking of *you*, so why do you of him?"

She did not answer, but only pressed her lips together.

"I am not going to let you do it," he said. "I am not going to let you waste your youth and your strength in a stinking trial of a stinking Rebel all summer, and break your heart watching his heart cut out. That's all you saved him for, my dear," he said curtly, as she gasped, "I tried to tell you; didn't you know?"

She stared at him, her grey eyes all pupil, beneath their heavy curling fringe, but she did not say a word.

"Oh, lord, my dear," he said, looking back at her, "you are a lovely chit." He sighed. "You can do better than be a camp follower. You can get out of this, and forget it. I wish you'd let me help you. I wish I were not so tied up here, I wish I had time to make you do as you ought and as you could. I can give you a letter to a woman who will help you."

"Where?" she asked.

"In Aberdeen."

"Are there prisoners in Aberdeen?"

He did not answer.

"I think instead I'll go with your captain up to Inverness, if you won't take me. I'll start there, and work my way down."

"You *fool*," he said, looking as if he would like to shake her, and kiss her all at once, and after a moment he did both. "Oh, sweet," he said, after a time, "oh sweet, I have a wife, or I would marry you myself."

"And I have a husband," she said, and felt him strike her.

"Be damned to your husband," he said. "I have done all

that I could for him, Mary Elisabeth, he picked the wrong side."

"He did not, he was not for either side," she said stiffly, "and you knew it."

"There is no such side as neither side," he answered briefly. "Neither side is the wrong side. There is only the King's side. Pick the right one now yourself. You were born on it, and you lived on it until when? A week ago? A month ago I saw you at your mother's house, remember? If you continue this way, you will end in jail yourself, and a Scottish jail is no place for any woman. It is no place for you, Mary Elisabeth."

"I'll remember that," she said with an effort at lightness. "I'll try to keep out of them." She saw she had reached her limit with him, and the end of his helpfulness. "Slap me again," she said, to divert him, "but in another place." She lay beneath him then, quiescent, her mind thinking furiously.

That night, when he was out of his quarters, taking her money and hiding it beneath her skirt, and wearing the simplest of her clothes, leaving all the others, she stole out and removed herself to the camp followers just outside the camp itself. She believed, rightly, that for all his words and hers, it was the one place Colonel Grant would not look for her, both for her own dignity and his own, or think to find her; and she believed, rightly, that he intended to force her to return South to be cared for. She did not intend to wait for that, when escape or elusion would be harder. She knew she had only one way of reaching Inverness safely and quickly, with inconspicuous transportation and food easily obtained by a single woman, and young as she was, and that was to march with the army. The Colonel himself had ironically suggested it to her. Otherwise, she would be picked up by the army, or worse, by a small patrol. She had already seen too much death by the road not to know what the attempt to travel alone and unprotected by George could mean.

She had little trouble finding a dragoon to sponsor her, and by now, no trouble meeting what that involved. She was a woman, she had discovered that essentially she meant one thing and had one commodity, and she accepted that. Between the dragoon and the Colonel she found little difference. On the long march, short to him, long to her, she found him in his way as kind, and she was grateful to him for that and for unconsciously furthering her purposes, as he furthered his own.

When they reached Inverness, she left him, quietly, without a word, as she had left the Colonel. She was not feeling quite herself, but she did not wonder at it. In fact, she no longer was certain who she was, in her self, for the self of the month of April bore no relation to any self she had been in any of the seventeen years before. She did not, as a matter of fact, think of herself at all, or of her family. That world seemed ages now removed away from her, by her experiences, rather than space or time. She seemed outside of time now, with no relation to anything but the present moment, but in this seeming she was mistaken. She was very much in time, and close to becoming the prisoner of time in the way peculiar only to women, for though she did not know it, at some time she had become pregnant.

Meanwhile, she stood in the cold windy streets of Inverness, and shivered, and drew her cloak about her, and wondred what to do. She would have liked to find a place to have something hot to drink, but she saw no likely place, and she had never tried to find such a place on her own. She was not downcast; she had known how hard it would be, and she had known she had to come. Diarmid might be here, or he might not, and how she was to find out she had no idea, but find out she intended to do.

If to find a hot drink was hard, to find the main jail where the Rebel prisoners were was not hard at all, she found. Everyone was glad to oblige her, and knowledgeable. She stood in the street, not realising that Cumberland had had them swept of their customary litter, in the little rain falling softly, that reached the earth as heaven's pity did not, not wincing at the smell like what she thought a charnel house must smell like, for it might be the air that Diar breathed, and stared at the walls of the building before her, and at the white faces at the little windows that stared back at her, without expression. Was Diar's one? She could not tell, they all looked alike, but she could not imagine him standing and staring so. But then she could not imagine herself standing and staring so, as she realised she was, either.

She could not breathe in the foetid air, and she felt herself becoming overcome by an unaccustomary faintness, when she saw the doors of the jail open, and soldiers emerge, escorting in their midst a wretched little band of unhappy men. She could hear the sound of their chains, inside the marching square of soldiers, but after the first glimpse she could not see them, for a crowd, of all sorts, and particularly children suddenly appeared, silent at first, then becoming noisy, jeering the prisoners.

"Where are they taking them?" she asked faintly to a woman near her, her heart seeming to be in her throat with a sudden fear.

"They are taking them to the transports," the woman said. "My man is there among them." The woman looked about hastily, as if she had said too much, as if she had been caught cursing the King, and without Diar's wife being aware of it, she melted away into the back parts of the street. Mary Elisabeth's eyes were not on her any more, they were strained to catch the glimpse she could not find. On more than impulse, on a compulsion she did not reason with, she followed the little group, in the crowd, past the Cross and the Stone, past the apple tree beside both among whose last pink and white blossoms and young leaves hung the naked mutilated body of what had been a Highland man, pushing ahead of them, and after a time, as she had somehow known she would, she saw Diar's black head and his unlaughing face set in lines she almost did not recognise and his eyes that swept over her and past her, unseeing, and did not see her, and his large hands

lost in the heavy bands of iron constraining him, and his leg
irons about his neck, for him to carry.

There was nothing she could do. She could not go to him,
and she knew from his face he would not want her, even if
she could, in this humiliation. She could not even cry out his
name, even if she could have found voice, choked by pity
and a helpless instinct of protectiveness. But she followed.
She knew now, without being told, what Colonel Grant's first
order had been, on arriving in Inverness, and she wondered
if she had hurt him again, worse, as the Colonel had said she
would, by her interference. She saw him put with the others
into the boat, and the boat go, and then capsize, and the
prisoners weighted with their chains, and some chained together, sink and not reappear. She stood watching, from the
little hill above the quay, unable to believe what she had
seen, and so she saw what those on the quay did not, what
seemed to be a face against the waves, that rose, and disappeared, and rose again. She marked the direction the man
was swimming towards, and ran down towards the shore,
intent, watching, forgetting she might be seen. She saw the
figure swimming closer, tossed by the waves, and then strike
the rock, and she cried out his name again and again, unable
to reach him, floating face down in the windy sea. The two
soldiers, however, who had followed her curiously, saw too,
and one leaped into the sea without hesitation, and struggling out into the windy surf, pulled the figure away from
the rock and let the waves push them both in, until the waiting soldier and Mary Elisabeth could pull the both up onto
the ground.

She knelt beside him, her dress dragging in the wet, her
hair blown in the wind and wet with the spray, the rocks
cutting her knees, and pushed the hair back from his forehead, kissed it, and took his head in her arms, cradling him,
until the soldiers pulled her away.

"It's another damned Rebel," one said, "that was a kilt
once, that thing about him."

The other looked at Mary Elisabeth suspiciously and

asked how she knew he would be there, and who she was and who he was.

"I don't know," she said, and it was all she would say. "Have you any brandy? If you don't want him to die, if you want to keep him so you can hang him, if he is a Rebel, don't you want to give him some brandy, out of that flask I see you have?"

They did not seem particularly to care whether he lived to be tried as a Rebel, or died as a man by the sea, or perhaps they thought there was little danger of it. But they did try to give him brandy, which he could not swallow, being senseless from the blow.

"Well, Missy," they said, "you're going to come with us, and tell the Sergeant why we found you here, a-kissing of this man."

"I kissed him because I thought he was dead, and I was sorry. He looked like my brother but he isn't."

They laughed, and looked as if they didn't believe her, and as if they didn't much care. And then, with a look at one another, they fished out the lengths of rope that George's soldiers seemed always to be carrying with them, for Rebels, and bound Diar's hands and feet. Then they took her behind a rock, and in turn had her, the other watching. She did not fight them, for she hoped they would then leave her, but they did not. When they had finished, quickly, like a quick drink snatched on the march at a bar, they made her get up, and go with them, one holding her arm, the other carrying Diar slung over his shoulder.

"I doubt he's from the transport, and someway slipped his irons. There's one already got out on pig bladders he kept from the food, they are saying," said one. So they took him back to the second boat that was ready to go out, and threw him not gently in the water at the bottom, and then they took her to their Sergeant, in a room in the lower part of the Tolbooth outside of which she had stood watching the faces upstairs.

The Sergeant was as displeased with the soldiers as with Mary Elisabeth, not that they had raped her, which he dismissed as only natural if she would go down alone by the sea, but because they had sent the man out to the transport, and if he was in the hold now, there would be no distinguishing him from any other.

"We might know him," they said uncertainly. "The girl would know for sure. She could be taken to the transport."

"I wouldn't," she said, "I never saw him before, and what you did to me has put his face entirely out of my mind."

"You didn't seem to mind so much," one of the soldiers said with a glance at her. She bit her lip, and did not answer.

The Sergeant cut through the arguments by dismissing the soldiers. He then turned to Mary Elisabeth, and told her, his voice entirely cold, that he believed she did know something of the man, and he intended to have it from her.

"You can't have from me what I don't know," she said with spirit, "and I haven't any knowledge of who he is at all. Cannot a girl go by the seashore if she likes?"

"No," the Sergeant said curtly.

She did not answer immediately. She had already perceived what Diar would not topple to for weeks, that his situation, unrelieved in all respects but one, in that one offered some hope. If Colonel Grant believed him drowned, then Diar, she thought, would be tried as a Rebel, but not perhaps as MacLyon who had killed two of his men. If they did not know, she was resolved they should not know through her, if she could help it. She realised the Sergeant was looking at her, waiting for an answer.

"Well," she said, looking at him back, wondering what material he was made of, and deciding he was cut differently from Colonel Grant and not susceptible, "it is the truth all the same, and you will just have to believe it."

"We'll see about that," he said, and he ordered her taken to the Bridge-Hole.

She did not know what the Bridge-Hole might be, and so

she was only moderately afraid, being too weary and too disheartened out of all but her desperate resolution, but when she understood what was to happen to her she became very much afraid. Nevertheless, she only bit her lip and said nothing, looking down at the coffin-shaped narrow hole they were prepared to lower her into sunk into the bridge, just beneath it in its supports.

She stayed there for two days, with the noise of the carriages rumbling like thunder or like cannon over her, deafening her, and the tramping of soldiers' boots, and Rebel cattle's hooves, forced to stand, with her weight on her legs, unable to move, her arms over her head as they had lowered her in, refusing to eat or drink what they offered her, or to answer the questions the Sergeant put to her, or his kinder Captain who also visited her and tried to reason with her. The first hours she was able to answer spiritedly, but after a night there, the next morning she was beyond answering at all. That second day, she miscarried of the baby, screaming in cramp and pain.

At first they thought she was pretending, to be let out, but then, when they came again to see, she had fainted and had stopped screaming.

In the late afternoon Colonel Grant came to visit the stubborn Scotch lass in the Bridge-Hole, and if possible to persuade her to be reasonable. He could not see her face, only the colour of her hair, and he stooped beside the opening in sudden premonition.

"Oh my God," he said, "is it you, Mary Elisabeth?"

"I don't know," she said, her voice hardly audible. "Who is it?"

"It is Colonel Grant," he said. "Mary Elisabeth, is it you? Answer me, and I will have you out."

She began to cry, faintly, but she did not answer, and he signalled then to the soldiers they should bring her out, her legs so swollen they could hardly pull her up, and covered with blood. The Colonel took her hand, and stooped to one knee beside her, unable to speak, at the sight of her condition.

"Oh, Colonel Grant," she said, "I have been so sick. I think I've lost a baby." She began to laugh, in hysteria, between her tears, gasping. "I didn't know I was having one. And I don't even know whose it was." And then she began to cry in earnest. He did not try to answer or to ask her anything at all. He only held her head against him, and patted her hair helplessly, while he sent the soldiers to bring a carriage to carry her to his house in.

When she was better the next day, and the doctor seemed to think she could be talked to, he asked her if the man had been MacLyon.

She looked at him straightly, with her candid grey eyes. "I thought it was, Colonel Grant, and at first with his black hair and his white face he did look a little like him, but it was not Diarmid after all. But I kissed him, because he looked like Diarmid, and Diarmid was dead. I saw him drown, you know, and so I knew."

The Colonel sighed. He did not entirely believe her, but he forbore to question her farther, as clearly useless, and privately, he put a question mark by Diar's name.

X: *Carlisle, The Castle Gaol:*
The High Road and The Low Road

To BE ON A TRANSPORT WAS TO BE IN HELL. A MOVING
TRANSPORT, DESPITE THE SICKNESS OF THE MOTION IN
THE CLOSE HOLD, WAS PREFERABLE TO A STATIONARY
TRANSPORT, ONLY BECAUSE THE VOYAGE WOULD IN TIME END
and then one might get out. That was all. The journey down
to Carlisle was short, and that was all that could be said for it,
in Diarmid's opinion. But he was not asked to give it. He was
required to sit on his ballast stone, and not complain, and not
ask to come up topside to make his messes, in fact not to ask
for anything, nor was he given anything worth mentioning.
The weather was not stormy, and in less than a week the transport had arrived, the prisoners had been unloaded, dazed and
blinking in the sudden brightness of the morning, gasping in
the sudden freshness of the air, the plenitude of it choking them
in the rush of it. Those that could still walk, Diar among them,
walked to their new quarters in the Castle Gaol, again the subject of stares, and catcalls and rude names, and worse, sticks
and stones hurled at them, and boots, for the Rebels had advanced on Carlisle, breaking its city gates, and had held it long

enough, and had made prisoners of their own. There was a hostility here not felt in Inverness, out even of the Lowlands now, in England, and what Scots there were were many of them Armstrongs, and Lowlanders and hostile on those separate accounts too. It was a terrible experience to be mocked at for his suffering, and for his discomfort to be a source of delight to those about him. They were chained together in small groups of twos, but the boat this time did not go down, and they marched their hurt swollen legs through the streets prodded by swords behind them. If the gaol after the march seemed a relief they discovered soon enough that that was a delusion and that it was not.

The presence of the boy Rawn saved Diarmid's spirit from dying there completely, though he did not know it. His shock at seeing the child roused him from the lethargy beginning to take him, and to the child, except for the alteration in his looks and the heavy chains on him, he seemed much as he always had. His main concern continued to be to keep the child alive.

"I can't eat this," the child, hungry, had said in dismay, his stomach revolted, the first day they were given offal instead of meal.

"Of course you can, Rawn," Diar had replied cheerfully. "If I can, you can. Watch me. You didn't use to be so choosy. Anyway," he added, the clinching argument, "you want to be here when your mother comes, don't you? You don't want to fade away first, do you?"

The child had picked up the ill-smelling ropy stuff, and resolutely chewed at it, trying not to gag, shamed by his older cousin.

As the days passed, the jail grew fuller, and in August, the trials began.

They had been lotted for trial shortly after they arrived. A Baillie had appeared with a hat with little scraps of paper in it that each one drew, obediently, not knowing what they drew, and since most did not understand English they would not have known any more had they been told. It had been determined that each one out of every twenty so lotted should stand trial for his life, while the other nineteen should without trial receive the King's mercy of transportation. Even the King's justice and the outraged moral right of the King's people at the proposed treason against his person boggled at the prospect of several thousand trials and executions, and so the milder system was arranged. They stood in the jail, bewildered, holding the little slips of paper, while they were separated into groups, those to go for trial, and those for transportation, to sign their names into the separate books then, pleading or accepting the King's mercy.

Diar had drawn a white nineteen, and the child Rawn the black number twenty. He looked at the two papers, and with the voices and activity about him something of the nature of what was happening dawned in his mind, although the haphazard callousness of it and in both their cases the injustice of it made him still unable to accept it as possible. How soon the black mark was to be redeemed or in what way he did not know, or what would happen to the white, but he could not bear it for the youth of the child, and he knew it, and for himself, one fate suited him about as well as another, if he could not go free as he chose in the hills.

"You've gotten the wrong slip," he said quietly and conversationally to the child, taking it in his palm as he spoke, "give me mine. The white one's for a child, and being older, you know, I get the higher number anyway." He had taken it as he spoke, and began to talk of other things, and the child who spoke only Gaelic still, English only haltingly, did not know what he had done.

"What do they want?" the child asked, when the Baillie came to him.

It's just a silly game the English play," Diarmid said, "don't trouble about it, just say your name when the man asks you, and give him your slip, and hold up your fingers for your age." He could have wept when he saw the child's name signed to be transported, but he did not know what to do. But perhaps he would yet think of something. When he was asked for his own name, he thought of his father, and wrote down only the word Lyon. If he stood trial under his own name, the word might reach Colonel Grant, and he thought his own name would not help him, either way now. It was past; another time. Occupation, he put *none*; gentleman's rank, he put *none*. Let them think what they liked. In the end, he believed, that would be what they would think whatever he said.

The days then dragged on, those to be transported continuing as they were, beside those to stand scapegoat and be tried. Of the two fates, in the end, he thought, there might be little to choose. Tried, one might get off entirely; but he did not think so. From the little that crept in from the outside world, and the reports of the fresh prisoners who came in by land, not off the transports, the hot itch of the conquering country for their blood seemed no way abated. And he had seen already the nice distinctions of their justice, which put active and passive, thought and action, the innocent and the guilty, the eager and the reluctant, the young and the old, of both sexes and all estates of age, into one terrible basket of death and dirt together.

"Am I truly to be transported?" the child asked one day, having overheard something about it.

"I don't know," said Diarmid, or Lyon, as he schooled himself to think of himself, "I think so." He concentrated on picking his lice.

"What does transported mean?" the child asked, his eyes frightened.

"Well," said Diar-Lyon, "I don't exactly know myself, having never been done it myself, but if it is the King's mercy it cannot be so bad. Why, perhaps you'll get to travel on the sea, and see fine sights, and other countries. You'll have to work there, to pay your passage off, but then you'd be working here. It could be a fine time you'll be having there." He was lying, and he knew it, and the child knew it. They knew all round it was a bad time, and that they were in a bad way. Abruptly, he gave up the lie.

"Is that true, Diar?" the child asked, creeping closer. His foot was not healing, in the damp and the dirt, and it pained him always.

"Lyon," he corrected absently, and ran his fingers through the child's matted hair.

"It isn't true, is it, Diar?" the child asked again.

He decided on a part truth, leaving out his own experiences.

"No, Rawn, it isn't, not exactly. I don't know what it means myself." But he could guess.

"Will you be transported too, Diar?"

"I don't know. Perhaps, Rawn."

"I shall die without you, if you are not with me. I know I shall."

"Nonsense! You, a MacCullough? Die of anything you don't have to?" But privately he was afraid of the same thing.

And so the time continued to pass, and the child grew frailer, and he himself grew weaker, and he taught the child the English he knew, as the only help he could give him.

Then in August the trials began. He had still a rag about his waist, and that was all. They appeared in court, some twenty-five of them, making a smell that surrounded them like a room, withering the onlookers and the curious who crowded into the courtroom, who put little bouquets to their noses, including the Judge and the Jury, and their trials did not take long.

Diarmid gave his name briefly, protested his innocence, had no witnesses and no way of proving it, had witnesses who swore they knew him and saw him fight for Charley, and he was with the others, condemned. They returned to the jail, knowing now their fate, if they understood the English, that was now clearly spelled out to them. He heard the white-faced man beside him whisper, "But it's two deaths, not one." It was not real to him. Pain was something one got through with. One thought one would die of it, and either one did or did not. This time he would. There was no more to it than that, no more to think about it. One suffered, and tried to escape, and could not, and finally one died of it. The staging of it meant nothing to him now, and held no terrors for him. The fire, the faggots, the crowd, the masked executioner, the rope, the stripping, and the second death with the knife were bogies to frighten children with. If that was what these mad English wanted, who thought him a savage, they could have it. He could die. He could do that. And as for his dignity, he had lost it in April, four months before.

In the jail he did not talk about it. They were all heavily ironed now, but he had been so before, and that was no change. He knew the child knew, that someone had told him. They met now only in the yard, being put in a separate room.

"Aren't you afraid, Diar?" the child said, looking at him wonderingly, as they took the brief air in the courtyard together.

"No more than common," Diar said.

"Will it be soon, do you think?"

"I think so." He looked at the child. "You must not mind for me, Rawn. I don't for myself. It is no worse than what happens all the time to men by accident."

"I could not bear it for myself," the child said. "I could not bear for someone to hurt me."

"The planning of it is the bad part," Diar agreed. "But August is a nice month, not so cold or wet. One won't shiver," he said with a little smile.

"I know what you did, Diar," the child said. "I understand it now, what the black slip was."

"Do you?" Diar said, his voice unreadable.

"Should I tell them now?"

"I don't think I should, you know. They didn't care whose name they got. They didn't care at all, then, and I doubt they do now. They wouldn't change now if you told them. So put it out of your head."

"Oh Diar," the child said weeping, "I don't even want to tell them now. I don't want to be killed. I just want to go home to my mother. But I couldn't be a state's witness, against you or against anyone, not even to go home."

"Did they ask you that?" Diar said, holding down his anger.

"Yes, all the time, while you were gone. They knew I knew you, somehow. They were at me all the time. But I wouldn't. I wouldn't tell them anything at all. Not even to go home."

"Oh God," Diar said, the irons heavier than he could bear. He sat down, to relieve the weight, and the child sat beside him. "I don't think, Rawn, they would have let you go home, even if you had. And I doubt if your mother is there still in the old places, even if you could go, or your home now. They're not the same now, or ours, you know. She will be looking for you, and she will perhaps be finding you more easily than you could her. But you might have gone into the King's army. Would you have liked that?"

"No," the child said. "I would rather be transported, whatever that is, or die here." The passion in the child's voice surprised Diar. "I know three here who are going to be King's men, but I could not ever. I was born of a good house, and I saw what they did to your father and your wife and to you and to your house, I saw what they did before, too, and after. I have seen too much, I will be no part of such men. My father would not wish it—would not have wished it, and I do not." His voice grew young again. "I am glad I don't have to die right away, Diar, but I wish you did not have to either."

Diar began to laugh at the honesty of the remark, with a sudden reckless merriment he had not felt since April. He had, then, done something then.

They were all more reckless now and more merry, those who were to die who were young. Those who were older were soberer. They had come near to reaching the end, where they could not be touched any more, after that last cruel handling. There were men from the Manchester Regiment, that had held Carlisle. They had a bond together that Diarmid did not feel; they had been through battles together and survived them, and had fought for the same things. They sang now, until the older prisoners cursed them for silence, and danced the fling in their fetters, still strong enough, making true the claim of one death didn't shock him in the least, his own or any other's. Some made speeches for themselves, some bought them, and some, like Diar, had nothing any more to say.

During that week they were visited by travelling evangelists of a sect Diar did not know or care to know. One of them, a slight young man with auburn hair set back from his face falling to his shoulders, in a black frock coat with a white collar, came by Diar, where he was lying on the floor, and attempted to talk with him, but they made no impression either one on the other.

"I am here to die," Diar said curtly, his eyes flashing dangerously with a sudden sparking of anger. "Can you stop that?"

"I have no interest in interfering with the King's justice or that law which you have transgressed against his health," the minister answered, "my interest is in what state of soul you pay the debt you are owing, and what justice you must meet thereafter, according to that state of soul you die in."

"Oh, lord," Diar said, "must I listen to this?"

"I think you must," the other said calmly. "I think you should. I wish you would."

"Look you," Diar said, "you can't do me any good, even if I wished it. You are frocked wrong for me."

"A papist?" the other said with sorrow in his voice. "I did fear it."

"Not enough of one to fear it much," Diar said. "I wish you would leave me alone. I have this dying to do, and I can't be bothered with your arguments. Can't you English spare me even that, my faith, what faith I've got? I have enough. I am at peace there already. I don't need yours."

He saw that the other man seemed disposed to argue the point, and he sighed impatiently and got awkwardly to his feet, and turned his back on the evangelist, and shuffled away to another part of the ward. The minister seemed to have had more effect in other parts of the ward and the prison, for he talked long and earnestly with two men throughout the afternoon, with the result that they cried aloud and dropped to their knees, their eyes streaming, and prayed with the minister both aloud and silently then and by themselves all that night, and sang hymns together. Diarmid was glad when the next day sheer weakness choked them back to silence.

The last night the fathers of two of the youngest soldiers, young enough to be students rather than soldiers, came to sit with them, holding their hands, saying little. The night passed, the morning came, they were taken to the fetteryard to have their irons struck off, and a glass of white wine, in the cool summer morning, and their hands were bound loosely then with rope, shaking hands for many of them but Diar's did not shake.

He lay down, as directed, on the sledge that was to draw him through the town to the scaffold that had been set up for them. He could not yet feel fear, among the jailors suddenly courteous and kind, for there seemed nothing to fear, nothing to see or hear in the air about him. He could not even any longer see the white frightened faces of the other men who had to do their dying that morning too, only the blue sky, with a few white clouds in it, and the sweet scent of late summer flowers and trees, mingling with the stifling ugly odours of the jail. He had not put on finery, as some of the men had; he had no one to bring it to him or buy it for him and no money himself now. He was a hero to no one, not even to himself, and he had no wish to dress for the occasion. He had been told a rich dress to take made the executioner kinder and quicker, but he had never bribed anyone, except perhaps the clergyman that night, and he had no wish to end his life with the act. In truth he had no wishes at all, except that he not be troubled with looseness during the time of it, and he lay there quietly, in the awkward indignity of the position, with few enough clothes about him now to bother the executioner's assistants with in taking off, the air cool on his coated skin, while the other men were fastened down. He could hear one crying, and another sighing heavily, and another praying aloud, but the rest were quiet like himself. He watched the sky above him that in that position was all he could see, and did not think, not even when he heard steps near him he could not see and hurried, harassed voices. He was unbound and taken from the sledge, and he did not change expression. He stood there, numb, not knowing what had happened or why or what was to happen next, watching the men he had come to know drawn away, as he had expected to be, past thinking or past relief; and past fear.

XI: *Diar's Wife, Inverness to Carlisle*

DIAR'S WIFE STAYED ON IN COLONEL GRANT'S HOUSE IN INVERNESS, AS HIS NIECE, THAT SHE WAS, DURING JUNE, AND HE CALLED HER BY HER MAIDEN NAME, AND TREATED HER AS A DAUGHTER. THE PASSAGE BETWEEN THEM AT Ft. Augustus, and the way he found her in Inverness, was not mentioned between them, nor was Diar's name. He paid for her care, and gave her money for frocks and "female fripperies," as he called them, and hired an abigail for her. But he did tell her, without explanations or names, that since he was giving her in public the name of Grant, she could please him by foregoing black, and spare him embarrassment. He also looked at her shrewdly to see how she would take the request.

Diar's wife lowered her eyes and made no comment. She was as lief herself that he should forget her marriage and forget Diar's name, and all about him. She had no wish to remind him, either way. After a moment she lifted her grey eyes and looked into his, allowing them to fill with tears. She had no difficulty weeping over Diar's fate, living, or her own, when she felt she could let herself cry. He melted at her tears himself, and cleared his throat, and grew redder than usual, and patted her hand awkwardly.

"I will do anything to please you, Colonel Grant," she said softly, and dropped her eyes.

"Then don't wear black, m'dear. It depresses me. I don't like it, and it don't do anybody any good, and people would ask questions, that's a dear."

She did not deceive him entirely: she did wish to please him, and she was grateful. Beyond that she submitted to the overwhelming necessity of her life. Her instincts antenna-sharp, made keen by danger and necessity, she knew that he watched her, to see if her behaviour fitted with Diarmid's death, and that he did not wholly accept her story. But she had been brought up to live in society and to be a wife by her mother, and that training to play the female part as men required it under all strains stood her in good stead, now, in her need, and he seemed satisfied at her reactions. But though he gave her accounts and paid her bills, he kept her in short supply of money itself.

"I don't want you running off again, my dear," he said, when she complained prettily.

"Why should I want to run off?" she asked, her eyes opening wide under their thick lashes, and her pretty mouth guileless. "I am very well here. And when I am better, you will let me go to my mother's."

"Would you like that, Mary Elisabeth?"

"Yes, I would now," she said, lying without hesitation. "I have no reason not to now, it is my place. But I think I cannot yet endure the jolting of a carriage." She sank weakly into a chair, and pressed her handkerchief against her lips. She made a lovely picture, and had he not been afraid to touch her, his public standing as a kinsman might have galled him. Over her handkerchief, looking at him through her lashes, she saw the look on his face, and wondered if he would give her money, but she decided the venture too risky, too liable to raise suspicions, and too likely to produce nothing easily negotiable, so she remained weakly in her chair, her eyes downcast, and after a few moments, she excused herself from the room.

She had been there a month now, and she felt quite herself again, in body, and she had regained her looks. She knew she had to do that, and to keep them, for the days ahead, for men did not like gaunt unhappy sickly creatures with unkempt clothes. But she was growing quite desperate as the days went by, at the waste of time, and the possibility of being sent home. And then she learned that the trials of the Rebels were to be held in London and in York and in Carlisle and in Newcastle only, and that Diarmid would then have to have been taken to one of those towns.

"Colonel Grant," she said, the next day, "I would like to go home, I would indeed now. You have been so very kind, but I want to see my mother." She saw no reason to tell him, if he did not know, that she did not particularly enjoy her mother's company, or know how to confide in her.

He looked at her narrowly. "Do you, Missy?" he asked, his voice concerned. At the naked look in his eyes, stripping her, she felt a brief pity for him, and she wondered if she was to go through her life feeling pity for all kinds of men, one way or the other, but she steeled herself.

"Yes, Colonel Grant," she said, "I do. My nature is all disordered"—she lowered her eyes and let herself blush—"and I think I could get better there, around her."

Feminine disorders distressed him, as she knew, and he had her on the coach the next day. He could not go with her, but he sent his First Lieutenant to escort her, and the abigail he had hired, in the rented coach.

She found, to her dismay, that she was not as well after all as she had thought, and that the coach trip over the rough roads was as hard on her as she had said it would be. "That will teach me to tell stories, I suppose," she said to herself grimly, clenching her teeth against cramp.

The Inn they stopped at in Perth had bad beds, the sheets

ill-aired and damp, and the featherbeds lumpy, the service suspicious and surly, and the food scant, ill-flavoured and ill-seasoned. Nevertheless she hardly noticed these discomforts, discounting them, her mind intent on the necessity of obtaining money, and of either eluding her escort, riding in the day beside them, before Edinburgh or enlisting his support. She had no opportunity to observe him at supper, for he suggested she take it in her room with her abigail, the parlour and the barroom being crowded with soldiers, and she did not herself feel like demurring.

She tossed the problem to and fro, getting no further with it. She supposed she should take her baggage and simply go away with it in the night and hope to fall in with a man who would support her and not give her the pox, but she felt too tired from the journey to cope with the unknown elements in the plan. The lieutenant had a frank, honest face, but he was subordinate to Colonel Grant and likely to be questioned or disciplined if his report turned up with discrepancies in it, such as an inquiry later to or from her mother about herself. Nor did he look at all rich, though she supposed he had moneys from Colonel Grant. They were *for* her: if she stole into his room and stole them, would he pursue her and have her apprehended for theft? Soldiers might steal with occasional impunity, but not always even them, and never anyone else. Her desperate plans at any cost must not become known to Colonel Grant, whose shrewd wit might well guess the reasons for them and revive his suspicions, and yet she could not go to the house of her mother and father. Once there, the surveillance would be impossibly complete, and her story one way or the other pulled out of her, she knew. So her thoughts tumbled about, as her hair tumbled on the reeky pillows, and the moon rose and shone into her window.

"Well," she thought, "a girl could try." She would do as she could, and think as she went. She took her nightgown off and pulled her wrapper about her, and slipped her feet into her shoes, her pulses pounding with fright and her throat dry,

and slipped past her sleeping abigail to the door and peeped
into the hall, which was empty in both directions. She understood the Lieutenant's room was to be next to hers, but she
did not know which.

"Oh, God," she whispered, "direct me, for Diar's Sake,"
and put her fears aside and breathed easier and turned the
handle of the door a little the closest. It was not locked, the
lieutenant either inside too drunk to think of it, or outside of
it too drunk also, or else it was another room. She slipped just
inside it, closed it gently, hearing the catch snap with to her
a thundrous sound, and leaned against it. The moon fell
through these windows with a clear light, as in her own, and
showed a humped figure in the bed, breathing heavily and
stertorously.

She listened in dismay, wondering if the figure, should it
be the lieutenant, would turn out to be too far under to lend
himself to her plans. "Well," she thought again, "she could
but try." She slipped her feet out of her shoes and left them
by the door, and stole across the rough uneven boards on soft
naked feet to the bed and surveyed the sleeping figure.

Whether luck was with her or not, it was the lieutenant.
What now to do? Would he wake in a panic, shout, and run
her through, if she touched him? She hoped not. He seemed
in no condition for niceties in any case. She let her wrapper
drop to the floor, and lifted the cover and slipped in bed
beside him.

To her surprise, her presence was accepted, like a puppy
put to nurse at an alien teat. The young lieutenant, younger
than Colonel Grant, though older than Diar, without seeming to wake put an arm about her, drawing her to him, a leg
over her, and performed the work, falling asleep again on
her, if he had ever not been asleep. "Well," she thought to
herself, "what next now?" After a bit she disengaged herself
to be more comfortable, firmly clasped in the crook of an
extremely strong arm, resigned herself to the bony prison,
and fell asleep herself, to be used twice more in the night in

the same way. She was waked in the morning by an exclamation beside her.

"Oh, my lady, Oh, Miss Grant," the young soldier was saying in mortification and alarm, over and over, "oh, what have I done. I didn't know that you were here." His words made very little sense, and his senses had not come round to reproaching her, but his dismay was clear.

She lay still, turning her head and her lovely eyes upon him, and smiled full in his face. "I had thought you did," she said sweetly.

"Oh, Miss Grant," he said blushing a fiery red, and bunching the covers about him, "did you mistake the room, and would I not let you go?"

She did not try to answer, or in fact say anything at all. She continued to look at him, her eyes smiling, her lashes half lowered, and as she had to the Colonel, she held out her arms, and as he bent forward a little unconsciously towards her sweet smiling face, she put them around his neck and drew his blushing protesting lips down to her own.

After that, there was nothing really to say. This time he was awake, and made a longer affair of it. When they had finished, he propped himself up on his elbow, in command of himself now, and looked down on her, his face contented and amused, but his voice very much the lieutenant's and demanding an answer, as he said, though gently: "Now, Miss Grant, tell me why."

"Tell you why what?" she asked, still prevaricating, moving a little against him. He put his feet against hers, and captured them.

"Why this?" he asked. "Why me? What do you want?"

So she had not misjudged his honest face, when sober. So what now?

"Would you believe me," she asked, "if I told you I had been swept away by your manly charms?"

"No," he said.

"I thought not," she said. "But it is very nearly true," she added, to placate his feelings. "Would you believe me," she asked thoughtfully, "if I said that I did not want to stay with Colonel Grant and that I did not want to go home with my mother, either one?"

"I might," he said. "You will be having some strong reason. Will you be telling me what it is?"

"Will you help me," she asked, "if I do?"

"Yes," he said. He might have said, "I might," but looking at her face, instead he said "yes," and bent and kissed her. His arms slipped around her, and she moved against him. "Tell me what you need, I'll do it if I can."

But all the same she was afraid to tell him or to trust him entirely.

"My brother," she said, "is in jail and I don't know where. I want to find him. That's all."

"Your brother?" he asked, with a question.

"My brother," she said firmly, and saw he understood.

"And where must you go?" the Lieutenant asked. "Where is this rebel brother of yours being kept? He is a Rebel?"

She shook her head, the tears perilously close behind her eyes, genuinely there without her wanting them. Her eyes swam in the pools of them, and they overflowed.

"Oh love, oh lassie," he said, "don't grete. We'll find your sweetheart for you, no matter what George says to it, or Colonel Grant either."

"No," she said, "I would not cause you trouble. Only take me to Newcastle instead of Edinburgh."

"Why Newcastle, lass?" he asked, genuinely surprised. "What's there?"

"I thought there were trials there," she said hesitantly. "I heard there were to be."

"Of Rebels? But he is no Rebel," he said, quoting her. "Well, I've known of that happening, too, lass, it is a hard time for some who don't deserve it. But we soldiers do our orders. But Newcastle will do you no good, I am a Newcastle man myself, and Mayor Smith is having no Rebels

and no Rebel trials brought there. So it's York or Carlisle you
want, or maybe London and the Common." He thought for a
moment. "There's transports putting into Carlisle, in the
Firth, that picked up at Ft. William, and it's as close to us as
Newcastle, lass. If I'm to take you, and I will, because I said
I would, suppose I take you there. If you don't find him,
York's no further than it was. The London trials I hear are
started, but Carlisle's have not, and York's will follow Carlisle. Shall we do that?"

"Oh, yes," she whispered, holding to him as to her guard-
ian angel, "oh yes."

So the Lieutenant took Diar's wife to Carlisle, and left her
there, and took the abigail back with him to Inverness, per-
suading her on the way to say nothing of the change in much
the same way as Diar's wife had persuaded him. On the way
back he visited Edinburgh, with a perceptible lady, and
passed by the Grants' house, and was able to give a circum-
stantial report to his Colonel of his mission.

The lieutenant had not asked the young lady whose plans
he had acceded to so surprisingly what she intended to do
once she found her "brother," if she did. He did not see what
she could do, in so hopeless an endeavour, except perhaps,
with unusual luck or persistence, gain access to speak to him.
From his small dealing with her he thought it likely she
would. He could not, from his experiences and the sights he
had seen, consider that would give any great comfort to
either of them, though, but with a certain native tact and
kindness he forbore to speak of that, and kept his opinions
and his questions to himself. He respected her spunk, if not
her means, and hoped himself, if he was in a spot, to find a
leman half so resourceful or so plucky. He also kept his
doubts to himself about her "brother's" appreciating the
means at hand she used, and parted with her with reluctance
when the time came. He had a short supply of coins with
him, and he gave her those he thought he could spare.

If the lieutenant did not know her plans, Diar's wife with a sinking heart knew she did not know either. He had not abandoned her on a stone, but had found an inn of moderate price to lodge her in, while she had yet the respectability of his presence, the carriage and the abigail about her, and tested out the comfort of the bed with her quickly, and kissed her, and left. He returned, though, within the hour, to tell her the first trials would probably begin the week follow-ing, retested the bed, ordered her supper sent up to her, and began his drive back, taking advantage of the late hours of evening daylight. When he had gone, and did not seem to be going to return again, she lay quietly weeping with exhaus-tion and fright at being alone again, until she fell asleep.

She was wakened by her supper being brought to her, and after she had eaten, she felt more heartened, and some of her spirit returned to her. She realised with a little start of sur-prise that it was her birthday, and that she was now eigh-teen. The thought made her want to cry again, as she re-membered the celebrations of her other birthdays in the center of her family, but she did not think she could let her-self weaken herself again with the luxury of tears.

She stood at the window, to divert her thoughts, and she was still there when the little serving girl came in to clear away her supper dishes.

"What are the buildings," she asked. "That one?" pointing. The servant girl told her. "And that?" And with her heart a little in her throat, "And that one there?"

"Oh, that's the Castle, ma'am, where the Rebel prisoners are."

She had known it would be. So it was there, and in it might be Diarmid, but she could not see him, she could not even look. There might be a registry, but she was afraid to ask, not knowing what name he might be using. She held tight to the window, holding on to the sill with her hands.

"Where will the trials be held? Can you see that too?"

"Oh yes, ma'am, it's just there," and the serving girl pointed it out to her. "If you want places, you'd best go early, my cousin says."

"Go early? But the trials aren't this week, I was told they were not."

"Well, I don't rightly know, ma'am, but there are some trials to be there tomorrow. My cousin says so, and he says one must go early. Yesterday he could not get in, but today he did."

"Oh God," she thought. "Had it happened already, and did not know? What had the lieutenant been about, what had he meant? Could he want to deceive me, or had he been merely mistaken?"

"I think I'll go," she said. "Will you call me at three?" The girl promised to see it was done and courteseyed and went out. She stood at the window a little longer, in the late twilight. He might not even be there, he could as well be in York, or even in London. She could not let herself think of his trial having already happened. She laid herself down to sleep while she could then, but she slept fitfully, in the depression of spirits she still felt after the miscarriage of the unknown baby, although her conscious feelings about it were purely relief, and the uncertainties before her.

When she awoke, or rather, when she was awakened, it was twilight again, the silver twilight of the pre-dawn. She dressed as carefully as she could, but in haste, breakfasted in haste, and paid to have a chair brought to take her to the Court. She could not afford one every day, but she did not know yet how to go. Even at that hour of four the court was nearly filled, the trials to begin at seven, and she thought that the next day she would have to come earlier.

She waited until the trials began, afraid to leave her place for anything, and then she waited through them, watching the miserable prisoners and their pitiful defences, some of them offering no defence, standing to their fates with dignity, but some wanting no part. And probably they had wanted no part of the Rebellion, she thought. Diar had not. He had not cared. She thought she would faint in the hot crowded ill-smelling discomfort of the court, but she did not faint. She watched each prisoner carefully, and in their sick starved unhappy faces she could find no lines at all that might be Diar's, even what misery might have reduced him to.

She stayed all day, and when the court recessed, she followed the crowd and the prisoners to the jail and stood there looking, but she saw nothing but the outside of the building, and having no permission, she could not go inside. She did find, however, the names and the addresses of the officers to apply to, and of the judge presiding on the trials. She had had nothing to eat all the day, and she went back to the Inn and had supper downstairs, to hear what was being said, and then she went to bed at once, and to sleep quickly.

She had asked this time to be awakened at two, and she arrived at the Court in time to take a seat where she could see well. She did that for three days, all the rest of that week, not knowing if Diar had appeared before or not. And then she learned that the prisoners to be tried had been lotted, and that it was more likely that Diar would have been sentenced without trial to transportation rather than that he would appear for trial. The next day was Sunday, and she went to the Judge's house, but she could not get admittance. She waited all day, a little away from his door, in the street, hoping he would appear, wondering what she would do, what she should say, if he did come out or go in, and if he would stop and hear her, now hoping, now despairing in her feelings but her determination not wavering.

XII: *Diar's Wife: The Judge*

THE JUDGE, HOWEVER, HAD ALREADY LEFT, TO BREAK-
FAST AT A COFFEE HOUSE AND THEN TO PROCEED TO
CHURCH AND TO DINNER WITH FRIENDS. HE DID NOT
RETURN UNTIL LATE AFTERNOON. HE WAS NOT WEARING HIS WIG
or his robes, but she had studied his face and she recognised him
and was going forward timidly towards him, realising by the
unbending aloofness of his glance that he would not speak,
when fortune intervened for her, as if pitying her unrewarded
courage, in the form of two fighting curs. They appeared out
of an alley, snapping and snarling at one another, and backed
into her, throwing her forward, stumbling, tangled in dogs, as
she uttered a small real cry of terror.

He perforce held her up, and with immediate forethought,
she shut her eyes and fainted. It was an old nursery trick,
learned in defence against nursery punishments, handed
down as useful knowledge among children, and feeling faint
already naturally, she was glad of an excuse to let go. She felt
dimly the gentleman pick her up in his arms, and carry her
somewhere, into his house, she hoped.

She was laid down on a sofa, rather hard and slippery and

uncomfortable, and she heard voices come and go about her. She lay still, holding to the faint as long as possible, while fingers loosened her dress and stays, and burnt feathers were brought, and a hartshorn found, someone holding to her hand and patting it. She hoped it was the judge, and that he had watched her stays loosened. She judged it was time to recover, and she reluctantly opened her tired eyes, looking up through their long dark lashes at the judge's face observing her with foolish concern.

She had been wondering, being dressed like the young lady of quality she was, which line of attack to pursue. Should she be pathetic? And if so, how? Daughterly, Sisterly, Wifely? An orphan? Would she do better to appeal to him directly, and to throw herself upon his mercy and his generosity and his justice? Her recent experiences with all three qualities, the general lack of them in men in general for their own sakes, led her to be doubtful of such an approach's success. Particularly since she imagined he had many such approaches and many such appeals. Yet could one attempt to seduce a judge? It appeared one could. The question then was how. How best, and how quickly?

She caught his eye upon her bosom, and she wondered if she were in disarray. She let her eyelashes fall back over her eyes, fanning her cheeks, and her lips part slightly, and let her fingertips press slightly the fingers of the hand holding hers. To her surprise, they pressed hers back. For a few moments her eyes lowered, she played that game, press, wait, press, repress, and then she felt a knee move against her leg. Lord! she thought. A judge, older than my father, and on Sunday? What is he thinking of. She moved her own leg a small way closer and felt the leg beside her rub hers gently. Encouraged, resolved to put it to the test, she took the hand holding her fingers and moved it gently up to where she judged her breast to be, with her eyes closed, and placed it there. She was disarrayed indeed, she discovered, feeling fingers then at her bare skin. Abruptly she felt him leave her.

Had she gone too far, too soon? Was there anyone else in the room? She heard the door close, and the sound of the key, and of curtains being drawn, and she knew she had not. Sighing inwardly even as her heart filled with a faint hope, she braced herself for an uncomfortable passage on the un-yielding rounded horsehair sofa, the stiff points of the stuffing pricking her through the satin, and loosened her drawers. Her eyes still closed, her lips still parted, breathing shallowly, she felt him return beside her, and without a word, her eyes still closed put her hands up to his face. His own hands covered hers, and then his lips her hands, moving back at her guidance to her exposed breast, opening the dress still wider, letting him hold her and play with her, not a word yet spoken. After a time of that, she felt his hands between her legs, stroking them, tentatively, and in answer, she put her knees up and apart. Her skirt was pulled up then and bunched about her, and her loosened drawers pulled further down, and she felt the man upon her. Well, she thought to herself, justice was not much, either way, but like the court it seemed to go on and on with no resolving, only finally an end to it.

Well, she had burned these bridges now. She wondered what he would find to say to her, and what the voice she had heard pronouncing sentence would sound like when it spoke to her. She brought his hand up to her lips in her small one, and kissed it, and put it against her cheek. It rested there, and then she felt the fingers move into her hair, among her loose chestnut curls, disarranged now and bonnetless. His words, when they did come, surprised her, his voice quiet and gentle, cultured in tone, unlike the stern unbending voice of the Bench.

"My dear," he said, "I am ashamed."

She drew his face near to hers, and whispered against it, "Do not be."

"You were in distress, and I meant to help you. I do not know how I could have done this to you."

"I wanted you to," she whispered. "I am glad. Please don't be sorry."

"I do not understand," he said then, after a little pause. "A child like you, like this. You are experienced." He stated, he did not ask.

"Yes," she said simply.

"Oh, Lord," he said aside, in a genuine disturbance of spirit. "So lovely, and so young." He looked at her in a sudden suspicion. "Are you a Rebel, child? Is that why?"

"No," she answered truthfully, "I am not."

"Have you someone in the jails then, who is?"

"No," she answered truthfully again, "I do not have," for Diarmid was not, though they might call him one. She opened her grey eyes suddenly on him, clear and candid, dark beneath the lashes. "May I put my skirt back down now?" He hastily adjusted both her dress, and his, and seeing he was not averse, she took his hand in hers and held it still.

"Why then an old man like me? I see no sense in it."

"May I not love you, sir?"

He dismissed the possibility, without a word, but he stroked her hair with his free hand.

"I would you did, my dear, I would you did."

"May I not, then?"

"May you not what?"

"May I not stay with you and love you?"

He stared at her, shaken at the prospect and the possibility.

"Where is your mother, child, and your father?"

"They are not here. I do not know where they are." Which was strictly true. "I am alone now, and I have no one to protect me and no money."

"I had thought," he said slowly, "that you came here to seduce me, for some purpose of your own, and being lonely and much burdened, I was willing to be seduced, for you are very lovely, my dear, but I had intended when we finished to give you to the constable and have you whipped at the cart's tail for daring to try."

"I cannot stop you," she said quietly, "if you wish to do that. Do you mean to still?" She had been right then to hesitate to embark upon it, for he was no young officer, neither gullible nor stupid nor kind. She lifted her lovely eyes again, with their soft innocent look of trust, to him.

"No," he said just as quietly. "I do not. I tell you because I do not." She shivered inwardly at the narrow bridge she walked, but her face remained calm, and she waited without speaking for him to tell her what he did mean to do. His next question surprised her. "Where are you staying?" he asked.

"At the George Inn," she replied truthfully. "My way is paid there two days more."

"A good name," he remarked. "You had a protector then?"

"Yes," she answered again truthfully, "but I do not now."

"He has left you?"

"Yes," she said, letting her eyelashes fall.

"Poor child," he said, "poor child. How old are you?"

"I was eighteen yesterday."

"That is too young," he said with sudden decision, "too young and too lovely to be left to the streets and to your own devices." Oh, God, she thought, is it to be an orphanage? In true despair she held to his hands tightly, and let the unshed ready tears fill her eyes and overflow.

"Oh, do not send me away," she pled piteously. "Not now. Oh, please do not." Had she overdone it this time? She hoped not. Her breath came quickly, naturally, without pretense, and she thought, if it would serve, she could easily go into hysterics.

"I did not intend to, my dear," the old man said heavily. "You have bewitched me, and my better judgment. If that is your good fortune, it is mine as well." She began to laugh and to cry all at once, kissing his hands in passionate gratitude, since he seemed, strangely, to enjoy her emotion. She wondered why. Was it because he believed she meant to make no claims upon his profession? "Oh, my dear," he said, almost humbly, "do I please you so much?"

"Yes," she whispered, "yes, you do." She thought then he

was going to be on her again, but he was, after all, old.

"My dear," he said, "we must think then what is best to do. If you have your Inn Room, it is already evening, and I have an early Court tomorrow. You should go back there, I think, now, and I will send you in a chair. I will give you money now, for that, and for a chair to return here in tomorrow. Come at this hour again tomorrow, and we will dine together, and discuss how we should best conduct this arrangement between us, and to amuse yourself, buy yourself a new frock, while you wait for me."

She could have laughed, thinking how she would amuse herself, but instead she only smiled at him and answered, "What contents and pleases you will also content and please me."

He took her then to the door, when she had refastened with the help of his trembling fingers her stays and the front of her dress, and saw personally to his servants finding her a chair, bowing courteously to her, his fingertips just touching hers.

She was more than relieved to be allowed to return to her room. The Inn was quiet that Sunday, and she took supper in her room, and paid the little serving girl to obtain a widow's dress and veil for her, which she promised she could do, with part of the gold coins given her. At three the next morning she was again at the Court, waiting, a small silent figure, the veil hiding her expression when later that morning, she saw Diarmid take his place with those also to be tried before the Judge. She wondered that she had thought she might not recognise him. There was the fall of black hair over the brow, the square jaw rounding into the cheek, the fair skin, underneath the dirt, and the broad black brows that could cock so merrily. There was no merriness left to him, brows and mouth and eyes a straight narrow line, dark hollows squared about his eyes, pinching against his nose in black marks of illness and fatigue, his big-boned hands helpless in their heavy fetters, his clothes filthy and torn and falling apart away from him. She heard his brief defence, which he made without the help of the interpreter, and the tearing apart of it, and his sentencing, a word here, a word there.

"I have as much courage as the next, I think," he said then when he saw it was finished for him, "when it comes to dying, but it is a messy death, and one I do not deserve. I am no traitor, I have been none, and you should not put me to a traitor's death. But I ask your mercy then, if you will do it, that you do it quickly."

If he gave his name, she did not hear it, but she heard the judge call him by the name Lyon. She watched him stand wearily, his legs a little apart to steady himself, his hands holding to the bar for support, while the procedure continued with the others brought with him. There was really very little to watch, for he made no motion, and his face read no change of expression. Yet she took comfort in being near him, though unobserved, in the sight of him, and that he had strength of some kind left and showed no distress, not weeping, or falling to the floor, or attempting to sit. The day passed, the prisoners were returned to their wards and cells, and she returned to the Judge.

She did not need after that, to return to the Court. She could not find out, no one in the streets or at the Inn seemed to know, when the sentences were to be carried out. She did not dare yet to ask the Judge, either directly for information or for help. She went to his house, and lived with him, cheering his suppers and his evenings and his bed, playing all manner of games with him, piquet and whist, and other games, and she saw him seem to grow to love her, both as a daughter-like companion and as a playmate. He began to talk to her, more, as he discovered she was content to listen, and occasionally she dared insert a comment or a question whose answers or directives told her something of what she died daily to know. While he was in Court, ostensibly at the shops, she haunted the entrance to the jail, in her veil, a pitifully familiar figure there, begging information of anyone who would speak to her. When the executions began, without warning, and she saw the crowds, she ran in desperation after the crowds towards the scaffolds, her heart failing her, but she did not that day see Diarmid among them, desperately seeking a place to see their faces through the crowd, pressing and pushing and screaming like a madwoman, to see before they hooded them. At her relief he was not there, she fainted, and ignored in the crowd, was nearly trampled, except for the kindness of a burly butcher by her who picked her up, like a string of sausages, over his arm. After that she dared not then delay to put her power with the judge to its testing.

She came to him that night, without subterfuge, her eyes dry and pitiful, and knelt before him and clasped his knees with her clasped hands.

"My dear," he asked, distressed, "what is this?"

She bent her head lower, her hair falling in waves, and did not answer. With his hand he took her chin in his fingers and tilted her face upwards.

"Am I to know now why you have humoured an old man?"

"Yes," she whispered.

He sighed and said nothing, and released his fingers from her chin, but she did not hide her face again from him, but remained quietly looking at him.

"Well," he said, after a little. "Well, I should have known. I suppose I did know, always. Which of the rascals is it that you want? Does it lie within my power?"

"I don't know," she whispered. "You will tell me. I pray it does."

"Well," he said testily, "who do you want?"

"My husband," she said, her voice shaking. "His name is Lyon."

The old man said nothing, his eyes on her face.

"Oh, sir," she said taking his hand that did not resist her, in hers, and that did not respond either, "he is not a Rebel. What he said when he was tried was true. It is true still. I was there, at his house, I knew his father, I knew all the story, all that they did, and all that was done to them, and they were none Rebels, none of them. Oh sir, his father is dead now, do not make him die."

"I cannot pardon him," the old man said, "not now, not without the King's pardon, even if I would, and there may not be time for that. It may not be obtainable, even if deserved. There is your word only, and you are prejudiced."

She forbore to say she thought both him and the King also prejudiced.

"I did not expect a pardon, I was not asking for that," she said, "I ask only not for death. If his cause is just, perhaps I can win the King's pardon for him. I want now only to have his life kept in him." She began to weep then, the tears falling slowly, unable to hold them in.

"Transported, you mean, Mary Elisabeth?"

"Yes," she whispered, wondering if Diar would hate her, for cheating, or trying to cheat, him of death yet again.

"Tell me the story," he said slowly, "in your words, just as you know it. Tell it to me all." His personal warmth seemed to recede from her, and the judge sat before her, and to the judge she told the story, omitting only the violence done to her, and to the soldiers, and Colonel Grant's name. When she had finished, he looked at her, not the judge, just an old man again, and asked her, his voice sad:

"And when I have done this for you, if I do it, what then? What will you do? Will you leave me then?"

"No," she whispered, "I promise I will not. I will stay with you, as you wish me, as long as you wish me to."

"Well," he said, "let us go to bed then and I will think on it."

"Oh, sir," she said, in ashen fear, "is there time?"

"You don't want me to think on it?" he asked, his tone unreadable.

"I am so afraid." Her lips quivered. "If Lyon dies, I shall die. I cannot bear for Lyon to die."

"You are a brave little girl," the judge said. "I wish you were my own, though then I would not want you to behave this way after all, even to save the life of a man who may not want it so much as you think. But I will transport him for you instead. There. Will that satisfy you?"

"Oh, yes," she said, "oh, yes." The image of the fire and the scaffolding and the halter began to recede from her mind, and her breath came easier.

"And I suppose you want me to put on my glasses, and write it out now, even though I am tired, and seal it, and all."

"Yes. Oh, yes, please, I do."

"You are a persistent little girl as well, but I like that in you. Be glad I do." He took himself to his desk as he spoke, and after a time, he folded and sealed the paper, transmuting the order of execution to the King's mercy of transportation for the Rebel Lyon. But he did not give the paper to her, but put it in his desk.

"May I not take it tonight?"

"You may not," he said. "It is late, there is no need to wake anyone there, and I doubt very much if the young man is set for tomorrow in any case. But George shall take it over to-morrow before six, and you shall go with him too, if you like, to be certain he picks out the right man. Now come to bed now."

She had no choice. She could not make him, more than he had; she knew when she had done all she could, and could go no further.

"Besides," he said, "the young man may deserve his death after all, and we shall give him half of it, the expecting of it, as long as may be. It will not hurt him for it, either way." He put on his nightshirt over his thin legs and waited for her to come to him, which she did. She did not herself sleep. She lay awake, watching the little dark change into twilight, and then she roused him and reminded him of his promise.

"It's in my desk," he said crossly, "why need you ask. Take

it and be off with you, and don't dally," he added needlessly.

George was waiting as instructed the night before. "Oh, hurry," she prayed silently, to the chair bearers, "hurry." "We will not be too late," she asked George, even though the question was no use.

But they were not early, the prison had waked earlier yet than they, and gone about its business, and by the time they had seen the officials and answered questions, and George's identity had been established, and they went to the yard, Diar had been strapped to the sledge.

He did not see her, strapped as he was, but she saw him, from inside the prison room, as the officials went out to him, and she knew then, as she looked at him, that she loved him, and that it was not pity as she had thought, or was not now. She longed to go to him, and put her arms about him, as he stood there, bewildered, his face blank and dazed, let up from the sledge and his death. She cursed the Judge inwardly for his cruelty in waiting the night and letting the matter advance so far, even as she blessed him for stopping it in any way at all. Without his name, his signature, or the King's, it must have needs gone forward. But she could not go to her husband, it was not permitted to her, and remembering his last words to her, she did not believe he would have welcomed her then, could she have gone.

XIII: *Carlisle Castle Gaol*

"I AM NOT A GHOST, RAWN," DIARMID SAID TO THE WHITE-
FACED BOY, WHO PUT HIS HANDS UP AS THOUGH TO PRO-
TECT HIMSELF, "DON'T SHRIEK. I AM JUST BACK AGAIN.
SOMEWAY I WAS LEFT OFF, THEY DIDN'T TELL ME WHY. I AM TO
be transported now too, like you. When they do kill me," he
added bitterly, "after this they had better weight me down
with stones, or I will rise, even with the ocean's weight over
me. I have had enough of these half-measures."

He did not seem particularly grateful, and he was not.
Once again he had readied himself for death, and again it
had not arrived. He was exhausted with the strain of it. He
had been taken back in, too dazed to wonder if he had been
pardoned or why he had been unstrapped or if he was
wanted for some questioning, the thoughts in his head, but
himself not thinking them. He was to be transported, he was
told, the King's mercy, and he was to sign his name here,
please.

"The King's mercy!" he had spat, reviving at the words,
remembering the transport he had already been on for an

endless fortnight, putting in, putting out, waiting in this place and that. "I'll not sign, I will not go. You can't make me. Take me back out there and finish me now." He could have cried, then. But instead his eyes flashed, and he looked very dangerous, for all his unbound hands.

The official shook his head again, looking as if privately he agreed with Diar about what should be done with him, indicating again that he should sign and show respect for the King's mercy, and a proper attitude of gratefulness.

"Mercy be damned!" said Diar, and took his fist, freed for the first time since April, and hit a blow with all his strength, not at the official, who was out of reach, but at the book, knocking it away a few inches. As a gesture, it expressed his feelings, but as an act it was ineffectual, his fist being weak as the new-born's. The heavy book slid to the edge of the table and stayed there. As for Diar himself, he found his arms seized, his hands each in a fetter of another man's hand.

The official, weary of Rebels, did not trouble himself even to slap his face. He took the book and the pen, found Diar's name Lyon in the paper presented him, and inscribed it himself for him.

"There," he said. "That will do just as well." He looked at Diar with distaste, and he was indeed a distasteful object. "You Rebels," he said carefully, "have never learned when not to waste effort, when the result is impossible or useless."

"I am not a Rebel," spat Diar, "I never was, I am not now."

"So you say," the official said quietly. "So you say. I daresay you would like not to be now. I have met with many of your kind now, and of the two, I prefer you Rebels who acknowledge it. But it is no matter. Either way it is wasted effort. Now I," he said carefully, "understand what is useful, and I am not going to waste my effort or my men's in having you flogged. I see no purpose it would serve. There is nothing you can do." He turned his back on the uncringing un-Rebel. "Take this man out, this rash, ungrateful Rebel," he said, "and iron him heavily, and take him back to the ward for the transports."

So Diar accepted the King's mercy, and rejoined Rawn in a black humour. Exhausted entirely by the second scene, he let his legs slip out from under him and sat down beside the child, his wrists aching under the double irons. They made no difference, however, for his necessities, for he had fought then, to the delight of his escorts. He had hoped to be killed, but he had merely in the quick scuffle of subduing him lost the last scraps of his clothing, and that was all his provocation got him.

"Lord," he said after a time, swearing softly, as was not his custom to swear, so perhaps it was a prayer, "this floor's cold. I shall have to get more dirt on me. I wish I were dead, Rawn. Do you?"

"No," the child said. "I think my mother will find me, and I want to be here when she does. I want to see her with my eyes."

"You are very brave, Rawn," Diar said. "I think perhaps you will be then."

"If they don't transport me first," the child whispered. "I am not brave really. I cannot bear the cries of these grown men, it is terrible when grown men are brought to where they will cry and no one will help them. I wonder if my father is somewhere, crying. And I am afraid every day they will come for me, and put me on a ship, and take me away where I can't be found, ever."

"You are a true Rebel's son," Diar said, admiring, with a touch of envy, "not a neither-nor like me."

They stayed there another two weeks together, trying to keep one another's spirits and strength up, not to let bitterness overcome them, and then a group of names was called out for transporting, those who had been there longest waiting for it, since May and before. The child's name was among them this time.

When he heard it, his white face went white and cold as

death, though the change was hardly perceptible, and his eyes large and dark with terror. He started to rise, but Diar held him down.

"Don't move, Rawn," he said quietly, and turned and kissed his forehead. "You wait here for your mother. There's no one looking for me, you know. I've no one to come, and no place to go back to. They don't know us any more by name, and one of us is as good as any other for this purpose, a man like me better to sell off than a wee feckless thing like you. You are Lyon now. You are me. Don't forget that. And do well for both of us." He stood up, pulling his chains with him, and smiled with all his eyes into the child's frightened face in which relief was creeping. "That's all right then, isn't it."

"You don't mind, Diar?" the child asked in a whisper.

"Rawn, now," Diar corrected. "I don't mind," he said, lying. "It will be an adventure. Sure you wouldn't rather come?"

"No," whispered the child. "I am sick even when I go on the Loch."

"I have to go, then, now," Diar said, "if I'm going. I don't want to make a fuss here, or be conspicuous. Goodbye, Lyon," he said, taking his hand in a brief clasp. "Goodbye, God be with you." (And with me, with us both, if He can, he thought. But a man can take care of himself better than a child.) He turned away and walked to the door and stood with the group about to go, and gave his new name. He was not questioned or even looked at. The quota was filled, and his name checked.

XIV: *Diar's Wife: Carlisle, London, Carlisle*

DIAR'S WIFE LEFT THE PRISON, AS SHE HAD TO DO, WHEN SHE HAD IDENTIFIED THE PRISONER THROUGH THE WINDOW OF THE OFFICIAL'S ROOM, BEFORE DIAR HIMSELF WAS BROUGHT IN. SHE WENT BACK TO THE CHAIR, WITH THE Judge's servant, and returned in it to the Judge's house, where she waited all day for the Judge's return. She did not eat lunch, and she sat in one chair, hardly moving all the afternoon.

"You are sad, Mary Elizabeth," the Judge said that night. "Don't be sad, or you will make me sad."

She looked up from the game of chess that he was teaching her to play, and gave him a bright watery smile, and did not answer. She bent her head again to move her man.

"That was a stupid move," the Judge commented. "You are not attending, I think. I think your mind is not on the game."

"What am I to say, sir?" she asked. "I do not dare contradict you, yet I do not want to offend you by agreeing to being in a condition you dislike."

"Don't be pert with me, my dear," the Judge said. "Your words are insincere."

"What do you want me to say?" she said then, her lips

quivering, her head bent over her queen, and her tears falling on the board. "Do you want me to say that I am like to die of grief?"

"And are you?" the old Judge asked.

"Yes," she said simply. "But I do not wish to burden you with it or any further with my troubles."

"This young man is fortunate," the Judge remarked. "I hope he knows his fortune. Did you speak with him?"

"No," she whispered.

"That was as well," the Judge remarked. "Come here, my dear," he said, "don't ruin my board—the wood is inlaid, and all this flood will raise the little squares. Come drench my coat. I can have that pressed."

She rose slowly, and came round the table, and at his gesture seated herself on his knee, her choked-back sobs getting in the way of her breathing and near to choking her. He patted her, and gave her his handkerchief. Then a sudden thought struck him.

"You were surely not too late?"

She shook her head. "No," she whispered, her voice unsteady. "We were in time. Just."

"I am sorry, my dear," he said. "I had not thought it would be so near a thing. You must have seen sights that distressed you."

"I did," she said.

"But your young man is safe," he said. "He will be transported merely, and you will live with me, this way for a while, later perhaps as my daughter, or if we can set the previous lines aside, as my wife. Does the prospect distress you?"

"Oh, do not ask me," she said, gasping, "I have said I would stay, I have promised you. I will improve my spirits."

"But it is not enough. I see that. And to have you this way, my dear, is not enough for me, old lecher tho' I daresay I seem to you. What is it you still want to do, or have me do for you?"

"You make me seem ungrateful," she said, "and truly I am not. Truly I am glad. I am very glad."

"It is only what, then?"

"I saw his face, and he looked as though he still had to die."

"And so?"

"And so I am unhappy tonight, even so, because I know he is. You should not ask me, sir. We have grown to speak too freely. I cannot be as you wish me, if we do. And I would please you."

"Move your pawn," he said in reply, "so, and I will show you what I will do. Or shall I for you?"

"Yes, please," she said.

"Mate," he said, "and then you move, and it is mate again, and now, however you move, checkmate now. Tomorrow I shall teach you how to do this yourself and guard against it, it is the 'Fool's Gambit.' What you want to do," he continued, his tone not changing, "is to go down to London to find a King's complete pardon for your young man. That is it, is it not? That is what is in your heart?"

"Oh, do not be cruel," she whispered, trying to slip down, but he held her on his knees.

"What I have done is, after all, not enough, and you regret your promise that keeps you here."

"You have said it," she whispered, "I have not."

"If I released you, how would you go? You would find a soldier here, a drover there, a barman somewhere else, or some young buck, and catch the pox perhaps? And who would you try in London? You could not reach the King this way, I assure you that, nor Cumberland either. What then? What Fool's Gambit? And who then?"

She bowed her head and did not answer.

"I cannot bear this for you, Mary Elisabeth, I cannot bear for you to do this to yourself, to so little purpose. I will not release you from your promise."

"I did not think you would," she whispered. "I have not asked you."

"I cannot take you myself," he said musingly, "I have these trials to finish. Not until next week, or the week following. I suppose you could not wait until then?" He sighed. "You need not answer. I see you cannot. Yet I myself see no rush. There are men in Carlisle Castle who have been waiting since before April to be transported, and the ships not yet found. Suppose," he went on without a pause, showing he had known all along what he would say, "I should send you tomorrow with my servants and my carriage and letters to my nephew who is a lawyer to the Crown in London, suppose I should do this?"

She lifted her head as he paused, her eyes questioning, her face wet with tears, a new hope shining like a rainbow through her eyes.

"Do you think, if I should sleep upon the matter, that you could dry your tears and help a doting old doddard to consider it and make him glad he did?"

"Oh, sir," she said, her voice choking with relief, "oh, sir, I think I could." She felt his hand slip between her legs, beneath her dress, and she leaned back against him, and let him do as he liked. "And when you have come back," he continued, as though unaware of the activities of his fingers, "with a pardon for your young man, and he is released, what then, my dear, what then? Will you be leaving me then or staying?"

"I will be staying," she said, "with you, if you want that. I want only for him to be free again, and to be happy. That is all I want." He picked her up then, and carried her to the bed.

"And will he not be unhappy, free, and without you, as unhappy as he is now?"

"No," she said, lying back and letting him disrobe her, "no, I don't think he will be. You will think it very strange but I do not think that he will care. If he is free, I will not try to see him."

"I do think it strange," the Judge whispered in his turn, "almost inconceivable, Mary Elisabeth, but if he is to be freed, if that is what we are now to try for, the thought indeed relieves me. I will think on it hard." And he shortly did.

Having thought about it several times in the night, in the morning the Judge with his characteristic dispatch had arranged for her transportation and her escort before she had dressed and breakfasted.

"I do not know why you should be so good to me," she said, as he handed her into the coach.

"Nor do I," he agreed. "I trust I am not cutting off my own nose. The law is slow, Mary Elisabeth, and you must not become discouraged. If you are not back within the fortnight, I shall come to London myself to help you, after the courts close here."

"You trust me to return," she said.

"But of course. I have a pawn in hostage," he said smiling wryly, "who can't get out unless you do."

"But I think you trust me, all the same," she said, "and because you do, I will not ever play you false, or ever deceive you, as I did once." She reached up her face and kissed him. "You are very kind to me."

The journey to London passed with its usual speed, which meant slowness and delay. When she arrived, the letters of the Judge procured lodging and entrance for her, and although the days seemed to her to slip by in an endless string, with the lawyer-nephew's help she did receive a comparative quick audience. When finally, after a week, she did secure it, and then, put off once, and then a second time, finally stood with the lawyer to place her cause before the King's final mercy, she found it granted on her testimony of non-rebellion swiftly and almost carelessly. The mood of London in parts was shifting. July and August had witnessed the executions on Kennington Common of the Rebels, and more were scheduled to come. The Capital had discovered that it was one thing to cry for the blood of the disaffected Papist Rebels, and another entirely to get it in the person of a runaway student from a good college, needing a sharp redress and instead disembowelled. Though the executions would continue, as the tension and the hysteria of imminent invasion relaxed, and the pleasures of a glorious victory took their place, and as reports of the savage rape done on the prostrate defeated began to trickle slowly down, and of possible mistakes now irreparable, the Crown and its representatives were becoming ready to show mercy and to listen. A mistake was not admitted, but it was the week before the official celebration of the day set for National Public Thanksgiving for the victory at Culloden, "which was to us a day of solemn joy," clergy, crown, and common alike, and in that mood, the King, not admitting error but allowing graciously the possibility of misunderstanding or misidentity, granted the mercy of his pardon.

She took it, and though it was late in the day, she took coach and left immediately, travelling through that night, stopping only the next day for quick meals and quicker changes of horse, and again through the next, sleeping in the coach, her escort and the driver taking turns to sleep. They were delayed by rain washing out a bridge on roads already poor, by cattle blocking the way, by wheel blocks failing on a hill, by a broken axle. She thought of sending it on ahead, trusting the identity could be established, by horse, but her escort refused to leave her, having the Judge's orders, or to let her ride, and she was forced to hold herself in patience. She did persuade him, by the whiteness of her face, to take her directly to the Castle jail, and while she waited outside in the carriage, he went inside with the piece of parchment.

XV: *Prisoner Lyon*

AFTER WHAT SEEMED AN INTERMINABLE TIME, THE DOOR OPENED, AND TWO FIGURES CAME OUT. NEITHER BEING DIARMID, SHE PAID NO ATTENTION TO THEM UNTIL THEY CAME DIRECTLY TOWARDS HER CARRIAGE, APPROACHING her. She did not wait then, but got out of the carriage, descending the steps, and went to meet them, although her escort was not with them.

"I am bringing the prisoner Lyon to be identified," the official said. "The gentleman will be here presently." He waited, but though she nodded her head slightly, she said nothing, not even noticing when the official went away. She was staring at the figure before her, a small, ragged, filthy boy dragging a useless foot, as hard as he was staring at her. Even as she looked, she saw the eagerness fade from the child's face and eyes, in a brief showing of disappointment as keen as hers, before expressionlessness shuttered his face.

"You are not Diarmid," she said in amazed accusation. "Your name is not Lyon."

"No," the child agreed quietly, his eyes blank, "I am not. I am Diar's cousin Rawn. How did you know?" he asked without much curiosity.

"I know because I am Diar's wife," she answered, her eyes on his frail bones showing through the scraps and tags he held about him in the cold air that hung on him but concealed nothing.

"Oh," he said, his eyes briefly on her. "Then I know who you are. I remember now." He said no more and he did not seem interested.

"Where is Diar?" she asked urgently. "Why are you here, and not Diar?"

"He went in my place on the transport," the child said, "with my name, and left me his."

"Oh, God," she said, "why, why did he do it?" hopelessly, the answer there before her.

"Because my ma would not have known where else to look for me, outside of here, and he said no one was looking for him, he doubted, since there was no one left of his, and he was strong enough. He did not think I'd last. I thought you would be my ma," he added, his voice trailing away.

"And was no one looking for you, Diar," she thought, in bitter grief and disappointment and new fear. Aloud she said, her voice little more than a whisper, "When was this, how long ago?"

"I don't know," the child said, "I don't remember. Not yesterday, or the day before. Not recently."

"Oh, God," she said again, trying to hold back her disappointment and her fears.

"They said there was a pardon for me," the child said, his voice as bleak as hers. "I forgot it wasn't me. I thought it was my mother got it. I suppose now you'll send me back." His voice, questionless, was a pathetic question in its lack of one, and the snuffing of its hope. He did not seem to show much interest, for he was too ill now to care.

The thought had been momentarily in her mind, but with the child before her, swaying on his feet, only momentarily.

"No," she said, "I have you, I will keep you. You are out now, you are not going back."

"What of Diar then?" the child asked surprisingly, his face not changing. "I cannot take his pardon, even if you will let me."

"Diar would wish it so," she said. "I will get another in your name," somehow I will, she thought to herself, "and when I find him, I will give Diar that."

The answer seemed to satisfy the child, for the set look went a little out of his face, and the tired lips smiled just a little at her, tightly and fleetingly, a wan ghost of a child's smile. He looked as though he would faint, but instead, he began to cry.

"You are not going back," she said again firmly, to herself and to him both.

She took the frail stiff little figure in her arms and kissed his pale grimed face. "There now," she said, "there now, love," and stroked his filthy hair. "I will find your ma for you," she said (if she is there to find any more, she thought inwardly), "you will tell me all about her. And until I do, I'll take you to my mother and she'll take care of you and make you well."

"Thank you," the child whispered with small pathetic courtesy, "you are very kind." He shut his eyes, against the soft grey light, and did not seem any more to be there.

By this time the escort had finished his work inside with the officials, and he returned and helped her lift the child into the carriage. The escort would have laid him on the seat, across from her, but she sat down, and indicated he should put the child in her lap. She held him close to her, as she would have liked to hold the true Lyon and had hoped to, her arms strong and warm about him. He was breathing lightly and unevenly, his lips colourless, his eyes shut, light as a featherweight in her arms, fragile as a small bird, and he seemed now that he was safe to be slipping away from them.

"Oh, what shall I do?" she asked, frightened.

"A touch of brandy," the escort said, offering his flask, "is helpful, for too much joy."

He pressed it between the child's lips, and the child swallowed, and coughed, and turned his face away against her.

"I was thinking we'd come for an older man, somehow," the escort said, hesitantly and somewhat curious. "But when they said his name was Lyon, and there was no other, I sent him on."

"You did right," she said. "I think we must take him home at once now and put him to bed."

"Well," said the Judge, softly, when the child had been put into bed, unwashed, with hot stone bottles wrapped about his feet and sides, and he might speak with her quietly and privately, "you were gone a long time for not very much."

"It is not Lyon," she said.

"I did assume that," the Judge replied. "And I have not seen the face. Who is he?"

"It is Lyon's cousin," she said. "Lyon went on the transport in his place." She looked very unhappy, her face wan and bleak.

"I am glad to see you back," the Judge said. "I have missed you very much, Mary Elisabeth." He took her in his arms, and she rested her head against him and let him stroke her hair. "The child is resting easy. Come into my room, and let me comfort you."

To let me comfort you, she thought wearily, in exhaustion, but she was so unhappy, one more thing seemed very little, so she went with him for an hour. When he had comforted her sufficiently to his satisfaction, she went down to the kitchen to supervise the making of a scraped beef tea to feed the child with, waking him to force a little of it down into his starved body.

The Judge, while she was doing this, had summoned a doctor, and arranged for a nurse. For the next week, Diar's wife's days were spent in a dream-like attendance either upon the child in the sick bed or upon the Judge after court hours in the big bed behind its hangings in the Judge's room. She did what the moments required of her, and afterwards she could not in her weariness tell what it was she had done. It was days before they dared to wash the child, despite the possibility of taking a fever from him, days when every hour Mary Elisabeth fed him small spoonfuls of weak broth every hour. But finally he was sitting up in bed, his black hair washed and combed, his skin the colour of skin, able to smile again, and to eat without cramps or looseness, and he began to put on a small amount of flesh, and then to leave his bed. The doctor had examined his foot, and had suggested treatment to relieve the pain and swelling in it. It had knit crookedly, however, he said, and the bone had shortened, and there was no help for that now except to order a crutch.

Rawn did not seem to mind about his foot. He was very quiet, very docile, anxious to improve to please them, but otherwise he did not seem to be with them. His thoughts, and sometimes his eyes, seemed always to be looking inwards at things he had seen and would not tell them and they could not guess at. His reserves of resistance and endurance had been totally called up, to survive, and now that he had survived, in the relief of it and the disappointment of it not having been his mother who found him, there seemed little left of him.

"I want to take him to my mother's," Diar's wife said to the Judge, "before the winter really sets in. He will be more at home in Scotland, even in the Lowlands, and I have brothers and sisters to amuse him and bring him out of his brooding. I am poor company, being broody myself, and you are gone all day."

"You are looking broody these days, much too pale yourself," he agreed with concern. "Are you breeding?" he asked directly.

"No," she answered, "no, I don't think so." She did not say anything else.

"I wish you were," he said. "Then you might be content. I wish I were less old."

"I do not think I will have children for anyone," she said, "I do not think I can any more. I was hurt in the Spring, you see, before I met you." She did not explain further, her face withdrawn.

"A forced bargain, my dear," he said, "and an unmerry bargain, is no bargain at all. I think I have told you so once before. What is on your mind?"

"Nothing, sir," she said, forcing a tired smile. "I am only very weary. I wish myself I might go to my mother's, instead of sending him with George, but I do not wish to ask you to let me."

"If you go, Mary Elisabeth, I am afraid you will not come back."

"I am afraid I will not either," she said frankly, "and that is why I cannot ask you to let me."

"You have ideas and plans and schemes in your little head that you know I will not approve of." She was silent. "I will never agree to them, Mary Elisabeth. I will not help you to it, in any way, or supply you with money for them, it is a fool's venture, impossible to execute. You cannot get a pardon now, your case and your story have been used up. And the child's name is no good at all, the MacCulloughs did fight for the Prince. The child is lucky to be out, and I will turn a blind eye and know nothing of it, but I must tell you flatly that if you were so determined, then you should not have let pity make you give up that pardon. Now even if you could make the trip across and even if you could find him, you have nothing to show. But you can*not* find him, Mary Elisabeth. The colonies are too vast. You do not even know where he has been sent, to which part of the world. He is a lost man, even if he lives. And myself I doubt very much he will survive the transport over.

"And now I have made you cry. But I am keeping you here for your own good, as well as my own. Any person of sense, any person of any attachment would not let you go on such a hopeless wild goose's errand."

"Well, sir," she said, "almost you persuade me. Shall we

take him, the two of us together then to my mother? And if you like, since my husband is gone, you may take me if you wish it still as your affianced wife."

"I will do that," he said, his eye kindling. "I had not hoped for this consent, so soon on your disappointment, or I should have suggested it myself."

She knew, however, then, that she meant to deceive him. Her honour gone, as a woman's honour counted, she counted it less a sin to deceive in words than a man would have. And though she knew it was a deception and a breaking of a promised troth and agreement, she was unable not to. All the force of her being was still centered in the direction Diar was, and that way, like the magnetised compass, now pointed West across the Atlantic Ocean. Her whole energy was concentrated within her, unseen and unknown by those looking on, into finding the means and the way to continue. But she had first, because Diar would have wanted her to, to bestow the child Diar had benefited comfortably at her mother's and to do that she would have first to go there with the child herself. She did not mind the Judge's presence with her. It would tend to throw off suspicion and questions from her that she could not and would not answer.

So they went together, and after she had settled the child, and accepted their congratulations on her new estate in life, and their reproaches for her silence, both meekly and dutifully, and started in motion enquiries towards finding the child's mother if she was to be found, after she had done all these things, she turned her mind on escaping from her loving keepers.

She did not dare steal, afraid of pursuit, afraid of blame and the terrible penalty being laid to someone else, as before. But she took her pearls, and the diamonds her father had given her, thinking to sell them in London. She knew this time the Judge did not trust her, and meant to keep her, for he kept her without money. She went in to Edinburgh, supposedly to shop for her wedding clothes, but she lost her

maid in a crowd on the street, and went instead to a disre-
putable-looking Inn where she sold herself to two soldiers.
The experience left her shattered, and fearful of disease, but
with two gold coins. When she found her maid again, she
was convincingly distraught.

Nevertheless, the next afternoon she did the same thing, at
a different Inn, letting her maid secretly have the afternoon
free for her own concerns, which were much the same, and
yet the next. Then she came in flowers, and judged it time to
go back to Carlisle with the Judge.

Her excuse gave her an acceptable reason for vapours, and
for requesting a separate room, although the Judge pointed
out that flowers did not disturb him.

"But they disturb me," she said, "and I am weary after the
coach. Had I known," she said untruthfully, "I would have
delayed the trip, but I have been much disarranged since my
miscarriage. Truly, I would like to sleep alone."

She kissed him gently, with sincere gratitude, wishing for
a moment almost that she might stay. In the morning she was
gone, and no trace to show how or by what means or in what
direction. The Judge was shocked and genuinely grieved for
a happening he had hoped to prevent, but not surprised, and
he did not attempt to pursue her, judging it both useless and
cruel.

XVI: *On Board the Transport*

IT WOULD HAVE BEEN TRUE TO HAVE SAID THAT DIARMID, NOW RAWN MACCULLOUGH, WOULD HAVE PREFERRED DEATH OF ANY SORT TO TRANSPORTATION, AS HE WALKED OUT OF THE JAIL IN PLACE OF THE CHILD. HIS RELIGION AND HIS own heart forbade him to kill himself, even had he had means, which he did not. He had therefore to wait for it to come to him, the slow way or the fast, and endure the life that had for months now become to him unbearable, and what he knew lay before him. He had been on a transport, and he knew, as the child had not, what that would be, only more of it.

The procedure was much the same for loading him on. His shackled wrists were chained to the man beside him, and in twos, soldiers before them and behind them, their swords pricking those who lagged, they marched or walked or staggered to the quay. The only difference for Diarmid was that this time he was completely naked, but his nakedness was viewed not as a man's but as a beast's would have been, or a black's, something alien and divorced from the curious throngs on the streets, alien, not human, not of their race.

And he was not, for they were English, and he was not, he was Scotch and a savage from the wild Highlands. He kept his eyes lowered, and paid no attention to the things thrown at him, words, stones, bottles, pieces of chairs. A book with a metal clasp hit his forehead, and made a cut over his eye, which began to bleed, but he did not attempt to raise his hands, which in any case he could not have done.

He was ferried out in a small boat again, which this time did not overturn, and taken up the side of the ship and put again into the hold, which was already full, the ship having come up from London. The conditions were the same, the only difference this time being that they were to remain in them for months at sea, not weeks. The ship stayed in harbour for two days, while the crew was put again in order, and for those two days the prisoners in the hold fasted.

The next day the Captain came aboard with the merchant who had bought the original papers of bond, and the merchant, inspecting briefly his property of some eighty bodies, men, women, and children, mixed and stacked with the ballast stones in the dark hold, insisted his cargo be kept alive and fed. For that day they received each a biscuit, in the confusion of setting weigh, with their half-pound of meal to begin the next.

The ship crossed the sea then to Dublin, to pick up more prisoners for the already full hold, putting into the overcrowded hold ten fresh fiery Irish spirits from Carrickfergus jail who with an enterprise better fed and not cowed, as the ship cast anchor led a rebellion of the prisoners against their masters. It was briefly and surprisingly successful. Though chained, they outnumbered the crew, which expecting no such rebellion was not armed, and their shackles proved effective weapons, both as clubs and as garrots. They unlocked their shackles, or struck them off, and put them on the captain, the mate, and the crew, and forced them to steer a course towards one of the outer isles. They had taken a boat and filled it, with women and children and the Irish, and sent

it ashore, and were filling another to go, when fate intervened in the form of a British frigate, one of the warships
patrolling the coastlines against the French and looking for
Charley, yet. Receiving no answer from the ship in rebellion,
they had fired upon it so heavily the boat being loaded
could not go. It overturned in the water half drowning, half
being pulled aboard either the rebelling ship itself, or aboard
a boat sent from the frigate. Under pressure of the firing and
the disaster, the rebellious Rebels left surrendered or were
overpowered, rechained, and replaced in the hold, Diarmid
among them, and left again without food to consider their
sins while their owner counted his losses in terms of the
profit of the voyage and resolved to go up to Inverness, being
well-started on the way, and pick up more heads to replace
those he had lost.

Three weeks later, the prisoners wholly subdued by the
second fasting, they set out a second time towards the open
sea. But in those second two days without food or water a
change came over Diar, sitting on the cold stones and dirt in
his chains, a calm anger at the treatment of them that he had
been too numb before and too bewildered to feel, and a settled determination to outlive it. He was not to lose it throughout the entire hideousness of the three months' voyage, in
which he saw others die and rot beside him, and he did not
die. It gave him a patience of spirit and an iron of soul
which endured without retort the mockery of the sailors who
fed them, laughing at their pitiful naked efforts to catch the
meal thrown to them in whatever scrap of cloth still hung
about them. Lacking the scrap now, he made a cup of his
chained hands, and of his knees put together, to catch what
fell.

The conditions of the sailors above were not that much
more comfortable than those of the prisoners below, but they
did have a hole in the freezing deck they might use not to
have to live with what they had done, that the prisoners
were not allowed out of the hold to use. The spray might
sting them and freeze them, but the air was fresh. The hold

itself festered with illness and sickness of several kinds, with excrement and pish, and bugs. The air became so foetid the sailors detailed to feed the prisoners revolted, and after that once a week half the prisoners at a time were taken on deck while the other half worked at the hopeless task of cleaning the hold. Those on deck were cleaned summarily of dirt and lice by a method that gave much amusement to the crew. A rope was tied to the prisoner's waist and he was lowered from the yardarm into the water, and kept there supposedly until the lice drowned. Several of the prisoners drowned before the lice drowned, and before the official who owned them stopped the practice, but Diarmid did not.

After that, they were not washed again, and their hole was not cleaned. The sailors, however, who did not like them, found other ways of annoying them, using their bucket of drinking water as their urinals before they brought it down, and sometimes where they could see, in case they did not know.

"They are better fed than we are—we may be grateful at least we are getting some of it," Diar said wryly, and helped himself to his portion.

Life settled down, as it does even in its meagerest condition. They played games at importing and exporting one another's lice, in the dark hold, and they talked softly to their immediate neighbours in Gaelic about the places they had come from, lands now too aptly named: Tirnadris, land of the briars, or thorns, and Meall nan Luath, the Hill of Ashes. They kept these pictures before their eyes, when there was nothing else to see, and sang softly when their lips were not too parched or too blue and shivering, and were thrown against the hard stones in the gales, some of them dying from the blows, or drowned in the seas of water pouring over them in the hold which, in their weakened crowded state, they could not avoid, and were rocked in the calms, encased in the womb or the tomb of the hold, the outside only a memory, and waited and died or endured.

The day came in the end that the ship docked and those

who were still alive were called up on board deck or carried up, to learn what was to happen next to them, in the King's mercy. Diar was one of those still able to keep on his feet, the gift of God to rascals, and he climbed up the rope stair out of the hold, this time no one pushing him back, and stood on deck, dazzled by the light, in the sky and breaking on the waves, breathing in the cold crisp air. It was the day after Christmas, but he did not know it. The climb up had exhausted him, the unusual exertion, and with the rocking of the ship in harbour, he could not keep his feet and slid across the deck. But no one, to his surprise, hit him, and he picked himself up and held on to a rope on the side of the ship, and no one said him nay.

He learned shortly the reason for this kindness. The official who held their bonds to make his profit needed their agreeing signatures on the new bonds of sale exchanging their indentures into the hands of separate masters. He painted in glowing pictures their chance at securing their freedom for some of them after only seven years, but many of them knew their sentenced indentures were for life. The prisoners looked at one another, as if bewildered at this turn of affairs and the sudden need for action on their part, and those few ahead of Diar like children, stumbling and obedient with shaking hands affixed their names or their marks.

Diar watched them, his eyes narrowed both in resolution and against the sun, his lips set, the wind, welcome at first, whipping and chilling his nakedness like fingers of ice. The pen then was given to him, but he ignored it held out to him. It was then thrust into his hand and a hand laid on his shoulder, but he dropped it, so that it fell, splattering its little load of ink on the deck, and with a sudden pitching of the ship, pursued by scrambling feet and hands, fell into the sea.

"You clumsy!" said the official, saying other things beside. "Now what's to do?"

"It don't matter," Diar said indifferently but firmly, "for I don't sign."

"You don't sign?" the official repeated, his face turning red near Diarmid's. "What do you mean you don't sign? Of course you'll sign. That's what you were brought here for."

"I did not wish to come here," Diar said, his voice soft and quiet, "and I never signed to come. I refused then and I refuse now. Do what you like about it. I am a free man and I will not sign myself to be a slave."

His words reaching the ears of the other prisoners found seeds of agreement waiting for some such action to bring them out and into sight. They nodded and spoke quietly among themselves, and the personal rebellion of one seemed rapidly to be spreading, like a spark among ready tinder. The official gave Diar the benefit of his opinion, and he looked ready to give him the benefit also of his fist, but he held himself in, needing the signatures, checking his rage, in the hopes of settling the affair quickly and moderately. His hopes were vain. The men stood silent and sullen, their chained hands at their sides, waiting in a quickening resolution what he would think to do next.

There was little he could do. The Captain, uninterested in his financial problems, refused to give him the help of his crew in forcing the men to sign, pointing out he had brought the prisoners over and that was all he had agreed to do. He would like to unload them now, so that he could clean his ship out for the return voyage, fumigate their quarters with gunpowder. The official's problems were none of his; he and his crew had enough of their own.

The official requested patience and a few hours' grace. He went with the Mayor's official who had come out for him in a small boat to the shore, threatening to incarcerate them all in prisons on the shore, and to secure the Mayor's cooperation.

Diar looked at him with eyes of scorn, and his lips twisted. "I doubt there is nothing you can do to me here you have not already done to me there, and I will not sign for any man," he said. "Take your threats elsewhere than to me."

"You will see what my threats are worth," the official said, and went over the side of the ship into the little boat, with those prisoners who had already put their names.

Diar looked at the cockleshell tossing on the sunlit waves and followed it with his eyes as far as his weakened eyes could make it out towards the land he seemed destined with no recourse to shortly enter. He did not know where he was, and no one troubled to tell him. After a half hour had passed, the official returned, again with the Mayor's official and with the boat filled with some rough frontiersmen of the colonies, "buckskins," the Captain commented scornfully, watching them come.

They had offered their aid in subduing the rebellion with rough force, but the sight of the naked chained men, with faces not unlike their own, more bone than flesh, what rags some had left fluttering in the bleak wind, the sun disappearing behind the scudding clouds, with their simple refusal to sign over their lives, unnerved their intentions, and they seemed reluctant themselves to touch them. The Mayor had seemed dubious when approached about prison quarters, despite the assurance of George II that such would be provided as required (for the stubborn or the recalcitrant). For a moment it almost looked as though the little rebellion was under weigh, but it was resolved as simply as Diar's earlier short-lived and ineffective one at Carlisle Gaol. The prisoners were taken, will they nill they, over the side into the boat, as many at a time as could be handled, and were sold with their indentures unsigned to the higher bidders without scruples about a technicality in a land little biased towards technicalities.

By the time Diar's turn came to go in the boat, blue with cold, and resigned again, past caring and past showing rebellion any more, except for the simple refusal of lifting his fingers to write, word of the prisoners' stand had gotten around. When they learned a ship docking at Wecomica was about to sell out the indentures in Annapolis, certain Catholics from Prince George County, and Highlanders and Scots already settled in Maryland and North Carolina, and Georgian Jacobites had been making it their practice to meet the ships when they came in, and to outbid the buckskins for those prisoners they could secure, buying out their indentures and setting them free as soon as the technicalities of it could be dispensed with. It was into such a port in Chesapeake Bay that the ship Diar was on put in, and it was by such an old gentleman that Diar's indenture was bought. He did not know it.

He stood there in the cold, before the well-dressed gentlemen in black and lace, with their ladies, mixed among the buckskins, shamed, sick, sick at heart, and to his further humiliation, frightened, he found. He held his head up and his eyes were open, but he saw nothing. He heard voices, loud, calling figures, repeating, replying, exchanging, and after a time was pushed forward, and the bidding was for him. He thought he must die of it, so ill and so ashamed, but he kept his inner mind fixed on a picture of a hill by a loch in a mist with the heathers and the golden gorse in bloom, and after a time, a considerable time for even as he was he looked worth buying, the bidding was over and he was pushed, sightless, and dying inside, towards the person who had bought him and was to own him now and use him like an animal. He was unaware that any intentions towards him any longer could be kind. Had he had any strength then, he would have brought his chained hands down in brutish dumb rage upon the head of the man who had dared to buy him, who had once been Diarmid Mac-Lyon of Lyon, and let them then do with him what they liked. But he had not the strength. The ground was wobbling under his feet, swaying and rising like the waves about him. He could not see the land or the figure in front of him through the bright brown fog gathering all about him, and what he did was for the first time in his life to faint.

XVII: *Wecomica–Annapolis:* *An Indenture Bought*

HE AWOKE TO FIND HIMSELF IN A BED. HE FELT LIGHT AND DISEMBODIED, AND UNLIKE HIMSELF. HE WONDERED, HIS EYES SHUT, IF HE HAD DIED, BUT THE BED SEEMED REAL ENOUGH, AND WHEN HE PUT OUT A HAND, OR rather moved the hand that appeared to belong to him that was lying loosely on top of a coverlet, he discovered that his hands were free of shackles, and no longer chained or bound, and that that was the reason for the extraordinary lightweightedness he felt, besides the lightheadedness of his condition. He moved a foot tentatively, and found that the same was true for it. He wondered if he could manage to somehow get to the window he now found his eyes focussing on, an enormous fuzzy square of blinding glaring light, but the effort of moving the little he had exhausted him, and he put the idea aside. He turned his head a little to one side, and saw an immensely large woman sitting in a chair by his bed, nodding.

The motion of his head turning seemed to rouse her, for she left off nodding and looked at him and smiled at him. He could not smile back. He only stared.

"Well," she said, "you're awake. That's good. I'm going to feed you then, and then I'm going to bathe you, so that you're decent, for when you are, Mr. Smythe wants to see you."

"Decent?" he asked, as if he did not know the word, and it had been out of his vocabulary and his ken now for months.

"Well, you cannot say you are that now, and Mr. Smythe is a gentleman. I could not bear the being in the room with you myself," she said, "except I have the asthma, and I cannot smell anyway."

"Oh," Diar said, for want of anything to say, or strength to say it. To stink had become a natural part of his insane world, and now it appeared he was among some kind of sanity which once again objected to it. He felt a spoon pressing against his lips and his teeth, and he opened them, and swallowed with difficulty the thin hot broth poured into him, and a spoonful of water. The effort exhausted him past resisting when the strange woman and a man she summoned uncovered him in his nakedness and between them put him into a hot bath they brought in, and scrubbed him like a child, body, face, hair, all of him, and rinsed him with cider vinegar. He shut his eyes, wincing, and the tears ran down his cheeks like a child at the roughness of their scrubbing, helpless in their stringent hands, until they relented and left off and dried him with towels and put him in a nightgown and returned him to the bed and covered him with blankets to stop his shivering.

He shut his eyes, not to see them, not to think, the only thought in his head that Colonists seemed to protect their property better than the English proper, and fell asleep again. He had had the brief thought again that he should try to escape these lax captors, but the warmth of the bath enervated him over and beyond his weakness, and he again gave the idea up. He woke, and was fed a few spoonfuls again of the broth, and water, and like a child helped to relieve himself, and re-covered, and left to sleep again. The light in the room passed, and it grew dark, and then, after hours of feverish discomfort, in which he slept and woke fitfully, the light came again, and the red-haired large woman. He was again fed, and relieved, and re-covered, and the fever seeming to leave him somewhat, he slept again. He seemed to see another figure in the room during the afternoon, but he could not be sure of that or of anything. He was delirious again in the night, as he had been so many times, in the jails and on the ships, but this time a hand took his and held it, and when he fought the hand, it transferred itself to his forehead with a cool scented cloth, and he relaxed and let himself fall again into sleep. Three days or more passed in this manner, and then he woke one afternoon to find the large red-headed woman gone, and in her place an old man was sitting, thin, erect, with shoulder-length white hair, his intelligent grey eyes fixed kindly on Diarmid.

"Ah," the old man said, bending forward, "you are awake. Good. We can make acquaintance now in a proper manner. I am Mr. Smythe, George Smythe, and you are?"

"Lyon," Diarmid said, his voice remote. "A Lyon in mourning."

The old man looked surprised, but he only said, "I thought your name was MacCullough. Rawn MacCullough. Your papers had that name."

"It is my name too," Diarmid said, his voice flat and ungracious. "You will call me as you like. I do not care." He had been treated kindly, but he had been bought, and he did not forget it, if the old man with his courtesies seemed to.

"Mr. MacCullough," the old man said, "before we speak further, I wish to set your mind at rest. I have your papers of indenture here which I have bought only with the intention of releasing you from them as soon as you are well enough to be able to go with me to accomplish it. I have bought them for no other purpose."

Enough of the measured sentences reached Diarmid's mind to wake his dulled expression into an incredulous dawning hope.

"You must believe me," the old man said, "I assure you it is so. We are here in an Inn. I came up from my home in the County only to meet the ship, and only for this purpose, hearing there were Scotch Catholic prisoners aboard it being shamefully mistreated. I am Catholic myself, Mr. MacCullough, and I have known in my family what persecutions that could bring."

Diarmid raised himself briefly on his elbow to look at the man beside him, his Saviour come in this strange guise to relieve him. He held out his hand, recovered it in shame seeing the ugly marks of the fetters left on his wrists, and felt it clasped and held. He lay back down, feeling again in his eyes the tears kindness brought in his weakness filling and overflowing. He wiped them away with a rough gesture of his arm in the white nightshirt put on him that was not his, and smiled directly at the old man, his old smile.

"I am much obliged," he said simply. "I am indeed. My hand, at your service, for what it's worth."

His progress in recovery thereafter was rapid but to no purpose, for the old man took the fever he brought with him out of the hold of the ship, less virulent in himself from long usage than to one less used, and died of it. Sorry for the death of the one man who had been kind to him, after so much unkindness, he had no thought at first, or idea, of the personal disaster it was to prove to him.

At the first signs of the seriousness of the illness, word had been sent to the old man's nephew in Georgia, who came post haste, arriving the day after his death.

He looked Diarmid up and down, straightly, with cold eyes. "You are the man my uncle came to buy?" He did not wait for Diar's answer of affirmation. "What are you doing then in this room? You are not a house servant, or if my uncle thought so, I think differently. Please go outside, and wait for me in the courtyard by the stables. I will see you by and by."

Diarmid did not move, his mouth setting hard.

"Well?" said the new nephew, a man of some thirty-five years, still in riding boots and riding coat, with his uncle's eyes without their expression, a square full face, its lips pressed tight together, and his uncle's hair but dark with youth, and tied at his neck with a ribbon. "Go on, then."

"I am no servant," Diarmid said. "I have my papers here that Mr. Smythe has bought, to cancel out. He has told me this, and if he has not told you, as I doubt not he did, there are many in the house besides me who know it. It was my illness first, and then his own, that held it up and has prevented it."

"Let me see the papers," the nephew said. He held out his hand, and as Diarmid hesitated, he took them. Without examining them closely, after only a cursory glance he folded them and put them in his pocket.

"I'll have them back please now," Diarmid said, quietly but firmly, "being mine."

The nephew turned a look of contemptuous dismissal on him that hardly seemed to see or to consider him.

"I think you do not understand," he said. "My uncle is dead, without issue, and I am his heir. His property, all of it, is mine, and these papers not being cancelled out in law, included in it. His intentions do not concern me. This is a perfectly valid indenture, paid for, I daresay, knowing uncle, paid too much for, and legal, and I intend to hold it myself for what it is. He is dead, I say again," he added at Diarmid's startled face, "and his intentions are dead with him. Forget them. His intentions are not mine, nor his foolish charities. We are in no way alike, and do not think it."

"I want my papers back that you just took," Diarmid repeated as if he had not heard, his hand out, but his tone startled.

The nephew shook his head. "I have told you what to do and where to go. You'd do well to go there before I have you dragged there."

"Then I'll take my papers," Diarmid said, desperately, and

he proceeded to try. But however bonny a fighter and reiver he had once been, he was no longer a match for anyone. Groggy with the blows directed on him, he fell swaying to his knees, despair circling him again. Two servants were called, and his wrists were bound together with a cord behind him, and he was taken out to the stables. There he was fastened with a stronger piece of rope to a horsepost, and left there, his mind savage but dismayed.

He remained there all the day, sometimes in the sun, sometimes in the shadow, and all the night, as the dews fell, and all the next day, back in his old posture and his old filth, while the nephew arranged for the sale of his uncle's County land and house. He was released at noon to eat, when word of his recent illness prompted his new owner to take some precautionary care of his property. His old shackles, found discarded in the stables, were put again on his hands and his feet, as a punishment and a restraint both, and he was left for the rest of that day and night locked in a horse stall, his feet fetters additionally secured to a ring in the wall, his face black with bitterness after the brief taste of life again as he had known it, to think over his future.

It made no difference to him then whether his papers were for seven years or seventy. It seemed then all the same to him. He did not hope to die, but he knew that nothing whatever that could be done to him could make him, the son of his father, serve as a bondsman, not to anyone and not to this man perpetrating on him the double injustice the law allowed him.

For the remainder of that week, no one paid any attention to him, except to feed him from time to time. The stall grew dark and grew light and grew dark again, and his spirit resurrected by the week of kindness he had had, and the care and feeding, it burned with bitterness against the new cruelty of fate. It was no comfort or source of resignation to reflect that it was only what he had been sent for originally that he was now to experience anyway. Had he had power and opportunity he would have killed the man aiding in the forcing of bondage upon it. And something of this spirit communicated itself to the younger Smythe when he came finally to see his bondsman.

He looked at the smouldering eyes of the chained Scot, measured the length the chains would reach, and kept at that range.

"We have gotten off to rather a bad start," he said, conversationally, his manner considerably changed from his initial one. "I thought it would be just as well if we had a talk."

Diarmid did not answer, and he looked remarkably dangerous.

"I am sorry about this," Smythe said, indicating the chains. "But you did not look to be going to be reasonable about it, and I have had other affairs more pressing than you that had to be done at the time. I couldn't look over you myself just then, even if it would have made a difference, which I doubt. Let us have this clear now. You are a valuable piece of property, and mine, whether you like it or not, for the time being. It seems to me you might as well accept that, but I am not certain that you are going to. You did not look like it then, and you still don't." He looked with a certain compassion that was lost on Diarmid. "I know that you don't like this. I should not myself."

"Then why do you not follow your uncle's wishes about me?" Diarmid said, his voice quietly dangerous.

His master sighed. "I have told you. You are valuable, and the law has given your service to me. I am not a philanthropist, I am just trying to manage a plantation and keep it going despite my uncle's charities. He lives where there are slaves, which he did not set free, I may tell you, but the land I have from my father is in a Province which does not permit the use of Negro slaves. You look to be strong, and I need you, and I have you." His eyes were thoughtful. "The question in my mind, though, is whether I am going to be able to use you; how much trouble I will be put to convincing you that you have to work now, if not for me, for someone else. You will be made to, you know, one way or another, in the end. But it may involve so much trouble, the making you, that I might do as well to sell out your indenture again now, if I can find a buckskin fool enough to buy it now."

"You will do as you please. But I have already been made once, and I don't need making again, by you or anyone."

Smythe's eyes raised in brief surprise.

"You were quality then, where you came from?"

"No," Diarmid said, "not as you would count it. But I was not made to work as a servant for anyone, nor was my father, nor his, and I will not for you or anyone. I will not bend my back."

"It is no matter, in any case. Whatever you were, or whatever your expectations were, and whatever life you were used to, this is where you are now. You were simply on the wrong side, where you were, and this has happened to you, and you look strong enough, even after the transport over, that I am going to use you if I can, no matter how you feel. Your name is *Lyon*, isn't it? Something like that, *Lyon* MacCullough, isn't it."

"Lyon MacLyon," Diar said, abandoning the masquerade.

"Well, MacLyon," he said, "there are some who think a Highlander is a savage, but I do not happen to be one of them. I have known Highlanders here, and I know they are not. That is why I've come to try to talk to you, and to get you to accept this thing that's happened to you. It will be so much better for you, and for me, for us both, if you can."

He might as well have talked to a stone wall, and he saw it. He dropped his conversational manner, and his voice stiffened.

"So be it, MacLyon, then. If I choose to keep your indenture, I can have you imprisoned and tried if you refuse to serve it. I can do much as I like now, and in Georgia, when I take you there, if I do, I can do more. Think about it. Most transports, even those as proud as you, choose to serve." He had gotten up from the stool on which he had been sitting, as he spoke. " 'You roar? You storm?' " he said, quoting softly, looking at the chained Scot, " 'Fret till your proud heart breaks,' then, it will be all the same. I thought I could help you, but I see it is no use."

"I want none of your kind of help," Diarmid said. "You did not pay a penny for me, and you'll get not a pennyworth out of me."

XVIII: *Diarmid Indentured*

THE NEXT DAY TWO OFFICIALS CAME FOR HIM, AND HE
FELT A TERRIBLE FEAR. HE WAS TAKEN TO THE JAIL IN
THE TOWN, AND THEN INTO COURT BEFORE THE GRAND
JURY, WHERE A TRUE BILL WAS BROUGHT AGAINST HIM FOR CON-
spiring against the sentence of the law. But instead of imprison-
ing him again, the court granted an order to his master in his
hearing to take whatever actions or precautions were necessary
to assist in his fulfilling his indenture, and allowed two soldiers
to be sent as escort on the boat until he reached the boundary
of Georgia. He saw Smythe only across the courtroom, and
Smythe did not cross to speak to him, though he looked across
at his bondsman curiously from time to time, in black now for
his uncle, his eyes calm and impersonal. He was also sentenced
to be whipped in the public square, and when that was done,
he was taken between the two soldiers, hardly able to walk,
still chained, onto the boat waiting in the harbour.

He did not see his master again on the trip, but he had
begun to learn what kind of teeth backed the indenture law
besides the torn bite in the paper itself. The boat put into

Charles Town to wait a storm, and then made as straight for Savannah, pulling against the winds of winter, as adverse winds and waves allowed. Buffeted again in a knocking hold, the salt water blown in stinging the cuts made on him, ill as everyone else was in the violent weather, Diarmid emerged finally at New Savannah, momentarily as tamed as his master could have wished him.

"Well, MacLyon," Smythe said, looking at him as the soldiers brought him up, "are you coming with me, or shall I keep these gentlemen?"

"I'm coming with you," Diarmid said. "I would think these soldiers would have something else to do," he added, softly and bitterly.

Smythe looked at him sharply but he said only, "Then come with me if you are coming," and Diarmid turned and followed him off the boat.

The sailing ship had landed them at a small island, and now they took a flat-bottomed barge-like boat up the river to the town itself, much smaller than the port he had come from.

"That was Tybee Island," Smythe said to him, throwing the words, "and we call this kind of boat here a pettiawga, we use the Creek word for it."

Diarmid looked at him without comprehension, and without much interest.

"Indian," he explained, and at the involuntary look crossing Diarmid's face, he smiled.

"You know what Indians are, don't you? Didn't you know there were Indians in America? I forget, but I suppose of course you've never seen even one. You will. You will see the Creeks, who are friendly to us. They come frequently into Savannah, even the Chicasaws occasionally."

He stood beside Diarmid, speaking conversationally to him as though he had not had the skin stripped off of him, leaning back against the cabin wall of the barge as Diarmid's shoulders were yet too sore to, rolling off unfamiliar words that Diarmid did not understand, as the unfamiliar land slipped by with nothing in it that Diarmid recognised. All strange, even the blank bright colour of the sky, and the temperature of the air which in that early February noon was almost mild, and the trees green like Spring. He was choked by the strangeness of it and the homesickness that welled up all through him frightening in its growing swelling intensity through all his organs and his breath. His mind was drowned in it. There was nothing, not a face, not even the ship, that he could hold to as something recognisable, to steady him. The dislocation was of a sort he had never experienced, not even in the English jail, and though he seemed to be standing beside a man talking to him, on a gently rocking flat boat, he felt as though he were being whirled around, in a giant wind roaring in his ears.

"These islands are marsh," the voice beside him said, "but we are coming now into the pine-barrens, before Savannah. You will see it now, there, look up, on the bluff above us. When I first came here, I did not want to come either," the voice continued, surprising. "It was strange to me, and I did not like the landscape, the monotony of the pines, and the big cypress in the swamps, which you have not seen yet. I wanted to stay in Prince George County, which I knew, but my uncle wanted my father to take care of a property he had here, and my father insisted I come with him, to learn it, thinking of such an eventuality, I suppose, as has come about. When I came here, had I believed one day, my father dead, I could have left, I would not have believed then I would have chosen to stay; or that inheriting my Uncle's property in Prince George it would be this I would choose to keep. But I have come to like Georgia in a particular way, MacLyon, and you may come to, too, MacLyon, though you do not think it now," he said, reading the young man's thoughts. "I have great hopes, and with the support of the sale of my uncle's property, I intend to try things I could not before. I want to try growing rice in the river swamps as they do in

South Carolina and in the cane swamps if I can clear them; and indigo, perhaps, as Elizabeth Lucas had tried two years ago in South Carolina, and I think tobacco may grow in the oak-land here as it does in parts of Maryland and Virginia. But I need labour, MacLyon. It is a good land, with possibilities, but one cannot stay afloat in it financially to any degree, the land as it is, under the laws of the present charter and the policies of the Trustees. It is my hope that we may yet become a Royal Colony, with all those advantages. To make loans merely to insolvents is not enough."

They put up for the night at the house of a friend of Smythe's in the town, there being no good Inn, and for all his conversation, Smythe did not unchain him. He was put in a small shed-like room off the main floor, and locked in, and left to the piercing cold of the night, which was surprising after the mildness of the noon. His presence seemed to excite no interest. The next morning early, the man Smythe came in with a rope and another man, and Diarmid felt again the pull of fear, of being in a single person's hands; more than before in those of the law, in the alien land. Smythe said nothing, but took out the key to the fetters, and his pistol, and handed the key to the man he had brought. He stood with the pistol cocked while the man unlocked the fetters from Diarmid's hands and feet, and took the rope and bound his hands together in front of him, but loosely, with play between them, as his hands had been bound in the Carlisle Castle Gaol yard the morning he had been to die.

"Do you see the absurdities you put me to, with your stubborn mulishness," Smythe said. "Come along now, the horses are mounted, and we have a day's ride. I'm not going to put a lead on your bridle, but if you try to bolt, I'll shoot you. I don't think you'd like to anyway, MacLyon, you don't know how the land lies yet, but with a young fool like you one doesn't know."

Diarmid said nothing, and felt again a horse's flank beneath him, and felt his heart turn over within him. His spirits were so raised that he could look about him with interest, despite the bonds on his hands, and listen with a half-ear to the agricultural lessons the man leading him seemed to want to give him.

"This is oak-land," he said, "not your Highland oak. It is the most valuable land in the Province, oak-land, but the most trouble to clear. I have some that I am clearing slowly. It is worth the labour, for unlike pine-barren, which will grow only one good crop and then begins to lose the yield, it will bear any grain for three, or four, or even five years, without needing any manure laid on it. One acre will give ten bushels of Indian corn or five of peas in a single year. I have thought, as I said, it should also do well for tobacco like Virginia land, and I am trying it out."

MacLyon turned his head and looked at the man and his interest without comprehension, his attention not on the land but on the horse beneath him. His own interest had nothing to do with farming or cropping. One hired people to do it when it had to be done, or rented out to them. With a shock, he realised that was much what had been done to him, against his wishes.

"In the fresh pine-land," his owner and hirer continued, "Indian potatoes grow well, that is a potato larger and more luscious than the Irish, and also a crop we have of water melons and sewee beans. Pine-land near the coast has a dry whitish sand, as you saw, not like the black we are in now. It grows naturally a spiry, coarse grass cattle don't like, and low shrubs, but they are easily cleared off, not like the oak, one can clear there four or five acres a year, easily, but the yield does not hold. Most of the coast land we have is pine-land, though, but in between, mixed with the pine land we have savannahs which are low watery meadows, and this soil is of a better kind, and grows hurtle-berries like the English, and Chincopin nuts which are like a small acorn, with a harsh dry taste."

He noticed Diarmid's attention pricking, and he smiled

slightly, reading his thoughts. "When you try to escape me, MacLyon, if you go through pine-land in the right season, you will find peaches, vines and mulberries. Don't try to eat the white mulberries, only the black. The grapes are all red and harsh to taste, both the Fox that grows in twos and threes on a single stalk, and the smaller Cluster. At this season you wouldn't of course find anything at all." He looked at Diarmid sardonically, but the young Scot's face was set without expression again.

"You will find persimmons in the moister parts of oak-land, and a few mulberries and cherries, as well as the grape. Do you know the Medlar fruit, MacLyon? Very luscious, like a clear yellow plum, after the frost, very bitter before. It will pucker your mouth inside, if you try it too soon. But I would advise you at no time to try to escape from my plantation or from me. I shall treat you hardly when I find you if you do," he added.

Diarmid said nothing.

"The oak-land grows in narrow strips between the pine-land and a piece of water, a river or a creek or a swamp. It is like gold, like a narrow band of ore, MacLyon, and as beautiful. In the Spring we have a tree we call the dog-tree, that is covered entirely with large white flowers, and also bay, laurel, ash, and walnut trees grow there, and sumac-trees, and gum-trees that are like a sycamore, and hickory-trees that have a poor nut like a bad walnut. You will learn to know all these trees. My oak-land borders on one side a river, on the other a swamp."

Diarmid, listening again attentively, lifted his eyes at the word. Crops he would not attend, trees were another matter. Next to horses he loved them. Wild trees, or the tame trees of his father's orchard. He winced, his face whitening, remembering then the tree that had borne his father, and briefly himself, shut his eyes against that picture of that fruit rising before his eyes, real again in the clear air among the trees. He swayed and would have fallen, had not a hand steadied his bridle. He opened his eyes then and the stark pain in them startled the man by him.

"A swamp is a low, watery place, MacLyon, to stay out of, they go neck-high and deeper, and have snakes," Smythe said, ignoring Diarmid's face. "We have three kinds: Cypress swamps, which are ponds around which cypress grows, a tree I doubt you know; river swamps, which are usually overflown every tide by the river that runs in or near them, not safe to go to sleep there; and cane swamps. They would drain well and produce good rice, I think, as I said, and I would like to try that, but meanwhile they make the best feeding for all kinds of cattle."

He saw the young man's face relax, and wondered briefly what he had said that had called forth the expression he had seen.

"You have cattle?" Diarmid asked, his attention caught. He smiled, a touch of his old gleam in his eyes. "We have cattle in the Highlands too, but myself I did not tend it, I took it."

"Well, we don't take it here, MacLyon, we buy it if we want it. Then there is a fourth type of land here," he said, going on with his lesson, "but there is none of it on my plantation. That is marshland. There are two kinds of marshes, the soft, that is quagmire and dangerous and good for nothing at all, and the hard marsh that is firm but barren sand bearing only sower rushes. The Sea Islands particularly have marshes, and cedar trees and juniper trees, that you will not have seen, and then many of the Sea Islands have the other kinds of land as well. St. Simon's has particularly good oak, which Oglethorpe himself when he is here lives on."

They had stopped for lunch, cheese and a slab of a kind of gingerbread, and had ridden on, Diarmid beginning to tire from so many months without exercise, but the quiet, and the trees about them, and the crisp cool clear air were a pleasure to him that imperceptibly soothed him.

"This is I, Diarmid MacLyon," he thought, "and I am riding in a flat land with nobody in it called after a King who has sent me away off here for no good reason, I am riding a horse good enough to steal, if I were home, with my hands bound beside a fool of a man with a pistol who bound them who insists on telling me all kinds of things I have no interest at all in knowing about a place I don't want to be." It struck him suddenly as so ludicrous he almost laughed aloud.

XIX: *Georgia, 1747*

I N THIS WAY HE WAS TAKEN DOWN TO THE TOBACCO PLANTA-
TION IN GEORGIA THAT HAD BEEN THE OLDER MR. SMYTHE'S
AND WAS NOW ENTIRELY HIS NEPHEW-MANAGER'S, AND
PUT INTO THE STABLES TO WORK UNTIL THE SPRING PLANTING.
Here he surprised both his master and himself. He loved
horses, and he knew them, and he did not consider working
with them below his dignity. He stopped his resistance, yield-
ing to fate, indicated what he could do, and did it, his fetters
removed.

The stables were under the chief care of one Martin Hird,
a middle-aged Moravian. In the evenings Diarmid found
himself talking to the older man, his crabbed stiffness that he
would not relax around Smythe disarmed by the Moravian's
gentle humour and impersonal kindness. Also, he wanted information, not about crops but about people and places.
Once several miles outside of Savannah itself, he had seen no
evidence of any person anywhere at all, although he had
seen cleared land and evidence of plantings, until he had
reached the plantation and been taken to the quarters where

he was to stay, under Hird's care and observance. He was free during the day, although he was never left alone, and he knew Hird carried a pistol.

"But I don't need it," Hird had said. "If you go walking off, I'll stop you this way," and he took a stone from his pocket and threw it with unerring aim at a mark he indicated some distance from them. "To the side of the temple, so."

"Hird to ride herd," Diarmid had commented bitterly, and set his lips, but he had not gone walking off, as Hird put it.

At night his feet were fettered still, and his wrists too.

"He is not a bad sort," Hird commented one night, fastening the fetters on his feet, his old ones that had been brought from Savannah in a saddle bag behind Smythe, "you could do worse for seven years, much worse. You had best accept it."

"I have been transported for life," Diarmid said bitterly.

"Yes, that may be, but you are indentured for seven years only, and that is no great time in a man's life. How old are you, MacLyon? Twenty-five?"

"I don't remember. I was twenty-two when I last had my freedom. I suppose I am twenty-three."

"You will be thirty then. That is a good age for a man, and still young enough, and this is a good country."

Diarmid did not think so, to any of Hird's remarks. Seven years was almost a third of the time he had been alive at all.

Diarmid had sat with his elbows on his knees, and his chin on them, brooding, while the irons were put back on him. He got up now and walked over to the bed and lay down on it, his head resting on his chained wrists, staring upwards, while Hird sat in a rocker by the fireplace, smoking his pipe quietly.

"It is no trouble to me," Hird remarked, "but are you going to spend seven years being chained at night?"

"I don't know," Diarmid said, "I don't know at all. I don't

like the country here. I don't like the look of it at all, any of
it. I am homesick, Martin Hird, down to every inch of me, for
my own kind of land and my own kind of sky. I am sick with
wanting to be home, I ache with the very wanting. Can you
understand that, how that feels? I did not want to come here,
I did not deserve to come here. And I cannot go back. No
matter what I do, I cannot go back any more." He stared
upwards, his eyes blank and barren, seeing the images of
another country against the dark, the loss more keen now
that his physical agony and the necessity of its endurance
had relaxed, threatening now to devour him.

"You seem very used to having what you want and doing
what you like, before this came on you," Hird remarked. "I
did not ever have that problem, myself. It must make it
harder. I am a little sorry for you, MacLyon, but not much.
You will just have to come to grips now with what most of us
had to learn long before you, that we can't do what we want
or what we like, and we must make the best of what life does
to us, where it chooses to do it, and like it as best we may."

There was no sound from the figure on the bed.

After a time, Hird said, quietly, as if addressing himself or
the air, " 'Who can bound a thought, and to an understanding
spirit what matters here or there?' " his words falling with an
aptness against the images before Diarmid's eyes.

"What is that?" he asked sharply, lifting his head, struck.

"Words of Jacob Boehme, a German like myself," Hird
said. "I have found comfort in them myself."

Diarmid said nothing more. After a time, he turned over,
trying to make himself comfortable, since there seemed some
possibility of it, having never been both in irons and in a bed
until now, before it having been just one or the other, before
his falling in with Smythe.

The next day as he worked with Hird, he asked him,

"Where are the people?"

"Here, you mean? Mr. Smythe is clearing another acre of
oak-land, that he did not finish in the fall clearing."

"No, I meant anywhere."

"There are not many, anywhere," Hird said, "two thousand, maybe, all told, except for Indians. There are some settlements, small ones, out of Savannah, to the North of us. There is Highgate, with fifteen families now maybe. There were nine when I was there last, that is five miles West of Savannah. They spoke only French, when I was last there, except for one family. Then there is Hampstead, a mile nearer, they are all German there, seven families then, double now maybe."

He looked at the dark young Scot and smiled at him. "It has been ten years since I went up to Savannah. Things could have changed, one way or the other. Abercorn was deserted then, all except for the plantation of two Scotch gentlemen near Abercorn Creek at Joseph's Town, and Old Ebenezer where the land was barren except for two English families, and they may be gone. New Ebenezer had sixty huts then, it was on a bluff, near the Savannah River, six miles eastward near Savannah, twenty miles from it, maybe, and that sixty put up in a year, near. It bid then to thrive, then there are the plantations, the inhabitants come and go; Irene stands near an Indian town, and there is an unfinished school upon it that was to be for Indians. I do not know what became of it. It is not far from Captain Watson's house he did not finish, and not far from Musgrove's that was called the Cowpen. There is an old fort near Thunderbolt, which had three families there, left out of ten, and then there is Ft. Argyle, on a high bluff by the river Ogeechy, the freeholders near it had left when I was gone. Also Houstoun's plantation, and Stirling's."

"Argyle," said Diarmid thoughtfully. "That is Scotch."

"It could be," said Hird without comment. "You are not the only one."

"That is to the North of us then," said Diarmid again thoughtfully. "What to the South?"

"To the South," said Hird, "there is very little on the land.

There is St. Simon's Island, with Frederica, and the Fort, and the soldiers, and below that is Cumberland Island, also long, with Fort St. Andrew. The Province grant stopped below the Alatamahaw on land, but we hold St. Simon's Island, all of that, and also Cumberland, with the forts, where General Oglethorpe pushed off the Spaniards at Bloody Marsh. They don't trouble us up here any more as they used to now."

"Is that all?" Diarmid asked. He made no comment on the name of Cumberland Island, he was beyond comment there.

"There is a settlement of Highlanders at Darien," Hird said slowly, "that is twenty miles or so North-West from St. Simon's near the mouth of the Alatamahaw, and a mile from Fort St. George that is abandoned. But they have a fort themselves that they built in thirty-six when they expected the Spaniards to come up."

"Is it so?" Diarmid said thoughtfully.

"It is a hard four days' walk with a guide," Hird said, "and more people are lost trying than not. You would not find a boat that would take you, or a guide. It is well known in parts about that Mr. Smythe has a servant who will not serve."

"Is it so?" said Diarmid. "Then why are you telling me about a place you know I will be wanting to go to?"

Hird shrugged. "You will hear it from someone. They are there. You are here. They have been there a dozen years, more maybe."

"Do they wear the kilt?" Diarmid asked.

"I don't know," Hird said, "I have never been there or seen them. Should they?"

"We cannot now," Diarmid said, "I have heard. I wondered about how it was here."

"I don't know," Hird said, "Would it matter?"

"It matters to me," Diarmid said. "I like the short kilt, I do not like these trousers. The Loyal Scots, in the Royal Scots of George, may wear the kilt still, I hear, but that's all."

"It seems a poor thing to me," Hird said, "to be directing

what a man should be wearing, particularly a man transported. I will ask Mr. Smythe about it."

Mr. Smythe, however, when approached, was not receptive. "MacLyon is too Scots as it is," he remarked. "The King has the right idea there, I should say myself, and I will hold to it. Keep him in trousers." But that conversation was some days later.

"Mr. Smythe the elder," Hird remarked, his eyes on the fire thoughtfully, "was Jacobite in his Sympathies, as also was Mr. Oglethorpe. Did you know, MacLyon?"

"No," MacLyon said, "I did not know. He did not think to tell me, nor did anyone else. He may have just assumed that I would know it. I myself am not."

Hird looked at him sharply, but he did not comment. "I do not know the sentiments politically or otherwise of the Scotch at Darien," he remarked, only. "Mr. Smythe the young is not Jacobite, nor ever was. He had occasionally long arguments with Mr. Smythe his senior when he would come here, but they never neither one of them succeeded in convincing the other or moving either the one of them one whit from the first position."

"What is this to me?" said Diar. "I say," he added bitterly, " 'A Pox on both their houses.' They have cost me mine."

Hird glanced towards him, enquiring.

"I saw it burned," Diar said softly and bitterly, and he did not say any more. They worked on, at various tasks, without speaking. With considerable tact and patience, seeing he had won this much, Smythe had not yet asked his bondsman to leave the stables, and the saddlery and leather work, not even to go about the anvil and the horseshoeing, for Diar had indicated he could not and would not attempt that. Nor did he visit him himself, leaving him for the time, as he put it, to simmer down.

The evenings were growing lighter, but they were still sharp, and fires were needed and lighted after dark, and the ground in the mornings was still white with heavy white frozen dew like hoarfrost.

"Bring up a chair," Hird said that evening, as the light faded. Smythe let them have fires, for wood was easily come by, but not light, for candles and oil were not. Once the dark came, work ended, and did not begin until the sun gave light enough to see by. In the winter, therefore, the work day was short, growing longer in spring, and in summer lasting sometimes sixteen hours.

"I thought I would go to bed," Diarmid said, but he drew up the chair indicated, and sat down, his hands hanging loose between his knees, staring into the flames catching the logs.

"Are you so keen on it then?" Hird asked. "I cannot sleep yet myself. What do you do, lying there? Brood?"

Diarmid did not answer.

Hird lit his pipe at the flame. "Smythe's tobacco," he said, "last year the first there was enough for us. Do you smoke?"

Diarmid shook his head. "No," he said.

"What would you be doing if you were home, in your house, as it was?" Hird asked curiously.

Diarmid stared into the flames, but surprisingly this time he did answer. "There would be lights," he said. "We had the candles from France, and we did use them. We were not all like the MacDonald."

"How was that?" asked Hird.

"He had a visitor from England, who was describing his chandelier. The MacDonald called up his men then, each with a lighted torch, and they surrounded the table in a ring, holding the torches up. 'This is my chandelier,' he said, 'Can you boast such?' or they say he said."

"A fine story," said Hird, "tho' showing somewhat the sin of pride. What then would you do with your candlelight?"

"Eat, if we were all in together," Diarmid said, "at the big trestles, and tell about the day. For hours, with ceremony, and then there would be drinking, with the horns, and dancing, and maybe fighting. And we would sing. Always we would sing. And then those who had women would go to bed with them, until dawn, and then we would be up again."

"You seemed to need little sleep at all, then," Hird commented dryly.

"I didn't," Diarmid said briefly.

"I suppose you would not show me how you danced, or how you sang?" Hird asked.

"No, I would not," Diarmid said briefly. "I have not the mood at all for it," he said more kindly, at Hird's disappointed face, "tho' the soldiers did in the prison. But we was all together then, and, as it were, the same."

"Well," said Hird, a touch wistful, "my religion does not permit it, but I thought this once, I would like to see the sight."

"I am sorry," Diarmid said, "but there it is. My legs would not move for it. And I have not the kilt neither. Go down to Darien, yourself, you might yet find it there."

"I do not travel about," Hird said. "I stay much right here."

"Then how do you know about these places, if you have not seen them. Who told you? Mr. Smythe?"

"No," Hird said. "We do not talk together. I heard about them from Mr. Wesley, who travelled all over the settled East Coast of Georgia, many times, and in the unsettled parts too."

"Did he now?" Diarmid asked. "Who was he?"

"He was a religious, a kind of rebelling clerk it seemed to me, of the Anglicans, very interested in us and in the Moravian Church. When I came over, with Mr. Oglethorpe, on the ship in thirty-five, he was aboard it with his brother, Mr. Oglethorpe's secretary. He had come to instruct the Georgian Indians, he said, but he was never allowed to go near them, beyond the coast, or past Augusta, near Old Savannah, which was deserted then. And he said finally," Hird remarked, chuckling slightly, in reminiscence, "when he left some two years after, that he had neither 'as yet found or heard of any Indian on the Continent of America, who had the least desire of being instructed.' Which I daresay was a true fact."

"I met a religious enthusiast sometime not long back myself," Diarmid said, not chuckling, "in the Carlisle Castle Gaol, who was desirous of instructing me also, and I had not the least desire of being instructed either. Chain me up, Martin Hird, if you are going to, I would really like to go to bed now." He put out his long legs, and his arms, and shut his eyes until it was done.

He continued the conversation the next day. "Who is this Oglethorpe you speak of, and Mr. Smythe speaks of?"

"Mr. Oglethorpe is a Londoner, an army man and a Parliamentarian, who received a Grant from the King to start a kind of colony here, MacLyon. He originally thought to bring the poor debters here from the London prisons, where a friend of his died in bad circumstances, but that did not prove so feasible as he first thought, but he picked his first settlers very carefully, about a hundred. I came myself in another group of twenty-six Germans, two years later. Mr. Oglethorpe was on board ship then, as was Mr. Wesley. But it was a terrible trip, we were two months on ship in winter storms before we reached the high seas."

"Is Mr. Oglethorpe still here?" asked Diarmid. Hird's difficulties aboard ship held no interest for him.

Hird shook his head. "He went back two years ago, to answer questions about a battle with the Spanish, below the province, which I never rightly understood. And I think the Trustees were somewhat displeased, for Mr. Oglethorpe was a very strict man in the practices he would allow, which has kept some settlers out, not wanting to come in because of them, and forced others out who could not keep their plantations. He does not allow hard drinking, or Negro slaves, but he does allow the French, and some Catholics to settle here, without seeming to see them, and he has a good army, despite the traitor he had in it, who he put to good use, and has kept on good terms with the Creeks. Half his army is Indian, but they like to do things their way and are impatient with restraint. I hope myself he will return, but there are some who think he may not. Mr. Smythe had the news when he came back with you, that he had been put in charge of a regiment against the Jacobites, and being one himself in sympathy, or having been, he did not pursue them as the King thought he should do."

Diarmid seemed less interested in General Oglethorpe than he might have been. "Where are the Indians? Do you know? How many are they? Is there one tribe? What are they like?"

"The Creeks and the Cherokees are nearest to us," Hird said. "You will see the Creeks perhaps if you go again into Savannah. They are tall, well-proportioned men, with a softness of speech and a gentleness of behaviour that would contradict the cruelty we hear of them in war. The Territory of the Creeks goes down to the Alatamahaw River, we hear. It is all by report. They have no letters themselves, and no history, that we know. They say they have fifteen hundred fighting men and many towns. They live in a central plain that is well watered, about four hundred miles from Savannah and from us. They have three or four Meekos or head men to each town but no authority anywhere, and being closest to Europeans they have picked up their vices and kept their own. They are bounded on the North by a small tribe of only forty fighting men and one town that is two hundred miles from Savannah, the Uchees, they are disliked even by other Indians for their cowardice, their thievery, and their lying. About and beyond them are the Cherokees, who are some three or four hundred miles, they tell me, from Savannah. They live in a kind of Highlands, mountainous, fruitful, very pleasant by report. They have three thousand fighting men, fifty-two towns, each with three or four head men. They are civil to us, and for pay they will do any service, being well advanced in the particular sin of covetousness, as no other Indians. They are as cruel as the Chicasaws to the West of them, but they are not so valiant."

"They sound not unlike some Highland tribes," said Diarmid. "The Chicasaws, who are they?"

"They border the Creeks on the Northwest. They live in a land of meadows and springs and rivers, flat, very far inland, some six or seven hundred miles in, they say, yet there are seashells on their meadows. They have nine hundred fighting men, ten towns, with at least one Meeko in each, and they call their gods 'the beloved ones' and talk to them and claim they help them. They live to smoke and to eat and to drink, stopping only to sleep, and then to begin again, except when they are at war, when they are the most tireless, the most courageous, and the most cruel of all the tribes. They are frequently at war with the Choctaws to the South of them, who border the Creeks on the West and who are in league with the French. They are very strong, these Choctaws, most like a nation, least in contact with our civilisation. They have six thousand fighting men and many towns, and are eight or nine hundred miles from Savannah. It is extremely dangerous, our traders say, to go near them, although the French have sent some priests among them.

"All of these tribes, patient of pain themselves, enjoy inflicting it in most exquisite ways. If they have gods, as they claim, their gods in no way inhibit their actions either towards their enemies or their own. They murder their old, and their young, even the unborn child, and one another for any excuse. Mr. Wesley, who was much interested in learning what he could about the Georgian Indians, said finally that each seemed to know only two short rules of proceeding—'to do what he will, and what he can.' But the accounts we have contradict each other in many respects." He looked at the Scot listening intensely to him with a studious indifference.

"If you are thinking to go among them, that you can somehow buy their help, I would forget it, MacLyon. I knew a Frenchman who made his way here who had been taken by the Chicasaws in a battle between the Chicasaws and the French, after the friendship between them was disrupted. He himself and another were unaccountably saved by the warrior who took them, but he saw the others most miserably beaten and burned, even a priest among them, in ways you would not imagine, MacLyon. After being beaten black, he said, they were burned, little by little, with lighted canes applied to their arms and to their legs and to the several parts of their bodies, for a while, then taken away, then re-applied, and burning pieces of wood stuck in their flesh all around. And so they were kept all the day. This was done to some twenty-five, he said, they took away to their towns, putting only the commanding officer to death immediately on the field and one other."

Diarmid shivered. "That is even more cruel perhaps than King George's soldiers, for what they did they did quickly or ignorantly for the most part, but they burned several Scotch-men slowly, I was told on the transport, by those who had been made to lift the sheet and see them, and they burned many in the huts where they had hidden, they smoked them to death like salmon, and paid no attention to their screams and would not let them out. Soldiers in war are to be avoided, I think, anywhere."

Mr. Hird looked at Diarmid's pale face in astonishment, as he matched tales about the redface, and forbore to say any more.

XX: *"I will not bend my back."*

THE SPRING PLANTING, WHEN IT CAME, WAS ANOTHER
STORY.

THE NEXT DAY SMYTHE CAME DOWN TO THE
STABLES TO SEE ABOUT HIS HORSE BEING READIED WITH NEW
shoes. The smith was in the field that day, and he looked at
Diar consideringly, sitting on the stable steps patching harness.

"Shoe my horse for me, MacLyon. You know how, surely,"
he added, as Diarmid stayed as he was.

"No," Diarmid said, "I do not. We did not shoe our horses."

"Well," Smythe said with a touch of asperity in his voice.
"We do here. I would like you to learn now."

"I could not, and I would not," Diarmid said in his soft
voice. "It is not what a MacLyon does."

"It is what a MacLyon does here, if I say so," Smythe said,
losing patience. "Hird!" he shouted. The Moravian came out
from the stables where he had been within easy hearing.

"Sir?" he said.

"Can you shoe my horse, Hird?" asked Smythe testily. "I
cannot wait for Williams."

"I think I can do that, sir," Hird said quietly, his eyes on neither Smythe nor Diarmid.

"When you do it, have MacLyon help you. I want him taught. See to it, Hird, and see that he attends. I will ask about it. I am going up to Virginia," he added, "to fetch more seed for the planting, and some young plants. When I return," he said, his eyes on MacLyon's bent stubborn head, "there are other things you will learn then. Stand up, Mac-Lyon, when I speak to you, and answer me," he added sharply.

"Yes," said Diarmid, standing up, unfolding himself with his quiet ease.

"Yes, what?" snapped Smythe.

"Yes, I stand up, as you say."

"Yes, *sir*," snapped Smythe still more sharply.

"No," said Diarmid, his voice still soft.

Smythe, turning to go, turned back. "No *what*, MacLyon?" he asked.

"No *sir*," Diarmid said, "to anyone."

Smythe chose to ignore the ambiguous phrasing. "I hear you will not clean my stables either," he said instead. "You will do that for me now, after my horse is shoed."

"No," Diarmid said softly, biting the words between his teeth.

"No *what*?" Smythe said again, his voice warning.

"No, I will not work muck."

"No?" said Smythe quietly. "I will ask you again when I come back for my horse. I trust you will consider that again." He addressed himself to Hird, turning his back on Diarmid, as he turned to go: "I do not want you, Hird," he said, "to clean my stables again while MacLyon is in your charge, and I expect my stables clean." He left then, taking up no other issues, having raised enough. Diarmid stared after him, with pure hatred in his eyes.

"MacLyon," said Hird, "you are a true fool. What do you hope to gain by this?"

"Nothing," Diarmid said, sitting back down on the steps. "Purely nothing."

"You will gain more than nothing, at the least," said Hird. "Come with me now and we will get this horse shoed."

"No," said Diar.

"MacLyon," said the Moravian, his voice beseeching. "I do beg you not to stir this up, and out of nothing, over nothing. Mr. Smythe is not a harsh man, as I know, having been indentured to him myself, but you are pressing him too far, and you will force him to act on you."

Diar shook his head. "A MacLyon does not shoe another man's horse at his bidding." He could not be got to say anything else or to move, and Hird shook his head and shod the horse himself. Smythe returning found Diar still sitting on the steps, the harness laid by, his hands idle. When he learned the state of things, in insurrection, he ordered Hird to have MacLyon whipped.

"Do it now," he said, "while I am here, to see it has been done."

"O my God, sir, Mr. Smythe," the Moravian said, upset.

"Do it yourself, or call Rodgers in, but get it done. I will wait."

"I will do it," Hird said. Ignoring Diar's eyes, he took his shirt from him, and strapped his hands to a stable post, and laid on with the stable's horse whip until Smythe told him curtly to stop, it was enough. He walked over to his Scot whom he had knocked to his knees, and said curtly, his eyes averted from his ripped shoulders,

"That is the second time, now, MacLyon. Must there be a third? I will see you when I get back."

"Damn your horse shoes," Diar said softly, his teeth shaking with rage and pain, "and damn your seed."

Smythe answered by pouring a cup of vinegar from the stable barrel and throwing it over the raw cuts. "Vinegar cures, like the whip," he commented, and turned away from the writhing Scot.

When Smythe had left, and Hird was free to go inside again, half an hour later, he found Diarmid had fainted. His weight, dragging on his arms, had pulled the leather knots too tight to be easily untied, and the stableman cut the strap, sacrificing it to time.

"Poor stubborn Scottish fool," he said softly, bathing his back, diluting the acid with water, which stinging roused Diarmid back to consciousness, and then, throwing down a horse blanket for him to lie on, he annointed the cuts with bear grease.

Diarmid folded his arms under his head, raising it a little, wincing under the pressure of the gentle hands.

"Why did you do it to me, Martin Hird?" he asked. "I thought you were my friend."

"Better me than another," Hird said. "Rodgers is a bigger man, and a harder whipper. There is no escaping Mr. Smythe when he is aroused."

"I would not have done it to you," was all Diar said, "or to any man I had sit and talked with before a fire."

"Well," said Hird, "you have not had it all. You are to be kept close, while Smythe is gone. He says he'll have no more incidents."

"Kept close how?" asked Diarmid, feeling fear creep over him. "Where?"

"Down cellar," Hird said.

"Why? I have been whipped. Isn't that enough?"

"He remembers Mr. Lacy's bondsman, David Jones, that was a saddler of Nottingham."

"Who is he, and what is he to do with me?"

"He was tricked here by a Captain, and made an indentured servant against his will and the promises made to him, and sold to Mr. Lacy for land clearing. He was a middle-aged man, educated, MacLyon, and skilled in a trade. He did not fight Mr. Lacy, as you have so foolishly done, but he was as unhappy as you. He had a gun, which he stayed to kill a deer with on an island they were clearing, off from the plantation, but instead they found he had shot a great piece out of his head."

"Then he was not a Catholic," commented Diarmid, "and the Welsh have a melancholy turn. I am not that unhappy, and I have no gun."

"Nevertheless, you are to be kept close until he returns, MacLyon, and there it is. But he will be gone a week, at the least, or ten days, or more, and until the week I'll keep you in our quarters."

"Thank you very much, Martin Hird," Diarmid said, his soft voice sardonic. "You're a true friend indeed, I do not think."

"I've never said I was your friend, MacLyon. That will be just about enough," Hird retorted. "You will come with me now and have your fetters on again, and behave yourself. It is all your own doing, and not mine, and I warned you of it

Diarmid stayed in the room the rest of the afternoon, which was curiously still, his thoughts black, and when Hird unlocked the door and came in himself that evening, he would not speak. Seeing in what quarter the wind lay, Hird was quiet himself, and himself tired by the day, went at once to sleep. A little after eight, the storm of whose building up Diarmid had been unaware broke, immediately over their heads, suddenly and without warning, with an ear-splitting crash of lightning and thunder that shook the walls.

Diarmid sat bolt upright in bed in terror, the room drenched in blinding light flashing on and off.

"O God," he whispered, "what is it." The first bolt was followed by a second, and in quick succession a third, and a splintering crash that seemed to be in the room itself. In the eerie green light that came and went, illuminating the night like a little day, grass and trees and sky briefly their colour, he saw that Hird was by his bed, and fumbling with his chains.

"Help me," Hird said, "I've got to get these off you, before you're struck. The lightning is very close." He threw them towards a corner of the room by the door that had blown open, with hands shaking, and to Diarmid's horror, he saw the Moravian's fears justified, as the chains, in the next crash, seemingly caught in air, glowed blue, with a flickering light and sparks falling, as they fell.

"O God," whispered Diarmid again. He shut his eyes, feeling the end of the world had come, as the skies ripped open above him and the roof of their room seemed to be besieged by gunshot, and a noise that he imagined like the cannon and shot Rawn had described to him, rolling and flashing continuously. He felt a hand pull at him, and saw Hird indicating he should go under the bed.

"Not I," he said, shaking his head, "it will find me there. I'll wait for it as I am." The lightning seemed in the room as well as outside it, continuously cracking, rolling from one corner of heaven across to the other. In his amazement, he forgot his terror, and watched astonished in wonder at the display. As the storm gradually withdrew, the grating thunder rumbling in the distance, as if giant rocks and boulders were tumbling over the floor of the sky, and the lightning flashing flickeringly, but not in the room, the rain falling in a steady drumming on the roof, but the shot sounds over, and a peace stealing over him with the freshening air, suddenly he was aware of a hand fumbling upon him, beneath his shirt, handling him.

"Leave be," he cried in outrage, and sick disgust, trying to move and sit up, "get off me, take your bastard hands away from me."

To his amazement, exceeding that at the storm, the white figure he assumed was Hird slid to the floor, pulling him with him, kneeling on the floor and holding him there too, and began to pray aloud, fervently, in a loud voice, for help in temptation for himself and the young man beside him.

"Pray for yourself," he said angrily, "it's no temptation I am in at all, let me *up*," he cried more angrily still, as the hand clutched him with the strength of catalepsy, "this is *absurd*. Pray for yourself, if you like!" He wrenched himself free with a sudden jerk, and stood up panting, wondering if he was going to be chased about the room in the dark. Abruptly the praying stopped, and before he knew what to expect, the heap of his chains by the door were thrown at him, striking his head, causing him to fall and strike his head again against the corner of the table as he fell.

When he woke from the force of the combined blows, he found he was chained again, and in his bed again, and the hand upon him again, his head aching abominably.

"You dirty old man," he whispered weakly, "you liked whipping me this afternoon, you liked it. O God help me, what have you done to me while I was out?"

"Nothing more than this," Hird said, not taking his hand away. "We will be still now, and salvation will come. I fought temptation and I lost," he added, as though explanation were needed.

"Then fight it again," Diarmid said weakly, "and take your hand off me, or I will bite you." He felt the hand removed, and he struggled to sit up, and found he was alone again in his bed, the storm dying away in the distance.

In the morning he looked curiously at Hird, at his kind, soft face, and he thought he must have dreamed or imagined the night. Hird did not speak of it, and he did not himself. Hird was busy during the day, with other servants of the plantation, both hired and indentured, clearing away the oak that had been struck in the night, and fallen on one of the smaller huts. MacLyon was not asked to help, but left in his chains in the room. After a time he went out into the dripping fresh morning and offered the service of his arm.

"Is this something a MacLyon can do?" asked Hird.

"In an emergency, yes," Diarmid said. His fetters were unlocked, and he was given an ax, which he applied with energy and relief, not much impeded by his tender shoulders, until the only part left to do was the cutting in small into firewood. This he declined to take part in.

"As a MacLyon, I suppose," Hird said, and sent Rodgers to rechain him.

That evening, Hird addressed him in direct apology. "I have a weakness, a kind of demon, that sometimes comes over me, when God lets the Devil into me. I am sorry, I will pray for it not to happen again."

"I would pray hard, if I were you," Diarmid commented. "Does Smythe know of this—this weakness?" he asked curiously.

"I would rather not say," Hird replied. "I would appreciate your not speaking of it with him."

"I doubt the occasion arising," Diarmid said. He looked at Hird in a sudden suspicioning. "Are you telling me that you do the same with Smythe?"

"Mr. Smythe has not a wife," Hird said, "and he has sometimes been pleased when the fit was on me to have me with him."

"Oh, Lord," said Diar softly, "deliver me, I am fallen in a mad land among mad men."

He did not talk any more after that to Hird except to say yes or no. At the end of the week, after which the plantation's owner could be expected to return, Hird had him put down cellar, and they were glad each to be mutually quit of the other.

It was merely a small dirt dug-out with a door, a flat slanting door with a hasp lock, and dirt steps leading down, used for refuge in the worst of the storms, and otherwise for storage of root vegetables and potatoes. It had a pleasant earthy smell, cool but not cold, but with the door locked above him it was almost entirely dark, even when the sun directly overhead filtered through the cracks. Diarmid sat on a box he pulled into the middle of the floor, remembering Hird's parting words: "We have both the tarantula and the widow spiders, as well as the trap door and the dirt spiders, but they won't bother you, if you don't bother them." It was in some ways the worst place he had been yet, entirely alone, but he shut his lips and endured it, and said nothing when his food was brought him once a day, and his bucket changed, and if he dreamed the spiders walked over him, and woke in a sweat, he said nothing of that either.

After three days of that, however, Smythe himself returned, and Diarmid was brought out of the cellar and returned to his room and a bed. That night Hird looked at him, a faint maliciousness under his face and his concern.

"You are going to be asked to go out in the fields tomorrow," Hird said. "Will you do it?"

"No," Diarmid said.

"You are asking for trouble then," Hird said, "and you will get it."

XXI: *The Field*

THE PROPHECY WAS ACCURATE, AND FOUNDED ON CLOSE OBSERVATION. SMYTHE DID NOT COME OUT HIMSELF, BUT HIS OVERSEER TOOK ALL THE MEN WORKING THE PLANTATION IN ANY CAPACITY OUT TO THE FIELDS, INCLUDING Hird, including Diarmid again out of his chains.

He stood in the fields, in the furrows others made and he did not, watching with a remote eye the men stoop and bend and stoop and bend, dibbling in the little plants, in the warm sun, his eye indifferent to the vegetation and all the life around him, waiting for trouble. He received the overseer's warning, with an indifferent face, and then a sharp blow of his stick, which sent him sprawling. When he refused again, he felt the stick across his mouth, leaving the taste of blood on his lips, and the corner catch him in the groin. He saw Hird watching, and he thought, "Enjoy your self, little man," and then he was sorry, remembering the line he had liked, that had so struck him, and he wondered at the contradictions in the man. The blows fell upon him hard and fast, and as he fell under them, he said the lines to himself, moving his bruised lips, "Who can bound a thought, and to an understanding spirit what matters here or there." The *here* or *there* would seem to matter very much, but the words comforted him curiously under the blows, until they stopped. He lay in the black sandy dirt where he had fallen, hearing hammering next to him. He did not look up until he was pulled roughly up, and his hands bound behind him around the stake that had been driven into the middle of the field beside him. He could sit or stand, sliding his arms up or down the pole, but he could not raise them high enough behind him to slip them over the height of the stake.

So there he stood, in the sun which grew warmer, the object of furtive glances at "Smythe's Scotchman," as he had become known. No one came near him again, and when it grew dark, the overseer and the workers went in, no one still coming near him. The night grew chill, and a heavy dew fell, freezing his clothes to a stiffness, and he hoped the little plants. He fell, finally, in a heap, crumpled against the foot of the stake, missing the grey twilight of dawn, until the sun's rays struck sharply against him and the overseer's stick more sharply yet.

"Will you plant?" he asked.

"No," Diarmid said faintly, "I will not. Do what you like. I can't stop you. But I won't plant, for you or anyone."

"That is your answer?" the overseer asked.

"Yes," Diarmid said, his soft voice little more now than a whisper.

"Stand up, then," the overseer said then, cracking his shins with his stick. "If you won't bend, we'll see that you stand."

Diarmid pulled himself wearily to his feet, the overseer offering no assistance, except to check the binding on his hands. He stayed there all that day, through the afternoon when a rainstorm passing over drenched him as completely as in a bath, not a misting rain like the Highland rains but a rain like buckets of cold water poured over him, soothing his parched throat, but soaking him. The workers had left the field, and there was no one left to watch him or strike his legs, and he crumpled once more in a heap on the muddy ground, held to the post by numb things that he knew had once been his hands but that had no feeling in them. He saw across the grey sky to the East where the rain was still lightly falling, a rainbow form, covering the entire sky, like a bowl, from end to end, so distinct all the colours, even the indigo shone, and as he watched, he saw a second form within it, and knew its promise for him to be a mockery, its beauty causing him to catch his breath even so. He shut his eyes, away from the rainbow, thoughtless, enduring, opening them sometime later because of a brightness pressing in on them. He looked, and saw that all the sky was a bright gold, the sun reflected in a particular way against the clouds so that they turned into a soft blaze of pure gold that shone back down on the trees, the pine needles like glass reflecting it back, and the pools and rivulets made in the field, and all the earth glowing with it, encasing and bathing himself in its gentle encompassing brilliance that as he watched began to deepen, and turn to rose. He had never seen anything like it, like the world and sky on fire together in a heavenly illumination. He pulled himself up to see it better, his head thrown back to see it. When he lowered his eyes, he saw Smythe standing before him, watching him, bathed also in the deepening heart of light.

"It is very beautiful, is it not," Smythe said, his voice quiet. "It happens rarely, even in Georgia. Do you *like* to be tormented, MacLyon?"

"No, I do not," Diarmid answered. "I have not done this to myself."

"I think you have," Smythe commented.

"No," Diarmid said. The light about them was already going, the rose fading to pink, and again to ash-grey.

"Are you going to stay here another night?"

"I hope not," Diarmid said. "I cannot help myself."

"Cannot you say *yes* to me?" Smythe asked, genuinely curious.

"No," Diarmid said, "not if I die for it."

"You are a curious man," Smythe said. "I have not met your like before. I do not understand this thing you have on planting or field work. I do not mind planting myself, in fact I have myself often done so."

"It is your choice, and your land," Diarmid said, his voice remote. "I will not be at your disposal."

"But you are, you are," Smythe answered. "What do you call this?"

"I call it murder, a miserable killing," Diarmid said, "that's what I call it."

"I have no wish to kill you, MacLyon," Smythe said, his voice serious. "Believe me, I do not. I want your hands and your legs working for me. Dead you are of no use to me, and I have lost my effort in getting you. But you have put me rather on the spot, you know, and now here we are. How many more days and nights of this do you think you can stand? Just how tough are you?"

"I don't know," Diarmid said. "Are we to find out?"

"I hope not," Smythe said. "That's why I've come to talk to you again." He looked at Diarmid. "I thought, MacLyon, that the Scotch were a practical people. I thought they used people for themselves, and sided with the winning side to suit themselves."

"Not all of them," Diarmid said. He added with a slight glint returning in his dazed eyes, "You may be thinking of Lowlanders, Edinburghian Scots."

"I have said, you know or did you know, MacLyon, that you would stand here until you planted or until the planting is finished. I said it, and I was heard to say it."

"It is your spot, not mine," Diarmid said.

"I rather thought it was yours."

Diarmid shook his head. "If you do not mind killing me, I do not mind dying. I have been weary of my life for some time now."

"If you die unnecessarily, it is as much a suicide as if you took a pistol to yourself, or starved yourself. We have a story we tell here, MacLyon, about some silly goslings that drowned in a rainstorm because they did not have the sense to put their beaks down. Do you?"

Diarmid did not answer or argue. He put his head back against the post and shut his eyes and shivered in the cool wind springing up. There was a silence for so long he thought Smythe must have gone, and when he opened his eyes, he did not see him, but after a time Smythe came back, his boots and trousers splashed with mud.

"I want you to serve me, MacLyon, and I am willing to bargain with you, since I see I cannot force you. What will make you do it?"

"Nothing," Diarmid said. "Nothing on this earth."

"That is strange," Smythe said thoughtfully, "I could have sworn earlier you were not so positive. You worked in my stables for me when you chose your work."

"I repent now I did that," Diarmid said. "I would not do it again."

"What has then so changed you. My having you whipped?"

"In part," Diarmid said, "but, in part only. I will not serve such a man as you."

"Now what does that mean," said Smythe thoughtfully. "Before, I thought it was any man you would not serve. Now it is only such a man as me. What brings this change about? I wonder, and I would like to know." The air was dark now, and he could not read Diarmid's face or Diarmid his.

"Come now, MacLyon. I am being very patient, and I have come to help you if you will let me."

To his surprise Diarmid did not snap him up, but said only, "Ask Hird then."

"Ask Hird?" Smythe repeated in surprise. "I am asking *you*. Tell me."

"Martin Hird took advantage of me when I could not help myself," Diarmid said then, "and tho' he asked me not to speak of it to you, he said that he had been with you and you had liked it."

"*Said*, or *said as much*," Smythe said, surprisingly, his voice surprisingly calm.

"It does not matter," Diarmid said wearily, shutting his eyes again.

"It matters to me. I regard that as a libel. Open your eyes and face me with it."

"It does not matter," Diarmid said again, but opening his eyes. "You seem to know what I am talking about. I will not serve such men as you and he in any way at all."

"Now look here, MacLyon," Smythe said, his voice still calm but a touch of testiness in it that lent it conviction, "it is you exaggerating now. You said a good deal in a sentence, shall we separate it out? You will not ever convince me that Hird did more than touch you in a still way. He is not capable of any more. And do you really believe that I would so involve myself or put myself in such a position with a man like Hird who is my stableman?"

"I can believe it, yes," Diarmid said, and wondered if he would be hit for his words.

"Then you do not know me very well," Smythe answered without rancour. "We will let that side pass until you know me better. Let me tell you about Hird, MacLyon. You know he is a Moravian."

"I know it but I do not know what it means," Diarmid said, quietly.

"I will tell you then in a moment. You do not know, though, that he is a spoiled Moravian."

"Like a spoiled monk?"

"Something like that. They are a German sect. He came with a group of sixteen with Spangenburg in thirty-five, to live in a community on two plots of land arranged for them, but his wife died on the voyage or shortly after they arrived. Even had he wanted to rewed, MacLyon, they had no extra women. So what with one thing and another, he made what they call a scandal, but I would not call so much as that, and he left them and tried to indenture himself out in the world out of the community plots. I agreed to take him. I find him a good worker, very quiet, very honest, sober, desirous of doing well, except for the religious part of him which generally works well for him from time to time going awry. Do you follow me, MacLyon?"

"I follow you," Diarmid said quietly.

"But he is a Quietist, and it takes no form of action. He just lies there. Weird, but harmless. They tell me. I wouldn't know myself. It has happened twice before that I know of."

"He hit me over the head," Diarmid observed.

"Well, I daresay you resisted him. When he had you quiet too, then wasn't he quiet?"

"You are mad," Diarmid said with weary conviction. "Go away, and let me die. I'll not be talking of such things."

"I am not mad, MacLyon," Smythe answered, his voice this time earnest. "That should prove to you how much I need you and how far I am prepared to humour you. Without the privilege of slavery, and with settlers in short supply, and most of them in religious colonies or in the army, I take what help I get. I have told you that. I put up with Hird because I need him, and he is rarely troublesome, and he is ashamed himself about it. I am prepared to humour you as well. This early rain has finished my planting. The seeds are in, and the plants are washed away, and the ground can't be worked now until it dries. I shall have to go back for more plants, and perhaps I shall stop by Charles Town for Indigo seed. It is finished for two weeks, at least. I am not going to ask you then to plant."

Diarmid thought suddenly of the rainbow, and hope stirred in him again for the first time in days. He met Smythe halfway.

"If you ask me to do something I may do without dishonour, I will do it," he said. "I do not want to die myself, whatever I have said, or to be needlessly stubborn."

Smythe forbore to comment. "Hird told me that you helped them cut the tree that fell. Can a MacLyon do that without dishonour? Will you help me clear?"

"I will cut," Diarmid said, "but I will not grub or haul." He felt movement behind him, and though his hands felt nothing, the next moment his arms were his to move again, stiff, with shooting pains beginning in them.

"Raise them over your head," Smythe advised, "and slow the circulation returning." He again forbore to comment. "I will accept your cutting, and you need not shack with Hird. You may shack by yourself, if you like. I will trust you, Mac-Lyon, and not chain you, for I think I have misjudged you, and that you are a man to be trusted or not dealt with at all. You will spend your time at the field I am clearing, and though I need you, I will not ask you to weed or hoe in the tobacco or pick worms, or replant. But I will warn you now, MacLyon, this concession goes this far. When the tobacco is ready to be picked and cured, I use all the men that I can get. I will not excuse you from it then."

"Tie me back," Diarmid said, the hope fading. "I am not agrarian, and I will not do those things. I can tell you now."

"No," Smythe said, shaking his head. "Give yourself a chance. You may change your mind. I hope you do. I will go easy on you until then. For now, I hold you to your word that you will cut for me." He held out his hand briefly, and Diarmid took it.

"You may trust me then," he said, "I will cut for you and I will not try to walk away from you so long as you ask me only to do that. Nor will I try to shoot myself," he added, thinking of the story of Mr. Lacy. "But I will not call you *Sir*," he said with a return of his provocative stiffness.

Smythe laughed slightly. "So be it," he said. "Come follow me now, and have something to eat."

He turned and started towards the edge of the field, and Diarmid followed.

XXII: *Diar's Wife Travels Again to Carlisle and Again to London*

WHEN MARY ELIZABETH LEFT THE JUDGE, IN THE COLD WINTRY MIDDLE OF THE NIGHT, SHE WAS MOVING BY INSTINCT ALONE, WHICH ALONE SUS-TAINED HER DROOPING SPIRITS AND HER DROOPING FLESH. SHE made her way down to the front of the Inn, past her sleeping abigail in the upper deserted halls of the Inn, down to the courtyard which was bustling with the imminent departure of the public coach to Carlisle, departing in the dark even before the grey light of dawn. She surrendered one of her gold coins for a seat whose owner had apparently overslept, asking for no change to insure she would not be disturbed if he should come; and her bandbox, in which she had packed as much as she could, besides her largest reticule, which she kept with her, having to leave all else behind because of lack of strength to carry anything heavier, and the fear of making a commotion. She had put on a double set of petticoats and two overdresses, against the cold and to take that much more with her, and over that her redingote and her most becoming and her most dura-ble bonnet, and her mantle over her arm. She felt as plump as a poulter pigeon, and more uncomfortable, but she had done as well for herself as she could. Her pearls were hidden under the high collar of her redingote, and her coins in her reticule, held closely in her gloved hands. Despite her lack of attendance, she looked immanently respectable, and her first concern, after the coach had moved off with its crowded occupants and also with the mail, was how to find a potential protector before she had spent all her coins herself, and to dispel that look sufficiently in his eyes.

She settled back in her seat, tightly wedged, her eyes downcast, and through the lashes surveyed the travellers on the seat across from her. There was immediately across from her a thin white-haired clergyman, whose glance down his nose was disapprovingly directed upon her, above the white flaps at the neck of his rusty black coat. She turned her head slightly away from that piercingly and alarmingly awake gaze, towards the passengers next. A twelve-year-old boy with a bad cold, pressed against the side of the coach near the door and the steps, a schoolboy she supposed, in the company of his bearleader, a young anemic-looking clerk, was complaining querulously that he had been promised he might ride outside and that he wished to tool the coach. She wished he might ride outside also, without tooling the coach, and hoped part of his wishes would be granted, but the clerk from his watery eyes looked to be catching his cold. On the other side of the clergyman were two middle-aged red-faced gentlemen, commercial looking, one holding yesterday's newspaper in his fat ungloved fingers, the other, black-gloved, asleep again and snoring with a soft whistling sound. It seemed less than promising. Her side had numerous baskets and boxes stored uncomfortably under their feet, one basket in the middle having a lid, and a hole cut in the lid, with the neck of a white duck sticking out of it, who returned her covert look with a beady eye. Who was beside her on either side she could not see, wedged too tightly between thick caped great coats that towered above her, to see. Several students returning home for the Christmas terms appeared to be on the roof, from the noise of shouts and gusts of laughter that wafted down to her, which the juvenile listened to avidly and commented on to his suffering tutor.

What she was looking for she did not know, but she was open to suggestion, and when, after an hour of rough jolting, pressing the passengers more closely against one another, she felt an unseen hand steal under her and surreptitiously pinch her, perceptible even through her layers of clothing, without raising her eyes, she whispered "Yes." The hand continued as it was, in its muffled activities which she thought must surely be unsatisfactory, and after a time came to rest possessively behind her. Her own hands remained demurely clasped in her lap, and her head downcast, throughout all of it, wondering whom she had got or who had got her. She did not find out until a strong pair of arms lifted her down, some hours later, at the first stop, holding her possessively several moments longer than necessary.

She lifted her face under the bonnet rim and looked straight into a whiskered heavily-lined grey-skinned middle-aged face whose black eyes under their black brows glanced with amusement into hers. He put her arm more possessively yet through his, and strolled off with her towards the Inn, followed by the startled glance of the clergyman.

"You are a young woman of decision," he said cheerfully, "no shilly-shallying. I like that, myself. I know what I want, and I take it if I can, with no waiting about or fooling with speeches. Nothing ventured, nothing gained, say I. I put it all to the test at once, and there we are then, or there we aren't. I knew what I wanted, myself, when you got on the coach. Why is she alone? I thought to myself. We'll find out, I thought, what's in it, and I did. That's how I am. What shall we do now?" he said. "It's a short stop here."

"I have to find the geeks," she said with equal candour. He laughed, amused, and called the chambermaid over.

"I'll find some coffee while you're out," he said.

When she returned, there was time for nothing more than a short swift swallow of the hot cup, her eyes meeting his over the brim, as he held it, her gloved fingertips touching his, and then they were bustled back in the coach, with an extra passenger added, pushing in at the last moment and separating them. At the second stop, she was reclaimed, taken behind the baggage that was strapped to the back of the coach in the boot, in its bulky shadow and summarily kissed, without preface, while the students still on top of the coach cheered, and scrambled down and pretended to form a line.

"Be off with you," the man said, not uncheerfully, "find your own bit, this is mine. Just checking the merchandise," he added for Mary Elisabeth's benefit, "to see it was there still and how it was."

She stood on her tiptoes, and put her fingertips against the sides of his face, and kissed him back lightly. "I have the flowers," she said, "it's a nuisance on a trip."

"Plucky chit," he said. "Never give 'em a thought myself. Five daughters. Be off with you then."

When she returned again, he picked her up off the ground and lifted her whole up into the coach, swinging up after her and taking his seat beside her in a positive manner.

The big lumbering coach was slower on the road than a horse or than a private carriage, many of which passed them, and the dark had fallen again when they pulled into the Inn at Carlisle. The unknown unnamed man who had taken her on helped her out of the coach, stiff and white and half-fainting, and looked at her wan cheeks with concern.

"Worse than a ship, these rocking barrels," he said. "Will you make it through?"

"I think so," she said gamely, and let him lead her in to the Inn and up to the room he had arranged for them, hoping he did not with his decisiveness intend to board her at once.

"You'll stay here, now, won't you?" he asked anxiously. "I have to leave you now, I've affairs to be checked on at once that won't wait, but I'll be back by the time supper is here and have it with you. But I'll have it ordered now, and if it comes before me, and you're hungry, you go ahead with it, right, now?"

She smiled palely at him, relieved for the respite, and requested a bath sent up for her. She had eaten, and bathed and undressed and put herself wearily to bed before he returned, looming large in the little room that seemed as if it would crack open with his clumsy lumbering presence, his shadow in the flickering candlelight breaking into several pieces and duplications on the walls, and all, it seemed to her, coming at her. She looked very small and fragile without all her clothes heaped on her in the big bed, like the frightened child she was, with weariness and waiting.

"Had a bath, have you," he commented with comprehensive jovialness, "a good idea, perhaps I might myself, it being a week, or perhaps I won't wait," he added, looking across at her, "it being late now."

"A week?" she said faintly. "Oh, sir, I pray you prithee do."

He ate his supper then, with evident enjoyment and considerable noise, not seeming to observe its coldness, gesticulating with the chop bone towards her, his mouth full. He had a ship, he told her, while he ate and later as he bathed, that he was sending out, a merchant ship. In fact he had three, but not all at Carlisle. One was at Dublin, and one at Balaclava. He had come back from overseeing the loading at Balaclava, and after Carlisle, he would go to Dublin, by which time the Dublin ship should have come in. His wife lived at York, with his daughters.

She lay there, her eyes shut against his nakedness in the bath which he did not trouble to conceal from her, aware of her luck if she could bear it, that seemed once more with her after its crooked fashion. If he did not know what she should do to find Diarmid's ship, he would surely know what she should do to find out, and perhaps if she pleased him well he would do the finding out for her. He came to her then, still damp, just as he was, not noticing or minding her shrinking at the size of him, and as he had said, he did not mind flowers. Despite the end of her condition, he gave her a rough time, as rough as any she had had, waking her again and again in one fashion or another, insisting on the difficult accommodation and using her in ways she had not been used. In the end, finally, she fought him, crying, heedless in her distress of her need for advantage, but he ignored her struggles and her tears, and forced her with his big arms and legs to do as he wished, neither he nor anyone else seeming to mind her cries.

"Hard on a woman, ain't I," he said in concern the next morning. "My wife says so, and I suppose she must know. But I am generous. I give her two carriages and all the bonnets and feathers she wants, and the girls too, and French lessons and music lessons and art. I give them what they want, all of them. And I'll give you what you want. What shall it be?" he asked, his voice earnest and clumsy, his big fumbling fingers again on her, demanding and seemingly inexpert.

She began to cry, wondering if she could bear any more of him and knowing she must.

"If you don't like it, I'm sorry," he said, his voice testy now, "but that will teach you, little girl, not to go picking up strange men in public coaches, or letting them pick you up. What else do you expect, or they? What do you do it for, if you don't like it?"

She did not want to make him angry, and she swallowed her tears and her disgust, and let him put his fingers in her and play with her.

"Soft little thing," he said after a time, "but you don't like it, do you? Tell me now why you let strange men have you when they frighten you. What do you want? What shall I give you? Money?"

She shook her head. "I do want money, but I want something else more. And I think you can give it to me. But I can't tell you," she said, gasping suddenly, "while you're doing what you're doing. Please stop."

"Yes, you can," he said, paying no attention to her request, "try," his voice said kindly, as though he did not know what his fingers were about.

"Oh, stop," she cried then, in a panic, writhing and trying to evade him as strange unfamiliar pains shot through her, twisting her and making her pant and move against her will in awkward rhythmic motions she could not stop. She threw her head back, gasping again, her hands that had been pushing against him futilely, rubbing her own eyes and face now frantically as the shooting pains increased and her body went completely out of her control, until finally they subsided and he let her lie still.

"There, Missy, I thought you could," he said with satisfaction. "Wasn't that nice? You never have, have you?"

"No," she said, dazed and bewildered.

"You will learn to do that with me," he said, "and we will both enjoy it more."

"Oh no," she whispered, "not ever any more."

"Oh, yes," he said, his ugly lined face near hers now, "many times, Missy. You will come to like it and to want it. You will see. I promise it."

She shivered and lay back, curiously relaxed, as if no problems pressed on her, and it was with difficulty she roused herself, as she saw him making preparations to dress.

"You promised me you would give me what I wanted," she said with difficulty, the initiative taken from her and her vulnerability shown her. She sat up and drew her knees up and clasped her hands about them, pulling the stained sheet about her. She looked like a child again in the big bed, her hair falling about her shoulders in loose tangled curls, damp with sweat as with a fever and curling in tendrils about her temples. He looked over his shoulder at her, pulling on his breeches, and said.

"Why, so I did. Do you need it this morning? Can't it wait?"

She shook her head, but he paid no attention to her. "Well," he said, "it will just have to. I'm late, and I've already given you something, even if you didn't like it. Tell me at lunch, when I come back."

"I want to go down to the ships with you," she blurted out, desperate, her voice not like her own. He was going but surprise stopped him.

"Down to the ships with me? Why, that's no place for you. It's rough down there. What do you want with ships, Missy?" He came over and rubbed her head roughly with his fingers, kindly. "You didn't know I had a ship, did you, Missy, on the coach?"

She shook her head.

"My husband has been transported," she said again baldly. "I have to know where, and on what ship."

"Oh, Lord," he said, "I should have known. A little thing like you, and acting like you do. He's not much husband for you. I can tell. Let him go."

"Oh please," she said, her voice stark with fear, "oh please help me. I will do anything you like, but please help me." She was not crying, and the fact she was not touched him. He took her hand, and held it in his big one.

"What's he done, Missy? Did he deserve it? Was he a rebel, or did he do a worse thing?"

"He didn't do anything at all," she said, her voice trembling.

"Oh come, Missy, the government is bad but not so bad as that. What's he done? You'll have to tell me, or I just won't mix in it."

"They said he was a Rebel, but he wasn't." Her lips trembled uncontrollably now. "I got a pardon for him, but when I took it to the jail, he had already gone. They had already sent him off."

"And you are going to America to take it to him," he said

slowly, his eyes inscrutable on her, "but you don't know where to go. Is that it?"

"That is it," she said simply.

"What's his name, Missy?"

"MacCullough," she said without hesitation. "Rawn Mac-Cullough."

"And when did he go? From where? Here, in Carlisle?"

"From Carlisle, I think. I don't know when. I found the pardon in October, but the coach was slow, and when I reached the prison, he was gone."

"Well, Missy," he said, "you have picked the right man. I'm taking sixty Rebels on the ship I'm floating now. I'll check the books there at the Castle for you, while I'm there; I'll see what I can do for you, and what ships have left, with transports, and the colonies they were bound for. If they kept the records, Missy, I'll find it for you."

When he came back at lunch, however, he had not found out much, only that one Rawn MacCullough, age uncertain, had signed for the King's mercy and obtained it, and been checked out. The date was not marked, nor the ship.

"He's gone, Missy, that's sure, but where and when is harder."

"Can't you ask the Captains or the sailors?"

"Lord, Missy," he said. "That Captain could be gone two years with his ship, trading and coming back, or he might not make it back at all."

"I can't wait two years. I know Diarmid. He will die there."

"I thought his name was Rawn," the shipman said.

"Diarmid Rawn."

"You wasn't married long," he observed, his eye keen.

"No," she said. "Hardly any time at all."

"And you want him back?" he stated, observing her again.

"Yes," she said.

"And this is how you're going about it," he stated again.

"Yes," she said.

"Well," he said. "I like my facts clear. I will ask about the harbour. And my god, yes," he said, "I'm not using my head now. I'll ask the King's agent who holds the bonds."

It took him three days more, however, to find out what she wanted to know, and three nights. In the day, while he was gone, without his knowledge, she went out as she had at her mother's, and sold herself, where she could, to whom she could, to seamen off the ships when she could, holding to the coins like a miser, and to the scraps of information about the transports. On the third evening, he laid his findings before her.

"Your man," he said, "would seem to have left on the *Alexander*, which sailed October 5. He was released from the Castle to the King's Agent on October 1, and that is the first ship that being in the harbour at the time left with transports on it. The *Oliver*, which sailed October 12, was bound for the Barbados West Indies, but of the two it is more likely he went on the *Alexander* which was bound for America. The names, however, are on the ships, the Agent only has the receipts and numbers. If I had to choose," he said, "I'd put my money on the *Alexander*. The *Alexander*," he continued, "had a spirited history. It stopped to pick up more transports, both criminal and rebel, from Carrickfergus and suffered a rebellion out of Dublin, when the convicts took the ship. Now here, my dear," he said, his eyes avoiding hers, "you have a choice. Of that rebellion, some ten or twenty escaped onto an island, and disappeared. Another number, about the same, drowned when their boat was shelled and overturned. The rest surrendered and were taken on again as planned, when a leak a cannon of the rescuing warship caused had been repaired in Inverness and the Agent had picked up more transports. A spirited story, I should say, but not exactly helpful."

"They don't know which ones drowned," she whispered.

"I heard the first boat was entirely women and children except for two men and the second half, with some men in the second."

"If he escaped," she said, "he does not need me, and if he drowned, he does not need me. I shall act as though he went on, on that ship, for if he did, he does need me."

"Brave girl," said the shipman. "Sensible Missy. Just how I'd think it out myself."

"For where in the Colonies was the *Alexander* bound?" she asked. "Do you know?"

"For Wecomica, in Chesapeake Bay, outside Annapolis," he said. "That's Maryland," he added kindly. "If she was not blown off her course on the way, or changed ports."

"Or sank," she said, "you're thinking that too."

"Well," he said, "the time was pushing winter. The possibility is always there. We would not have heard yet, altho' we might have. Come, Missy," he said; "I've done my part now for you. Come do yours. I've written the names for you, and the Captain's name. I can't do any more for you. Unless you want me to give you Ship's Passage," he added casually.

"Would you?" she asked, her eyes widening.

"I would," he said. "I have to go back in any case to York, after Dublin, and I cannot keep you. But my ship in Carlisle is going to Barbados."

"I have in any case," she said, flushing, "to go again to London."

He did not ask her why. "My ship from Balaclava is going to London in a month, to pick up transports there. It is bound for Boston, but I will route it down from there into the Bay, if you would like." He smiled at her. "Would you like that?"

"I would like indeed," she said, "oh I would indeed."

"Then finish your affairs, Missy, whatever they may be, and be prepared to sail then, when it sails, or miss it, for it will not wait for you or any man except the weather. It will be a bad time, though, to sail," he added looking thoughtfully at her. "The transports can't help themselves, but you can."

"I think I cannot any more than they," she whispered. "I

must go as soon and as quickly as I can, before his traces are all lost in that vast place."

"You know, Missy," he said, "I'll be honest with you. I like you, you're a nice chit, but I would not like a wife of mine doing what you are, even for the reason you are. Have you thought, he may not want you back, when you find him, after this?"

"I know that," she said. "I think indeed he may not, but all the same I have to find him."

He went to the table of the room, and took a packet of papers from the pocket of his coat, and spread them out, and began to write.

"The name of the ship," he said, "is the *Helen*, after my wife. You must not lose these," he said, "they are your boarding and your passage papers. I will pay the captain for you myself in Balaclava. He is an honest man, as they go these days, and he will know me, and so he will not try to cheat you out of your way or to indenture you."

"Might he try?" she asked, her eyes horrified, at a possibility she had not considered. She had known she had to find passage money, one way or another, before she could sail, for she could not afford the time lost for an indenture.

"It has been done," he remarked briefly, "but with me to account to, he'll not dare, in any case." He showed her the papers and explained them to her, and then he folded them and opened her reticule and put them away inside.

"They are for you," he said, "in the morning."

When morning came, he left her, putting her on the stage for London, paying her passage for her all the way down. "A rest, Missy," he said, his eyes twinkling, as he kissed her off and goodbye. Her reticule seemed unusually heavy, and when she looked inside to see why, she discovered he had put money in it for her as well. He was, as he had told her, generous, and she wished she was not so relieved to be parted from him.

XXIII: *Diar's Wife: London*

S HE HAD ALL THE TROUBLE AND ALL THE DELAY SHE HAD
FEARED, MAKING HER WAY IN AMONG THE THRONG OF
WAITING PETITIONERS, SOME WAITING FOR MONTHS, TO
SEE THE KING. SHE USED BOTH HER MONEY AND HER BODY FOR
bribes, to enlist interest, fearfully aware of the passage of time,
and able to do very little, it seemed, to stay or prevent it, her
desperation as both her beauty and her money as well as time
seemed to be leaving, working against her and threatening to
wreck her plans. She remembered the Judge's pessimistic
words, and they lowered her spirits even further, yet she continued to try, unable to remember the faces after she left them,
accepted by some, rebuffed by others, helped by none. She
approached yet again a lawyer leaving the chamber with a
young man with him, her intentions unclear now even to her,
and was startled to hear the voice beside him say her name, and
looking now at the second face, to see her older cousin Val,
her father's sister's son.

"Mary Elisabeth!" he cried again in surprise and shock and
considerable horror at the alterations in her. "What are you
doing here?"

"Oh, Val," she said, "I am so glad to see you," and fainted. Between them they took her into the chamber so inaccessible to her. She woke, hartshorn held beneath her nostrils, the Queen's ladies hovering about her, and her cousin standing near her solicitously. She wondered, looking at his face, why she had not thought to come to him before. But she had not known he was in London, or thought of any of her family, since the day of the April assembly ball after Easter at Edinburgh. They had become like a dream of other days that she did not redream, but seeing him standing beside her, she realised she had been foolish and told him almost everything.

She had her audience then, the King both touched and amused by her persistence and determination.

"Let us get all this young man's possible names upon the paper," he said, smiling slightly, "so that when you are far off in that land you will be equipped for any contingency. I have no fears that you will keep him well in line for me, if you find him."

She could not herself smile. She had been too frightened, and she was too weary. Prompted by her cousin, she made the proper responses and gestures, until he shepherded her from the room. She looked at him fearfully, but he did not say very much to her, but called a chair, and took her to his rooms near Temple Bar, by a way she would not see the spiked heads, not knowing she had seen them on Carlisle Gate already, and ordered a restorant for her.

"Now, Mary Elisabeth," he said, when her colour had a little restored, "just what was all that about? I think, you know," he added gently, as she hesitated, "that I have a right to know. We have always stood by each other before, have we not, was it not 'always and ever' with us always? What is this cock-bull story about your being married to someone besides me, and going off on a ship from Balaclava? You have outdone yourself this time, little cousin, you leave me in a fog. I went along with it, but now I would really like to know. And," he added very gently, "I would also like to know why, if you were in trouble, you did not come to me before, instead of bumping into me and my friend Trot in a public corridor."

"Oh, Val," she said, "I forgot you might be here. I forgot all about you entirely, and I did not believe anyone who knew me in my family would want to help me, anyway, even had I thought."

He whistled slightly, his face stiffening. "Are you telling me then, Mary Elisabeth, that what you told us there is only true?"

"Yes, Val," she said nervously, her eyes lifting briefly to his and at the look in them returning quickly to her fingers, "yes, Val, it is."

"I cannot still believe it. I thought it was arranged between us."

"I could not help myself, Val," she whispered. She could not tell him what had happened to her. She did not dare. She kept her eyes lowered before her cousin, five years her senior, a tall red Scot.

"I see that," he said bitterly. "He must be a fine fellow indeed, to have swept you so completely out of remembering everything else."

"You are not so disappointed as that, Val," she said wearily. "It was not so arranged. You did not even know I had left home."

"Well, no, I did not, but then I have been here in London for two years. I thought you understood, I thought you'd wait."

"Let us not quarrel, Val," she whispered. "Please let us not quarrel. I cannot help it now. I was never so glad to see any man. I have had a terrible time, Val, and I have a ship docking tonight or tomorrow morning that I must be on. Are you going to try to stop me?"

"No, Mary Elisabeth," he said, "I have stood by you in all your scrapes, ever since we were mere bairns together, when you would visit me, and you have done the same by me, and

I will stand by you now, however much it hurts me and however much I don't like it, if it is what you really want to do."

"Oh, Val," she said, her eyes filling with tears. He took the hand she held out to him, blindly, and pulled her up to him, and held her against him, breathing hard, and found her lips angrily. She did not resist him, nor did she respond.

"Does he do this so much better? He must, I suppose. Or was it money," he said bitterly.

"Don't, Val," she said, "please don't, it is done now."

"You have changed so, Mary Elisabeth," he said, holding her, "I can hardly believe it yet." He pushed her away at arm's length, looking at her. "I thought, you know, for a moment, that you were out to seduce my friend Trot, the way petitioners sometimes do."

"I was, Val," she said quietly. "You were not mistaken."

He dropped her hand and she walked a little way away from him and sat down on one of his chairs, her face turned away from him.

"Do you want me to go away," she said, her voice low. "I have hurt you, and you helped me, and I loved you all my life, Val, even before you loved me, even before you asked my father and he told you to wait. I would have waited for you all my life, had you asked it, had not this happened to me. But it has. I do not want you to remember me as I used to be, or to imagine things that are not possible. I was married one night, Val, only, and after that the soldiers came, and raped me. It seems to me that the whole world has had me now, that wanted me. I have had no other resource. If you want me too, if that would help, one more will make no difference to me."

"And that is all I would be to you," he said slowly, "one more?"

"That is all, Val, now. I am sorry. You said I was not the same, and I am not."

He looked as though he would slap her, but he did not.

"I am going to go now, Mary Elisabeth," he said slowly, "down to the London Docks, and see if your ship has come in. I will come back and tell you. Don't go away, please."

"If you wish it, Val," she whispered. She was sitting in the same place, in the same position in the same chair, when he returned an hour later.

"She has gone into Yarmouth," he said, "because of weather, but they think she will be into Gravesend the day after tomorrow." He paused. "Will you have supper with me, Mary Elisabeth?"

"Yes, Val," she said, her voice and eyes reserved. "Yes, if you wish it."

"I am not going to write your mother, Mary Elisabeth, or send for her, or your father either."

"I am glad, Val," she said. "It would be no use. It would only make a big blow, and help nothing. I was there two weeks ago, or three, perhaps now."

He left the table, and walked a little way, while his servant cleared, looking out of the window at the silhouettes of the buildings against the evening sky.

When the room was empty again of anyone but them, he turned again to her. "I did not think this morning," he said, "that this day would end this way."

"Nor I, either, Val," she said.

He came over then and sat beside her. "Do you love him, Mary Elisabeth, this MacLyon, or whatever his name is."

"Yes," she said simply.

"What does he look like? I would like to know."

"He is tall, Val, not so tall as you, perhaps, and he is a tight man, well-built, like you, but somewhat sparer. He has white skin, that does not freckle," she said, looking at his with a small smile, "and eyes that crinkle up in the corners when he laughs, that are grey-blue, but they seem black behind his lashes which are long and very black, and that lift upwards. His teeth are very strong, and white, and even, and when he laughs," she broke off. "He has a smile I like, Val, but when I saw him last, he was not smiling. His brows are black, thicker than yours, but not a bushy black, well-shaped, straying a little, and his black hair falls over them, a little to one side. He looks much like any Black Scot," she said shakily, "except for the way he laughs, with his mouth and eyes, and that is his own way."

"You do love him," he said again.

"Yes, Val, I do. I could not help myself."

"Poor Mary Elisabeth," he said, "all that, and he has been transported."

"He was much spoiled," she said, her voice shaking even more, "when I saw him last, but I found I loved him more. I don't want to talk about him, Val, please, any more."

"Poor lass," he said again. "There was a time, and not long past, when Trot and I thought it politick not to let our voices be heard in the streets here, loyal Scots that we were, or call each other by our surnames publicly, but that hysterics I thank God is past, and there is some rationality again. I am sorry for you, Mary Elisabeth, and for your young man, caught up in these things. Is it a marriage my uncle would have approved, things being otherwise than they are?"

"I think so," she said, "being otherwise. His father was a fine man, in all ways equal to my own, Val. You may tell them that, Val, sometime if you will, if it should turn out that I myself should not be seeing them again to tell them."

"You will not be saying these things, Mary Elisabeth," he said, his own voice shaking a little, "a fine foolish thing to say. Ships go to and fro and nothing happens. Where is his father now?"

"The soldiers hanged him, Val, the ones that were not raping me, before me, by his house."

"Oh dear loving God," the young Barrister said.

"And then my husband came down from the hill, where he was, and they were doing the same to him, but Colonel Grant came up and stopped them."

"Poor lass," he said again. He took her hand in his and held it hard, for a long time, in silence, and after a time, somehow it found itself slipping down of its own accord to her knee. "Did you mean what you said, this afternoon, Mary Elisabeth," he said hesitantly.

"Yes, Val, if you wish it. If it would make you any happier. I do not think it will, it does not seem to anyone, but you have done me as much service as anyone has, and I love you, Val, tho' not any longer, Val, for this."

"Well," he said with a sigh, "I will take it anyway then. I will at least have something. You will no doubt think the worse of me for it, Mary Elisabeth, but then I have thought the worse of you, too."

"Had you been condemned unjustly, and transported, you would not have wanted me to do this to try to save you, Val?" she asked, her tone wistful.

"No, Mary Elisabeth, not on any account. A man has to take his fate, however much he does not like it, or change it himself, but not have a woman and his woman ruin hers for him. That would be a heavy load for any man to bear, for many reasons."

"The soldiers had already spoiled me," she said, "and before him, while he saw it, else I might not have myself gone the way I did. But after that, it seemed that nothing could be done to me that was any worse than that, and I could not bear, Val, that they should hang him for a traitor, even had he been one I could not have borne it, and he was truly none. But I think myself too," she said in a small voice, "that he will feel the same as you."

He looked at her then. "Mary Elisabeth," he said, "if you find him and he will not claim you, or if you cannot find him as I think may likely turn out to be the case, come back to me and I will marry you all the same."

"Oh, Val," she said, half laughing, then, half crying, "you to say that to me, after what you have just said to me. I will remember it always."

"I hope you will," he said. "And will you promise me to come back?"

"No," she said, her lips turning in to hold their trembling, "no, Val, I promise you I will not. I shall never be any other than Diar's wife, regardless."

She went to bed with him then. As she lay there, waiting for him, underneath the sheet, he paused, standing beside her, before he came to her.

"I wanted so much more from you than this, Mary Elisabeth," he said, his lips like hers tightening, "But if it is all I am to have, I will take it then. For for all either of us know, you may after all drown in the seas."

"I have said to," she said quietly, "if you like. But I beg you to make no big thing of it with me now, no more than if I were the harlot that I know you have. There is just a harlot's body here, that you can have as well as any other; if it is Mary Elisabeth you want, you will have me better than this way sitting in a chair and talking, for it is only in my mind that there is any of me left."

"I will take what I can get," he said, his voice muffled in her hair, and he did. He loved her, and he found what she said was true, that she no longer loved him as a man, but her body was warm and comforting and very dear to him, folded to him.

"You are not like a harlot at all, Mary Elisabeth," he whispered to her. "That is not true. Remember that."

"I will, Val," she said, crying, and kissed him.

She stayed in his rooms with him the next day, and the next night, when the *Helen* docked. He went with her to the quay at Gravesend, having found a trunk for her and helped her buy necessaries, although he had little ready money himself. On the way down they passed the prisoners that were to be transported being marched from their prisons to the ship.

"You see those poor wretches," he said. "Look at them, Mary Elisabeth. They are in no shape to stand such a voyage. Half of them, I think will not live." His voice became urgent. "It is not too late to hold back, Mary Elisabeth. What if this voyage is already pointless," he asked, pleading cruelly what they both knew to be too possible. "What if he is dead now? Do you think you would know?"

"No," she said. "I cannot trust feelings. They come and go. I have no feeling he is dead, I do not, I cannot believe he is, but I do not know. I just have to try to see for myself."

After the transports were loaded on, which she watched with dry eyes, but her hands shaking, she went aboard herself, to the part of the Captain's cabin she found had been reserved for her, having kissed her cousin Val goodbye.

"Do not tell my mother you saw me, Val," she whispered, her hand to his cheek, "please? It would only worry her."

"I will not tell her," he said unhappily. "I could not very well explain my part in it, or why I let you go. I hardly can explain it to myself," he whispered.

"You could not stop me, Val," she answered, "there's nothing can, I think, that's living. I have to go, you see. That's all."

He caught her hand as if he would not let it go, but after a moment she gently disengaged it, and he did.

XXIV: *Diar's Wife: Across Atlanticum*

THE SMALL ROOM SHE HAD IN THE CAPTAIN'S QUARTERS WAS PLEASANT, AS QUARTERS ON A SHIP GO. IF SHE WONDERED WHAT THE ARRANGEMENT MIGHT SIGNIFY, SHE WAS QUICKLY ENLIGHTENED. THE SHIPMAN WHO OWNED the *Helen* had apparently given the Captain to understand that if his passenger was privileged, privileges also went with her. That night, while they lay still in harbour, awaiting the first tide, he came into her room without knocking, and without a word or any expression visible on his face by the light of the lamp he carried, he undid himself, imprinted himself on her quickly, and still without a word, did himself up again and left. She lay back amazed, too startled to protest, even if she had judged protest wise, as she did not. It seemed now to be her lot, to be thrust upon by men and have them in and upon her at all hours and in all moods and in all ways, and it seemed best to be used to it. She wondered sometimes what had happened to her inside, that she no longer conceived, but in the circumstances it seemed as well, and so she turned over, and went to sleep, with the waves rocking the ship gently.

It was as well she slept well that night, for it was many nights before she slept so well again. The next morning they sailed past Goodwin Sands, when the wind suddenly dropping, they were in danger of being run aground, but the gale springing up again carried them into the Downs. Diar's wife had until now never been on any ship at all larger than a rowboat on a quiet loch, and the rolling sea on which they now sailed made her head to ache acutely, so that she kept her cabin, in an unhappy condition, disturbed only by the Captain's occasional swift laconic visits which followed the pattern of the first. They passed St. Helen's Harbour, to which in her misery she gave hardly a glance, on into the Cowes Road, where they picked up the man-of-war that was to sail with them, and thence into the Yarmouth Road. Here contrary winds forced them out of the Yarmouth Road back into Cowes, while the storm raged in which she learned later two ships on the Yarmouth Road were lost. The ship at harbour tossed, and the wind roared, and she thought to herself she had never known such misery, even in the Bridge-Hole, which had stayed still beneath her.

The Captain, more talkative now, coming to see how she did, laughed, and told her that she had seen nothing yet, but he took her ashore to spend the next night in an Inn at Cowes, and the next day, the storm letting up, brought her again on board before the tide. They sailed then from Cowes, and in the afternoon, passed the Needles. Here the Captain came for her, and supporting her on his arm, insisted she leave the cabin long enough to see them, her eyes blinking at the ragged rocks jutting upwards, with the waves dashing and foaming at their base, and the white side of the island rising straight to an immense height, straight upwards from the beach.

" 'He spanneth the heavens, and holdeth the waters in the hollow of his hand!' " the Captain remarked piously and pertinently, and led her back then, her legs and her stomach collapsing, to her cabin and her basin. For four days more, being in the rough seas of the Bay of Biscay, she kept entirely to her bed, so ill with the motion the Captain, who was busy on deck, forbore to disturb her, but the sea then calming, he came to see her to tell her that they would soon shortly be on the high seas themselves. For several days, a contrary wind held them back, but as impatience grew, it was settled by a violent storm rising in the evening that for two hours increased until the sea itself broke over the ship from stem to stern, bursting through the windows of the cabins, and covering them all over, from Mary Elisabeth in the Captain's quarters to the prisoners drenched in the hold. Towards midnight the storm abated, but six days later it was followed by a second storm which put the first in proportion.

All night it increased, so that in the morning the Captain was forced merely to let the ship drive. Towards noon the sea did not break as usual, but came with a full, smooth tide over the side of the ship, stunning all those in its path, observed by Diar's wife round-eyed before she shut them from the cabin window. At midnight the storm ceased, but after only twelve hours of peace, at noon the next day a third storm began, rising rapidly to a more violent peak than either of the other two. The waves seemed one moment to reach heaven, the next to part and reveal if not hell, at least the bottom of the ocean. The wind roared insistently and continuously around the ship, and whistled with the sound of a human voice, crying among the ropes, until she put her hands over her ears to try to shut out the sound. The ship not only rocked to and fro violently but began to shake with an unequal grating motion, jarred by the waves, that she was thrown from her bed, and slid about the floor, unable to keep her hold anywhere. An old sailor, sent by the Captain, came in through the door that was flying open and shut, and picking her up, rocking himself with an easy motion with the rocking of the ship as though it were a difficult horse he was riding, lashed her with a rope to the bed, and told her to "rest easy." Shortly after began a series of shocks, one coming regularly every ten minutes, against the stern or the side of the ship, with such force as seemed each time certain to dash the planks of the ship in pieces and send them floating. Yet the ship held, even when the sea broke over the entire ship, splitting the main-sail in pieces, and covering the entire ship, pouring in between the decks, as if the deep had swallowed them up. Yet the ship continued to ride and the water receded, leaving Diar's wife and all the occupants drenched and gasping.

She lay on the soaked bed, in the wet ropes, and began to pray, silently, for some sort of courage to come to her terror-stricken heart, afraid to drown in the vast spaces of the sea, bound as she was, until she thought of the prisoners chained in the wet hold, and then her terror for herself ended. Towards noon the wind fell at last and the sea calmed in a molten bright light falling on it from the scattered running clouds.

For three days they sailed on a calm sea, and then the next day, in the early evening, they fell in with the outer skirts of a hurricane. At once the sky grew so dark with wind and rain that she could see nothing out of her cabin or in it. The ship began a rebounding, starting, quivering motion much like she thought an earthquake must be, like what the ship's owner had put her through, the sea breaking over, and against the sides of the ship like the sound of large cannon going off. The Captain, though he went on deck instantly, could not make his voice heard above the voices of the winds and waters. The wind, veering all directions of the compass, in less than a quarter hour, and the sea running mountain high upon the ship on all sides, the ship would no longer obey the helm, and the steersman, unable to see the compass through the violent storm of rain, was forced to let the ship run before the wind. Diar's wife learned later that the sailors could not see the ropes in the thick rushing darkness of it or set about furling the sails, so that the ship had likely have been overset and foundered, had not the wind fallen as suddenly as it had risen. In the strange eerie calm, she rose from her sodden bed, and made her way to the door, with the sea legs that had been growing on her, and looked out, to see appear as she watched on the tips of each the masts a small ball of white fire, like a star.

"The Castor and Pollux," the Captain said, appearing at her elbow. "When it comes on the masts like that, it means the end of a storm. During the middle, it stays down on the deck, if it appears." He seemed weary, but relieved. The next day, however, yet another storm blew up, but this one, brief in duration, did no more than split the fore-sail. The beds, however, were now so thoroughly wet, that the floor was dryer to go to sleep on.

The ship had been driven considerably South off its course in the storm, and was beating its way North again, after its seventh week on the open high seas, towards the port of Boston where, its sails needing repair and its compass broken, it limped into harbour.

There she watched the broken shells of the prisoners brought up out of the pit of the hold, wondering if Diar had looked so, and cried so. She thought he must have, and she felt faint, and clung to the door for support, wondering that she could have been seven weeks on board above them and given them so little thought, in her own misery, even on the errand on which she had come. She had seen them when they were put on, and she saw them now, and knew by the alteration in their looks wretched even then and by the smallness now of the group, in part what they must have suffered to produce the change. She saw them taken away in boats, and driven by an urge to know what Diar had known, asked to be taken ashore, and watched the bidding and the prisoners taken away by the well-dressed gentlemen and the buckskins. They were in Puritan country here, and there was no setting free of Catholics out of charity. It was a cold day, with a bitter wind laden with ice, and snow everywhere on the ground, the boats going in skirting the floating cakes of ice, the harbour itself almost blocked by the grey spreading ice. She shivered in her clothes, and looked about her, at the brick buildings and a high steepled church, not altogether unlike some she had seen in London, and wondered what to do.

"The weather is bad," the Captain said, appearing beside her, "and my ship has repairs to be done to her. I shall be in Boston Port a month, two perhaps, and then I will take you to the Bay."

"How shall I live while I wait?" she asked.

"You may live with me," the Captain said. "I will treat you well. And when spring comes properly I will take you down as I promised your friend. You had best do it," he added, "for this is Boston and your kind is not well thought of here." She flushed but she held her tongue. "I shall say you are my niece," he said thoughtful, "or perhaps my daughter."

"If I should decide to travel instead down by land, would you refund to me the price of the voyage?" she asked.

He shook his head. "There was no money paid for you, my dear. You were only given space."

She was not certain that she believed him, but whether it was so or not, she was in no position to argue. The snow was deep and seemed continuous, and she did not know what else to do. She had perforce to do as he said, at least in the bad weather, and to conserve the small moneys she had.

The papers of pardon were in her reticule that she kept always with her. Her trunk was brought ashore, with the Captain's, and a carriage arranged for. She turned her head to look again towards the *Helen*, floating in harbour, not knowing it would be the last time she would see it, and felt no affection for it and no regrets to leave it. She felt no affection for the Captain either, but he seemed no worse than other men. He installed them in a small house, not far from the harbour, on a quiet bricked street, and for two months she lived there quietly with him.

The solid ground was welcome beneath her feet, of whatever continent it might be, and the thought began to grow in her mind and strengthen into a resolve that she would not go aboard a ship again, with its terrors of wind and wave, until Diarmid stood beside her. If she could travel from Edinburgh to London, it seemed to her she must somehow be able to travel from the town of Boston to the town of Annapolis, other than by boat.

She was disturbed, however, by the Captain's veiled warning about her profession, and when he showed her the Frog Pond and the stocks, and she saw a woman whipped, she believed him and settled into a quiet life in the cold air as his housekeeper. She spent what time she had to herself attempting to purchase more cheaply than he expected, and she saved a penny here and a penny there, which she privately claimed. She kept her eyes and her ears open, especially when visiting Sea Captains came to the house, and in March she was rewarded by hearing the name of the ship *Alexander* fall between the two men sitting before the fire.

"Is the *Alexander* in at the port?" she asked that night, in a fever of anxiousness.

"I hear so," the Captain replied. "Is the name something to you?"

"My husband I think sailed on the *Alexander*," she said, her eyes desperate, "and I cannot have any news of him."

"I will look up the Captain of the *Alexander* and bring him here," he said kindly, and the next evening he did that, for supper and a quiet talk. She was silent until they had finished eating, and then the Captain summoned her and indicated she might ask her questions.

"I am looking for my husband," she said, "whom I have reason to believe may have sailed on your ship."

"Crew, you mean?" asked the *Alexander*'s Captain.

"No," she said flushing, but her gaze straight, "as a prisoner, as a transport."

The Captain's friendliness abated and his glance stiffened, as did her own Captain, to whom the story was new.

"I am bringing a pardon to him from the King," she said, "and gentlemen, I am most urgent to find him."

Their looks relaxed somewhat at her words, though their faces remained guarded.

"He is not likely to be here," the *Alexander*'s Captain remarked, "for we unloaded at Wecomica and at Annapolis, in the Bay."

"I had heard that," she said, half afraid to speak. "My husband's name was Rawn MacCullough, though sometimes he called himself Lyon. Would you remember a prisoner by that name?" Her voice faltered as she saw by his surprised face and the emotion running on it that he clearly did remember a prisoner by that name. She waited, numb now, the air humming about her, for what she might hear.

"Oh, my lord!" he exclaimed, "MacCullough! I do indeed remember him."

"Is he," she paused and began again, "is he, do you think, alive now?"

"Well, my dear," he said, "I would not know of course about now, but I should think that young man hard to kill. I should imagine he is very much alive."

To their consternation, she fainted, toppling right off her chair onto the floor. They brought her round, fussing over her like two old hens, and took her into the captain's bedroom and laid her on the bed, and started to tiptoe heavily out on their boots.

"Oh Captain," she said weakly, trying to rise, "please do not go. I will not do it again." To her consternation and theirs, the tears were flowing down her cheeks, but she was not crying. "I am so glad he did not die, coming across."

The *Alexander*'s Captain, used to distresses of all kinds, came across the room then, and drew up a chair and took her hand.

"My dear," he said, "you said, I understood you to say, that you have brought a pardon for this young man. Is that true?"

"Yes," she said, "it is true. I have it with me."

"May I see it?" he asked.

"You will not take it from me?" she asked, frightened.

"Of course not, my dear. I only wish to see if it is really so. It is a matter of some interest to me." He took the paper and read it carefully, nodded, and passed it to the *Helen*'s Captain, glanced at it again himself, smiling slightly at the several names, and returned it to Mary Elisabeth.

"A valuable parchment," he said, "which I know you will keep safe, and one he would have been very glad to see some months back. I daresay it will still come welcome. And you have found this for him," he said looking at her with a curious smile, "and you have come all this way across Atlanticum in winter to bring it to him. You are a woman of spirit, Mrs. MacCullough, I should say, like your husband. I shall tell you a little story about your husband, which it may interest you to hear."

He told her then the story of Diarmid's rebellion on the ship at Wecomica, even remembering some of the exchanges of words. "I was by this time, Mrs. MacCullough, myself sympathetic. It is no mean thing to come through a voyage, tho' not so long or so storm-ridden as I hear yours has been, with so much spirit left, and I would not let my crew be used to beat them down." Observing the look in her eyes, he moderated both his language and his story, omitting parts.

"But in the end," he said, "the indentures were all sold, your husband's, Mrs. MacCullough, among them, although I understand that quite a few were bought by Papist gentlemen and released out within the week."

"Would you know who bought my husband's?" she asked.

He shook his head. "Not in my head, Mrs. MacCullough. And I was not required to keep a record of it. But the young man interested me, and it is possible I put the name down then in my log. When I go back to ship, I will look it up. Or if you like," he said, "you may come with me tomorrow, and see the ship that was your husband's home."

"I would like that very much," she said.

"And you are his wife," the Captain said again, "and you have come to find him, in all this immense land."

"Yes," she said.

"It is curious," the Captain went on, "that it should so work out. He protested his innocence and the injustice, as he called it, most vehemently. I will say I did not believe him, yet it was clear that he believed himself, and his attitude about it was in itself interesting, as you see, for you see I have remembered it, and him. And a mistake *was* made, then, as he said, and you are here and bring his pardon." He sighed, as tho' he thought it unlikely she should deliver it. "I wish you every success, my dear, that you do find him."

The *Helen*'s Captain that night offered the *Alexander*'s Captain a bed, and the next morning, together the three of them walked to the Quay and took boat out to the *Alexander*. This then, she thought to herself, had been the prison that Diar, sick-at-heart as she knew he was, had been brought to, and put into. She was not shown the hold, and she did not need to see it. She knew how little except discomfort was there. The Captain took them to his cabin and produced his log, and let her read the entry with him, and after a time of perusing it, a page farther on, he produced with an exclamation the name of Smythe. "It was a Mr. Smythe, bought him. The name is marked without notation, but I know that is what the name means, for I remember I put it down, thinking someday when I was again in port I might reinquire. He was an old gentleman, Mrs. MacCullough, that is all I know."

He had tea brought to them and served to them in his cabin, and the talk passed to other things, but when they left to go, the *Alexander*'s Captain walked a little way apart with Diar's wife, and without the *Helen*'s Captain observing him, he slipped a small purse into her hand.

"I am sorry about the young man your husband," he said simply, "and about his sufferings, which were beyond my power to alleviate, even had I tried. It is enough to suffer for what one has done, and too much for what one has not. And I am sorry for the trouble you are put to. Don't go by sea to Wecomica. The weather is very bad this Spring along the coast, and my own ship was very nearly wrecked this trip along of Hatteras. You could be yet several months that way, delayed and putting in and out of port, and this month there is doubt in my mind you will make it at all. I shall advise my friend the *Helen*'s Captain of this opinion which I doubt he heeds. But you heed it my dear, and don't drench your paper any more which I see you have brought in carefully in a good oil skin. Use care for yourself, and take the Mail down the Post Road as far as it goes, to New York, and then go as you can. I cannot advise you do this instead too strongly, Mrs. MacCullough, and as earnest of it, please accept this money towards your fare. Blood money, if you like."

She flushed with relief at the way opening before her, overcome with his kindness that had asked nothing of her.

"You wonder why I do this?"

"Yes," she said.

"It is a small price to pay for having witnessed what I saw and heard. I have thought much about it, since."

They left the *Alexander*'s Captain then, and returned to the small house. The *Helen* had now been repaired, the snows were less frequent, and they did not last when they came. Buds on the unfamiliar trees to Diar's wife were swelling. The Captain was anxious to be gone. Mary Elisabeth, however, declined to go, telling him truthfully that she was too frightened of the sea to go aboard again. He believed her, and not knowing what the *Alexander*'s Captain had done, bought despite his earlier words a passage for her on the Mail down the Post Road to New York, and told her laconically goodbye.

"You will do better in New York, out of New England," he said. "Go to my friend Nicholas Van der Voort, who should be still at this address, or his family, if he is not in port, and say I sent you." He gave her two letters, whose contents fortunately she did not know, one to deliver personally to the Captain if he was home, which read, "A jolly bit. Use her well for me." The other, to the Captain's wife, was more sedate.

It was the last she saw of him, or that anyone saw. A month later the *Helen* was wrecked off Hatteras, and all those aboard her lost. She read about it in the Boston News-letter in another town weeks after it occurred, and shivered, for both herself and Diar's pardon and for him.

XXV: *Diar's Wife: Boston, New York, Philadelphia, Fort Christina*

THE POST DOWN TO NEW YORK ON THE KING'S HIGH-
WAY SHE FOUND NOT SO DIFFERENT FROM POSTS SHE
HAD RIDDEN IN SCOTLAND AND IN ENGLAND, EXCEPT
FOR THE UNACCUSTOMED SCENERY, TURNING THEN TO EARLY
spring, its beauties and its curiosities falling on uninterested unseeing eyes. In New York, quiet now after the riots by and
against the Negroes, Captain Van der Voort, perhaps fortunately, was out; but his family honoured the Captain of the
Helen's requests, and fed and lodged Diar's wife for a night
until she could discover a coach to Philadelphia, which she
paid for out of the purse given her by the Captain of the *Alexander*. The Van der Voorts offered her no money, having none
to speak of themselves, but they packed her a lunch in a basket
to carry with her of boiled eggs and bread and a slab of boiled
beef and two withered apples from the barrel still remaining
from the Fall harvest before. She arrived the next day, travelling
all night, in Philadelphia, which she discovered to be a large
city, almost as large as Boston, numbering though she did not
know it some fifteen thousand souls. She was met, to her sur-

prise, by a Quaker family, a gentleman and his wife and his older daughter, who though she did not know them insisted with gentle persistence not needed upon her needful grateful heart that she lodge with them.

She had never been treated so by strangers, and she went with them wonderingly to their large grey stone house with the wide white paned windows that reminded her of her own. She was taken to a room and given facilities to wash herself with and her clothes taken from her to be washed and pressed, both those she wore and those in her trunk. She lay in the high four-poster curtained bed, in a shift loaned to her, resting, and waiting for her clothes, and watched the shadows of the white flowering tree outside her window and a large fat brown red-breasted bird sitting in it, and she fell asleep, watching.

When she woke, not herself but wakened by a tap upon the white door pushed open and the entrance of the young girl Hannah who had met her at the stage, with her dress and a hot cup of something unfamiliar to her in taste, the light had changed and the shadows had moved across the room. She watched the young girl move like the shadows about her room in her plain grey dress, her hair smoothed back and almost hidden by her cap, fifteen, perhaps, slender and very innocent-looking.

"I was like that too, once," she thought, "only last year—no," she thought, correcting herself. "I forget there has been another year since, almost. Two years ago. Only I was always more worldly," she thought, peacefully watching, "even before I came out, even when I was a child, riding my pony over the heather and the hills, with Val, and my hair let to fly free." The memories caused her no sadness and no pain and did not disturb her present peace. They seemed as remote as tho' they were of another person she had known and loved once, whom she had now grown apart from, but remembered with a vague kindly affection. They had very little to do with her now.

She had supper with her hosts, whose name was Howard,

she found, breaking bread with them according to their custom, and afterwards she told them where she was going and why, and they discussed what she had best do next. Unlike the Quakers of London who had regarded with some justification a Papist rebellion as a personal threat to their liberty of conscience, the feelings of the Howards, removed from persecution in Philadelphia, were impersonal and unengaged, except towards the humanity of the individuals caught up in it.

"Diarmid may have come here, if he has the freedom of his bondpapers," the head of the house remarked thoughtfully, using MacLyon's first name easily and naturally. "There is a group of the Scotch-Irish I understand settled in the west of Pennsylvania, near the Cumberland, in that valley," he said. "John Brinton went down just the week passed and bought the papers of a transport, a Protestant Scot, and I understand the young man has gone to join them with a party a guide is taking."

Diar's wife shook her head. "I know he may," she said, "but I cannot guess what he may do or may have done until I talk with Mr. Smythe. He may yet be in Annapolis or near it."

"That would seem unlikely," her host said, but his wife intervened.

"The child is right, Edward, one must go always to the source, first. What thee wants, Mary Elisabeth, it would appear to me, is to take a coach as far south as the road goes, and then thee may find a guide down the rivers, perhaps a boat, to Annapolis. But it may be some weeks before the public coach goes again."

"Then we must find a way to help Diarmid's wife to go there," Edward Howard said, and to Mary Elisabeth's surprise, she saw them cease talking and bend their heads. After a quarter of an hour had passed, or something like it, they began to speak again naturally, and whatever question they may have had appeared now to be answered.

"My ship is not yet in harbour, but John Brinton will advance the moneys from the Meeting stock," he said, seeming to have no question in his mind about it.

The next morning they put her in the private carriage they had hired, together with a family also going South as far as to Fort Christina and sharing the expense.

She held out her hand to them, and she asked then the question that had been in her mind, not wanting to ask it before, until she was safe on her way, lest she wake from this dream of kindness.

"Why have you done this for me?" she asked, "when you did not know me?"

"You have Bibles in England and in Scotland," Edward Howard said, his eyes smiling at her, "and New Testaments too. You will find your answer there." He spoke naturally and unaffectedly, his face kind and serene beneath his silver hair.

"But how did you know I would be there, needing you?"

"We did not, daughter, but we take no chances of omission. One family meets every stage, we share among us that responsibility in turn."

At Fort Christina her worries and her old life began again. Her old-new life, rather, and the way she had found to travel by. She stood on a corner of the central street, with its central gutter like Edinburgh's, among the refuse and the pigs wandering about, and paid no attention to these things. The family had themselves spent the night at the Inn, but contrary to the Howards' expectations, or to all charity, they had not offered hospitality to Mary Elisabeth, being large and full of personal expenses and embarrassed.

The night before, she had been robbed in a bad Inn on the road where they had stopped, having started late from Philadelphia, delayed first by the family's preparations and then by a lame frontwheeler. She had been waked suddenly in her bed, a hand over her mouth in the dark, her heart beating as though it would break, no idea who held her.

"I want your money," the voice hissed in her ear. "Don't scream. Tell me now."

"No," she said bravely and tremblingly, "I haven't any," as the hand released its hold a little.

"I know you do," the voice said, "I watched you at supper. Give it me or I slit your throat," and she felt a knife beneath her ear.

"Oh God," she whispered, "help me, I need it for myself, and I have so little. Surely you will not kill me for so little." She felt the knife press more sharply, and she said then, desperately,

"All right, it's underneath my mattress, in my reticule." Her hands and feet were bound then with a strip of cloth, and some cloth stuffed in her mouth, and the man got off her and began to search in the dark, swearing, his voice a low whispering stream, but he could not find it. He came back to her then, and took the sheet from her mouth, and she felt the point of his knife again in the same cut, twisting, beneath her ear.

"You tell me where it is, now, truly," he said. "I'll not be tricked. I think I'll kill you anyway for trying."

"I did not try," she said, desperate with fear but her voice cool, "you frightened me so, I forgot. It is underneath my pillow, I put it there tonight." She felt it pulled from under her pillow, and the clink of coins, the coins the Howards had given her for the guide and a boat, and the rattle of the parchment paper, and the knife again at her ear.

"Leave the paper," she said, her voice cool and valiant, despite her terror, "that's no use. And you can have me, if you like. I won't scream, and I won't tell tomorrow, and I won't try to find you. Only leave the paper and let me live."

"Why should I want you?" the voice said, beside her, still rattling the paper between unseen fingers, creasing it.

"Many have," she said, "try me and see." She felt the point of the knife trace across her throat then, lightly, and lightly trace her features out, and then press between her teeth and in her mouth against her tongue. She lay very still, and did not speak or move, the man's elbows pressing into her breasts, his breath heavy but unliquored near her, and after a time the knife was removed.

Her legs were unbound then, and her gown slipped up, and a hand put between her legs.

"Loose my hands too," she whispered, "I'll not fight you, whatever you decide to do."

"I'm not afraid of how you fight," she heard the voice say, though her hands were cut or pulled free. The hand was again between her thighs, this time holding the knife, the cool blade passing over and moving against her thighs, and then without warning she felt the handle of the knife inserted in her. "That for a whore," she heard the voice say, as she gasped with pain, trying not to struggle, more frightened now than she had ever been. The knife was twisted, pushed, withdrawn, pushed, and then she was turned over roughly and a finger put up her roughly and relentlessly. She began to cry in terror and in pain, but softly, almost without a sound.

"You know who I am," the voice said by her ear, "you saw me at supper and you know."

"No," she whispered, desperate that she not be tied again and gagged, believing now he would try to kill her in the end, desperate somehow to find a way to escape that end, and afraid to scream, to hasten it.

"You heard my voice, and you knew it," the voice continued, putting both his fingers now, and with the other hand fingering and moving the knife.

"No," she whispered, sick, praying she would not faint.

"Yes," the voice whispered back. "It was because you knew me you said that I might have you. You liked my voice and my face."

"No," she gasped, "I never did."

"But I don't want you," the voice said smugly. "I don't want a whore. But I'll have you where I doubt no one has," he said, giggling slightly. He put himself in her now, as he should not, and between himself and the knife handle, she thought she would die, but instead her body went out of her control and responded to the intolerable pressures.

He cursed and took himself but not the knife from her abruptly, and turned her over, and she knew then she was going to die, even before she felt his hands about her throat, and that she had waited too late to try to scream.

"Diar," she thought, gasping and struggling in the dark, "Diar, help me, Oh God, help me," unable to break the pressure. "I am being punished," she thought, in wild dismay and terror, the thought paralysing her, "I have been wicked, and I am being punished for it now, Oh God," she pled, her spirit fighting still against this new despair, "do not make me die now and go to hell without ever finding Diar, which I did it for." But then the thought came to her, still, even in her panic, "He cannot. I left the window unfastened myself, and he cannot, even if he would. I must help myself, or I will die." "I am not going to die," she thought then, as the blood throbbed in her face in her pain, "I cannot," and she reached her hands under them both, and pulled at the sharp blade, all that she could reach, that he had thrust in her, and pulled it out of her, and plunged it into the back of the man on her, throttling her, and then a second time, and a third. He gave a scream at the first blow, and at the second, still screaming, released her throat. She could not scream herself, but his screams had roused the Inn, and there were knocks at the locked door, even as he pulled himself up. But instead of leaving her, he took the ribbon from her hair that he had tied her wrists with, and swiftly knotted it about her throat pulling it hard and fast and tight. His hands were covered with blood where he had pulled out the knife from himself, and he rubbed them on her choking face and her exposed belly. "Die," he whispered in a hiss, "die, whore, and never tell. Had I time, I'd carve you right," and took her money and stumbled to the window.

When those at the door had brought a key and forced the door open and found her pulling frantically with weakening fingers at the tiny hard knot she could not undo, and had cut it with the bloodied knife, and pulled down her gown, the man had gone from sight. She lay there, in the midst of the moving hurrying figures, her eyes wide in horror, unable to speak, her caught breath returning to her throat, seeing before her the image of Diar lying on the ground, her fingers unable to undo the rope at his throat choking him.

The Innkeeper and his wife and her fellow travellers crowded about her, with candles and lanterns, looking ineffectually in her room and outside. The older daughter of the travellers found her reticule on the floor, turned inside out, and her paper and gave it to her, unhurt and unstained. She began to cry then, the painful sobs of relief shaking her, holding it to her shaking breast. "Oh, Diar," she thought, "Diar, I did not die, I did not, and I have it still, I am still coming with it."

The women then examined her, despite her entreaties, when the interested men had gone, and the Innkeeper's wife brought hot cloths and hot stone bottles and hot tea, against her protests that she was not much hurt, as she was not, the pressures removed, except for the bruises on her throat.

"I think not, indeed," said the traveller's wife, her face stiff with disapprobation. "It seems to me you should be more hurt than you are. It is my opinion you made the appointment yourself, or how did he get in, and that you are no better than the man thought, and that you deserved what you got, travelling alone without your husband or your maid, and entertaining strangers in your room."

"I am sorry for your opinion," Mary Elisabeth said wearily, "truly I am, that you should think it. I thought I was not alone, I thought I was with you. I am travelling to find my husband, and I have had a child, and you have said too much to me, I think." But she thought herself that she must not continue to travel alone.

But for her money, it was dark, and nothing could be done. The man, whoever he had been, was gone. She lay in her bed, terrified he might return, despite his wounds, and "carve" her, no one offering to take her with them or to stay with her, weeping softly in afterfright and the pain of her throat, until she fell asleep for pure weariness. Twice she woke screaming, feeling in her sleep again the man on her, at her and at her throat and the knife in her, his wounds gaping and bleeding on her. The third time the Innkeeper's wife took her in her big arms and comforted her, and stayed with her until the Innkeeper called her to come back to bed. A short time afterwards, however, the door turned with the key and opened and the Innkeeper himself came in, it being then about three in the morning.

"I hear you have no money," he said. "How will you pay?"

"I don't know," she said faintly, shrinking.

He carried a candle, and saw the movement and her face.

"I think you do," he said, "my wife thinks so," and then he said, not unkindly, "Always get back on a horse that throws you, it's the only way," and proceeded to show her the truth of the saying, in reverse. She lay quiet beneath him, curiously soothed as he predicted by the now familiar not unkind warmth, the images of the night and its sensations receding. And when later yet the husband of the family travelling with her appeared, after his wife's description of what his eyes had seen with a similar comment and offer, more hesitantly and somewhat ashamed, she let him also into her bed, more asleep than awake, and hardly felt him.

In the morning the solicitous Innkeeper found a trail of blood leading from her room, and through the garden into which the man had leaped from the window of her room and leading on into the wood, where there were marks of a horse, and then no more. There had been several strangers in the Inn room the night before, and there was little to be discovered, then, or ever. Mary Elisabeth told no one of the violence done her that was not evident, and she minimized the loss of her money, for she did not want to be held as a witness in any attempt at finding the man and delayed. The

Innkeeper's wife treated the cut beneath her ear, and the cut on her fingers, and made her a lunch to take. That evening they reached the Fort and the destination of the family travelling with her, a coolness between them after the wife's words and the husband's action.

When they had gone upstairs to their room, glad to put her embarrassing presence and her embarrassed state out of their sight and remembrance, she stood a moment watching the empty stairs, her empty reticule, empty except for the pardon, clasped in her two hands. There was no one else there, in the Inn, except a travelling Clergyman and the Innkeeper's wife. She walked out, wondering what to do, most people seeming to be in their houses, and she was almost relieved when the Constable accosted her, questioned her, and took her to his house that was also the town's lock-up.

If she had no funds, or visible means of support, he was willing to show her a way. In the morning he also offered her a proposition of marriage, but she told him she was already married enough and declined.

"You were better take it," the Constable said darkly and suggestively, "unless you have a husband produceable."

In the lock-up itself there was a young Buckskin, who had been shut up the night before for disturbing the peace. He had been listening to the exchange with considerable interest and amusement, and now he unfolded his long deer-skinned legs and stood up, leaning against the bars.

"What the young lady needs," he said, "is a guide, and there is no better one than Jim Hawkins." His blue eyes twinkled at her, out of his long brown face, their weathered corners crinkling somewhat in the manner of Diar's. "At your service, ma'am," he said, with a flourish, his lips folding into a little tucked-in smile.

"Pay the fellow no mind," the Constable said, and then a thought struck him that Hawkins, whom he knew well, might be a way out of a situation that might prove embarrassing to him, particularly if Hawkins had been paying attention the night before. "Unless you need his services," he added, hopefully and somewhat doubtfully.

"I might," she said, going over to the bars and standing by them, her hands on them, looking in and liking what she saw. Apparently he liked what he had seen, for he put his hands around hers on the bars, warm and calloused. She did not remove hers, and a little pause began to race through hers, that was echoed in his, at this strange bargaining.

"I can't pay you," she said, "I haven't any money."

"Haven't you?" he asked sympathetically, and he did not seem to care. "You shouldn't have to travel alone, though. A lady needs a guide."

"Well?" said the Constable.

"Well, Jim Blucher," said Jim Hawkins, "I would like powerfully to oblige both you and this lady, but I understand I have some stock-sitting to do today."

"I would be willing to overlook certain items, maybe, Jim Hawkins," the Constable replied mildly in retort, "if you could see your way clear to taking the little lady where she wants to go."

"Can she ride a horse," Jim Hawkins said, over her head, his hands still warm and reassuring over hers.

"Yes," she said, determinedly forgetting her bruises.

"And will she leave her luggage, if she has it," he said to the air.

"Yes," she said.

"And travel rough, without asking for a bed?"

"Yes," she said.

"Done, then," said Jim Hawkins. "I'll take her." He rattled the bars impatiently while the Constable fetched his key, and inserted it in the big lock and turned it.

He looked at the key, and then at Diar's wife, below her waist, with a meaningful glance, that she found herself blushing to meet, and laughed aloud.

"Off we go, then," he said, "out of the frying pan into the fire," and tucked her hand under his arm.

XXVI: *Diar's Wife: Annapolis*

"YOU WILL NEVER RIDE IN THOSE CLOTHES," HE SAID, SURVEYING HER AT HIS CAMPSITE OUTSIDE OF FORT CHRISTINA. "TAKE THEM OFF."

"HERE?" SHE SAID. "LIKE THIS? IN THE LIGHT?"

"Well," he said, "go behind a bush if you like, but if I'm to spoil a pair of doeskins, I'd like them to fit. We will know each other soon enough, and why not now?"

"Why not indeed?" she said slowly, her body throbbing, her throat dry. She took her dress off, and stood before him, in the green thicket of spring, in her shift, her breast shaking through the thin cloth.

"Is this my luck?" he said slowly, "is this my fortune? To have found this in the Lock-up at Fort Christina. Indians, look on," he said softly, "if you are there. This woman and I have business here together." He spread a blanket beneath a small white tree in flower, and then he walked across to her and put his hands on her shoulders, looking into her face before he kissed her, touching the bruised places on her neck with an unspoken question. Her arms slid about his neck, and with a sigh he picked her up in his arms, one arm beneath her knees, and carried her to the blanket and laid her down.

"Who hurt you?" he whispered. "Who dared."

She did not answer, but put her mouth to his and let his lips have hers.

"Will I hurt you?" he whispered against them.

"No," she whispered into his lips. "No," her head back, her eyes closed.

"Have you drawers on?" he whispered.

"Yes," she whispered back.

"Then slip them off, and I will mine. My key must meet your lock." She did so, her hands shaking.

"I am a whore now," she thought to herself. "I want this man. And he is not my husband, and I almost do not know him. Except a voice and a smile. I have paid a higher price than I thought." And then she put her knees up and gave herself entirely to the man entering her, shaking with him, letting herself drown in his strength and in his gentle touch, the little white petals of the blossoms drifting on them.

"I love you," she said shakily, her arms about his neck, "and I do not even know you, and I have come to find my husband."

"I would say you did know me," he said, "but you will know best, ma'am." His eyes crinkled at her. "You are a little foreign girl, you are just overbowled by your first woodsman." His face grew serious. "And I am just a woodsman, and I am overbowled entirely by a little foreign girl." His lips found hers again, and his sex hers. "Where are you from, little foreign girl?"

"From Scotland."

"From Scotland. And what is your name, little Scotch girl?"

"Mrs. MacLyon," she said, her voice a whisper, Diar's face not near her.

"Not a name like that, not now," he said, "not like this. What is your real name?"

"Mary Elisabeth."

"Mary Elisabeth," he said, "here with me in the woods and I in her, forever and ever, until we find her husband. Why is your husband at Wecomica, or Annapolis, or wherever it is you want to go, and you not with him, and you with bruises on you?"

"He was transported," she said, "it was there his ship landed. And I was robbed of all my money by a man who hurt me." Diar's face was suddenly before her again, and she began to cry.

"There, love, there," he said, understanding. "No one shall hurt you while you are with me. I shall love you, and you shall love me, until we find him, and no one will think the worse of anyone, and then I'll slip away, love, like a shadow in the woods and leave you with him. But I wish," he said, "that I had found you first. Perhaps," he added with a grin, "I shall leave a little Hawkins on you. That will make his eyes pop rarely."

"I cannot bear children any more," she said, "I do not seem to."

"Then you would be little thought of here in the colonies," he said, "where we breed fast and often, trying to outnumber the Indians. Why can you not?"

She told him, and he was shocked to a short silence. "Do they do such things there? I thought only Savages were so cruel, to their enemies. You've had a shock, Mary Elisabeth, you may recover from it one day when things are calm again for you." He traced her features with his finger. "If we don't find this Mr. MacLyon, I shall declare you a widow and rewed you for myself. And we shall see then about the little Hawkins."

"Where are you from, Jim Hawkins," she whispered.

"I was born in Pennsylvania," he said, "my father was a blacksmith and a Quaker there. But he liked his freedom and he used it too freely and was read out of Meeting. So we moved to North Carolina when I was ten. But I like my freedom quite as much as he, and when I was fifteen, I left him and my stepmother and took out on my own, where I've been ever since. The Indians used to come right up to our house, in Pennsylvania, but the treaty held there, and I was friends with them. They taught me much of what I know."

"Do you think we will see Indians?" she whispered, her eyes enormous and frightened.

"I hope not," he said, "the treaties don't hold well outside of Pennsylvania. One is much like another, now the settlers are pushing West on them. If we don't start, we shall get nowhere today." He picked up his long limbs and picked her up and set her on her feet.

He outfitted her in his second pair of pants, cutting the legs with his knife, and the sleeves, and rolled her dress and her petticoat into a bundle that he placed in his saddlebag.

"Not to shock the good MacLyon," he said. "Now," he said, "for your hair."

"Oh, no," she cried, "not my hair!"

"It will get thorns and spiders and twigs in it, and catch on trees, and the Indians will catch sight of you and scalp you for it," he said, watching her eyes widen again and enjoying the sight.

"Do it, then," she said resolutely, and stood still while her curls fell in long locks under his knife. "It will be easier to clean, and not so hard to brush," she added, with a slight quiver in her voice, as the locks continued to fall about her in heaps.

"And you will find it harder to seduce men," he said, "and I shall like that, except only me. You are doing it far too easily." He stepped back and looked at her and at his handiwork. "There. You make a very proper boy, if I say it, if one didn't know." He looked for a moment as though he were going to be sure she was not, but he shook himself and smiled, and said, "Later."

She put her hand up to the short rough edges of her hair, that felt curiously light on her head, and then suddenly she laughed too.

"Why, Jim Hawkins," she said, "it feels *good*! I did not

know the easy life boys lead. I think I'm going to enjoy myself."

"Good," he said, "I hope you do." He put her before him
on his saddle, his arms about her, and they rode off through
the sweet-smelling greening woods.

And so down to Annapolis, with a second horse, and nights
spent together between blankets under the starry cover that
seemed almost to touch them, and dinners of fresh meat
Hawkins shot, and Indian Pemmican, and strips of barbe-
cued sun-dried bearmeat that they did not always stop to
boil, until they reached the Bay. Then a ride on a riverboat
without storms, in the peaceful tidewaters, before the mos-
quito season. She had not wanted to go again on any boat,
but he assured her it was the only sure quick way to go, and
looking at the wooded mountains rising on the horizon and
the twisting shoreline, she believed him.

"What would you do," she asked him, lying in his arms on
the deck of the boat on a blanket in the night, "if you were
made an indentured servant and it was against your will?"

"I'd work, and work the indenture off," he said, his elbows
under his head, his face peaceful and relaxed beside her
under the stars, the trees on the bank sliding along, it
seemed, beside them.

"Would you not care?"

"I'd not waste my energy in caring," he said. "The world is
too full of things to care for and to care about to waste one's
energy in caring for what can't be helped. And good things
come of things just when one does not look for them. Look. I
found you in a jail." He turned to her then, and threw his leg
over her.

"Pull the damned britches down," he said, his voice laughing and smothered, "and be a girl."

She put her arms around him, drawing him to her. "Can
one love two people?" she asked.

"Not at the same time," he said. "The heart has room, and
the womb does not care, but the attention cannot cope. It is

like trying to hit two bears, or two Indians, standing in different directions, or a little apart. It can't be done. One has to reload, and lift the gun again, and then, if they're not a fool, one of them is gone. I love you, Mary Elisabeth. Right from the start."

"I love you, Jim Hawkins," she whispered, "too. Right from the start. And I'm going to find my husband, but I cannot see his face any more. I only see yours."

"I would not think too much about it," he said. "I'd do each thing as it came. Was he good to you?"

"No," she whispered. "No, he wasn't at all."

"I did not think so. I cannot imagine a man not being good to you, Mary Elisabeth."

"He never saw me," she whispered. "He never thought of me at all. I was just a person who fell in his way. That is why I love you, Jim Hawkins, because you see me. You would be a good husband, I think, better than Diar would ever know to be."

"You disappoint me," he said lightly. "I thought you loved me for my face, and what you saw in me, and now I see I'm just a mirror."

"No," she said, "you know that isn't so. I love your face. I loved it then, looking at me through the bars, because your eyes, crinkling, reminded me of his. And I loved your legs, and your thing, swelling through the doeskin as you looked at me, and I wanted you on me. I could have gone to you then on the floor of the jail. I've never felt that way before, not for Diar, not for anyone."

"Are you trying to embarrass me, Mary Elisabeth? My thing, indeed."

"I don't think I can embarrass you. That's why I love you most. Unless it's that you want to love and to take care of me."

"And when we get to Annapolis tomorrow, if we find him, what are you going to do?"

"Leave you and go to him."

"Loving me better, loving me best?"

"I did not say that, Jim Hawkins. I only said I loved you."

"But you do."

She shook her head. "I don't know. I know you so much better, is not that strange? But he is an entire part of me, and I of him, I do not know why, and I cannot break that and I do not want to."

"Well," he said, "that may be so, but I have you. I could take you off in the woods and keep you."

"Would you try to do that?"

"I would not try. Either I would do it or I would not."

"Would you do it then?"

"No," he said, "not even if you wanted it, as I think a little almost you do, unless you said you wanted me to. I will have no wife or woman unwilling or by force."

"I will never ask it. I am Diar's wife."

"So be it, then," he said.

"Do you know," she said in a small voice, "how very many different men have had me?"

"I can guess," he said, "seeing how long a way you've come."

"And you do not mind?"

"I do not think of them. You are here with me, that is enough to think of. You are not my wife. They are hardly my affair."

"And if I were your wife—"

"I should be very happy"—

"If I were your wife," she went on as though he had not interrupted, "and I did these things, if I had slept with many men and held them and let them hold me and do as they liked, so that I could come to you, what would you think then? How would you be?"

"I would be very happy to see you, any way at all. I would think you very brave, and I would ask you how you were, and I would thank you. And then, when the night fell, or we could go away alone, I would show you you were still my wife, and that I knew it, and make you know it. I would make you forget all the faces but mine, even 'Jim Hawkins', and I would show you that they were not in my thoughts at all. That's what I should do. And it would in no way be hard."

She lay upon his breast and let his arms enfold her.

The next day the boat docked at Annapolis, a small group of buildings, hardly a town. She had changed early that morning back into her dress, her hand enlaced in the fingers of the tall man beside her, her heart beating strangely. But they could not find a Mr. Smythe living there. It was Jim Hawkins who thought to look at the Ordinary book at the Inn, and turning the pages backwards, found his name and his initials, and further down the page, the name of Lyon MacCullough.

"Is it his hand?" asked Hawkins to the shaking girl.

"I don't know," she said. "I've never seen his hand.

"Now what's to do?" she cried, ready to weep.

"Here love, cheer up," he said. "You'll stay here now, and rest, and I will take my horse and see what I can find.

"And my dear," he said, ruefully, "I am powerful short on money. If you wish to ply your trade while I am gone, I'll not ask you what you did when I come back or where you got the money. I am a good guide and a good trapper, but I am low on furs, and when I guide, I'm usually paid in money. So you see, things being as they are, I simply haven't any."

She looked at him, to see if he were joking or not, and she decided, uncertainly, that he was not.

"I am tired," she said, a little bitterly. "I don't feel like walking about the streets. If you wish to bring a man to me who'll pay for it, I'll let him do it."

"I may," he said, "if I have time. You are thinking," he said, "that there is some value in being stiff-necked, after all, and you are right. But one cannot have it all ways or even many ways. And you are not my wife."

She cried when he left her, and she cried all through the

reechy paddling of the commercial traveller he brought to her room. She had several such visitors, and she earned enough to pay for her room, and then some.

Two days later, hot and dirty and dishevelled, he returned. She looked at him and wondered how she had ever thought she had loved him. He saw the look and read it correctly.

"You would have done it without me, Mary Elisabeth, and you know it. You just mind my finding them. I told you, I was your guide; I am simply not in any position to be a patron to you or anybody. But it is not the same now, is it?"

"No," she said, "it is not the same."

When he came to her in the night, after he had washed himself, she yielded to him, as she had to others, but she did not respond.

"Stiff-necked little Scot," he said, his voice gentler. "Stiff-necked like your husband. You see, I would not be so good a husband after all, running away into the mountains among the Indians after bears and things, or little trails, you never knowing when I would be home or if I would be home. You had much better stick as you are."

"You know where he is," she cried, sitting up.

He shook his head. "No," he said, "but I know about your Mr. Smythe. He is dead, Mary Elisabeth, he died right here in this Ordinary, perhaps in this very bed. The Innkeeper has remembered him, when I found that out by riding in the counties. And what is more, he has remembered something else."

"What is that?" she said, her voice tense.

"He remembers the dark Scot the old gentleman bought the indenture of, how when he died and the old gentleman's nephew had come up, there was a fight here in the parlour, and the Scot who had the week before been ill in a bed here in the Inn, the old gentleman looking after him, did not win it."

"Diarmid ill," she whispered.

"Very ill, but he recovered, though the Innkeeper did not think he would. He is not a cheerful sort, this Innkeeper. He has bad thoughts about you and me."

"Diarmid in a fight?" she whispered.

"Yes, Mary Elisabeth. They all heard the shouting. It seems the old man did not mean to use the indenture, and the young man did."

"What then?"

"Then they took the Scot out to the stables and tied him to a horse post, and kept him there for several days while the young man whose name is also Smythe, we should have looked further on the guest book, settled his uncle's affairs and buried him."

"And what then?"

"A big thing, Mary Elisabeth, and much excitement for Annapolis. The Bailiffs got him, and took him into Court, such as it is here, and the court official told him he must serve, and had him also whipped in the Square. Then off they go together, on a boat, and the town has to talk about something else. But you can hear more from the stableman, if you like."

"Oh, Diar," she whispered.

"Well," he said, "that's torn it, hasn't it?"

"Yes," she whispered.

"You feel sorry for him, and that's an end of it. Trust a woman to. I could not have told you."

"But you would not have," she said.

"No," he agreed. "Go to sleep now. Tomorrow we'll find out what else we can."

She talked with the stableman who remembered Diarmid well, with a respectful and amused admiration, and then with Hawkins she talked to the Court Officials and obtained Smythe's full name and his general direction.

"Georgia," she whispered, in dismay. "Oh, where is that? I have never heard of it."

"South," the official said vaguely, "several thousand miles," he thought more vaguely yet. "It was not a colony yet, and a wild place, Indian infested, and few settlers."

"Oh, God help me," she said, sitting down.

"Why not ask me?" Hawkins asked. "I am more likely to."

She raised her eyes to him, drowned in unhappiness, to have come so far, and find she had yet so much farther yet to go.

"Would you?" she whispered.

"I might," he said. "I'll think it over. At least," he added, his mouth twisted in a wry smile, "if there are not many settlers, he should be easy then to locate." He questioned the official more carefully about terrain, and roads and harbours, and the coastline, on the way down.

"Bad coastline," he reported to her, "once we leave this enlightened state and large town" (his eyes amused), "undeveloped harbours, no roads, a bad climate, both too hot and too stormy, all the way down, and Indians in the interior. He thinks we should stay here. Shall we?"

"Don't tease me, Jim Hawkins," she said, near tears, "I cannot bear it."

He took her hand, as once before, and put it under his and walked a little away with her.

"I have a hankering to see more of America," he said, "I have thought for some time I might go down. This seems to me as good a time as any. But you, Mary Elisabeth. Are you up to it?"

"I don't know," she said frankly. "I don't know what to do."

"Well, for a start," he said, "I would strike while the iron is hot. I should go over to that ill-prophesying Court man there, whose eye I notice particularly on your neckline, and I should sit down in that chair by him, right there, so that he can see right down it, to the globes, and I should weep prettily, so that he bends right into it. And I should take the handkerchief he offers, putting my little hand against his, and when his arm went around me to comfort me, I should nestle. You are very good at nestling, Mary Elisabeth." She could not read his tone, but even in her distress the idea of tall lanky Hawkins nestling struck her as funny, and she smiled, just a little, tremulously. "There," he said approvingly, "more of that, that should do it. Myself, I shall leave you to a clear field, and go find another trapper or a guide, who will likely have more information and what he has more accurate, than this fool here. You stay here and make hay, Mary Elisabeth, while I am gone, and make him pay you first, while the merchandise's value is at its highest. If he boots you out, or has you put in lock-up, I'll be around. But he won't. And I wouldn't hesitate," he added. "There are not that many men about, well-heeled, with any cash to spare, ready to hand, and we can't do the trip *entirely* on a song. Little fool," he added, "do you think I *like* it? You want your husband, don't you? Do it then, and don't think about it. It's no time for land reform."

So she did as he said, and it happened as he said it would, and she stayed with the official for two nights in which he took his money's worth. The next day Hawkins returned and retrieved her, ignoring the official's looks.

XXVII: *Diar's Wife: Virginia, North Carolina, South Carolina*

"HAD A NICE TIME, MARY ELISABETH?" HE ASKED. HIS TONE WAS BITTERER THAN SHE HAD HEARD IT. SHE DID NOT ANSWER. "I NEVER THOUGHT TO BE A PANDAR," HE SAID. "BUT I HAVE THREE BUCKSKINS LINED UP AND waiting. They are in the stable at the Inn. They have just sold their furs, and they want a woman badly. I have praised you to the skies, and told them a quarter hour each, only, or the price doubles. They promise they are clean. God knows how you are. Come along," he said, not asking if she would. "You needn't put forth any effort. It is just the thing itself they want, no frills."

She lay down in the straw, in the semi-twilight of the stall, and he let them in to her, one at a time. Big, soft-footed men, who did not speak, who took her, and as silently left. When they had gone, she turned over in the straw and wept, sobbing into the straw, different straw than Diar, chained, had messed. She had never felt so low, in spirits or estimation. She heard someone beside her, and it was Jim Hawkins.

He put his hand on her, and she shrank a little and sat up, her head bent.

"I did not think it would come to this either, Mary Elisabeth," he said. "You have a choice now. You can stay here, in Annapolis, and I will find more men with money, and then you can take the boat, when one comes, all the way to Tybee Island and the Port of Savannah, which is in Georgia. Then you will have to someway find guide there to find this Mr. Smythe. Or you can go with me on a small boat down the Bay to Norfolk, and then we will pack across the land to Georgia together, as best we may."

"Don't you know the way?" she asked faintly.

"No," he said, "but I can find one."

"I thought you said you had been up and down all along the coast, many times, even to Florida," she said faintly.

"I am a powerful liar. I have never been farther South than the North Woods of Virginia. But I am ready to do some trapping, and I would like to see the land. I like to see new country. Take your choice, Mary Elisabeth. Think about it, and take your choice." He sat a little away from her, his knees cocked, whistling softly.

"How am I to come, if I come with you?"

"I am like other men, Mary Elisabeth. Does that answer you?"

"I am terribly afraid of boats," she said in a low voice. "If I drowned, the pardon would be washed down too."

"The sailing is uncertain," he agreed, "but this will be a small boat." He looked across at her and then he said, "It's time for you to turn into a boy, again, then," and tossed her deerskins to her. He came over to her, and unbuttoned her rumpled dress for her, and then, as she took it off, he looked at her, his eyes asking. "Will you be a girl first?" he whispered. "I want you too. Can you take another?"

She turned to him, without a word, and they embraced, as silently as the buckskins and as quickly.

He took her in then for a large dinner at the Inn, commenting they would find few such, and then bought passage for them and their horses on the river boat. He sold her there to the river captain of the shallop, for half their passage fare, for the duration of the trip, and himself stayed with the horses, his eyes on the river, whistling softly.

When they reached Norfolk, he camped a little way out from the cluster of houses that were the center of the town, and left her there while he went into town as before to talk with the buckskins, furriers and trappers and traders, about the possible trails and their merits and the likely hazards of them. He returned at dusk with five who were flush, spread a blanket for her, and let them at her, as before, one at a time, a few minutes each. Then he moved camp, so they could not return in the night.

When he had used her the same way, himself, she moved a little away from him.

"I think you do this because you are angry with me. I think you want to hurt me now," she said.

"What is *this?*" he asked. "Now, or before?"

"Before," she said, "but both maybe."

"You are in rough country, Mary Elisabeth, and you will find it harder to know who you have run into or their intentions. I am merely helping you to do things your way. I have told you I do not like it. You can believe that or not as you like. I can judge those who are safe for you, being a man, as you cannot. I have told you also that I do not know any other way to have money quickly, until I am back again in the back country where I can pursue my own trade. I won't be pestered with emotions. You will go my way now or go alone."

She was silent. She needed him, and she had not scrupled before to please men or to humour them.

"You may want to anyway," he said after a pause. "I am striking out now, tomorrow, through the hills. The game is easier, and I have bought enough powder and lead to last for a time. It is too rough for a woman, and I know it, but the second one who had you is the best guide of the area. And he tells me at this season I should avoid the coast because it breeds fever. In fact, if you do not want me, I can perhaps arrange for you to go with him. But then," he added bitterly, "he might not be such a fool."

"I do not want to go with another guide," she said, and reached out and felt for his hand. He took hers, and pulled her to him where she lay quietly against him.

The next days she spent in perpetual fright of seeing Indians or bears, unable to appreciate the beauty of the streams they forded, or crossed swimming on their horses, or the waterfalls they passed, or the flowering trees and bushes. She was in an agony of apprehension about disaster, which the night noises gave food to, and she willingly went in to the small ports first of New Bern and then of the new town Wilmington, to rest at the Ordinaries there, while he sold his skins. They had taken a route along a blazed trail to the West of the swamp, and not gone in to Edenton or Bath. The word, curiously, had spread before them that Jim Hawkins had a very pretty Scotch girl with him, dressed as a boy, who was not loath, and she was as busy as he, both when he was there and when he was not.

"I shall be glad when I can go home," she said, wistfully. "I do not like being known for such as this. But I have considerable money. If I continue like this, I shall have money for Diar's passage home."

"I wondered when you would think of that," he said. "I had, all along. I don't have to take your money, now, now that I have skins. Shall I find you more, then?"

"No," she said, "I am coming in flowers."

She stayed in the wood camp quietly the next days while he used them to advantage roaming wide for game. If he saw bears or Indians, he did not tell her.

He avoided the rice fields of South Carolina and the coastal plantations, both because of the fever again he had been warned of, and because, he told her, he could not stand by and watch the slaves.

"I am surprisingly a Quaker still," he said, "at least about that, if not much else.—And there is no money for *me* that route," he added. "I have my living too to make."

Hawkins had intended to go into the Port of Charles Town, to trade his furs, and replenish his ammunition, but his directions on the rivers he would pass and their branches proved faulty, and he pushed Westward, looking for a crossing of one particularly broad one, and for a landmark he had been told to find.

He became concerned in a way Diar's wife had not seen him. "I do not know where we are," he said with a faint smile, his eyes worried.

"Did you ever?" she asked. "I did not. One day is like the next to me, and the woods and the waters the same, and you firing your gun and setting wires."

He shook his head. "I have missed my marks. I have kept on for four days, hoping to recover them, and I do not know at all where I am now. I think we must go East as directly as we can, wherever it puts us. I feel we are not safe here."

"What do you mean, not safe?" she asked, having felt unsafe for days on days.

"I do not mean to frighten you, Mary Elisabeth," he said, "but I think it is better I warn you. I have a pricking about me about it, as though I were being watched. The woods seem full, where before they were empty, and yet I have not seen or heard anything. I am going to have a look about me, to see if I can discover any reason for this feeling, and you must stay quietly here."

Nevertheless, he found nothing, and heard and saw nothing. He came back to her, and was about to speak, when some yards away from them, materialising quietly out of the green woods, three quarters, stood five tall Indians, looking straight towards them, motionless.

"Oh, my God," he whispered. "I think they have seen me. And I am not sure they are friendly. They look dressed for war. And I think they know where I am." He took his knife and gave it to her. "Keep in the bushes, little one, down like a fawn, covering yourself, and if they find you, use the knife on them or on yourself. Don't watch," he said, "and when they have gone, if I cannot come with you, you must walk East, where the sun is, and follow the river. If I shoot, Mary Elisabeth," he said, "they will be on us before we reload, and you don't want to spend your life as an Indian Squaw." He did not tell her how few bullets he had left. "Oh, God," he said, his hands on her face, "I wish I had not brought you into this. God bring you out of it, for I cannot."

"What are you going to do," she whispered.

"I am going to take both horses, for they will have seen them both, and ride off, a little slowly, casually, and then fast, and lead them from you. If they haven't horses near, I'll come back when I can."

"Why don't they come, then?" she whispered.

"That is not their way. Until I move."

"What will they do to you if they are not friendly?" she whispered.

"If they like my face, they may adopt me," he whispered, and if he was afraid, he did not show it. "If not, Mary Elisabeth, it is a risk a furrier takes when he leaves the coast and goes in the hills. They think the animals are theirs. I have to go now, my dear, they look to me as if they're getting restless, and if they take me here, they'll beat the bushes and find you too. With any luck you'll meet another furrier in the woods. But remember, Mary Elisabeth, I did love you. And I am helping you still, the best way I know and the only way now, to still reach your Diarmid." He slid away so quietly she did not know he had gone, and yet it seemed to her the faces she dimly saw, knew it and their attentions sharpened. She hid her face then, her courage breaking, that she might not see their faces any more or draw their gaze to hers. She heard the noise of the horse's hooves, walking, and then riding, and suddenly the wood seemed full of horses and riders, the noise thundering about her, and then dying away.

She did not see his capture, or his desperate fight to live, as he had not wished her to, ringed in the hopeless odds. The Indians had had recent unpleasant experiences with trappers, and he was not adopted. He was taken to several of their towns, in triumph, and his ability to endure torture displayed in each, and then in the town of his captor he was burned slowly, the event lasting all day. His bravery was respected, and his scalp worn proudly by his captor, and his name put in their stories. Because of the respect he won, his mutilated body was brought near Fort Argyle, and left there.

XXVIII: *Diar's Wife: Chicali*

SHE STAYED THERE IN A SMALL HEAP, HOLDING HERSELF FROM SHAKING OR CRYING, THE ONLY THING SUSTAINING HER BEING THE COLD HEAVY KNOWLEDGE THAT SHE COULD NOT HELP HIM, AND THAT THE GESTURE WOULD COST Diarmid all as well. But slowly, as she crouched, hardly breathing, she was aware of eyes on her, on her exposed neck like the sun burning, and she raised her head then and looked direct into the face of an Indian standing a little way from her. She thought she would faint, in her terror, voiceless, yet her mouth open, screaming soundlessly, and in a single step the Indian was by her, his hand over her mouth.

"Be still, and not cry," he said in a soft voice near her, in her own tongue. "I am friend to you, I will not hurt." She stopped her frantic useless terrified struggling, and lay quiet in his grasp, and then he released her. "Come," he said, "your man taken by Cherokees, is no use waiting now, he not come back."

"Who are you?" she asked in a whisper. "How did you know where I was?"

"I Chicali the younger," he said. "I Chicasaw, my grand-father, Head Man. I learn English in Savannah with the blackcoats who go about, not like the black kings, and teach the good book. Then I go to live in Charles Town. I take you there, you want to go?"

"Oh, yes, please," she said, "oh, yes, please."

"Little bird," he said softly, "little brown bird. I wonder why the tall man take two horses and ride out letting Indians see him when he might stay and shoot, kill maybe two or three. I come to see. An old quail trick, and here I find the small brown bird."

He put his hand over her breasts, feeling them under the soft doeskin, with satisfaction.

"Standing there," he said, "I see all, and no one see me."

"Were you following us?" she asked.

"Two days now. I think, you lost, perhaps you want guide. Then you walk into Cherokee war party, everywhere, I melt, I wait. Much unrest is everywhere, among the Nations, much fighting, no time for anything but fight. My father, my brother three days ago killed by Cherokees, I hear, I go to see."

"Are they cruel?" she asked fearfully. "Will they hurt him?"

"Probably," he said. "Burn my father, burn my brother. Probably they burn your man. It is the war."

"Do you do that too?" she asked, frightened.

"But of course. It is the war. We have burned many Cher-okees, Choctaws too."

"But you said you would take me to Charles Town," she said, her voice faint with fear.

"I am not like my father and my brother," he said. "I listen, like my grandfather, to the men with the good book, and I have left the ways of war. But when I have heard of the battles with the Cherokees and the French, I come to see, and to kill those who killed my father and my brother, though I die. And then I see the man, and I stop to look, and find the brown bird. And I think, the beloved ones tell me this is the better way."

She walked beside him, very weary, her heart so heavy and so full of helpless fear and anguish, she could do nothing except move one foot after the other, her mind full of images so unbearable in the end they blacked it out.

They walked until the sun was near setting, and then the Indian made a camp a short way from a stream, cutting boughs for a shelter for her, putting his blanket down, and giving her to eat a strange cake of food he carried with him, not unlike that Hawkins carried, and strips of dried deer-meat. She lay down, and the Indian lay with her, naturally and without question.

All the next day they walked, and her heart was a little easier, for she thought, mistakenly, that if Hawkins was not to live, then he must be dead now, and out of pain. She wept for him, as she walked, because in the end she had not loved him after all, the tears falling silently. The Indian beside her seemed to take her tears as a matter of course, and paid no heed to them. At noon, he stopped, and slept with her again, tasting her tears with interest, and then they walked on. That night he told her about the beloved, as his tribe believed in them.

"We believe there are four beloved things above, the clouds, the sun, the clear sky, and He that lives in the clear sky. There are two with him, three in all."

"Do you think he made the sun and the other beloved things?" she asked.

"We cannot tell. Who hath seen?"

"Do you think he made you?"

"We think he made all men at first."

"How did he make them at first?" she asked, to distract her heavy thoughts, and charmed and strangely moved by his simple words.

"Out of the ground."

"Do you believe he loves you?"

"I do not know. I cannot see him. But he has often saved my life. Many bullets have gone on this side, and many on that side, but he would never let them hurt me. And many bullets have gone into young men I know, and yet they are alive!"

"But he did not save your father and your brother," she said. "And can he save you now from your enemies?"

"Yes, but we know not if he will. We have now so many enemies round about us, that I think of nothing but death. And if I am to die, I shall die, and I will die like a man. But if he will have me to live, I shall live. Though I had ever so many enemies, he can destroy them all."

"How do you know that?" she asked. She shivered, thinking of Jim Hawkins, and wondered if, as he had said, his thoughts were like these Indians. Had Diarmid's been so too? Was it how men thought?

"From what I have seen. When our enemies came against us before, then the beloved clouds came for us. And often much rain, and sometimes hail has come upon them, and that in a very hot day. And I saw, when many French and Choctaws and other nations came against one of our towns; and the ground made a noise under them, and the beloved ones in the air behind them; and they were afraid, and went away, and left their meat and drink and their guns. I tell no lie. Others saw it too."

"Have you heard such noises at other times?"

"Yes, often; before and after almost every battle."

"What sort of noises were they?"

"Like the noise of drums and guns and shouting."

"How strange," she said, shivering. "Have you heard any such lately?"

"Yes," he said, "four days after our last battle with the French."

"Then you heard nothing before it?"

"The night before, I dreamed I heard many drums up there: and many trumpets there, and much stamping of feet and shouting. Till then I thought we should all die. But then I thought the beloved ones were come to help us. And the next day I heard above a hundred guns go off before the fight began; and I said, 'when the sun is there, the beloved ones will help us; and we shall conquer our enemies.' And we did so."

"Do you often think and talk of the beloved ones?" she asked, the name stirring her strangely.

"We think of them always, wherever we are. We talk of them and to them, at home and abroad; in peace, in war, before and after we fight; and indeed whenever and wherever we meet together."

"Where do you think your souls go after death?" she asked.

"We believe the souls of red men walk up and down near the place where they died, or where their bodies die, for we have often heard cries and noises near the place where any prisoners had been burned."

"Where do the souls of white men go after death?" she said, her voice shaking.

"We cannot tell. We have not seen."

"Our belief is, that the souls of bad men only walk up and down; but the souls of good men go up." Oh Jim Hawkins, she thought in tearing grief, is your soul up? So recently he had been so entirely with her, and for so long now, she could not see how she could continue on without him and his steadying presence, forgetting how long she had continued before him, and very weary and dejected.

"I believe so too," Chicali said. "But I told you the talk of the nation."

"You are so wise, Chicali," she said then, touched by a brief surprise. "How did you come to know these things? How came your nation by the knowledge they have?"

"As soon as ever the ground was sound and fit to stand upon, it came to us, and has been with us ever since. But we are young men; our old men know more; but all of them do not know. There are but a few: whom the beloved chooses from a child, and is in them, and takes care of them, and teaches them; they know these things: and our old men practise; therefore they know. But I do not practise; therefore I know little."

Four days later, he showed her Charles Town lying a little below them.

"I shall not go further with you," he said. "I go myself now to seek my father's and my brother's spirits." He touched his fingertips to hers, and turned, and without a backwards look, went quickly from her.

XXIX: *Diar's Wife:*
Charles Town

H E HAD LEFT HER WITHIN SIGHT OF A HOUSE, A COUNTRY
SEAT, STANDING ON A LITTLE HILL, PLEASANTLY
SITUATED, A VALE ON EITHER SIDE, IN ONE OF WHICH
THERE WAS A THICK WOOD, THE OTHER PLANTED WITH PLANTS
she did not know, that she would learn were rice and Indian
corn. She chose the planted side to walk across, quite numb
now and forspent with weariness and sadness, beyond anxiety,
passing by the strange growths without a glance at them or at
the black Negroes whom she had never seen before either,
bending among the plants, her eyes unseeing of either one. The
Negroes paid her as little attention as she them, their overseer
at that time in the wooded side, and she walked, unstopped and
unhelped, through the muddy fields, losing the thin shoes Jim
Hawkins had made for her, moccasins he had called them.

She arrived before the house, the most solid and pros-
perous-looking house she had seen in several months, looked
at the closed front door and wiped her hot perspiring face
with one hand unconsciously, pushing the hair back from her
forehead with the same unconscious gesture, and then
turned and walked around the house to the back.

There her arrival created a stir among the blacks, old and young, whom she found there. Two white children came to the door with an older black, and she thought she heard a voice cry, "Ma, come see the little buckskin boy," as she stood on the steps waiting, not knowing what to say or to ask for, and then quietly, having reached hands that could help her if they would, and reached her endurance's end, she crumpled in a faint in a muddy heap on the white steps.

In her faint, she was dimly aware of voices and feet scurrying, and then black arms picked her up and carried her, not into the house, but across the yard. She struggled faintly, then, in terror, and the black arms put her down, and a man's voice said beside her,

"Well, little man, are you coming round?" She turned and saw a well-dressed middle-aged man a little distance away from her, looking at her.

She could not seem to speak, and the ground again began rising towards her, when the same black hands supported her. She walked then, with the support of the hands, into a low rounded hut made of canes, though she did not know it, pipe-like smooth sticks and knife-like leaves, twisted together to make a shelter, and put down on a bed made of the same material.

"Clean the boy up," she heard the voice say, "and feed him, and if he's not sick, if he's just starved, I'll see him tomorrow and see what he wants."

The big Negro said soft words she could not hear, and after a time, a woman came with a bowl of thin gritty liquid that she forced between Diar's wife's stiff lips, loosening her set teeth, that began to relax with the hot food. The big Negro had brought a kettle of hot water, and he came now by the cane mat to strip her dirty clothes from her, to wash her. She pushed him away with her weak hands, futilely, for without a word he took her shirt in his big hands to rip it from her, down the front where the opening weakened the skin of it. But when he touched her, his face took a startled look and then he began to smile, putting his big hands on her experimentally. His smile broadened, but he did not say a word, except to send the woman out. Then he stripped her leggings from her, and threw himself on her, his hand over her mouth, which she bit feebly, trying to scratch, in this rape that had no advantage for her, suffocating her, the strange rank smelling flesh on her, its scent different but as powerful as the Indian's. She felt the man leave her abruptly, unfinished, and she opened her eyes to see the same well-dressed middle-aged gentleman standing in the opening of the hut, and another white man, younger, who had pulled the black off her.

She lay there then, exposed, shutting her eyes against the eyes of the older man upon her, hearing from a distance howls outside, and after a time the younger man came back in, with a blanket, and picked her up in it and carried her into what seemed to be part of the kitchen of the house, the older man walking beside him, his eyes still on her, she found, whenever she opened her own. They seemed to be talking together in low surprised voices, but she was past understanding or listening to them. They seemed kindly in intention, and she let herself drift away while she was put in the care of a Negro woman in the kitchen, also talking in a soft running flow of voice she did not heed. Her clothes were taken entirely from her, her hands holding to her shirt then, crying, fumbling for the paper sewn into it. The older gentleman came forward then, and with a grave courtesy took his knife and cut the square free, not unfolding it.

"Rest easy, little miss," he said, "whatever it is, I will keep it safely for you."

The gentlemen did not leave the kitchen, and she was put in a tub brought in the room and set on the flags, and washed from head to foot, scoured, like she used to be as a child of three or four, her hair, her neck, her ears, all of her. She shut her eyes against the curious and interested gazes fixed on her, past struggling and past humiliation.

"A pretty child," she heard one of the men say with interest. "Where do you suppose she has come from?" She did not know that they were used to naked flesh, outside the situation of the drawing room, accustomed to examining and inspecting it assessingly before they bought it, the attitude extending over to her since clearly she was not of their station. A smaller Negro girl had brought a clean white gown now and that was slipped over her, and free of the dirt of the weeks of walking and riding, where she had had only the cold streams to wash in, and those in between days more of walking, she was judged fit to be taken into the house, and upstairs into a small bedroom, such as she had not been in since she left the Howard house in Philadelphia. She was fed by the smaller Negro girl, while several children at the partly open door stood watching through the crack, and the door closed, and she was left to sleep.

When she woke again, the lady of the house was beside her, questioning her, and she told her in part her story.

"I cannot believe it," the lady said, "that you should have come from Scotland and England to Boston and travelled down the coast by yourself. It is not a possible story," she added, a touch of severity in her voice.

"I was not always entirely by myself," she said, but that admission was received no better than the first.

"With your family?" the lady asked.

Mary Elisabeth shook her head, unable to speak or explain any further to the severe sharp unsympathetic face beside her, looking at her in horror and in shock. She did not listen to the words poured on her, or notice when the lady retired, except by the silence that fell. She slept again, and supper was brought to her, and she lay there, and remembered Jim Hawkins, and wished she could wish to die.

Apparently the lady of the house told something of her story to the master of the house, for in the small hours of the night, smelling strongly of hard spirits, in his nightshirt and dressing gown, he appeared in her room by her bed and sat down on it and took her hand tentatively.

"I have a paper of yours," he said. "Do you want it back?"
"Yes," she said, knowing what he meant, and let him in.

The next day, he took her in a borrowed dress in his carriage the thirty-mile drive into Charles Town and set her up in a room of a house he had there. She judged he must be an official of some kind, but she did not ask him. He told her his name, and suggested she stay with him. Her resources of all kinds were exhausted, for the Indian had taken her money, but he had not noticed the paper or thought it of value. She judged it time she return openly to the position of a woman, for which she needed clothes and for a time a place of comfort, to restore herself in, and this interested, well-positioned affluent official seemed better than she could have hoped for.

He brought to her his wife's dressmaker and brought her material he had had shipped in for his wife and his daughters, and in all respects but one treated her with the courtesy due a lady, and under this treatment she began again to flower. Two weeks later she looked at herself in the mirror, her short hair hidden under a wig, a tiny hat perched on it, like the highest fashion for the genteel, her waist nipped in, her petticoat and her overskirt flounced, her neckline very low, her feet shod with little heels, her hands gloved, ready to go in the carriage with her driver and her little black boy, and she did not recognise herself, either as Mary Elisabeth Grant or as Mrs. MacLyon, Diar's wife. The person who had suffered so many hardships and bitter griefs and the girl whose determination and pluck had moved and carried her on despite them did not either one show on the surface of this pretty young turned out thing. Nor did the innumerable violations made upon her.

"I suppose that is how it is," she thought. "What we feel does not show, if we can come about baths and foods and laundresses easily."

She had asked the official, who she had since discovered was the Lieutenant-Governor, the first night if he could not have a troop of men sent to recover Jim Hawkins. His face grave, he told her reluctantly that with the uneasy border situation he could not. He also told her it would be useless.

"They will have taken him inland, little miss, into one of their towns, and if we should happen to find a town and it should happen to be the right one, and he should happen to be yet alive, he would be removed or more likely killed before we could reach him."

"Will they burn him," she asked, her eyes piteous, "as the Indian who brought me here told me they would?"

"I do not know," he said, both truthfully and untruthfully, reserving his private opinion. "But I will tell you this, my dear, he would not want you to be upset for him, for a man who elects to be a woods trapper in these days knows when he does it the risks and that he can bear what he may have to bear." And in this opinion he was correct, and remembering the man, she believed him, and it somewhat eased her heart.

She told him, the second week, when she had somewhat recovered herself, why she had come to America. He was somewhat relieved.

"Well, my dear," he said, "you relieve my mind, for though I am content with things as they are, I have promised my wife and children to bring them into Charles Town for the hot months. I was wondering what to do about it."

Two days later she changed her patron to an unmarried acquaintance of his, a young man with heavy florid good looks, and moved into separate lodgings, where from time to time he continued to come to see her. She was making money now, and she thought she should not go down into Georgia until she had recovered her position financially that she had lost, for he led her to understand she would find Savannah a very different matter from Charles Town.

"We have the French Huguenots here, and some of them are strict, but many have married with the Anglicans, and laid aside some of their ways. But in Savannah you will find they are all surface-strict, and no spirits allowed to ease a man's problems, and ease him into things. Frederica I understand is another matter, with the fort, but it is Savannah you will go to."

"Well," she said then, "I suppose I must stay here a while longer." The young man had a large acquaintance, and he entered into the chivalry of the thing, not to the point of giving her the passage moneys, which he said, engagingly, he could not afford, and afford her too, but he did spread the word among his friends and increase her trade. She looked wistfully at the large brick church plastered like stone, when she passed it one day. It seemed large enough that in it she might be lost and not observed, but a family going in gave her a sharp glance and she did not go in, and after that she avoided the street and its bells.

In July, however, she struck an acquaintance with a French Huguenot Belinger who had seen her in the street and resolved to help her.

"If you continue as you are," he said, arriving not to purchase but to chastise her, "even in Charles Town you will be run out of town soon. You are becoming notorious, even the wives now know of you. You are much too pretty for your own good, my dear, or to be so completely immoral as I hear you are, not even keeping to one man at a time."

She was genuinely upset by this picture of herself, and she broke down without design and cried. The result was the usual one then, and left her censor enslaved.

"I don't know why I cried," she said, picking herself up off the floor, angrily, rearranging her disarranged wig and clothes. "You are the worst yet, in view of the windows in daylight. Why, you could not even wait to get into a bed. And you did not bother to ask my price." Her eyes glittered. "I am very high. And my price is double for those who criticise me first. And you have spoiled my dress. It is ripped here, and rumpled. I do not have so many, you should pay me for that too."

"I will pay it, all of it," he said humbly, and pulled himself back together, his eyes like a whipt dog's, sitting awkwardly on the edge of the little chair. He gave her the money without a word, but he did not go, and he sat there, looking at her, his eyes hungry, his face sad.

"What is it," she stormed, her eyes still bright with tears. "What do you want now? You have had it both ways now, you have abused me with your tongue, and then with the other. What more do you want now? To do it again?"

"Yes," he said, his eyes beaten and humiliated. "Yes, I do."

"Then come," she said, her anger suddenly evaporating, and her voice and her eyes kinder before his misery. "Come into my bedroom, properly, and I will make you happier."

She undressed, and seeing his shame, turned her back while he undressed, and then she came to him, like a bride to a bridegroom, under the clean sheets, in the soft warm afternoon light.

"You are not a whore," he said soberly then, "and yet you act like one, everywhere else, and though you do not look like one, you are known for one."

"Are you going to criticise me again?" she asked, but not angrily.

"No," he said in a low voice. "No, I cannot. I cannot criticise you when I want you too. I want to know why you are as you are, and I want to help you if I can."

She did not laugh. "I think you mean what you say. I do not know why you should, but I think you do," she said, and she told him.

He was thoughtful for a time, and then he said, "I was ten years old, Mary Elisabeth, when my father took my mother and myself and fled from France, and came, in time, on a ship, here to Oyster Point to Charles Town. I was only ten, but I remember well the dragonnades, and the rape of my mother that led my father to his desperate flight. It was desperate, Mary Elisabeth, because even though it was made intolerable for us to live there where we were, we were not allowed to leave. Yet we did leave. And I remember the rape because I was there, and I saw it. I have never had, or wanted to have, a woman until today. It is strange, and I do not understand it, why it should be. Had I not thought myself immune, I should not have come to you as I did. I am fifty-one now, Mary Elisabeth, and I have not yet forgotten, any of it, nor the indenture papers my father had to sign, for himself and my mother and for me, to bring us here. Nor the years I had to work, to work them out. I understand persecution, even if I do not love a Catholic as you say your husband is. I have stayed here because I love this city now, and because it will not allow Catholics here, for I do not want to look upon their faces, ever again. But I am sorry for anyone whose house is taken from him and his wife given to soldiers and all his living and his lifetime's work made useless to him, and made to be a bondsman when it was not his estate as he knew it or expected it. I am sorry for these things, and I think you are very brave, and I will help you."

"Can you?" she whispered.

"Yes, I can. I am not poor now, I have a plantation, outside of Charles Town at Chulifinny, a strange name, is it not, Mary Elisabeth. You should leave Charles Town now, and I will take you there until I can arrange for a sloop to take us to Savannah. And you will do this with no one, except me, so long as you are with me, and prepare yourself to see your husband again, if we may find him."

"I am to be your mistress then?" she asked, her eyes bright. "Should you not ask me?"

"Yes, God help me," he said, "you are, if you will. I would I might be so charitable as not to ask it, but I do ask it. But I will pay you well," he said. "I will pay all your expenses for the trip, and each time what I have just given you. If it is not enough, tell me and I will pay. I do not want you to divide yourself this way any more."

"It is enough," she said. "But I am afraid of the Sea. Can we not go by land?"

"No, my dear," he said, "I do not want you to take so rough a route, in our uncertain weather. There is no way to go except by foot or by horse, and though you have been used to it, you must become unused to it now. And even if we hire a guide, they have been known frequently to lose themselves. I will not take you by land. But the distance by sea is not far, and we will stay close in to land."

She sighed, but she did not protest any more.

He took her to Chulifinny, as he had said, and past the deserted remains of Purrysburg, that scene of death where no one had returned. Two days later he had hired a sloop, and they embarked. The winds, however, turned contrary, and they lost their anchor, beating out at sea all night and with difficulty two days later made their way back into Charles Town Harbour.

"I can't go again," she cried, but nevertheless, she did, for she was as equally afraid now of the wild land, and of meeting Indians. He could have assured her that the ones she met in the coastal swamps would have been friendly, but her fears served his wishes and he let her keep them.

The next day the winds seemed favourable and they sailed to Ashley-Ferry and to Cumbee-Ferry, but the winds becoming again high and contrary as they were crossing the neck of St. Helen's Sound, the oldest of the five sailors cried out suddenly, seeing the mast bend, "Now everyone must take care for himself." As he spoke, the mast fell, and Mary Elisabeth hid her eyes beneath her cloak hood, from the wind and sea rising about her, knowing neither she nor anyone aboard was likely to make the shore by swimming, although Jim Hawkins had taught her to swim.

She bit her lips, remembering the river in which he had taught her, his body white where the sun had not touched it, otherwise nut-brown, and making her strip too, and threatening to take her in the water if she did not swim from him, and then taking her anyway. She wondered if she was remembering these things because she too was to die now, and Diar's pardon with her, her salt tears mingling with the spray and on her lips, and then two men caught the mast, as the pictures hung like lightning, clear in that brief second, in her mind, and pulled it into the boat, while the other three rowed with all their might. In an hour, they were safe on land, and had reached Beaufort on Port-Royal, forty miles from Charles Town three days after they left it.

The contrary winds continued to Tybee Island, gradually diminishing as they went up into the river to Savannah, and with the blind eyes of one who had lost hope of reaching it, Mary Elisabeth arrived in Georgia and let Mr. Belinger lift her from the boat. She could not say a word. He hired horses and a carriage, and put her gently in it, and took her to the Ordinary. He fed her there, though she could hardly eat, and then left her to go early to bed while he enquired out the location of Mr. Smythe's plantation, if it could be discovered, and how it might be reached.

XXX: *Smythe's Plantation*

So Diarmid, having made a temporary truce with Mr. Smythe, went into the far south field and into the wood beyond its edge that extended to the far river branch, and with three other men cut trees and brush to clear another field. At night he came back, not to the small house he had lived in with Hird by the stables, but to the cane huts of the field workers. He was too weary at the end of each day to know or care where or how he slept. He ate the mush of Indian corn set out for him and the strips of bear or deer meat, when someone had shot one, and drank water, and threw himself down on the cane mat to sleep, and slept as soundly as though it had been eiderdown, for the workdays now began early and ended late. He was not chained again, after his release from the post in the field where he had thought to die, but neither was he given a gun. If he saw game, he could do nothing about it, and had to let it go. Neither, when game saw him, could he do anything about it except hollar, and he spent one afternoon in a shadgum tree, treed by a wild pig, and the next day, he was jumped by a bobcat, which the man four trees over, hearing his scream and the noise of the cat, came running and shot off him.

After that, while his back was being dressed, he addressed Mr. Smythe, who had come to see him, on the subject.

"Well, Scot," said Smythe, "I see someone else has ripped your back for you."

Diarmid winced as his owner touched his back, exploring the depths of the claw marks, and did not smile. "It is vinegar again for you, Scot, these marks need disinfecting."

"Go ahead, then," Diarmid said, "what are you waiting for?" and gritted his teeth.

When that was finished, he turned his head to Smythe and said, "I want a gun, sir." If Smythe noticed the concession he did not show he did. "I have seen three bears, which you could use, sir, and which to tell you frankly scare me, nosing about with those little eyes and big scraping claws, and deer past counting, and now this. I shall be finished off one day, before your other men get to me, and then you've lost your man and the game too. Most of these animals climb better than I do. I don't like the eagles either. It is a wild place you've put me in. It's not rabbit country. I'll promise you any assurance that I won't use the gun on you or any of your men or on myself. I could use the axe as well, anyway," he added, his eyebrows cocked, "if I had a mind to it. Scots are trained with battle axes."

Smythe regarded him thoughtfully, and after his next trip into Savannah, brought him a gun. Diarmid also became expert with rocks, reviving a childhood pastime, and killed two snakes with them, where the woods were swampy at the East edge. The third snake he did not see, and it bit him. The man working next him took a knife, and cut the bite deeply, and sucked the blood, ignoring Diarmid's cry and his astonished protests at the treatment, and then cut out the liver of the deer Diarmid had shot that morning the hour before, and put the liver over the wound now flowing freely.

"God!" said Diarmid, faintly, "I shall bleed to death. You have stuck me like a pig."

"Better that than die of snakebite," the other said, his tone grim and worried.

"Stay there," he said, "and don't move. I'll call Rafe and we'll make a litter for you."

"I don't need a litter," Diarmid said, "I can walk."

"No," said the other, "it makes the poison move, if I didn't get all of it."

So they carried Diarmid back, white and in a faint by then from the loss of the blood, still flowing. Smythe had it stanched with an iron, bringing Diarmid out of the faint with a scream, and suggested next time they go about it less drastically. Diarmid was ill for several days, from the treatment as well as the bite. Smythe kept him in the house itself in a room, and came to see him when he had time.

"I am accused of favouritism," he said, smiling.

"I do not see how anyone can say that," Diarmid commented.

"I have put you here because you know things I would like to hear about."

"Like what?" asked Diarmid. "I've nothing I want to speak of, myself."

"I would like to know who you are, and how you lived before the rebellion."

"I lived well," Diarmid said briefly. "Now I do not."

"I know that. I want to know what I do not know. Really, MacLyon; I asking because I would like to know."

"My father was a small king," Diarmid said, slowly, "and I was a small Prince. There were larger ones, of course, but it was enough. I had all that I could want, and when we wanted what we did not have, we took that, if we could. My father's house was larger than your house, with more land and more fruit trees, and much cattle, both the black and the blond, the wood and the stone of it more beautiful, the Library in it larger, and the silver shining and the linens thin.

When I wore the kilt, I wore also French lace, and jewells in it. And I had French wines and brandies to drink as I liked." He laughed mirthlessly at Smythe's face. "You do not believe me. You think as the English do the Highland Scots were illiterate savages who because we fought savagely should be treated like savages. We believed in living well when we were not fighting, and in fighting well when it was the time for that. And we did both, although my father was less on the fighting than some, and he thought the rebellion foolish; but he did not foresee that it would kill us all, as it did. We were not so grand as Keppoch, as the MacDonalds, or Lochiel, but we were grand enough. I had the freedom of the hills all my life, and you cannot conceive what that was. I will not try to tell you. I had tutors, brought in, and I was sent to France a year, to finish my education, after Edinburgh. And that is what you have," he said bitterly.

"If this is so, I do not understand why you were transported like a common man."

"There were others as good as I on the ship I sailed on," Diarmid said, his eyes dark, remembering his disowning, remembering the ship. "I told you, my father was only a little king. He was not one of the grand chiefs. Most of those died, anyway, in the battle, or in the afterwards, or on the scaffold, they told me on the ship. And I had killed two of the King's soldiers, when they killed my father. It would not have counted for excuse. I did not use my name. I don't want to talk about it any more. It is over. It is past. I am here, and I am cutting your trees, and bitten by your snake." He turned his head away and did not speak any more.

"Unfortunately, MacLyon," Smythe said softly, "it is not princes I need, but workers."

"I know that."

"Your mother, MacLyon? Where is she?" Smythe asked curiously, despite his bondsman's tone and his averted face.

"In heaven, I suppose," he said. "She died in the birthing of my brother Coll."

"And your brothers or sisters?"

"I have none such now, none brothers. Sisters perhaps. I had cousins, sister's sons and sister's daughters of my father, but I am the last MacLyon." His face this time did stop Smythe's questioning.

The next day he was well enough to go back to the field being cleared. Smythe however had gotten high boots for him made and for the other men, and he forbade them to take the boots off, despite the heat of the work, or to wear soft moccasin shoes or to go barefoot again, while they worked there.

The months of May, June, and July slipped away. During the winter months, had he known it, the air though unlike the air of his home had not been unlike England: warm at midday, the mornings and evenings sharp, the nights piercing cold. But late spring and summer brought a scorching sun that between ten and four burned fiercely, except that the sea breezes blew too, tempering it. The thunder and lightning especially so terrible to a stranger and which had at first so terrified him could be expected almost every day. He suffered from a discomfort new to him, that was called the prickly heat, a rash in all the moist and sweaty parts of his head and face and body under his hair and his clothes, and that once started, spread; and from the bites of sandflies. He would have liked to take off his shirt, and his hated trousers, but they protected him from the sandflies, and from the rays of the sun which burned his fair skin. The wet cloth, wet with his sweat, cooled in the sea breeze, and muted the rays, and the heat, so he endured the rash. The first hot days he had discarded his shirt, and all but a clout, working without fear of the sun, sent out to clear that week on one of the sea islands. The sun, reflecting back from the sand, had burnt him badly, without his knowing it, and that night he had been delirious with sunburn, calling and crying in the strange fever. For three days his skin was burned all over, red and fiery hot and tender to the touch. Then, with mud applied to it, and time passing, it healed.

"You will be tougher, after this," Smythe had said, when he came to see how he did, lying on the knife-like cane leaves, covered from head to foot with mud. "Your skin won't burn so easily."

But Diarmid had learned that lesson and he kept his shirt and trousers on. The summer passed in this way, and if Mr. Smythe was short of hands to pick bugs and worms off the leaves, in the field, he got a good deal of clearing done. His bondsman cut trees as he would have liked to cut men. In July, when the first tobacco leaves were ready to be picked, he did not disturb Diarmid or the arrangement, but as the skies grew sultrier and stormier, and the leaves ripened faster, he recalled all the clearers, as he had said he would, Diarmid among them.

XXXI: *"I do not work tobacco."*

Diarmid laid aside his axe and his gun, that evening, by the house as he always did, and went without a word into his hut, and lay down on his bed. The next morning he did not appear for work. The overseer came after a time to the door of his hut and called to him:

"MacLyon? Are you sick?"

"No," MacLyon answered, his voice remote.

"Then come out."

Diarmid rose obediently and came out and sat down on the dirt threshold of his hut, his knees bent and loose, and his hands hanging loosely over them. His head was a little bent, and his eyes shut. The overseer in the peace of the preceding months had forgotten Diar's earlier rebellion and it took him a moment to realise he had come up against it again.

"MacLyon" he had said, impatiently, "if you are not sick, what is the matter with you? You are needed in the field."

"I don't work tobacco," MacLyon said, his voice soft but definite.

"O my God!" the overseer said, equally softly. "Is it that again?"

MacLyon did not answer. He shut his eyes again. He was himself tired of the struggle, and had no wish for more discomfort or to be mistreated purposely again, but though he was afraid, for him there was no question of doing otherwise. It was the inner core of his being and all that sustained him.

He heard the overseer speak again. "MacLyon," the voice above his head said, "you will come to the field and you will work tobacco as we all do, and please to make no more question about it."

"No," Diarmid said, his voice a whisper, and waited for the whip to strike him, but no blow came. He heard footsteps leave, and he stayed as he was, having no safe place to go to, not caring to be dragged out of the hut, as he supposed could and would be done to him.

After a time, steps returned, and it was Smythe.

"Stand up, MacLyon," Smythe said curtly. Diarmid slowly stood up, his eyes still lowered.

He felt fingers lift his chin, to look into his face and his eyes, and he spat suddenly and viciously at the face opposite him, his eyes black with fury at being touched so. He thought he would be slapped, but again the blow did not come.

"It is to be this way again?" Smythe said slowly, and almost, it seemed, sadly. "There are some horses one can never break entirely, and they are never of much use. Are you a horse, MacLyon? Is that how you are and all you are?"

Diarmid said nothing. He lifted his eyes briefly and blankly towards the man standing before him attempting to direct him, and then lowered them and stood waiting again, more animal truly than man in the blind dumbness of his instinct for resistance.

"Look at the sky, MacLyon," Smythe said, "look at the clouds boiling up and the leaves bright and ready to be picked. You are wasting my time. Help me," he whispered to the bent face, "and I will make you glad. Do not, and I will make you wish you had. I will fight you every inch of the way until this time there is no inch of fight in you left. As I warned you I would. Well?" he said to the silent figure before him. "What's the answer to be?"

"I do not work tobacco," Diarmid said, his voice soft but distinct. He shut his eyes against the anger pouring against him.

"Take MacLyon to the field," Smythe said curtly. "He will at least go."

His hands were again twisted behind his back, roughly, and secured with small rope. He did not resist, feeling again the ache, once familiar, that he had grown used to being free of. He felt a rope then around his neck, a noose, bringing a year-old memory, and his eyes flew open in surprised terror, though he did not utter a sound or plead. He had not thought Smythe could or would do such a thing to him, and he found he had been right. He was merely led by the halter the long way to the field, forced to keep up with the man leading him, the noose drawing tight when he stumbled or tripped.

He stood then in the field among the broad leaved plants, the rope now hanging about his neck. He shut his eyes against the eyes staring at him, at "Smythe's Scotchman" out of favour and in trouble again. The flies settled on him, standing there, unable to brush them off, biting him, and he shook his head against them like an angry bull.

He stood there all that day in the sun, while Smythe's workers, Smythe among them, cut the leaves that were ready, and tied them, working in frantic haste against the clouds building up, too busy to look any more at the figure standing near them, carrying the cut bound leaves to the curing shed Smythe had had erected during the early summer out of the timber Diarmid and the four had cut. The storm that day did not break but passed over, with a great show of thunder and several cracks of lightning, darkening the field and splattering down a few drops. They could see it in the distance, letting itself down in a grey curtain over the river swamp. In the evening Diarmid was led home by the neck, and his hands still bound, put again in the house with Hird who grinned and lay with him, helpless and repulsed.

In the morning he was not fed, but was led out again into the field. He stood the sun for two hours, and then his spirit gave up within him and he fainted. If anyone saw him fall, no one had time to care. He was revived by water flooding over him, from a cloudburst that had broken overhead. The day had turned as dark as night, and the dry plants rustled about him. His mouth was full of mud and water, and he raised himself up a little and spat it out, his head splitting with pain and the noise of the thunder cracking about him. He saw a bolt, inches thick, hovering in the air, it seemed a few feet from him, and another struck the flue of the curing shed, and fell in orange sparkles across the roof and on the ground. Then the rain fell again, in a shower of hail ripping the leaves and pelting his face and head so that he crouched on the ground, his face hidden, among the little pellets whitening the surface of the muddy soil. After a few minutes the hail ceased, as quickly as it had begun, and was followed by a second cloudburst like a grey sheet, beating him down against the ground, drowning him in the thick wet air he could not breathe in, as though he had been forced under water and held under with a giant hand.

There was no one in the field, but he could not have walked away, bound as if to a stake by the force of the wind and rain falling from the low grey-green roiling clouds. He forced his way to his knees, choking and gasping for breath, the rain beating and forcing itself into his eyes beneath their closed lids, his nostrils, his gasping mouth, his ears.

"O God," he cried, his voice lost in the roar, "help thy servant," and then he bent his head again inward towards his knees, trying to find a place where he could breathe, in the little cave his back made, crouched above the flooding field. After a time, the rain ceased to fall in a solid sheet, like full buckets emptied, and he turned over and lay in the mud, his bound hands behind him, gasping in the freshened charged air, breathable again, and lost consciousness from fatigue in what was neither a sleep nor a faint.

When the men returned to the fields, they passed him without a word or a gesture, lying in the mud, half-covered with it, looking as if he were dead. No one had time for him, not Smythe nor the overseer nor anyone else, picking up and propping with canes the plants that had been beaten down, picking up and washing the leaves the hail had stripped and flattened in the mud. When dark fell, Smythe stopped beside him, felt his cold face and discovered there was breath in him, still tough, and had him carried home slung over the back of a horse.

He gave him to Hird to wash and to feed and to do with as he liked, and the next morning he came himself for Diarmid who was lying naked under the sheet, his wet clothes not yet dry. He looked up at his master, his eyes hurt with shame and blank with pain, past any kind of resistance now except his passive stubborn refusal.

"Get up, MacLyon," Smythe said, his voice without pity or any expression, and handed him a pair of breeches and a shirt and his boots. When Diarmid had pulled them on, he signalled to the Scot to walk beside him, back out into the field beside him, his hands this time unbound.

Smythe did not speak on the walk out. He made no attempt to argue or to cajole or to persuade. At the edge of the fields, he stood and looked at his damaged crop and then he turned to the indentured Scot.

"We have reached an end now," he said, "of many things, and of my patience, MacLyon. I am asking you now to go into my field and to do whatever work the time requires as I require it, and as your indentures state that you will do. Go now and let us have have no more words and difficulties about it."

MacLyon stood with his feet apart, his hands hanging

loose, and lifted his eyes black with rage and pain and once more deliberately spat. He had hardly done it before the back of Smythe's hand hit him full across the mouth. His glance did not waver and he did not lift his hands to his bruised mouth, but deliberately spat again.

"Take off your boots," Smythe only said then, and Diarmid, sick with humiliation and fear, obeyed.

Smythe turned then from him and summoned his overseer who took Diarmid over to the side of the curing shed, and put his old chains on him that had been brought there by the overseer earlier, as if in expectation of the event, and hooked the center of the chains on his hands to a hook on the side of the barn used to hang the stalks downward from for measuring their length. He could neither stand nor kneel, and he hung, his weight divided between his wrists and his bent feet, while the overseer, by Smythe's order, paraded his workers past him on the way into the field, each in turn given the overseer's whip with which to strike him, his shirt and trousers ripped apart by the overseer, some performing the act reluctantly, others with evident zeal. The whip remained near him, and as each sheaf of bound leaves was brought to be hung in the barn, the man bringing it might strike again, if he chose, "Smythe's Scotchman," some choosing, some not. Against his will Diarmid found himself cringing as the afternoon wore on, when footsteps approached, with the not knowing whether they would bring a blow or not or what severity. He was reduced finally to helpless crying and soft swearing, undistinguishable from praying, the tears running from his eyes, when Smythe came with the overseer and had the overseer unhook him. He fell helplessly to the ground, dust this time after the dry hot day, and hard.

"Had enough?" Smythe asked. "You'll work for me tomorrow?"

Diarmid could not speak. He was brought to his feet by the overseer, his eyes bloodshot and withdrawn, but as they focussed on Smythe they became wild again with anger, and he again spat, feebly, viciously in defiance. But his flesh cringed as he saw Smythe reach for the overseer's whip, and pushed only lightly with the butt end of the handle, he lost his unsteady balance and toppled over again on the ground.

"So where is the dignity now?" Smythe asked. "Work for me, MacLyon. Enough of this."

"No," Diarmid whispered, his soft voice savage.

"You will change your mind yet," Smythe remarked, his voice even.

"No," Diarmid whispered again, "Not to an English bastard of nothing."

"We will yet see," Smythe said. He had the overseer take Diarmid inside the shed, where Diarmid found preparations had been made as though anticipating his refusal.

"I had hoped not to use this," Smythe said, "but you see that I am ready. You can yet go back with me."

"No," Diarmid said, his voice flat.

A part of the barn across from the door had been set aside for him, on the raised floor to which the steps mounted. There was a small table, on which he saw a supper lay, meat, soup, milk, peaches, bread, water, and a chair, and a post supporting the arch of the roof.

"You'll not bribe me," he said, his voice strained, wondering if he was to be bound within scent and sight of the food and out of reach of it.

"I do not intend to try," Smythe said. "Make him comfortable," he said to the overseer, and walked away to the shadowy farther end of the barn, among the hanging leaves bound together in bunches, the stalks descending in tiers, looking up at them.

The overseer put a grease on Diarmid's back, as he had done once before, and gave him a clean pair of breeches to put on, and a clean shirt to replace the ripped bloodied one when he could bear the touch or became cold, and a pair of shoes. He took his hammer and mallet then and fastened a length of chain at one end to the shackles on Diarmid's feet

and at the other fastened it to about the post. It was long
enough for Diarmid to stretch out and lie down on the floor,
where two blankets lay, or to sit at the table and chair, or to
reach a bucket placed beside it.

"For your wastes," the overseer said. "Mr. Smythe don't
want you dirtying up his barn."

"This is your house now," Smythe said, coming up behind
them. "You will live here and you will die here, unless you
work for me. I am tired of your pride, as if no one else had
any, MacLyon, I have been patient long enough with you. I
am going to forget about you now, unless you choose yourself to have me remember you. I shan't starve you, and I am
not going to abuse you or try to force you by that way any
more. It demeans us both, and takes us nowhere. But I'll not
come back to see you, unless you send for me. You'll stay
here, unless you change your mind, and someone will bring
you food and water. You will be comfortable enough. For my
part, I shall see to the filling of my barn, without you. When
the rafters are full, and the barn ready, unless you have indicated to one of the men coming in and out that you are
willing to assume your responsibilities towards me, having
forgotten you are here, I shall proceed to finish the caulking
of my barn, which is done now except for the sealing of the
door, and to cure my tobacco. Think it over, MacLyon. You
should have several days yet. Myself, I would think it over
well."

He turned without any more word and left with the overseer, taking the lantern with him, and Diarmid was left in the
waning light to eat his supper, after two days without it.

In the morning he felt better, able to look around him,
able to resent his confining, and the restraint of his move-
ments. He was treated better than he had been for several
days, breakfast brought to him.

"It's the life," Rodgers said, slapping it down. "Food, and
no work."

When he returned that evening bringing Diarmid's supper,

however, the word had spread of what was to happen to the recalcitrant Scot, and he was the object in the afternoon of furtive glances his way from men bringing in the tobacco sheafs to hang. He did not understand their quality, and ignored them, his eyes lowered or staring unseeingly ahead of him and through them. He did not know what the curing of tobacco involved, but Rodgers that evening enlightened him.

"Don't buck Mr. Smythe any more," he said to the Scot, his rough voice curiously pleading. "You have gone too far too often. I don't like you, MacLyon, and I enjoyed the whipping you got yesterday, for you deserved it, but I don't like this and I don't want it. We none of us do."

"Stop it, then," Diarmid said, more horrorstruck than he chose to let out. "There are enough of you."

Rodgers shook his head. "No. You can stop it yourself if you have a mind to. I have one more year and my indenture is up, and I will have my axe and can get land and be a freeholder. You can do the same. I'm not going to be an outlaw for any stubborn fool, and lose that, if you care so little yourself for your own life. Why should we work, and you not? You can suit yourself then, and I won't waste being sorry over you."

The days dragged by, at once too slow and too fast, and the barn filled gradually with the flat hanging sheaves, until they hung over Diarmid's head, and about him and filled the space to the door, absorbing the air and making a gold-green dusk all the day, stifling even with the door open. Diarmid did not speak, and no one spoke to him, not even Rodgers who came to bring his breakfast, and empty his bucket, not looking at him, as the sheaves continued to be brought and hung.

That afternoon Mary Elisabeth arrived at the plantation.

XXXII: *Diar's Wife:*
Journey's End

SHE SWEPT UP, AS WELL AS ONE MIGHT SWEEP UP, THE
ROUGH ENTRANCE ROAD TO THE HOUSE IN MR. BELINGER'S
HIRED CARRIAGE AND HORSES, MR. BELINGER BESIDE HER,
AND SHE LOOKED LIKE A LADY OF CONSEQUENCE, THOUGH A
young one.

Smythe watched the approach from a window with interest. He had come in from the field early, the work almost
finished, and was at ease in his room. He watched the lady
and the gentleman alight, and went down the steps to receive
them himself at his door.

"I am Mrs. MacLyon," she said, going directly to the point,
her soft-lashed eyes on him. "I understand you have my husband here as an indentured bondsman, working for you. I
have come from England bringing him the King's pardon. I
hope I can arrange with you his release."

"You take my breath away," he said simply and truthfully,
sitting down in a chair. "In many ways," he added. "Please
do not make me rude, will you not sit too? Who then is this
gentleman?"

"Belinger," Belinger remarked, his eyes watchful, "from Charles Town, Belinger of Chulifinny."

"Why have you come through Charles Town?" he asked irrelevantly, "if you come from England? Why not direct to Savannah?"

"You do not know that I have not," she said gently. "Are you stalling for time, Mr. Smythe?"

"Yes," he said frankly, his eyes fixed on her in admiration. "I cannot imagine how you know my name, although I see you do, or that I have this MacLyon."

She sighed slightly, and as if with an unconscious hand disarranged the lace slightly at the low neck of her dress.

"I will tell you another time," she said. "I am most anxious to see my husband. Is he here?"

"I have no MacLyon working for me," he said truthfully, wondering if she would cry.

She looked at him thoughtfully, in silence, as if assessing his answer, her grey eyes on his.

"I have come a very long way, Mr. Smythe," she said, her voice soft, "I have travelled up and down the length of Scotland and of England, several times, I have crossed the Atlantic Ocean to Boston, and I have travelled from Boston to Annapolis and from there to your plantation. I do not know what your reasons may be for wanting to play games with me now, but I know that you brought my husband with you from Annapolis to your plantation, I even know the boat you brought him on, and I know that 'Smythe's Scotchman' is a byword in Savannah. I am not a fool, Mr. Smythe, and I would like to know why you wish to make me one. If my husband is dead, which I will not easily believe, please tell me so in plain terms."

"Very well, Mrs. MacLyon," Smythe said, "I will give you the answer you want. It is true what I said. MacLyon is not working for me. But I do have your husband here. And if you like, I will have him brought here, and you may talk to him."

"*Brought* here?" she repeated faintly.

"Brought here," he said again. "You appear to know something of my difficulties with your husband's unwillingness to fulfill his bond. Your coming may serve to help me. It is possible that if he knows he has a pardon, that he may be induced then to finish his years properly in the spirit in which he should."

Belinger had warned her on the drive, after the stories she had heard in Savannah, that she might find Smythe reluctant to have his bondsman bought out, and that the pardon only affected her husband's return. The situation did not dismay her or particularly surprise her then, and she said simply, "Yes, I would like to see my husband."

"I will have him sent for then," Smythe said, surprised at her coolness, "and while we wait, for he is in the field, I will offer you refreshment if I may."

An hour passed, while they waited, and the afternoon clouds built up, and the room darkened. Conversation was mainly between the two men, about aspects of plantation life. The subject of buying out Diarmid's indenture had been approached and Smythe had dismissed it.

"No," he said flatly, "there is no amount of money you can offer me that will be sufficient inducement. I do not need the money, I need the man. There are none available here to indenture."

"You could take the money and buy another in Annapolis, or in New Bern."

"I have not the time. I have your husband already. I cannot believe with this pardon he will continue his stubbornness, and I cannot believe you will withhold the knowledge of it from him."

"I will go myself then again to Annapolis."

"I might not approve the man," Smythe said. "I prefer to do my own hiring. The seas are getting rougher, and you do not know when a transport may be due in or in what port. A foolish idea, Mrs. MacLyon, and not one I am willing to give countenance to or offer hope on. But," he said, "I am not the heartless villain I may appear. I want your husband's body, as I take it you do, and I do not see why we may not share it between us, in different ways. Persuade him to the fulfilling of his indenture, and you may live here with him while he serves it, without yourself working for me."

"You are a generous man," she said, her tone unreadable.

"And you are a remarkable woman," he said, his tone quite readable. "I stand amazed at your feats, which I would hesitate to do myself. And amazed at your existence, of which I had heard nothing."

"I do not see why you should expect to have heard," she said, tho' inwardly shaken.

"I have heard from time to time considerably of other things. And so it was true," he added thoughtfully, "what MacLyon told me, about his not participating, and you do bring a pardon. It is remarkable. May I see it?"

"You may see it," she said, "but you may not hold it, and I must tell you that Mr. Belinger carries a pistol."

"I carry one myself," he said smoothly, and looked with interest at the paper she unfolded, not attempting to take it. "Remarkable," he said again, "remarkable. *Diarmid*, is it? Yet another name. Well," he said, "put your paper up, Mrs. Mac-Lyon, you have nothing on that score to fear from me. I do not want at all to take it from you. Quite the contrary. I think in fact it may serve to take me out of a difficulty of my own."

"I have not seen my husband for a year now," she said, pursuing her own thoughts, not interested in his difficulty, "longer even. May I see my husband first alone, in another room, please, just myself and him. Will you do me this favour, at the least?"

"I will do that," he said, "I will indeed do that. He does not know why he has been sent for, Mrs. MacLyon. Would you prefer that I not tell him?"

"Yes, please," she said, "yes, I would." She sighed. "You are most kind."

Her thoughts kept her silent then, her hands trembling and her throat dry, her stomach sick, at the remeeting at last to take place, not knowing what she would be called upon to say, unable to visualise what she had come so far for, and worked for so long and so patiently.

Smythe's eyes turned toward her from time to time, and her agitation did not escape him or her whiteness.

"You are ill, I think, Mrs. MacLyon," he said quietly, with concern. "May I take you to a room to lie down? You have had a shock, and my attitudes have not helped, I know."

She shook her head in demurral.

"Then let me bring you a restorant," he pursued, and he did so, which she took gratefully, her fingers shaking.

The rain still held off, and after an hour's waiting, perhaps a quarter hour more, Hird appeared at the door to speak to Smythe.

"He is here," Smythe said, "and I have had him put to wait in a small room down the hall." He dismissed Hird, who put his head into the room where Diarmid was to inform Diarmid with some glee that Smythe had visitors and he thought Diarmid's indentures might be being rebought.

"I will take you now, Mrs. MacLyon," Smythe said, indicating to Belinger he should wait. She put her hand on his arm, her gloved fingers resting lightly on it, and felt his pulse beneath them, but tho' she made an inward note of it, wondering if it might be put to account, she gave no sign that she noticed. They walked down the hall and to a closed door, where he motioned her to wait, and went inside himself.

MacLyon was sitting at a chair by the table in the room, his face tired and white and drawn, and he did not offer to get up when Smythe entered the room.

"You have thought better of it then," he said tiredly.

"No," Smythe said shortly, "I have not. You have a visitor, a lady to see you."

He took the key he had brought for MacLyon's fetters, noting he seemed hardly interested in the information and incurious, and unlocked the chains off the Scot, and put them in a cupboard whose door he locked. "Politeness," he said, "a courtesy to the lady's sensibilities. Rodgers is outside the window, MacLyon, and I am outside the door."

"I understand you," MacLyon said, indifferently. "I don't see what the trouble is for. Hird has told me what the lady wants, I cannot see the difference."

"Has he now?" said Smythe. He opened the door, beckoned to Mary Elisabeth with his hand, and closed the door behind her as she went in.

XXXIII: *The Remeeting*

S HE STOOD AGAINST THE DOOR, HER BREATH CAUGHT IN HER
THROAT, LOOKING AT HIM. SHE HAD TIME TO LOOK, FOR
HIS HEAD WAS A LITTLE BENT, THE LONG LASHES OVER
HIS EYES LYING AGAINST HIS CHEEKS, AND HIS FACE A LITTLE
turned away. She had wondered what she would think, and
how he would seem, if she would know him or if he would be
much changed. She had not been so close to him, with him
conscious, since they had stood in their nakedness outside his
house, and he had spoken his bitter words to her, three days
after his careless seizure of her person and his careless rape
upon it. And since then his image had with few days been con-
tinually in her mind and before her eyes, particularly as she
had seen him the day he was taken from his death. And now he
was here before her, the man himself, and he seemed simply
like Diar, no whit changed, his chest rising and falling with
his breath beneath the coarse unbleached shirt he wore, one
hand with its fingers resting on the table, his face pale but no
paler than she had seen it in the court and outside the prison,
his lips in a thin line, unsmiling, but they had not been smiling
either when she last saw them.

She could not speak or find her voice, and her eyes filled at the sight of him, alive and sitting in a room where she was and seeming unhurt. He raised his eyes then, when the woman, whoever she was, continued not to speak, looking at her indifferently in the half-light the approaching storm cast, and she saw he did not know her.

She did not know then what to say, or whether to laugh or cry at the sad absurdity of it. Then she remembered the wig she was wearing, and lifted her hand and loosened it from her head, with the little hat, shaking out her short hair, the tears spilling out of her eyes.

He watched the strange action, his unlaughing eyes registering no particular expression and no interest, and then, slowly, he recognised her. She watched it cross his face.

"O my God," he said, in his soft voice, startled into profanity, or a prayer, "it's Mary Elisabeth Grant. What are you doing here, Mary Elisabeth? What do you want? Come for revenge?"

He seemed still hardly interested.

"Mrs. MacLyon, Diar," she said, her voice shaking, correcting him. "I did not think you would have forgotten me, or that, but I see you did."

"It's been a long time, now, Mary Elisabeth. What do you want?" His soft voice even now was without interest and without expression, and in the face of his lack of emotion opposite her own, she stood mute, helpless in the feeling shaking her that left him untouched.

"They told me," he said, when she did not speak, "someone told me, that a lady and a gentleman had come to buy me. Is that true, Mary Elisabeth? Have you come to buy me? Do you like to own people too?" His voice still fell caressingly as a year ago like a brook over stones over the *r*'s and consonants of her double name, but his face and voice were both unbending.

"I have tried to buy your indenture, but Mr. Smythe will not sell it," she said, startled at his strange question into the fact.

"There is no one I would rather less be bought by," he said briefly. "Give Smythe my thanks." His voice in its coldness held her at arm's length.

"You misunderstand me," she said.

"Do I?" his voice asked, a slight inflection in it.

The tone reached her and she took herself in hand, realising in these moments, before his hard, cold, indifferent eyes, that whatever her hidden hopes she had indeed done what she had disinterestedly, as she had said she was willing to do, and that there was to be nothing in it for her at all. So be it, then she thought, her eyes on his face. So be it, then. And then, with the knowledge that her love gave her, she knew that he had been hurt in ways she did not know, besides those that she did, and she put aside the anger rising in her, and her own needs.

"I have come to bring you the King's pardon," she said, "Diar, I have it here. That is why I have come."

He looked at her, and he did not seem to understand what she had said.

"Diar," she said then, frightened at the strangeness and the whiteness of his already white face, after the days shut in the tobacco barn, "do you understand what I said?"

"I understand well enough," he said, and the tone of his voice eluded her. "What am I to say? Thank you? You seem to have survived. Have you come to own you have done me wrong? Well, Miss Grant? That you did me wrong? Is it finally the amends due me you come bringing for what you did to me, ruining myself and my father and my house?"

She gasped at his attack, in shock and sudden fury, that he should still somehow manage to blame her for his misfortunes, but she collected herself enough to speak.

"Diar," she cried, "how can you say that still, and here, when you know, and no one better, it is no whit true."

"I have no thing then to say to you. I do not know why you should come here."

"Diar," she said, "I have brought you a pardon. I told you."

"Why?" he asked. "Why put yourself out? It is of no use to

me here. Why interfere?" He looked at her curiously then, seeming somewhat to see her. "I am thinking," he said slowly, "you may have interfered before." He looked at her, and under his eyes she began to flush. "I am thinking it is so," he said again. "But let me tell you, if it was you, Mary Elisabeth, who cheated me a second time of my rightful death, making me die a thousand times since, in some way every day and in all ways worse than a brief choking, I will not be thanking you. If you come for that, it is disappointed you will find yourself. I am not thanking you at all for it. I am cursing you for it rather. Was it you?" He looked at her sharply, and she flushed again, going both pale and red.

"It was you, wasn't it," he stated rather than asked, and she nodded her head dumbly. He drew in his breath in a sharp deep sigh and then he let it out hopelessly. "I could never escape you, could I? It was a true revenge, was it not." His voice rose in a sharp cry. "Why did you do it, Mary Elisabeth, why? I did not never hurt you so much. Why would you *fool* with me? Why could you not let me alone, just the once, long enough to let them have it done for me, when I could not do it myself?" He put his face and his head then in his hands.

She could not doubt then, seeing his face and hearing his voice and the bitterness ravaging both, that what he said was true, that he meant what he said. She stood stricken, a little way from him.

"Would you have truly rather died, Diar?" she asked brokenly.

"Yes," he said simply.

"Oh, God," she said then, "oh God, what did I do to you?"

"You have put me in hell," he said, "as I suppose you meant to. And I have only stayed in it, for fear of having it eternally. You at least could not do that to me."

"No," she whispered, "oh, Diar, no. I meant well. Truly, I meant well."

"Did you?" he said, his voice dull. "I cannot believe it." He looked at her then searchingly. "But it was no mean feat, all the same, to accomplish it. How did you do it, Mary Elisabeth, when others could not? And a pardon too? All that, a little girl like you? Not alone, I am thinking."

"No, Diar," she said bravely, "not alone."

"And not for nothing, I am thinking either."

"No, Diar," she said, her voice low, "not for nothing."

"You have a gentleman with you now. I remember they told me that."

"Yes, Diar," she said steadily.

He looked at her with eyes full of clear disgust, his eyes seeming to strip her and throw her away, but on her still. "I am thinking you did not mind those soldiers. I want none of your pardon. I want none of you. I do not know why you should come here."

"Diar," she said, "you may pretend to forget it, but I do not, that I am your wife wedded by you and bedded—"

"Bedded by too many. And you are too familiar with my name—all my names." She gasped. "Mrs. MacLyon," he said formally, "if you will have it so, tho' I do not, I could never abide a whore. Have you used my name publicly, without my giving you leave, and used yourself so? Why did you do it, Mary Elisabeth?"

She looked at him helplessly, remembering all that had happened to him that she had herself seen, and to her, by him and through him, and then she said simply, despairing of reaching to him or reasoning with him or convincing him, "You have a bonny body, Diarmid MacLyon, I did not want it spoilt," and turned and walked away.

She did not look back. She had left the piece of paper and the money on the table, but as she opened the door, facing into Smythe who was waiting she felt something strike her in the small of the back.

His face shocked, Smythe bent and picked the little bag up and returned it to Diar's wife, who was biting her lip to keep from crying, as Diar, his face white with rage, his eyes blazing, limped about the table, the paper in his hand, thrusting it into hers that would not receive it.

"MacLyon," Smythe shouted, his own anger rising, in warning.

"I will take none money and none papers from a Lowland hussy, that is no wife of mine," Diarmid cried in a fury. "Do not let her at me again!"

Smythe's face, the blood rising darkly in it, looked as though he were ready to strike the Scot, and Mary Elisabeth, crying, took the paper from MacLyon, her stricken eyes briefly on his stern ones, and then she put her hands on Smythe's chest to hold him back.

"No," she whispered, "no, don't hurt him any more. Leave him alone. Please take me out."

"Rodgers," Smythe shouted, and as the man came running towards him, he said, giving him the key and leading Mary Elisabeth into the hall, "Get Hird and restrain that Scot, he has gone mad."

She fought back the tears, and attempted to smile, her eyes blind.

"Oh," she said, "I've left my wig, and my hat."

"You look very nice without them," Smythe said sincerely. "Why did you take them off? I'll have Hird fetch them when the Scot is gone."

"He did not know me," she whispered, "with them on."

Smythe was speechless.

"We were only married for a day," she added, trying to excuse her husband, "and so much has happened since, and come between us. It is no wonder."

The storm chose that moment to break, with a great crashing chord of thunder, and with a sudden impulse, she screamed and clung to Smythe as though in terror of the noise and the light flashing through the dark hall. Her breasts were warm and beating against him, palpitating as he thought with terror, and her nearness took his discretion from him. He found her mouth, which seemed to resist him, and held it and her before she pulled herself away.

"I—I beg your pardon, Mrs. MacLyon," he said in confusion, stammering in his embarrassment. "I cannot imagine how that happened. You must not think I will take such advantage of you again, or try to."

"Why not?" she said then, and put her arms around his neck.

He gasped, and then he grinned, and without another word, he picked her up, his hand under her skirt, and pushed open the door to another room, and carried her in, and kicked the door shut. He carried her to the bed of the guest room and laid her down. Without a word he put a leg over her thigh, under her skirts, over her drawers, and himself above her, as if to see how far at once she meant him to go, his hands behind her, and his lips on hers and his tongue inside. She lay quite passive, her head thrown a little back, all of her relaxed, while he explored, and then she said, her voice clear, pushing him a little back,

"Do you like what you find, Mr. Smythe?"

"Yes," he said, "I think I do."

"Then I think we had better talk before we go any farther with it."

"Talk?" he said, surprised. "What about?"

"About what I am worth?" she said. "What do you take me for?"

"I take you for a hussy," he said, "as MacLyon said, and a damned beautiful one."

"You are both mistaken," she said, "I am not a hussy. I want my husband's freedom, I have used what I had."

"Damned bit," he said, frustrated, "I can take you right now for no price, in my house. Don't you know it? I locked the door."

"You did not," she said, "but you can lock it now if you like. I do not believe you will do me any violence, Mr. Smythe, against my will. You are an honourable man, and a man of great control."

"What do you want then?" he said. "Be quick about it."

"I want Diarmid's indenture."

"You are mad, woman. I would not sell it. Why give it for what I can take? Besides, the man don't want you."

She put her hands under him against him, thrusting back. "I want to buy them," she said.

"Oh, God," he said anguished, "you bit. I will tell you then, one year off the six years left me, for it now, and no more bargaining. Afterwards I will talk."

"Done," she said, "get off me and let me take my drawers." She did, and he did then. She shut her eyes and gave herself completely to him, as if he had been Diar, and as if Diar were not three doors down still.

"Oh, lord," he said sighing, "you beautiful, beautiful bit. They do not make them like you in Savannah, not for me. I count the year cheap."

"Do you?" she said. "Let me up. Mr. Belinger is waiting."

She arranged herself as best she could, and he did likewise, while the rain poured about them, and they came out of the room as Diarmid was led out in his chains, his arms held by Rodgers on one side and Hird on the other. He saw the two of them, his gaze startled, then freezing. He spat contemptuously on the floor before them, and then, his face like a mask he turned from her, and walked shuffling down the hall.

She turned to Smythe. "Is that necessary?" she asked. "Is a servant to be chained?"

"He is a very troublesome man," Smythe said. "I wonder I keep him. He will never, I think, my dear, after this, have you back." His voice was slightly questioning. "There was a time we got along, after a fashion, but it has passed. He will never, I think, forgive you this with me."

"No," she agreed. "I want all the same to buy his indenture out."

"Why, my dear?" he said gently.

"Because he will not take the pardon without it," she said. "And he will die as he is now."

"I think he may," Smythe agreed. "I think he well may.

Well," he said, "it is raining too hard for you to leave. Surely your Mr. Belinger, is that his name, will see that. I will put you in separate rooms, being a moral man, and I will come to you tonight. We will talk of it then quietly, and see if we cannot come to an agreement."

XXXIV: *A Gift*

M<small>R. BELINGER WAS NOT HAPPY AT BEING PUT IN A SEPARATE ROOM ON THE OTHER SIDE OF HIS HOST, SOME WAY REMOVED FROM DIAR'S WIFE, BUT HE COULD NOT VERY WELL OBJECT, SHE BEING MRS. MACLYON AND</small> his host being an honourable man. He had to acquiesce, both in staying the night and in the arrangement of rooms, and being tired, he fell asleep and did not hear his host's door open when he went to join Mary Elisabeth.

He was surprised to find her asleep. He put his candle down, in the damp stuffy air following the thunderstorm, took his dressing gown off, and sure of himself, slipped naked into the bed beside her. He had not misjudged his girl. She did not scream, tho' she woke, but turned and put her arms about him.

"You were asleep," he said, surprised, kissing her hair.

"Why not," she murmured, "I was tired."

He kissed her face, and startled, found it wet.

"But of course," she murmured. "Should I not? My husband abuses me, and then I have to be abused by the man who has abused him. It seems to me I may cry."

"Well, be careful," he said, "or you will put me off. I don't like tears. Can't abide 'em. I liked the way you didn't cry this afternoon."

"And you knew I had cause."

"Yes," he said, "I knew," knowing better than she did how much cause from his side.

"Is Diarmid still chained?"

"Yes, my dear, chained and down cellar. Tomorrow he goes back to the field. He will be gone before you wake. Are you going to cry again?"

"No," she said, "it would be no use. I am going to fight."

"Who?" he asked.

"You," she said.

He laughed, amused.

"I do not find it amusing," she said.

"I have not very much to amuse me," he said soberly, "I have had a hard month. Storms and a shortage of workers. You are the only thing remotely amusing to come along at all."

"Oh," she said. "Well, then, I am glad. I have no wish for anyone to have a hard time." She turned to him and kissed him. "Not even you."

"Do you do this so easily with everyone?" he asked, amazed, and a little aghast, as well as pleased.

"Yes," she said simply, "if they can give me what I need and will give it, I give them whatever they seem to need that I can."

"And you want MacLyon's indenture," he said, not really asking.

"Yes," she said, "I need it and you can give it. You have told me he will not work. You will find life much more amusing without such a thorny person as Diarmid in a bad mood about—I should myself. But you don't have to give it. If you let me go away with Mr. Belinger tomorrow, and with Diarmid, Mr. Belinger will buy the papers from you. I have not enough, myself, to do that and still give Diarmid his passage money. But if you do not want to do that, and I have met men who did not, you can give me the indentures, just for myself, for the use of me, and I will stay with you."

"You will," he commented. "And your husband? Will he like that?"

"You have seen," she said.

"Well," Smythe said, "I shall have to look into the matter more before I decide."

"You may look," she said, and let him pull the sheet down. She was dressed in a shift, which he slipped up slowly and then from her, in the candlelight.

He pulled her to him then and there, and without a by your leave, took her. She did not resist him, to his surprise, though she did not this time act with him.

"You are displeased?" he asked.

"A little," she said. "Not much. I thought we were first to agree. But then I made a gift."

"I can make gifts too," he said. "I am not the hard man MacLyon thinks me, nor that you. I can make gifts too. You may have MacLyon, Scot-free, without paying anything more for him, you or Mr. Belinger. I hope you will stay with me awhile, but I will not require it of you in any way."

"Oh, sir," she cried, turning to him in true joy and gratitude and relief, "you are a good man. If Diarmid will have me, you will understand I will want to go with him," she gave a small shaky laugh, "but I think it is quite certain now he will not, and then I will stay with you if you like."

"I will like very much. He has been always a stubborn fool, and it is only what he deserves."

"I wish you would tell me about Diarmid here."

"No," he said, "it would hurt you too much to hear. It has even hurt me. He is a very stubborn Scot. I have never met his like before. He has also, I am afraid, from time to time made me angry."

"I know," she said meekly, "Diarmid is like that. Let us not talk any more of Diarmid now," she said, "for I see it does

not please you and I want now only to please you." He blew
out the candle then, and let her please him, as she did.

The next morning, she sent Belinger away. He was unhappy about it, but she was firm, and there was very little he
could do about it.

"I must change now," she said. "I cannot help what I have
to do. You told me I should at least stay with one man only.
You cannot help me, any more, for we are here, and this
Smythe will simply not sell them to you or to me. But he will
give them. So I must stay and give something too." She
caught hold of the collar of his coat and laid her head against
it, for she was genuinely fond of him, and he had helped her
greatly. "I shall never forget you, Mr. Belinger," she whispered. "I never shall. I shall always love you."

"And I you, Mary Elisabeth," he said. In the end, there
was nothing for it but for him to go away. He went, sadly
and reluctantly, having never seen Diarmid, and left Diarmid's wife behind.

XXXV: *The Shed*

I

"WILL YOU GIVE ME THE INDENTURES NOW?" SHE ASKED, HER EYES PLEADING, AFTER LUNCH, AFTER BELINGER HAD LEFT.

"No," HE SAID, "I AM AFTER ALL A HARD MAN. I WILL GIVE them to you, as I said, but not today. He is too proud, he will not bend. I say, he can wait, and wonder, a while longer. It will do him good. I did not like that scene yesterday."

She had perforce to wait. She did not ask him again for the papers, for she knew the ways of men well by now, and she did believe in his own time he would give them to her, as he had said. And if he should suddenly choose after all not to, she saw no way of forcing him.

The third day after Belinger's departure, he handed them to her. He had taken his part into Savannah, unknown to her during one day and had had the record made of its cancelling out.

"I happen," he said, "under the circumstances to hold Diarmid's piece as well. You can give the both to him. It should give him pleasure."

She wondered herself, for she knew Diarmid would know how she came by them.

He went with her, the two of them riding, across the fields, he stopping to pass the word to the overseer that from that time on Diarmid was not to be touched or disturbed. "Don't feed him, don't go near him, don't use the barn," he said, "until the Scot has vacated it himself."

"It is a pretty day, Mary Elisabeth," he said, as they rode on. "The weather is mild, and it does not look yet as if it will break today. A good day for beginnings. As all days are, but this one particularly."

She was unlike herself and unusually nervous. He gave her a little push.

"Go on, my dear. This hesitating is not like you. He is there, across the field, in the shed there. Take this key to him, in fact, take both. I trust in vindictiveness he will not burn my shed down. You may tell him, if you like, that I have been a week now ready to begin curing, and I will be more than grateful for him to vacate my premises and my shed, so that I can commence. I have been hard put to find excuses already for the delay."

So she got down from the horse, which he tethered for her to a tree, and began to walk across the field among the stubble of the plants in the warm sun towards it. The door was closed, but not locked, and she pulled it open, blinded by the sun, unable in the dim inside to see, though seen. She stood there, waiting for her eyes to clear, until she could make out Diarmid sitting in the chair, his hands and elbows in their chains resting on the surface of the table, the dim shapes of the tobacco leaves in their tipped bunches looming downwards from the dusky rafter beams.

II

She could hardly breathe in the close stuffy pungent air, even near the door that she left wide open, and she wondered that he could. The sunlight outside poured in in a square about her, breaking the gloom, and the freshness of the day outside and its air. She stood silently, letting her eyes accustom to the dimness, taking in the post, and the heavy chain on the floor, and the empty plate on the table, and the water jug. She did not speak, nor did he, their eyes on one another, hers wary, his hostile.

"Are you so dangerous, Diar?" she said finally. "Shall I keep out of reach?"

"I cannot stop you from standing where you like," he said then, in the voice she would have made the journey twice over to hear and that she was not sure she would be hearing again, "as you see. But this is no fit place, even for you. You should not come here. And I do not want to see you. I want nothing from you, and I will take nothing. I have told you. Why then have you come? Is it you like seeing me like this? Does it pleasure you?"

"Diar," she whispered, "what have you done, to be kept like a wild beast? Could you not bend, a little, to anyone, to anyone at all?"

"No," he said, "I cannot and I will not. Leave me alone now, at least; just go now, and leave me be."

"Not until I have told you why I came," she said. "I have your bond papers with me, cancelled, to give to you."

She was startled at the violence of anger that crossed his white face.

"Is it not enough that you come here and must flaunt your indecency before me. Be damned to you and your papers, I will not be beholden to a whore. Go," he said, lifting the pitcher, "get out of my sight," his voice rising, "and let me die." He hurled the pitcher at her, the chains spoiling and stopping his aim, and the plate after, which came nearer and glanced off her skirt. She did not move, and then she said,

"Will you throw the table too? And the chair?" she asked. "I know of no reason or anything I have done that you should throw things at me, Diar."

"No?" he said, his eyes black, his breath panting. "Go back, and paddle in the bed with Smythe, Miss Grant. I would slit your stomach, had I a knife and a way to get to you, down to the cleft, and lay your belly and your shame open. It is what we do to such as you."

"Then why did you begin it?" she asked, her voice quiet. "I never asked you to."

"Go away," he said, turning his head from her. "I have forgotten all that. But I took you in marriage to me, and you have claimed that and yet you have dishonoured me, and my name. I do not want to look again upon your face. Go away now, and let me die."

"What is this talk of dying?" she asked. "Who is speaking of any such thing but yourself?"

"I have set this as the place," he said. "I am going no further. I am to be dried out like a leaf of tobacco," he said bitterly. "He has himself said it, this man who sets himself with a woman who says she has my name, and I am content for it to be so. Leave me, now, woman, and go your ways."

Looking at his set face, she found her sympathies going not to him, despite her feelings, but to the absent Smythe.

"I think you are a difficult man and a hard man, Diar MacLyon," she said speaking her thoughts, "and I can find it in my heart now as I could not before, to feel sorry for those who have had the charge of you. Yet I could have wished, Diar," she said, her voice hesitant, "that they might have been your ways."

"If that is your wish," he said, his lips set, "you will be a long way to gratifying it, for it is not my wish, and it would not be, had I means to do it. But if you will come closer, I will put my two hands on your neck, which was always a lovely stalk, Mary Elisabeth, and I will snap it like a stalk, even with these hands."

"I have no wish myself to die," she said, "so I will keep you at a distance from me. But you will listen to me whether you like it or not, if I have to call Mr. Smythe or another man of his and have them put a rag in your mouth."

"And you would do it, whore," he said, but he shut his lips tightly.

She could only look at him in astonishment, while he stared back at her, eyes meeting eyes and no understanding at all between them, and then she walked over to the table, across from him. Despite his threats, he made no move to reach her, and he seemed very tired, despite the stiffness of his back and head.

"Say it then, and go," he said, when she did not speak. "And take your bastard papers with you, or I'll tear them up."

He said a good deal more then, nothing new, to the effect of her tearing what she had up herself if she would please him, and in explicit terms his opinion of her character. She listened patiently, the words pouring over her, half English, half Gaelic, until they stopped finally from exhaustion. Only then did she speak.

"Diar," she said, her voice very gentle in its love, but clear and demanding to be heard, "Diarmid MacLyon, you stiff foolish man, you have not been attending what I said at all, and you should. This paper here," she said, putting it down, "is a pardon, unconditional. For you, Diar. You can go back, any time you like, anywhere, in England or in Scotland, and no one anywhere will lift a finger to stop you or say you nay. You can go home now. You can go anywhere at all you please, that you have money and the will to take you to. Is that what I'm to take back or tear up? Anyway, it's not for me. It's for you. It's your name on it, all your names. I just carried it, and brought it to you. It's not contaminated, it won't hurt you.

"And this," she said, putting a second torn piece of paper beside it, matching the torn edges together, "is your indenture. I have bought it. You can walk on this place now, or in any hour, or any time you like. There's no one owns you now.

The paper is bought out, and here it is. I bought it for you, and I did it in a way you don't like, nor did I like it either. But there it is. You can do about it what you like.

"And here," she said, adding it to the papers, "is the key that will unlock those things on you. You can take them off yourself, whenever you like. I'll not be putting it in your hand, for from your black looks you would be throwing it off in a corner where you couldn't be reaching it then, even if you wanted it when I'm gone, or I finding it now to put it back. But you can reach it here if you try. There now.

"In this bag there is money, you can buy yourself some clothes and go to an Inn and have a bath and whatever you like to eat and order people about, as you choose. And there will be enough left over, when you've done that, still, to buy a passage back to Scotland. When you get there, there's an indemnity for you, to have back your land, and to have the value of your house replaced. The money is contaminated, I got it for you the same way, Diar, the indemnity is too, the way I got it given to you. You can take or leave them both.

"And here," she said, "is a pistol I was given, and a knife—like the one you said you'd like, for you in case anyone should think not to honour these papers on this property. But they will honour them—I promise you that. They would not dare not to.

"Now you do what you like about all this," she said. "It's there. You can sit there and never touch it, until it moulders and the spiders get it, or someone else comes and takes it. Or you can use it, all of it or part of it, just as you like. But it has nothing to do with me now, Diar, I have found you and I have given it to you now, and I'm going now, and I am never going to come around you again. You are a free man, Diarmid MacLyon, if you choose to be. It's nothing now to do with me, and I wonder now that I ever wanted it to be. But I did. Fool that *I* was, I did, until right now. If you hadn't wanted me, and I thought you might not, you know, Diar, for I know what I am, I was going to leave you yet another paper, telling you where you could find me if you changed your mind, but that paper, Diar, I'm taking off with me, as I am leaving you now your ring." She reached into the neck of her dress, and pulled it out and pulled it off its chain and dropped it on the table where it lay winking in a ray of moted sunlight.

She looked at him, sitting there, his face turned away from her, like stone.

"Well," she said, "I'm going now, Diarmid MacLyon, and if we're ever meeting with one another again, it will not be by my helping. It will be you going looking to the four ends of the earth for me, if there's ever any more looking, for I'll not be doing it. It's a distance I'll be putting between us now. But before I go, Mr. MacLyon, while you're sitting there like a hard stone, and you chained to a post and can't help yourself, there's one thing I'm going to take from you."

She knelt beside him in the dust of the floor, quiet and still now, and took his face in her two hands, feeling him shiver at her touch, and turned his face to hers, and kissed his limp lips with hers, unresisting, unresponsive, cold as stone.

"Well," she said, standing up. "I don't know why I wanted that. Goodbye, Diar," she said, and turned and walked out of the shed, down the little steps, and across the black fields, not looking back, wondering why she had ever loved him or thought she did, and forgiving him all in his hurt and humiliation, wishing he would call after her, and knowing he would not, brushing the hurt angry tears from her eyes that for this stock she had worked so long, and left her family, and ruined the honour of her flesh. And for a man she did not know, had no acquaintance with, had hardly ever spoken to, who had forgotten her. She could have laughed, had she not been so sad, to think of it now.

She walked back to her horse, tethered at the field's edge, and mounted and rode it back to the house, her eyes by the time she reached the house blinded with tears.

Smythe met her at the door, and helped her dismount.

"I see the visit was not a success," he said. "Poor stubborn Scottish fool." He put his arm about her, and led her into the house, and in the hall he lifted her bent face to his, and kissed her. "But I love you," he said, "I find you entirely lovable. And I am not married. Will you then marry me, my dear?"

"I am still Diar's wife," she said, her head resting on his chest, "for all he says I'm not. And oh Mr. Smythe, sir," she said, "you had best leave me now, for you tell me you do not like tears, and I think I am going to cry."

"Cry away," he said, picking her up.

"Oh, sir," she said, "I may cry all afternoon. I cannot any longer seem to help myself."

"My shirt is soaked already," he said, "you can't hurt it any worse," and pushed open the door to her room.

"Oh, sir," she said, weeping, "I could not now, please do not ask me. I am indeed too sad."

"Then I shall cheer you," he said. "You will find it will, though you do not think so, to find one man at your feet, when another does not want to be. And I have your promise, have I not?"

"Then close the curtains please," she said, gasping with sobs, "for Diar may come by."

"I shall indeed not," he said, his lips grim. "I should like him to see. There is no one else at this hour to pass by. But I think he will not, and the tree is by the window." He took her then, crying all the time, and when he left her, she yet continued to cry, all the afternoon, stopping for weariness, and then beginning again.

XXXVI: *Epilogue: Eighteen Months After*

WHEN MARY ELISABETH HAD LEFT, LEAVING THE DOOR OPEN, DIARMID SAT WITHOUT MOVING AS SHE HAD LEFT HIM, EXCEPT TO RUB HIS MOUTH WITH HIS SLEEVE. HE MADE NO MOVE TO TOUCH THE THINGS SHE HAD LEFT, and he did not look once towards them. The afternoon wore on, the square of light changed its colour, and lessened. No one at all came. The sun, beating down on the roof, heated the filled stuffy room as it had each day before, until he was gasping and sweating, as he had each afternoon. For some days past he had heard men working about the barn, checking the mud caulking and tightening it, but today there was no one near. No sound, except for the buzzing of flies. A small snake crept across the floor, found no crack in the walls, and slithered out the door. A field mouse put its head in and looked at him with its bright eyes, and seemed to find the place without interest for she left, and left him again entirely alone. He grew very thirsty, but he had thrown his water away. The air coming through the door grew cooler, with a slight wind in it, and the light outside turned gold. No one came to bring him his supper, or to refill his water, as they had done. The distant sounds in

other fields, and of an axe cutting wood stopped. He was entirely alone, in the stillness, and his eyes turned then towards
the papers on the table, the bag of coins, and the key. Had they
not been there, in his dazed state of mind, he might have
thought he had dreamed the episode. But they were there, and
they appeared to be real. He stretched out a hand, tentatively,
in the heavy chain, as though to touch them, but he could not
reach them easily, and the hand fell back.

"Oh, my God," he whispered aloud, through his parched
lips, "I am so thirsty, and I cannot reach the little key, now,
even if I would. O dear God, what shall I do?"

"Bend, Diarmid, bend, and you will not break. You bent
before me in the rain. Bend now." The still words fell into his
mind, with the clarity of a command, and he bent his back,
as far as he could forward, and his fingers touched the key
and he drew it to him, and schooling his fingers not to shake,
he unlocked first the shackles on his wrists and then those on
his feet.

He sat there then, again not moving, looking at the open
door, as though he did not know what to do about it, but the
light changing prodded his slowness. He took the papers and
put them inside his shirt against the band of his trousers, and
the bag of coins he hooked on their button. He slid the knife
and the pistol in also, under the band, and stood up, and
stretched, and no eyes still upon him and still no sound, he
walked down the steps and out. He took a path around the
house, not going near it, cutting North towards Savannah,
not knowing how he would find his way.

He stopped by a stream that blocked his way to drink, and
there Smythe found him, sitting wearily.

"Don't pull your pistol on me, MacLyon," he said. "I have
brought you a horse. You'll not find your way, I've come to
guide you. I brought you here, I'll take you back."

He opened his saddle bag and took out a small loaf of
bread and cold bacon and tossed it to Diarmid, without a
word.

Diarmid took it and ate it, while Smythe watched him curiously.

"What is the difference," he said, "MacLyon, to you between eating the food of a man who's had your wife and taking the help of the woman itself. I noticed you thanked neither of us, but you did not delay taking mine."

"Are you wanting a fight," MacLyon said, looking up.

"No. I would really like to know. Myself, I cannot fathom it."

"I decided to live," MacLyon said. "It seemed foolish not to. So I took the papers and I take your help. I know that I don't know the way. But I think less than nothing of the both of you for offering it."

"Well," Smythe said, "I did ask."

He went to the horse and took off two blankets.

"Here," he said to MacLyon. "I don't travel myself in the dark. I could myself lose the way easily. You go on, if you like, or go as far off as you judge your dignity demands you." He lay down between the folds of the blanket, his arms under his head, and after a moment, Diarmid did the same, a little way away.

"I am tired," Smythe said. "I have been watching at the window to see when you would decide, as you put it, to live, so that I could use my shed again, and you were long enough about it, I must say. And I had your wife to comfort. You are a hard man, MacLyon."

"Harder than yourself," MacLyon said, agreeing. "I should myself, being you, not have let myself, being I, get the upper hand."

"Oh," said Smythe, "but you see, MacLyon, I liked you, and you, MacLyon, like no one."

"I have been given no cause to."

Smythe let that pass. "You are mistaken on one count, MacLyon. Had your wife not come, you would this time have bent for me, or had no more chance to. I meant what I said."

"I thought you might. I made my choice," MacLyon said,

his voice noncommittal. "Your woman, Smythe, is not my wife. I will have none of her. She is the common whore."

"You are again mistaken, MacLyon. She is a most uncommon whore. You are losing more than you think for, but that is agreeable to me, if it is to you. I am more tempted, however, than you can imagine, to do a violence on you, for she will not marry while you are walking about."

"It is her decision. No priest has said the lines, the ceremony she speaks of does not bind me. Let it not bind her. If you think to provoke me, you will not do it. I am grateful for a guide." He turned over in the blanket and went to sleep.

The next day late in the evening Smythe left MacLyon at the Ordinary in Savannah.

"I will treat you to a dinner," he said, curiously reluctant to part from the Scot.

"I'll not eat with you," Diarmid said, "I don't need you any more." He turned and limped into the Inn, his ankles still painfully bruised from the shackles Smythe had set on him, unaccustomed to act for himself now, hardly knowing what to do.

Smythe entered himself then, having arranged the stabling of his horses, took a room for himself and ordered his dinner, passing by as if Diarmid did not exist in his rooted condition, or as if he did not know him. The little act of ignoring him woke him as nothing had to the reality of the new condition of his freedom. He walked up then to the master of the Ordinary and asked for a room, tentatively, having never done such a thing ever. He caught the Innkeeper's experienced eye raking his dirty disordered state and his rough clothes, and he flushed a little.

"I can pay," he said. "I have money. If you like, I can pay now."

"I do like," the Innkeeper said. "No boots in bed, the price goes up depending on the number to the bed."

"I want a bed and a room to myself," Diarmid said. "I can pay for it." He fumbled in the bag and brought out a coin.

The Innkeeper's manner changed, then, and became more accommodating. Would he have supper in his room, or in the public room, he asked.

"In my room," Diarmid said. "And I want a bath. And my clothes washed for me."

He was too tired to do more, or to think more. He washed himself, and put himself into the real bed, after he had eaten his supper, as if he were in a dream. He was suddenly hideously tired, and he felt, not like rejoicing but like crying, like an infant, to have so much before him and to be too tired to want any of it.

It had begun to rain, outside, and he was glad he was in the Inn in his bed, fed, instead of out in it, walking and hungry.

"Why would Smythe do it?" he wondered, "I should not have for him." The matter was beyond him, but whatever his reasons, he was glad Smythe had seen fit to bring him to the Inn. He could not remember ever being so tired, as he was now, when nothing was being done to him, and he could not understand it, or why now he should want to cry. Then he thought, "Why, if I want to, should I not? There is no one to know, or to see." He fell asleep, the tears staining his lashes and his cheeks.

In the morning, when his clothes were brought to him and he went downstairs for breakfast, he found Smythe had gone, and was relieved. He spent the morning arranging to have clothes made for himself, and the afternoon in sleeping. After dinner he went to his room. He bathed with more care, and this time he washed his hair, with soap and with vinegar, and then again curiously exhausted, he lay down and went to sleep, his mind still blank, but this time without the desire to cry. The next two days he spent exploring Savannah. He discovered that since he had money, he was now as good as anyone about him, in public estimation. He gave no thought to the person who had gotten him the money, but he expanded in the use of it.

After several more days of eating when he chose, and as he chose, and walking as he chose, when his new clothes were made and had been fitted, his spirit expanding further with the resilience of youth, he resolved to go farther afield to a place that had drawn him since he first heard of it. He spent two more days looking at the immediately available horse-flesh, settled his choice on a mare, hired out a guide, and began the trip to Darien, some four days down from Savannah.

He arrived, after difficult travelling in the coastal woods and swamps, he talked and fed his homesick heart, and he procured a kilt, of the MacCullough weave.

"Just don't wear it about the soldiers at Frederica, or any fort, there's no sense waving it," he was told, "otherwise, there's no one cares."

He stayed there a week, inspecting, exploring, visiting St. Simon's Island, and thinking, and then he rode back, this time not with a guide but a McLeod who was intending to make the trip to Savannah. As he rode, he whistled softly, feeling the mare's flanks move beneath his thighs, bare again of trousers, the plaid kilted about his waist and over his shoulder, and he threw back his head and laughed for the joy of it. The year and a half in between seemed to have fallen away from him, as if it had not been, or had been a bad dream he had finally waked from.

It was then, and only then, that he thought again of Mary Elisabeth, and that it occurred to him to wonder where she was and if she was still at Smythe's. The words he had said to her had slipped his mind, and it occurred to him now only that the woman he had gotten for himself at great trouble was being enjoyed without trouble by someone else. He had gotten her once, she was after all his, he would get her again.

"McLeod," he said, riding his mare close, "Smythe has got my wife. I think I'll go and get her back. Will you help me?"

"I will that," McLeod said enthusiastically. "A man should not be having another man's wife."

"Then cock your pistol," said MacLyon, "and we'll ride in and raid and get her back."

Which they did, in part.

"What the hell are you up to, MacLyon," said Smythe, as the two Scots charged down on him as he walked up the entrance he was laying out. "Put your pistols up. This is my land, and if you don't, I'll have you shot. I'd like to anyway. Suppose you keep them out."

"I've come for my wife," MacLyon said, "I'll have her back, if you please."

"I don't please," Smythe said, "you gave up the claim, as I recall. Go on, now, Scot, and don't disturb me."

He had not reckoned on a loose Scot, up to the ears in the joy of his freedom. With a wild yell, Diarmid rode his horse right over Smythe, the chest knocking him down, the mare's hooves avoiding him delicately. As he tried to rise, Diarmid overrode him again, and leaped lightly to the ground, throwing his reins to McLeod who watched with enjoyment.

"Up, with your fists," said Diarmid, "I owe you this for what you did to me when I was sick off the transport."

"No," said Smythe dizzily, "I'll not fight with you."

"Then I'll fight you with them down," Diarmid said, "I don't want you interfering while I woo my wife."

"She's not here," said Smythe.

"Is she not?" said Diarmid, hitting him hard. "Then where is she?"

"Back to Charles Town, with a Frenchie," Smythe said, spitting blood.

"I don't believe you," Diarmid said, hitting him again. "Fight me, Smythe, or I'll massacre you. Where's my wife," he asked again, with another blow, well-placed as Smythe's had been.

The man doubled up on the ground, groaning.

"Look for yourself," he said, between his teeth, "you damned Scot. I wish I'd killed you."

"You had your chance," Diarmid said. "Did you think I

could still like you? You don't seem to like me the whit so
well now either. You keep your pistol on him, McLeod, and
knock him, if he tries to shout or follow me. I'm off to get my
wife."

He found her in the house, in a morning dress, without her
wig. She looked very pretty, and very fresh, and looking at
her one would not imagine how she had cried, for days and
days, until Smythe had lost his patience and told her to dry
up her tears or leave. She had no money, again, and no place
to go or to want to go, so she had dried her tears and made
the best of what she had.

She looked up now, at the whirl of footsteps, in the sunny
room, to see Diarmid before her, his kilt bouncing with the
urgency of his step that brought him right before her. He
said no word at all, but put his hand over her mouth and
lifted her off her feet. His eye fell on the wisp of muslin and
lace at her neck, and he ripped it off, and stuffed part of it in
her mouth, and bound the rest around, then throwing her
over his shoulder, he stalked out of the house, to his horse
standing patiently, the reins down, at the door, threw her
across the horse, mounted behind her, and rode at a gallop
down to the waiting McLeod, riding over Smythe a third
time.

"If she don't want me," he said, to the angry prostrate
planter, over his shoulder, "I'll send her back tomorrow, so
don't bother riding after me, Mr. Smythe. A man has after all
a right to have his own wife."

He rode at a fast gallop with the amused McLeod until he
had put a distance between himself and the plantation. Then
he slowed his horse, and somewhat fearfully, righted his wife
and took her fichu from her mouth, his eyes cocked at her
waiting for her reaction to his peremptory action. He need
have had no fears. She said nothing, but she put her arms
about him, her face hidden in his chest, so that there was
nothing she needed to say. He rode with her thus, his face
against the top of her head, not saying anything either, the

pressure of her arms about him and his about her saying enough.

McLeod, however, had quite a bit to say, in an amused voice.

"I understood the lady was your wife."

"She is," Diarmid said briefly, his arm tight about her.

"Wedded and bedded."

"And does she not mind such treatment of a wedded bedded wife?"

"I have not asked her yet," Diarmid said again briefly, his arm about her. "I daresay she will tell me when I do, if she did. I did not want to stay there talking all the night. It is not a place I like."

The abused woman he held began to laugh, shaking in his arms, and Diarmid grinned, his eyes dancing with their old lost merry devilry.

"You are a pair of you," McLeod said admiringly, and laughed hard himself.

XXXVII: *Lovers' Meeting*

B UT IT WAS A SOBERER DIARMID WHO MET HIS WIFE IN HIS
ROOM AT THE INN THAT EVENING, AFTER A DINNER
WITH MCLEOD VERY LIKE A WEDDING SUPPER.

"I SUPPOSE," HE SAID IN HIS SOFT VOICE, "THAT WE WILL HAVE
to talk now, Mary Elisabeth."

"If you like, Diarmid," she said meekly, her head lowered.

"It is apologising I shall have to be to you now," he said
ruefully. "But it did not seem the place to find out what you
thought, with Smythe's big men likely to run in on me, and
only two of us. But you heard what I said to Smythe."

"I heard," she said. "Why would I want to be going back to
Smythe, when it is where I was wanting to be that I am
now?"

"I can think of several good reasons why not," he said, "a
long list of them."

"And one why I should," she said.

"What is that?" he whispered, his eyes on her.

"I am Diar's wife," she said, her voice a whisper too, her
eyes on him.

He came to her then, and took her in his arms.

"I love you, I think, little Mary Elisabeth."

"How so, Diarmid MacLyon," she said, "I have no reason to think it."

"Perhaps I do not, then," he said truthfully. "I do not know you very well. But if you are my wife, I'd like you with me."

She began to laugh, in his arms. "I do not know you very well either, Diarmid MacLyon, but I would like to know you better, being my husband as you are." She began as suddenly to cry.

"Hush, love, hush," he soothed her. "I have been a beast to you, always, and you being so good to me, and not even thought about you, except to hurt you. I shall try to make up to you for it all, if I may, if I can."

She choked back her tears and gave him a watery smile, and then she began to cry again.

"I cannot help it, Diar," she said, crying. "I had begun to think I should never be here again with you."

He held her in his strong arms tightly folded against him, looking out over her head, until her sobs died away, and they sat so while the light faded about them, not speaking.

"It is dark," he whispered then against her hair, "dark and time for bed for an abducted woman. We can talk as well there, in comfort, and tomorrow, if you are still of the same mind, as you may not be, there is a priest of my faith in Savannah, and I will take you there, as I said a long time ago that I would, Mrs. MacLyon, and seal it from my side as well."

"If *I* am of the same mind?" she said. "What of you?"

"I know my mind," he said, unbuttoning the back of her dress, "but you may not know yours. I would not take an advantage of you again, Mary Elisabeth. I am no one's bargain, and I know it, but I doubt you do."

"Why have you changed your mind about me?" she whispered. "What has changed it so completely?"

"I feel better," he said simply. "You cannot imagine how badly I felt, to have you come upon me, thinking I must die a silly death uncomfortably, for so little to anyone else and so much to me. I was in a true despair, as I had been for so very long a time. And when it lifted, when I was my own man again, and could have the use of my arms and my legs, as I liked, a simple thing but something I had lost, and could govern my days and nights, and will what I wanted to do and execute it again, I thought differently about it. I was willing to owe it to you, as I was not before, and not mind. I had had my back up against everything and everyone for so many months, it was a habit I could not at once break. I thought at first I would not even take the things you left, but I grew very thirsty in the heat, and I saw that there are two kinds of pride, pride that saves one and keeps one alive, and a silly pride that one can die of for no use. So I took your things and I used them, and when I felt better, I wanted you with me, all the same. It was that simple. So being myself, I came and got you. May I see what I got?"

"Yes, Diarmid," she said, letting him slip her dress down.

"You do not look much changed," he said, and the images when he had last seen her so did not shadow his face, "but I never really saw you, or looked at you, not for yourself."

"I know, Diarmid," she said.

"Would you like to see me?" he asked.

"Yes," she whispered.

He took his own clothes off, in the fading light, his eyes on her, his shirt, and let her herself let fall his kilt. "You see," he said simply, "I am no bargain. You will know what I mean."

"You are a bonny man, Diarmid MacLyon," she whispered. "I always thought so, right from the first, I think so now. And I have seen you, when you did not know I saw you, if you can forgive me for it, and learned to love you when you did not know."

"We will go to bed, then," he said simply, taking her hand. "And we will see."

"My dear," he said, when they were lying beneath the sheets, their hands clasped, but their sides not touching, "it has been so long now that I've been past that, I don't know that I shall ever be able to do it again, or want to, with you, or with anyone. I'm afraid I am going to be a disappointment to you that way, and not much use, and you have probably gotten used to it and need it now."

She began to laugh, wholeheartedly and with real merriment. "Oh, Diar," she said, "it has been a necessity for so long, I have not thought whether I had come to like it or need it myself. I know I shall not mind a vacation. Do not think of it, Diar, for I shall not. I have not been looking for you, thinking of that."

He took her in his arms then, and held her to him, her soft chestnut hair beneath his chin, in the hollows of his throat, clasping her loosely, very peaceful. After a time, he spoke, hesitantly, as though not wanting the answer.

"What of the child, Rawn, Mary Elisabeth? What became of him? Do you happen to know?"

"Yes, I do, Diar. I will tell you." She felt him tense, beside her, and she said quickly, "He is well, Diar. You shall see him, when you go back. But his foot is crippled. He cannot walk without a crutch."

"I am more than glad to hear it," he said. "I had feared worse. But your pronoun is wrong, I hope, my dear. I shall see him when *we* go back. Was it you who found him, in that hole?"

She nodded, and told him the story.

"Oh, my love," he said, "you have a kind heart. I am glad he was taken out, before the heart went entirely out of him, and that it was you who found him. Is his mother living?"

"I do not know, Diar. I have not been back. Will you be wanting to go soon?"

"I don't know, Mary Elisabeth. I have thought I did, that I would, when I could not. It was all that was before my eyes, and all that I have lived for. I could see nothing else. But now that I can, now that I am free to and have the way to, I seem to see things, myself, this country, that one, with new eyes. I think I might stay here for a while, at least, for there is more chance for advancement in the colonies. I can see that. Would you mind?"

"Are you saying I am to keep with you?"

"And what else have I been saying and asking, Mrs. Mac-Lyon. And do I not still have the right to?"

"I shall be happy to be wherever you are, Diar," she said, with a little sigh of relief and contentment, "whatever you decide."

"But I shall write King George and his officials, I think, and tell them not to be giving away my land for me to anyone else, for I'll be coming back for it. And perhaps I'll be writing my cousin Rawn and he will take care of it for me, until I come back to it. Are you able to have children, still, Mary Elisabeth?"

"I don't know," she said, "will it matter to you? I was to have one once, but I lost it in Inverness. I never knew whose it was to be, and I have not had one since."

"We are a pretty pair," he said ruefully. "The incapable and the incapacitated. Well," he said, "who knows, perhaps some day it may change for both of us. I just wondered. I wonder if it was mine, but it is no use wondering, and not very likely. The odds would be against me, I suppose. How did you lose it, my dear? Overuse?"

She heard the bitterness in his voice, that he could not keep out, but she did not remark on it. It was something they would have to learn somehow to live with, if they could.

"I lost it in the Bridge-Hole in Inverness," she said simply.

"Oh, my God, Mary Elisabeth," he said. "I did not know. Who put you there, and why, and when was that?"

She told him then, and he held her closer.

"Oh, my dear," he said, "I never knew, and I was rude to you." His heart stirred with compassion for her sufferings, and her endeavours.

"My dear," he said, "when you tell me what you have done, I can believe anything is possible with you. I cannot promise anything, but shall we see, now, you and I, what with your help can now be done?"

"If you like, Diar," she said, beginning to tremble. He felt her, and he shivered himself.

"You will have to help me," he whispered. "Do you know what to do?"

"Yes, Diar," she said, "if you would like me to."

"Help me, then," he said, "if you can."

He lay back, his eyes shut, beside her, and let her arrange him, stroking him lightly, her fingertips gentle and experienced, and after a little time, he turned to her and put his lips on hers, and found he loved her in all ways. And so they were at quiet and at rest.

Author's Note

I HAVE NOT invented the things that happened to Diarmid in Scotland and England and on the transport; nor the rapes of Mary Elisabeth Grant (let the clan's name involved in that first remain unmentioned for those who do not know it). I have merely combined together various abbreviated stories of various Highlanders at that time, into one, and turned them into a novel with voices. The springboard for the novel was *Culloden* by John Prebble (Atheneum, 1962), and many, though not all, of the facts dealing with the battle and the treatment of the prisoners come from the contemporary accounts quoted in this book.

The picture of Georgia in 1747 is modified, with the aid of other sources, direct from John Wesley's account of his two-year visit in 1735. With apologies, the account of the Moravins comes in its factual side from the same source. The dialogue in which Chicali (actually a Creek name, I preferred it to the two actual Chicasaw names given) gives the beliefs of the Chicasaws is taken almost directly from Wesley's conversation with five Chicasaw warriors and head men (July 1, 1736) and may be found in its exact form there, including Wesley's spelling of *Chicasaw*.

I should perhaps add for those who do not know it that though Lyon is a well-known surname, and the seat of the Scottish Court, standing therefore for Scotland itself, as in the volumes about the aftermath of the " '45" titled *Lyon in Mourning*, there is no Clan MacLyon, and to my knowledge no such name. The name Diarmid is a Scottish variant existing in 1745 of the name Diarmuid, pure Celt; surviving now in the more common form Dermot and McDermott. The old names persisted: in January of 1746, the son of MacDonald of Glengarry (killed by accident by a MacDonald of Clan-

ranald after the battle of Falkirk) was named Angus Og, the
name of the Apollo-like god who raised the child Diarmuid
of Celtic legend, a story found both in Ireland and in Scotland equally. Another MacDonald was named Coll, like
Diarmuid the name of another hero of the Fianna.

The interpreter at the Carlisle Trials was Patrick Camp-
bell, one of two spies for the Commander-in-Chief of the
King's Army in Scotland (the other one a MacDonald), an
interesting fact when one remembers the similar double role
played by the defense lawyer in the Irish rebel trials some
fifty years later.

An interesting final note, about Cumberland "the Butcher,"
"Billy the Martial Boy" of Culloden Field, exactly twenty-
five then, from the *Journal* of John Wesley for November 29,
1771:

> We viewed the improvements of that active and useful
> man, the late Duke of Cumberland: the most remarkable
> work is, the triangular tower which he built on the edge of
> Windsor-park. It is surrounded with shrubberies and woods,
> having some straight, some serpentine, walks in them, and
> commands a beautiful prospect all three ways: a very exten-
> sive one to the south-west. In the lower part is an alcove
> which must be extremely pleasant in a summer evening.
> There is a little circular projection at each corner, one of
> which is filled by a geometrical staircase, the other two con-
> tain little apartments, one of which is a study. I was agree-
> ably surprised to find many of the books not only religious,
> but admirably well chosen. Perhaps the great man spent
> many hours here, with only Him that seeth in secret; and
> who can say how deep that change went, which was so dis-
> cernible in the latter part of his life?

74-12512
Burford, Lolah
  MacLyon.

74-12512   sd   _____

Burford, Lolah

  Maclyon.

8.95